THE COUNTESS

AND THE CORSAIR

Sophia Sempeles

For the shy kid in class with a big heart and an even bigger imagination. And for those who celebrate Orthodox Easter weeks after Catholic Easter has passed. You know who you are.

Chapter One

The Fortress

Costa Brava, Catalonia 1315 AD

Elara Iliakos' feet were bleeding. Running around barefoot over the stone steps of Fortress Tossa de Mar had yielded that outcome. She cursed herself for not bringing an extra pair of shoes with her to the shoreline. How was she supposed to know she would be doing this much exploring on sharp rocks and that her shoes wouldn't be able to handle it? Saying a silent prayer for strength, Elara kept trudging painfully along to the place where her grandfather would be waiting for her.

First built decades ago, Fortress Tossa de Mar was beautifully made of warm sandstone and sat picturesquely on a cliff overlooking the Mediterranean Sea. Located in the last stronghold of the old empire in the west, other than Rome, Catalonia was the perfect place for a noble family to hide out and enjoy. Enclosed inside the fortress walls was a small quaint village, in which around two hundred Catalonians lived. Elara and her grandfather Count Basil Iliakos had recently moved into the fortress.

"It'll be a fresh start for us," her grandfather, or, as the Greeks say, "papou," had promised.

It didn't feel like a fresh start to Elara, especially when half her things were still in the old estate and the other half had been stolen by thieves during the various ransackings of her beloved city, Constantinople. The city simply wasn't as safe nor as powerful as it once was. With continued pressures from the Vatican over monetary debt and the looming violent threat of the Ottomans in the east, things in the city had taken a turn for the worse.

The last straw had been a life-ruining social situation that Elara had fallen into earlier in the year and they knew then that they needed to leave. When Emperor Michael Palaiologos IX offered Tossa de Mar in the south-east side of Catalonia to them, her papou, Count Basil, had decided it would be safer for them to live there.

"Elara! Where have you been? Come inside!" Her papou called out to her as she made her way to the main entrance of the fortress.

Basil was tall for an Eastern Roman man, with a round belly, gray mustache, and dark burgundy robes. His cheeks were rosy from drinking, and he seemed to be in good spirits even though he still mourned the recent loss of his wife, Countess Zoe Iliakos, and the loss of his son, Elara's father, many years ago.

"Sorry, Papou, I'm here!" Elara huffed as the sweet relief of soft rug graced her feet. "Did I miss Lady Celina's arrival?"

"No, you... you're bleeding, koukla mou! What have you been doing?" Basil let out a small gasp at the blood and dirt now soaking into the rug. Koukla mou, or "my doll," in Greek, had been a term her papou had been affectionately calling her for years. Even when he was upset with her, he still called her by it.

"My shoes broke, so I had to run barefoot. I'll freshen up." Heat rose in her cheeks as the feeling of shame overtook any physical pain she was in.

She looked down at her tattered blue gown, now dirty at the hem from running over sand and dirt, before excusing herself to the washroom where one of the serving women would help her clean herself up.

"You're a mess, my lady," the middle-aged serving woman with a hooked nose commented as she looked Elara up and down.

"Ha. Yes, I am." Elara didn't call the woman out on her rudeness as she wanted a delicate hand to help her clean her wounds, not an angry one.

The washroom, much like the other rooms in the fortress, was made entirely of stone and was not yet furnished or decorated. There were torches on one wall and thin windows on the other wall that let in some light. A small stone basin was in the center of the room with which she could wash.

"You did a lot of exploring today. Do you like the area?" Basil asked through the other side of the washroom door.

"Yes, it's..." Elara started, but there was a lump in her throat that kept her from finishing the thought. The serving woman got to work helping her get the blood and dirt off her feet. She didn't want to sound ungrateful or spoiled.

Clearing her throat, Elara continued, "It's certainly large, and... uh, spacious."

Basil chuckled softly at her dry and repetitive description. "Tossa de Mar will become more home-like in time, koukla mou. You'll see!"

"You are my favorite optimist, Papou." She hoped he would be right. She hoped Tossa de Mar would be a place where she could put her old life behind her and start anew, a place where she could prove herself worthy of being a countess, a place where people didn't gossip about her in the streets.

After her feet were clean, the serving women set to work wrapping them up in cloth. Her feet were sore, but they didn't hurt nearly as much as her pride did. It was embarrassing what a mess today had become. All Elara wanted to do was explore the beach and see what surprises her new home held. The sharp rocks and steep terrain had certainly caught her off guard.

"You've got a twig stuck in your hair," the serving woman said sternly.

Elara chuckled awkwardly and pulled the wood from her long dark locks. She loved to keep her hair down, even though she knew it wasn't fashionable to do so.

"So how long have you worked at Tossa de Mar?" Elara asked as the serving woman pulled Elara's mane into a delicate braid. Servants often served at manors and fortresses their whole lives, even if the original owners of the fortress moved away.

"We don't need to make conversation, my lady," the woman replied gruffly as she moved to help Elara into some fresh clothes.

Rude.

Elara took the hint and said nothing more as the serving woman helped her into a new dark blue gown with a matching pair of shoes. The dress was one of her favorites and had been made for her by the court dressmaker, Simon Metakis, back in Constantinople. He was great at making dresses that fit her tall, wiry frame. She wondered who would make her clothes now that she lived in Catalonia.

After she finished cleaning herself up, Elara was relieved to find that she had no trouble walking. Her feet, now bandaged and in proper footwear, felt only a little tender.

"There you are! Come join me." Basil greeted her warmly as she made her way into the drawing room. He was sitting in an armchair by a roaring fireplace, his feet propped up on a small footstool.

Elara moved to sit in the only other chair in the room. The room was still so bare as they had only moved in a few days prior.

"How are your feet?" Her papou asked with a furrowed brow.

His tone indicated that he wasn't upset with her, but she couldn't shake the feeling he wasn't happy with her either. Future countesses weren't supposed to run around rocky terrain like cavemen.

"It looks worse than it feels," Elara promised.

The count had to know that she hadn't done it on purpose. It wasn't like Elara was some sort of outdoorsy girl that longed for nature.

She hadn't planned on getting dirty and scraping her feet, but her life never seemed to go according to plan.

"I'll be more careful next time. It won't happen again."

"Don't make promises you can't keep, koukla mou." Basil chuckled, looking relaxed.

Elara tried to mimic his demeanor, hoping that some of his confidence might rub off on her.

"Excuse me, Count Basil?" A servant entered the room. "Lady Celina Oberon and her escort are here to see you and Lady Elara."

"Send her in!" Elara jumped up, feeling excited for the first time that day.

The servant looked to Basil for confirmation, not taking Elara's orders.

"You heard my granddaughter—send Lady Celina in at once," Basil said in a booming voice and a gentle smile. The servant gave a curt nod and exited the room.

Celina Oberon was a noblewoman around the same age as Elara and was to be Elara's first lady-in-waiting. Ladies-in-waiting were young, unmarried women of noble birth who went to assist higher ranking noblewomen with their day-to-day duties.

Elara had once served as a lady-in-waiting to Empress Maria, so she was looking forward to having a lady-in-waiting of her own. She'd start with her friend, Celina, but she hoped the group would eventually grow.

"I didn't think the baron's daughter was getting here until tomorrow," said Count Basil.

"Yes! Such a blessing she's early!" Elara stood and smoothed her blue dress, trying to look as presentable as possible. Her dark locks were already braided nicely out of the way, but she fiddled with them, nonetheless.

It shouldn't have been nerve-wracking. Celina was a close friend after all. That said, it had been some time since the girls had last seen each other and it would be the first time they had seen each other since Elara's exile from Constantinople.

"Hello dears!" Celina Oberon said energetically as she entered the room. She was accompanied by an older man in gray robes who was carrying two of her bags.

Unlike Elara and Basil who were olive-tone, Celina had pale skin and blue eyes that were common for those from Bulgaria. Her long blonde hair was braided like a crown around her head, and she wore a light green gown under a dark green cloak. A stunning pearl necklace wrapped twice around her long neck and matching earrings adorned her ears. Her eyes crinkled kindly in the corners when she smiled, and her cheeks were flushed from walking up the long fortress steps.

Basil dismissed her escort and then greeted her, as was customary, with a polite bow and handshake. "Welcome! How is your father, Baron Joseph?"

"My father is well, thank you!" Celina said as Elara threw her arms around her in a tight hug. "Oh, hello there. Yes, I'm very glad to see you too, Elara dear."

"I've missed you so much!" Elara breathed into the shoulder of Celina's cloak. She smelled like the ocean. Elara was tall for a girl, but Celina was a bit taller. "You have no idea what I've been through these past few months!"

"Oh, I think I might have some idea."

Elara pulled away from her to gauge her friend's expression. "What—what have you heard? Please be specific! What are people saying?"

"It's not healthy to deal with such trivial gossip, koukla mou," Basil scolded her gently. "Let's allow Lady Celina to get settled before we berate her with questions."

"I think I have a right to know what people are saying about me!" Elara tried to keep her tone light as she followed her papou and her friend out of the room.

Once they were in the main foyer, lit only by a large brass chandelier, Count Basil pointed to the spiral staircase, saying, "Lady Celina, your room is the second one on the left. It's just across from Elara's room so you'll be close should she need you. One of our servants will take up your things."

"Thank you, Count Basil. I appreciate your hospitality." Celina gave a small bow.

Basil smiled and put his arm around Elara. "Thank *you*, Lady Celina, for helping look after my little granddaughter."

"Little?" Elara groaned, annoyed. "Papou, you know Celina and I are nearly twenty years old, right?"

"You'll always be little to me, koukla mou." Basil winked.

- - -

"How have things been?" Celina asked once they were alone in her room.

"That depends...How much do you know?" Elara perched herself on the large stone windowsill as Celina unpacked some of her belongings.

The room was bathed in the comforting orange glow from the fireplace. Celina's room wasn't as large as Elara's, but it was still quite large with a wooden four poster bed, a dresser with a mirror, and two tall wardrobes. The dark green curtains that hung around the bed coincidentally matched Celina's dress proving that much like a chameleon, Lady Celina had the talent to adapt to any environment. It was a talent Elara both admired and envied.

"How much do I know?" Celina repeated slowly. "Hmm, well, I heard about the thieves taking your late yiayia's favorite art piece."

"Yes, and they took my mother's earring collection too!" Elara bemoaned.

Her parents had died when Elara was young, and her grandparents, Basil and Zoe, had raised her. The small earring collection had been all she had left of her late mother.

9

"What else have you heard?"

"I heard…" Celina paused thinking before saying, "I heard about the Prince Andronikos situation."

Ah, there it was. The real reason Elara and Basil had left their home in Constantinople. So, Celina knew, and if Celina knew, then many other people probably knew too. Elara's heart dropped to her stomach at the thought.

"What did you hear about all that?" Elara's throat went painfully tight as she wondered how many people around the Roman Empire were talking about her and her failed engagement to the prince.

Celina stopped unpacking and moved to sit next to Elara on the windowsill. "I heard you wanted to end the engagement with him and that the empress let you."

"Yes." Elara hugged her legs close to her chest. "It was a very difficult thing calling off an engagement to a prince. If Empress Maria had not allowed me to do it… I would be married to him now, I think."

"It must have been hard to call off a royal wedding like that—especially when everyone in the empire was looking forward to it." Celina wrapped her arms around her own legs, so they were both sitting as they once had as children. "What happened with him, Elara…if you don't mind me asking?"

Elara was quiet for a moment before saying dryly, "He chewed with his mouth open."

This response elicited a big laugh from Celina. "Cheeky! Fine, you don't have to tell me. I'm sorry if my asking made you uncomfortable. I'm your lady-in-waiting now and I've always been your friend, so you know I'm here for you no matter what."

"Yes, I know. Thank you, Celina."

She watched Celina get up and go back to unpacking her garments, putting them in the first wardrobe and putting her papers and jewelry in the dresser drawers. Celina had an elegant way of gliding about the room. Elara wished she was as put together and confident as her. It wasn't that she wanted to hide things from Celina, but she just wasn't ready to discuss what had happened with her ex-fiancé, Prince Andronikos Palaiologos. It was an embarrassing situation, and despite her papou's assurances, Elara couldn't help but feel it was entirely her fault. Everyone in the empire had been so excited to celebrate a royal wedding by partying and feasting for days. Now all they had was disappointment thanks to her.

"My papou says I'll be inheriting the title of countess now that my yiayia has passed," Elara said to change the subject.

"Oh, really?" Celina glanced over her shoulder as she put her last dress in the wardrobe. "And how do you feel about that?"

"I'm not sure I'm ready," Elara admitted quietly. It was the first time she had made this admission out loud. "My yiayia was so good at it. She ran our old estate with such ease. I'm not as skilled as her... I mean I don't have any experience running a household, let alone an estate."

11

Celina glided back over to stand in front of Elara. Crossing her arms, she said, "Lady Elara Iliakos, you served as a lady-in-waiting to the empress herself, *and* you have already taken care of so much for your papou. He would be lost without you, truly."

"Hardly," she kidded with a shake of her head.

"Elara dear, I'm serious." Celina poked Elara's arm, enunciating each word emphatically. "Give yourself some credit."

"Ow! All right, all right! Stop poking me!" She put up her arms to block her friend's jabs.

Celina grinned and gave a little mock bow. "As her ladyship commands."

"You are the worst. Seriously, is there a way I can request a new lady-in-waiting?" Elara asked with a wide, teasing smile as Celina once again sat on the windowsill beside her.

"Sorry Elara dear, but as a future Baroness of Bulgaria, I come with a no-returns policy." She matched Elara's teasing tone and mannerisms without missing a beat.

"Fine, you can stay," Elara laughed. "Will you come to church with me tomorrow?"

"Of course! Is there an Orthodox Church nearby or are there only Catholic Churches around these parts?" Celina scrunched her nose as if the idea of going to any church that wasn't Orthodox was offensive to her. "My least favorite part of the Latin Empire is its lack of Orthodox Churches, you know."

"I know." Elara rolled her eyes. "Don't worry. There's a small Orthodox Church on the far side of the fortress. Do you mind a bit of walking?"

"Not at all," Celina beamed. "As long as the weather is agreeable."

- - -

They lucked out with the weather. It was a perfect, crisp, sunny fall day. Exactly the kind of day for a walk to church. The little houses and shops they passed on their way were quaint, picturesque, little cottages with stone walls, clay tile roofs, and smoke billowing from the various chimneys. Count Basil had taken his carriage there, but Elara loved to walk. With the weather this lovely, it was hard to think of doing much else.

"Come on! We're nearly there!" Elara called back to Celina who was trailing behind.

"Oh, you're so much faster than me," Celina huffed in exasperation. "You know that I'm slow in my church heels!"

"You think your feet hurt? You should see mine," Elara half joked. Her feet had mostly healed from yesterday's escapade around the fortress, but they were still tender if she applied too much pressure.

"Why? What happened to yours?"

"Never mind." She laughed and continued full speed ahead, confident that Celina would eventually catch up.

The winding stone street was all uphill for the last few blocks of the journey, but Elara didn't mind. Even as her breathing labored a bit and her feet felt ready to rip open again, the cool breeze and promise of shade at the church kept her going.

"Money for the poor?" An older woman with a metal cup asked from a nearby stoop. The woman had messy salt-and-pepper hair, and a dark shawl draped over her shoulders. Her voice and appearance made Elara stop in her tracks, nearly causing Celina to walk into Elara's back. "Money for the poor?" the beggar woman asked again, pitifully holding out her cup for some coins.

"Oh, of course, dear!" Celina said as she and Elara pulled some coins out of their pockets to give to the beggar woman.

"Thank you." The beggar woman smiled, revealing a row of decaying teeth.

"Come by the estate after church and I'll give you some food and drink," Elara offered.

Instead of accepting her offer, the beggar woman squinted her eyes and said, "You know, we're very much alike, Countess."

Elara's throat tightened with dread. "How so?"

"We are both ladies with bad reputations. I used to be a noblewoman too but look at me now!" The beggar woman lifted her arms to show off her tattered clothes made mostly of rags.

"You used to be noble?" Elara's stomach churned and her palms were sweaty. She suddenly felt as if she was gazing into her own future. Perhaps the beggar woman wasn't a woman at all, but a premonition sent to warn Elara of what was to come.

14

"Yes, I was very wealthy before my ex-lover ruined my reputation," the beggar woman continued, her voice getting louder. "Unlike you, I didn't have an understanding papou to protect me! Lucky you."

"Let's go." Celina's tone became protective as she grabbed Elara's arm.

"It's only a matter of time before the count gets tired of taking care of you and you'll end up just like me!" The beggar woman laughed as if the idea of Elara getting thrown out onto the streets pleased her.

"I wish there was something more I could do to help you," Elara said to the beggar, feeling close to tears as Celina pulled her toward the church.

"Women with bad reputations either end up on the streets or dead!" The beggar woman's final words echoed off the stone walls as she disappeared from view.

"Don't listen to her!" Celina said, pulling Elara along as fast as she could.

- - -

They arrived at the church just as the bells for orthros, the pre-liturgy service, began to toll. The Orthodox church was a tall, cross-shaped building with a big dome roof in the center. The inside, however, was where the real beauty lay. Every wall was covered with mosaic iconography of the saints and bible stories. Over the altar was a mosaic of the Madonna and Child. The dome had a mosaic of Christ holding one hand up and the other holding the Scriptures.

15

It was a classic layout for an Orthodox church, yet Elara couldn't help but feel this church was extra special. Not as special as her church, the magnificent Hagia Sophia, back in Constantinople, but still special.

As the two girls made their way through the narthex, lighting a candle and kissing an icon by the entryway, their ears were filled by the sound of otherworldly Orthodox chant. Orthodox chant sounded much more other worldly than Catholic choirs in Elara's opinion. The best part of this particular church was no one looked at her when she entered.

After her failed engagement to Prince Andronikos, it seemed people always looked at her and whispered about her wherever she went, but the worst was at church.

"There's the girl... Yes, she was supposed to marry the prince, but she didn't want to... What's wrong with her?...Doesn't she know how shameful it is to refuse a prince?... We were all looking forward to the royal wedding feasts, but now all the celebrations are canceled...Her family must be so ashamed of her!"

The gossip was horrible, but the threats of retribution against her had become so overbearing, Elara and her papou had to move to a different empire to escape it. Now, even the beggars were taunting her.

Women with bad reputations either end up on the streets or dead. The beggar woman had been so gleeful in her damnation of Elara. It felt like a curse or a tragic prophecy.

"Good morning, all," Father Demosthenes' calm voice brought her back to the present. "The sermon today is about the Holy Martyrs.

We can learn a lot from their courage and how they cared more about doing the right thing than about their reputations in secular society..."

Elara often tuned the sermon out, distracted by her own thoughts and worries. She never really related to stories about martyrs and saints, people who always did the right thing and never made mistakes anyway.

Father Demosthenes kept talking, saying something now about the bravery of Saint George and how his comrades turned on him when they discovered he was a Christian, but his faith never wavered.

"Do you think the martyrs and saints knew we would be talking about them this much after they died?" Elara bounced a little on her heels, wishing for the umpteenth time that Orthodox Churches had places to sit down like the Catholics did. Standing the whole service was so cumbersome, especially when her feet were already sore.

"Hmm, I think not," Celina whispered back, looking equally uncomfortable. "Oh my, I hate these shoes... Do you think I'll get in trouble if I take them off?"

"Be quiet, girls!" An older woman in a black veil turned to scold them.

"Sorry!" they whispered, trying not to laugh again. Elara held her breath as she tried to steady herself. Perhaps if she counted to a thousand, she'd be distracted enough to not think about her poor feet.

"Let us pray," Father Demosthenes stepped down from the pulpit and returned to the altar. The sermon was over.

The sweet smell of incense filled the room again, transporting Elara to her childhood memories. She remembered staring at the stained glass windows, memorizing every detail of every icon. Her yiayia had taken her by the hand and tried to explain the Divine Liturgy to her. Elara never seemed to fully grasp its meaning, but she did love it.

Back in the present, Elara and Celina made their way out of the church once they'd had communion and the service was over.

Her papou was waiting for them by his carriage outside. He was standing next to a middle-aged, lengthy man with graying hair on his head and beard. The man had small dark eyes and lavish chestnut brown robes with a stone encrusted gold chain around his neck. His ears stuck out slightly, but he was so well dressed that it hardly mattered. The man looked eerily familiar, but Elara couldn't quite place him.

"Girls!" Basil called out and waved them over. "You remember Lord Nekros Epivlavis Palaiologos, Despot of Constantinople." A despot was the Eastern Roman version of a duke or prince and was yet another way Constantinople differentiated itself from the rest of the world.

"Oh hello, Your Excellency!" Celina gave a little bow and Elara followed her lead. "My father, Baron Joseph Oberon, sends his regards."

"So, you're Oberon's daughter! I should have known! You have his likeness." Nekros had a raspy voice of a man who either yelled or coughed often. "And you must be Lady Elara, the new countess of Constantinople."

"Yes." Elara smiled in what she hoped was pleasant enough. "Correct me if I'm wrong, but have I met you somewhere before, Your Excellency?"

Nekros smiled back kindly. "Yes, we met once in Constantinople early last year. Prince Andronikos is my nephew."

Andronikos. Of course.

The sound of her ex-fiancé's name caused her stomach to twist and her throat to tighten. Nekros could have said he was the younger brother of Emperor Michael or the brother-in-law to Empress Maria, but instead, he had said her ex's name.

Andronikos.

Elara was sure the despot hadn't said it to be hurtful, but it still rubbed her the wrong way. All she wanted was to go one day without being forced to think about the man that had broken her heart and sent her fleeing from her home in disgrace.

"I was also very dear friends with your father back in the day!" Nekros barreled on, seemingly unaware of her distress. "I was greatly saddened when he passed. Such a good soul. Surely you must miss him terribly."

Elara swallowed the lump in her throat and tried to steady her breathing. She hardly ever thought of her parents. Elara thought of her late yiayia, who had raised her, more often than she thought of her father or mother.

She had lost her mother at just three years old and her father when she was six. As she grew older, she started to forget what her parents looked like or what their voices sounded like. Now, they had faded from her memory almost entirely, but Lord Nekros expected to see her grief. Everyone expected to see her grief.

"Yes indeed, Your Excellency. I miss both my parents very much." Elara glanced over her shoulder, looking for an escape route.

"I've invited Lord Nekros and his wife over for dinner tonight," Basil told her, regaining her attention.

"Wonderful." She wasn't sure why her papou was telling her this. Back in Constantinople, her grandparents' friends just showed up and she never got much warning. "What are we having to eat?"

"Well, as countess and lady of the household, you oversee the necessary preparations for dinner. The servants and kitchen staff will help you, of course." Basil grimaced and furrowed his brow as if he was disappointed that Elara didn't already know about her responsibilities.

"Right...that's right." Elara flushed. "If you'll excuse me, I'll be walking home now to start making all the arrangements."

"I'm looking forward to it. Your yiayia, Countess Zoe, always prepared such wonderful dinners," Nekros said with a respectful tilt of his head.

"Yes, she did. See you both soon." Elara and Celina bowed respectfully before beginning their walk home.

"Do you want a ride back in the carriage, koukla mou?" Basil called after her.

"No, thank you, Papou!" she called back without a second glance.

- - -

20

"Will you tell me what's going on now?" Celina asked as they walked leisurely arm in arm back toward the estate. "You seem...distracted."

Elara shrugged. "People have a lot of expectations of me, and I feel like I'm letting everyone down." The beggar woman had left her stoop, and Elara was glad she wouldn't have to deal with her again today.

"Oh, don't be ridiculous! You're a lovely young lady of good noble character. It's not your fault your papou sprung this dinner on you last minute. You know that right, Elara dear?" Celina gave her arm a comforting squeeze.

It was hard for Elara to find comfort in Celina's words given that she didn't have the full details of the Prince Andronikos breakup. Perhaps if Celina knew the truth, she would judge Elara just as harshly as everyone else did. Besides, Elara *should* know her duties at least. She should know what is and is not expected of her as countess.

Instead of responding to Celina's question, Elara tried to enjoy the glorious weather and looked at the villagers bustling about after church. Most of the villagers were Roman Catholic and had been out of church at least a half hour before the Orthodox service let out.

She could smell the fresh bread they were making and hear the chickens they were grabbing for dinner. Children ran around playing games with each other while women gathered vegetables from their gardens or stitched the holes shut on their garments. Men chopped firewood and local blacksmiths were metal working. There was an older man playing the bouzouki on the front steps of his home, singing folk songs. The air was electric and buzzed full of life.

"There's a lot of work going on for a day of rest," Elara murmured, but she didn't mind the commotion. She could see herself growing to like this place—eventually.

"Elara..." Celina began again in a more serious tone. "You really can't take that beggar woman to heart. You're not going to end up like her. Count Basil would never allow it."

Before Elara could respond to that, there came a loud shout behind them.

"*Yasou!*" The Greek greeting rang out loudly, echoing off the stone walls.

Elara and Celina whirled around to see a young woman in a blue dress, with black curly hair that lay loose around her shoulders and tan skin racing toward them. The woman skidded to a halt before them with a wide grin plastered on her round face. She was shorter than the taller Celina and slightly fuller-figured than the more wiry Elara. The woman had warm brown eyes that conveyed the excitement of a child on Christmas Day. She didn't appear dangerous, but since Elara didn't know her, she still felt a little uneasy.

"Uh, hello," Elara said gently. "Can we help you?"

"Are you Countess Elara Iliakos?" The young woman panted, out of breath. She hunched over slightly but still appeared animated and in good spirits.

Elara glanced at Celina who looked equally confused. "Um, yes, I am."

"Great to hear! I am Rhea Ravi from India, and I would like to apply to be your lady-in-waiting." Rhea thrust her hand out to hand Elara a piece of parchment. "I have a list of my credentials and a letter from—"

"Oh, you can't be serious," Celina scoffed, snatching the paper before Elara could look at it. "Ladies-in-waiting are of noble birth. If you wish to apply to be a servant in Count Basil's household, that can be arranged elsewhere."

"I am of noble caste in India—"

"You'd also have to be an Orthodox Christian, not Hindu." Celina continued, barely letting Rhea get a word in. "And you'll need a certificate proving loyalty to the emperor."

"I am a Jacobite Christian and if you look at my credential paper, you'll see my family has close ties to the emperor and especially the empress. It was Empress Maria Rita Palaiologos who recommended I seek you out." Rhea pointed to the crumpled paper in Celina's hand.

"Empress Maria recommended you?" Elara raised both eyebrows. A friend of the empress was a friend of hers. "Let me see that, Celina."

"Elara dear, you can't be taking this loon seriously."

"Let me see it." Elara took the parchment and unfolded it, allowing her eyes to finally pool over its contents.

Name: Lady Rhea Ravi

Daughter of Indian Nobleman Kabir Ravi, Baronet

Religion: Jacobite Christian

Educated by: Governess Miss Padma Najman in Rome

Recommended by: Empress Maria Rita Palaiologos

"The paper bears the empress' seal," Elara smiled excitedly. "I'd recognize it anywhere."

She'd spent enough time as a lady-in-waiting to the empress to recognize Maria's seal and signature. The two-headed-eagle stamp of Constantinople was impossible to miss and intricately designed. There was no way Rhea would have been able to forge it.

"I can provide additional references if this is not sufficient," Rhea offered as Elara continued to read over the paper.

"No, this will do fine. I'd love to have you as a lady-in-waiting, Rhea." Elara handed her back the parchment with a smile. She had been hoping to have more than one lady-in-waiting and now it seemed one had fallen into her lap. "Can you start today?"

Rhea tilted her head back and squealed loudly with delight. "Ah! Yes! Thank you! Thank you! Thank you! Can I hug you? I'm a big hugger!"

Elara laughed. Rhea's excitement was contagious. "Of course!"

"Great!" Rhea threw her arms around Elara's neck and Elara hugged her back. She smelled of ginger and turmeric. "I'll go get my things and meet you at your estate. Is that all right? I can be quick!"

"Yes, that's fine," Elara said. "There's no rush."

"Thank you again, Countess. I promise I won't let you down!" Rhea was bouncing excitedly as she spoke. Elara wondered for a moment why this woman or any woman would think being her lady-in-waiting was so special. It was a glorified secretarial job, meant to promote companionship among unwed noblewomen. Elara had loved her time as lady-in-waiting for the empress, but it was hardly as joyous as Rhea appeared to think it was.

"Please call me Elara. We're both nobles here, so there's no need to be so formal."

"Well, Elara, I can tell we're going to be best friends already!" Rhea Ravi bowed and then skipped off in the direction from which she'd come and disappeared from sight.

"She seems like a real firecracker." Elara laughed fondly for a moment before turning to see a pale, stoic-looking Celina. "What is it? What's wrong?"

"*What's wrong?*" Celina repeated meticulously. "Are you serious? You just gave a total stranger my job!"

"I can have more than one lady-in-waiting!" she protested in confusion.

"Oh, how many do you need, Elara dear? Why not get another random girl off the street if you need help so badly!" Celina threw her arms in the air in exasperation before storming off to sit grumpily on a nearby stoop.

Elara wondered for a moment if she'd committed another social faux pas out in the open in front of the whole fortress. Perhaps countesses weren't supposed to have more than one lady-in-waiting. Empress Maria had six ladies-in-waiting, but she was an empress, so perhaps the rules were different for women of different ranks.

"I... I'm sorry, Celina. I'm new to this countess thing. I'm still learning." Elara lowered herself to sit on the stoop beside her friend. "As far as I know, I'm allowed to have more than one lady-in-waiting. Besides, two isn't a very large number really."

"Hmm," Celina grumbled softly but said nothing more.

"You know, I have a feeling you and Rhea are going to become good friends. There's nothing in the world quite so precious as friendship between women."

"Oh, please," Celina sniffed almost forlornly. "More like you and Rhea will become best friends and I'll be left behind."

"Now who's being ridiculous?" Elara rolled her eyes. Perhaps Celina wasn't as confident as she always let on. "Come on. I have a dinner to prepare, and I need *your* help."

"As Her Ladyship commands," Celina said sourly, but not nearly as angrily as before.

The two girls linked arms, making peace for now, as they walked the remainder of the way back to Count Basil's estate.

Chapter Two

Dinner Party

Celina knew only two things for certain: Firstly, Elara was entirely too trusting for her own good. Secondly, this mysterious Rhea person was clearly a con artist. Any seal or document could be forged, and anyone could claim to be noble even if they weren't. Celina was sure that Count Basil would see the truth at dinner and send Rhea away. Until then, Celina resigned herself to keeping as close an eye on both Elara and Rhea as possible.

"And this is the main dining hall," Elara was saying to Rhea. The countess had decided to give Rhea the full tour despite Celina's protests about trusting strangers.

The Iliakos dining hall was grand in size, but not in style. Since Count Basil and Elara had just moved in, they hadn't had time yet to properly decorate it. The long wooden table and hearth were both bare. There were spots on the stone walls clearly marked for tapestries that would be hung at a later date.

"So beautiful!" Rhea's eyes were wide in what Celina assumed was pretend excitement. "This reminds me of my father's dining hall back home, but ours is a bit more open air."

"Open air? Where do you eat—a field?" Celina asked with a tone of feigned innocence.

"Celina, please." Elara scowled in her direction, but Celina wasn't fazed.

"Oh, it was merely a question, Elara dear." She smiled at Rhea. "Well? Do you eat in a field?"

Rhea's cheeks turned a slightly darker shade, and she looked somber since the first time they'd met her. "The dining hall has no roof. It's beautiful in the day and the night."

"No roof? What do you do if it rains?" Celina asked with a frown and folded arms.

"It doesn't rain much in that part of India." Rhea shrugged.

"Really?" Celina crossed her arms and moved to stand right in Rhea's face. It pleased her that she was taller than Rhea. "I've studied many different types of architecture, and I've never heard of a roofless dining hall before. I scarcely believe such a place could exist in terms of practicality."

Rhea took a step back. "Have you never been to Rome, Lady Celina? There are many open-air courtyards there. I would think an educated person such as yourself would know that."

"Yes, but those are courtyards and meeting areas, not dining halls." Celina ignored the slight about her education.

"Well, we do things differently back home. We don't just copy Rome exactly."

"Oh, there's no shame in your family's lack of financial capability to make an exact copy of something as luxurious as Roman *courtyards.*" Celina probably should have stopped herself, but she couldn't help it, not when she was so obviously winning.

"I had no idea you were such an expert on my family's financial situation," Rhea quipped back. "Maybe you'd like to compare ledgers? I would be very curious to see how much money your family could possibly have in a meager place like *Bulgaria.*"

That struck a nerve. "Don't talk about Bulgaria or my family! My father is a nobleman of good moral character and vast wealth!"

"Enough!" Elara stood between them. "Ladies, please! I want us to all get along."

"You're right of course, Elara dear." Celina steadied her breathing. "My most sincere apologies, Miss Ravi."

"It's *Lady* Ravi, if you please, Lady Oberon." Rhea's nostrils flared, but she maintained her sunny composure. "I accept your most sincere apology."

"Oh excellent." Celina smiled before turning to look at Elara. "See? Everything's fine now."

Elara did not look convinced, but seeing as there wasn't much more she could do about it, she continued giving Rhea the tour of the estate. Each room seemed to impress Rhea more than the last. It was getting to the point that Celina simply couldn't tell if she was faking it or not.

"So how many people are you expecting for this dinner tonight?" Rhea asked as they made their way to the kitchens.

The kitchen area consisted of two large stone fireplaces and multiple tabletops for preparations, while sacks of flour and dry vegetables lined the floors. Dishes and utensils hung from the ceiling and walls, ready to be used. Servants and other kitchen staff bustled about preparing what appeared to be a five-course meal.

"It's only for six people," Elara murmured, clearly still feeling out of her element. "But you can never have too much food, I suppose."

Celina put a comforting hand on Elara's shoulder. "I'm sure Lord Nekros and his wife will be very impressed."

Elara shrugged off her hand. "Yes, but will my papou approve? I cannot mess this up."

"Don't worry, Elara," Rhea bumped her shoulder against the countess'. "We're here to help you and this kitchen staff looks more than capable of making a stellar dinner."

"Thank you, Rhea." Elara smiled and looped her arm through Rhea's arm in a way that made Celina's heart lurch with unnecessary jealousy. "Come on. I'll show you a secret passageway next."

Celina found herself trailing behind Elara and Rhea as the two girls giggled quietly and shared whispered secrets. It was like a self-fulfilling prophecy. By picking Rhea apart, Celina had inadvertently driven Elara away and she had no one to blame, but herself.

The three of them stopped in front of a large painting of an older woman with salt-and-pepper hair, a square nose, and freckled skin, in a dark yellow dress embroidered with light blue flowers. It was the only painting hanging up, but seeing as the Iliakos family had just moved in the other day, it made perfect sense to Celina that the walls would still be mostly bare.

"See this portrait of my late yiayia?" Elara pulled on the gold frame of the large painting and both Rhea and Celina watched in amazement as it swung open revealing a small hidden hallway. "Ta-da! Secret passageway!"

"Oh wow!" Celina and Rhea spoke in unison, much to both of their chagrin.

Elara chuckled, clearly pleased with herself. "Isn't it fun? It goes to my papou's room. It's meant to be a passage for the servants so they can quickly and discreetly attend to him if he needs them, but anyone could use it really."

"Wow," Rhea said again. "This is way better than the hallways back home."

"And this is the only hidden passageway in the whole fortress?" Celina asked.

"The only one I've *seen*." Elara shrugged suggestively. "But who knows…perhaps there could be more. We can go explore tomorrow if you'd both like."

"Yes, I'd love to!" Rhea said quickly and a bit too energetically for Celina's liking.

"Hmm, awfully eager to learn the layout of the place, are we? I hope you're not trying to *steal* anything from the Count and Countess."

"*Celina*," Elara groaned, annoyed. "Please."

Rhea sighed gently, taking Celina's dig in stride. "I'm just excited to get to know my new environment, Lady Oberon. There's no need to be hostile."

"My apologies, Lady Ravi." Celina felt a bit embarrassed now at being called out so bluntly. "It won't happen again." It would most definitely happen again, she just needed to be more careful.

- - -

Elara had a lot more on her plate tonight than just food. She had to impress Lord Nekros, prove herself to her papou, and get her two ladies-in-waiting to stop bickering; it was a bit overwhelming. Still, there was an air of optimism stirring within her that gave her hope. Perhaps it was Rhea's optimistic spirit rubbing off on her or the fantastic kitchen staff or the beautiful autumn weather; whatever the reason, Elara felt tonight could go well for her.

"Can you help me with this necklace, Celina?" Elara fiddled with one of her simple pearl necklaces around her neck but couldn't quite manage the clasp in the back.

"Here you go, dear." Celina finished the task for her.

"Thank you," Elara said a bit curtly, still annoyed at her friend for her earlier behavior. They were alone, just the two of them, getting ready in Elara's room. Rhea was settling in and getting ready in her own room.

Elara's room was larger than Celina's, but the layout was similar: stone walls, a roaring fireplace, a large four poster bed, two wardrobes, and a dresser with an elegant mirror. The windows were also slightly thinner, but Elara had a view of the mediterranean sea which she greatly enjoyed.

"I…I want to apologize for my behavior earlier." Celina paused, probably waiting for Elara to say something.

When she didn't, Celina continued, "I should have given Rhea a chance before making judgments about her. It's just…I find her very strange. She shows up randomly, out of the blue, asking to be a lady-in-waiting. I mean, who asks to be a lady-in-waiting? Normally, the lady of the house requests girls—"

"I thought this was supposed to be an apology," Elara interrupted her as she put on her matching pearl earrings from atop her dresser.

"Oh, you're right of course. I'm sorry. I'll try to be nicer—I promise." Celina fiddled nervously with her sleeves. "Can you forgive me?"

Elara sighed before pulling her friend in for a hug. "Of course I forgive you, Celina."

Celina relaxed into her embrace, clearly relieved. "Thank you."

Pulling back, Elara said, "Let's try to have fun tonight. I'm already stressed enough as it is."

"Everything will be perfect tonight," Celina promised. "I mean look at us! We look too beautiful to have anything other than a fun night, I should think."

Elara laughed and joined Celina in a short twirl around. Both of them were dressed in elegant evening gowns. Elara's dress was a dark blue with white pearls stitched into the sleeves. Celina's dress was a mustard yellow with little red flowers stitched at the hem. They both looked regal—a countess and future baroness respectively.

"Come on." Elara grabbed Celina's arm and pulled. "Let's go to dinner."

The two of them descended the spiral staircase, meeting Rhea at the bottom. Rhea was dressed in a long purple dress with little black beads sewn around the waist.

"Thank you for lending me this dress," Rhea said to Elara. "I'm told my bags should arrive with some of my father's servants in the coming days."

"It's no trouble!" Elara smiled. "I have more dresses than I know what to do with."

"I'm surprised your father didn't send an escort with you or a maid to attend you," Celina said this time with a measured, concerned tone rather than an accusatory one. "My father never lets me go anywhere without an escort."

Rhea shrugged as the girls walked together to the dining room, "I had travel companions on the sea, but once I hit land here it felt safe enough to go on my own...you're right by the water after all."

The first thing Elara noticed when they entered the dining room was the wafting smell of fresh baked bread and meat pastries. Elara had spent a good portion of the afternoon planning all the different dishes that the kitchen staff would prepare and what order the dishes would be brought out by the servants. Much to her relief, the order of things appeared to be correct so far.

The main dining room consisted of a long mahogany table atop an intricately designed rug with a large roaring fire behind it. The chairs all had wood carvings depicting different bible scenes with the head chair, her papou's, Count Basil's chair, depicting the Resurrection.

"There you are, koukla mou," Count Basil greeted her with a hug and a kiss on the cheek. He was wearing the outfit he'd worn at church but with a nighttime cape for warmth.

"I hope you'll find the meal pleasing, Papou." Elara said. "Shall I go over each course with you before Lord Nekros arrives?"

"That won't be necessary. I'm sure it will be wonderful." He greeted Celina and then noted Rhea. "And who is this?"

"This is Lady Rhea Ravi from India. She's going to be one of my ladies-in-waiting." Elara turned to Rhea. "This is my papou, Count Basil Iliakos."

"Great to meet you, Count Iliakos," Rhea curtsied and kissed the ring on his outstretched hand. "Thank you very much for allowing me to enjoy this feast with you all."

"Pleasure to meet you as well, Lady Rhea." Basil studied Rhea for a moment, taking in her appearance as if he was trying to decide what to think of this random girl Elara had allowed into their home without consulting him.

Elara felt a pang of guilt. Of course, she should have told her papou before giving Rhea the job of lady-in-waiting and letting her move into their estate. It was very presumptuous of her to think she had the kind of authority to do that in her papou's house.

35

"Sorry Papou, I should have—" Elara began, but before she could get another word out, the dining room doors opened loudly as a servant escorted Lord Nekros inside.

"Lord Nekros Epivlavis Palaiologos, Despot of Constantinople!" The servant announced before leaving the same way he came, closing the door behind him.

"What's a despot?" Rhea mumbled quietly to them.

"It's a noble title—like a duke. Now shush!" Celina whispered back.

Nekros had a dark tunic on with an equally dark cape and his hair was slicked back. His wife was notably missing. He spread his arms out saying, "Basil! So good to be here for dinner."

"So good to have you, Nekros," Basil greeted him with a firm handshake. "Please, let us sit."

As the servant brought in the first course, Nekros entertained them with tales and misadventures from his travels around the Mediterranean. Most of the stories were humorous and included Nekros stumbling about drunk in Athens or mispronouncing words in foreign languages in Rome. Some of the stories, however, were more serious.

"I'm telling you, Basil, the *pirate* problem has really gotten out of hand." Nekros took a sip of his wine. He was sitting at Basil's right. Elara was sitting on Basil's left with Celina and Rhea on her other side.

"Pirates?" Basil frowned. "Truly?"

"It's a huge problem. I can't even get my wife to travel with me due to fear of them." Nekros sat forward with a serious look on his face. "They've been ransacking different places all over the Mediterranean. I fear this place might be next."

"But Catalonia doesn't have any major shipping ports and most people in the area are making a modest living. Why would pirates target us?" Basil asked, perplexed.

Elara had heard of Ottoman pirates in the east that sometimes looted Constantinople ships or Eastern Roman pirates off the coast of Athens, but she'd never heard of them being in a remote place such as this.

"They're being led by a very specific corsair leader. A most dangerous man." Nekros' voice was strained as if this mysterious man had harmed him personally.

"Corsair? What does that word mean?" Celina put her fork down, giving the conversation her full attention. "I've never heard it used before."

"A corsair is a pirate who is working for another person or goal other than simple theft. They're more organized, more political—more dangerous." Nekros explained steadily.

"You are dramatic as always, Nekros," Basil laughed, breaking the tension in the room.

Elara always admired that her papou never seemed to be afraid of anything or at least not as afraid as other people seemed to be. He used to comfort her when she was small and afraid of storms by holding her hand until she fell asleep.

"This is serious, Basil." Nekros leaned forward. "The corsair I speak of is not to be trifled with."

"Is it Theodosius Kardia?" Rhea asked, speaking up for the first time since Nekros entered the room. She had an ashen look on her face. "He's the most dangerous and most prolific pirate in the Mediterranean Sea."

"You've heard of him?" Nekros' eyes widened as he looked in Rhea's direction. His face showed a combination of excitement and fear.

Elara had never heard of Theodosius Kardia. He sounded like the kind of person people talked about a lot but that you never saw much of—an invisible demon or poltergeist of sorts. Much like her papou, Elara tried not to worry about people that might not exist.

Before Rhea or Nekros could elaborate on who this Theodosius person was, servants began bustling in to bring the next course and refilling their wine goblets. All conversation stopped until the servants finished and left the room.

"So how do you know the name Theodosius Kardia?" Celina asked Rhea, a bit more pointedly than necessary in Elara's opinion.

"I've seen him…he and his crew robbed my father's ship on the way here from India…that's why I arrived here without an escort." Rhea looked slightly sick, and Elara felt her heart drop. Perhaps the infamous pirate was real.

"Oh," Celina said, sounding regretful. "How awful. I'm very sorry to hear that."

"What was Theodosius like? How did he look? Did he say anything particularly grotesque?" Nekros inquired, his interest clearly piqued, but Elara couldn't tell if his fascination was positive or negative. "If you don't mind sharing, of course, Lady Rhea."

"You don't have to share anything if you're not comfortable," Elara told Rhea. She thought it was quite rude for the despot to request Rhea relive what sounded like a fairly traumatic experience. The poor girl had been through enough.

"No, it's all right. I don't mind sharing..." Rhea took a deep breath. "It was the dead of night. The sea was calm, and we were sailing like normal. The captain let me sleep in his quarters while he slept with the crew below deck. Suddenly it got very hot, and I awoke to find the ship on fire—"

"Yes, but what of Kardia? Can you skip to the part about him?" Nekros interrupted impatiently.

"*Lord Nekros,*" Basil scolded the despot gently. "Let the poor girl finish her story."

"You're right, of course." Nekros gave an awkward laugh and leaned back in his seat. "Please continue, Lady Rhea."

Rhea nodded politely before continuing, "The ship was on fire...there was shouting above me. I ran out to find the pirates taking things and throwing things overboard. That's when I saw him..."

Elara's heart pounded in her chest as she imagined the scene that Rhea was describing. She pictured Theodosius Kardia standing on the burning ship, his hair wild, and his eyes glinting gold and red. She envisioned the wind whipping around him, his blood-stained coat making him look larger than life as he drew his blade above his head, shouting.

"I watched him bark orders…he was looking for something or someone, but he couldn't find whatever it was, so he was angry." Rhea swallowed. "My…servant, Sidra, pushed me into the last lifeboat, but she got grabbed by a pirate. I escaped alone."

Elara imagined Rhea alone in the lifeboat, shaking, crying, and watching the ship burn and her friends die. The pirates would escape the fire with their loot, untouched by the atrocity they had just committed.

"I'm so very sorry you went through that, Lady Rhea." Basil said softly, his eyes misty. "Please know you are safe here with us."

"Thank you, Count Basil." Rhea smiled, but it was clear she was still shaken by the memories of what had happened to her.

"Rhea, what did you say your servant's name was? The one that saved you?" Celina asked gently, but Elara could tell there was something simmering beneath the question. She hoped Celina would stay true to her word and not say anything out of line.

"Her name was Sidra," Rhea replied, not making eye contact with anyone as she spoke.

Elara wondered how long Sidra had worked for Rhea and how close the two may have been; she dared not ask. She knew she would be devastated if something like that happened to Celina or one of her other close friends.

Nekros finished the last of his wine in his glass before saying, "As I told you all, we must all be vigilant! You never know when Theodosius Kardia and his evil pirate gang may strike next!"

- - -

After dinner was over, the servants came in and started clearing the table. Rhea had excused herself early and Celina had also retired to bed soon after. Only Elara, Basil, and Nekros remained awake and talking in the main hall.

"It's been a pleasure as always, Nekros." Basil shook the despot's hand. "You're welcome here at Tossa de Mar anytime."

"Thank you for having me, Basil. I always appreciate your hospitality." Nekros turned to Elara. "Congratulations on your first dinner party, Countess. You did a wonderful job."

"Thank you, Your Excellency," Elara curtsied, pleased with herself.

Nekros smiled and nodded his head. "If either of you ever make your way back to Constantinople, please stop by my estate so I might return the favor."

"I don't think we'll be in Constantinople anytime too soon but thank you." Basil walked Nekros to the door, opening it for him.

41

Lord Nekros took one last look back at Elara. "Well, the offer still stands. If you're ever in the city, I'd be happy to host you." With another polite nod, Nekros disappeared into the night.

"I think that went very well, koukla mou," her papou told her as they made their way up the spiral staircase.

"Thank you, Papou." Elara grinned. "Are there any other important duties coming up I should be aware of? I'm still learning everything I need to do, you know."

They were at the top landing now, walking down the hallway dimly lit with torches toward Elara's room. It still didn't feel like home. The torch light cast a shadow over Basil's face, so it was hard for Elara to read. Normally, she could tell what her papou wanted to talk to her about, but now, in the dark, it was hard to say for certain. Elara had a feeling something was going on with him, but she didn't know what and was a little afraid to ask.

"There is something I need to talk to you about," Basil said softly as they made it slowly down the hall.

"What is it?" Elara wrung her hands worriedly. "Is something wrong?"

Basil shook his head and put his arm over his granddaughter's shoulder. "Don't worry. I have some business in Athens I need to take care of. While I'm gone, you'll be in charge of the estate, and it'll be your job to make sure everything runs smoothly."

Elara gave a small smile. "I'll take care of everything while you're away. No need to worry."

"Wonderful," Basil stopped in front of her door. "Goodnight, koukla mou. I'll be gone by the time you get up, but I'll be back in a month or so."

"All right, safe travels, Papou," she tried to sound more confident than she felt.

Basil frowned before pulling her in for a bone-crushing hug. "Everything's going to be fine, Elara. I have complete faith in your abilities as countess."

"I'm not sure I deserve your faith, but thank you, Papou," She muttered into his shoulder. "I promise I shall do my best."

"Wait a minute!" Basil said, suddenly remembering something. "I have something for you, koukla mou!"

"What is it?" Elara asked as she watched her papou dig through his coat pockets, looking for whatever it was he wanted to give her.

"Ha! Here it is!" He pulled an elegant ruby necklace that Elara recognized at once as belonging to her late yiayia. She remembered her yiayia telling her about it years ago.

"This necklace has been in our family for generations," Countess Zoe had told her as a little girl. "It has belonged to every countess in the Iliakos family and someday it will belong to you too."

The necklace was one of the family's most prized heirlooms and the most expensive thing they owned now that the thieves had taken most everything else of monetary value.

"Papou…I don't know if I can take this…" Elara whispered, feeling unworthy to even be holding such a necklace, let alone owning it.

"What do you mean? It's your birthright!" Basil slipped the necklace around her neck. "There! So beautiful on you."

"Thank you." Elara muttered in awe. It was heavier than it looked, and it sparkled more brightly than she had remembered. She wondered if her papou had had it cleaned.

"You're welcome, koukla mou." Basil smiled and then said in a serious tone, "Whatever you do—don't lose it."

- - -

Don't lose it. Elara fiddled with the brass clasp of her new necklace as her papou's parting words bounced about in her mind. *Whatever you do—don't lose it.* The necklace seemed to represent all of her new countess duties: beautiful, important, full of history—easy to break or lose. She couldn't afford to let her papou down, not again.

"Are you feeling well, Elara dear?" Celina asked from the doorway of Elara's room.

Elara jumped, startled, and looked up from where she was sitting on the windowsill. Celina was leaning on the door frame, looking at her inquisitively. She was wearing a simple light green dress and had her hair pulled back with a matching ribbon.

"Yes, I just need to find a safe place for this necklace." Elara stood and smoothed the fabric of her light blue dress with red stitched hem.

44

"It's a beautiful necklace." Celina stared at the necklace for a moment and then her eyes moved up to her friend's face. "But it is *only* a necklace."

"You don't understand, Celina. This necklace was my yiayia's and her mother's and her mother's and her mother's before her. I have to protect it," Elara explained as she got up and walked briskly into the hallway.

The fortress was quiet with only the occasional servant walking about. The walls still felt empty and not lived in. Perhaps she would do some decorating while her papou was away.

"Do you have a secret drawer or cupboard you can lock it in?" Celina asked as they walked down the spiral staircase.

"Good morning, Elara," Rhea greeted them in the main entryway, dressed in a pretty orange frock. "And good morning, Lady Oberon."

"Good morning, Lady Ravi," Celina said back with stiff politeness.

"Are you two still doing that? You're adults. Please act like it!" Elara quipped in annoyance.

Before either of her ladies-in-waiting could reply, Elara walked into the drawing room and began looking for a place to store her necklace.

The drawing room had two armchairs and a small settee. The walls were mostly bare, save a small tapestry next to the fireplace. She ran her hand along the opposite wall looking for a loose stone or something that was secret enough in which to hide her necklace.

Nothing.

"Hmm, what about this, Elara?" Celina pointed to a desk situated by the door. It had a drawer with a lock on it. "You could lock it up in here."

"What are we locking up?" Rhea inquired.

"That's the countess' business, not yours," Celina retorted before Elara could respond.

"*Celina*, we talked about this," Elara said her name like a final warning.

She didn't look at either lady-in-waiting as she slipped her necklace inside the drawer and locked it with the key.

Elara slipped the key in her pocket saying, "There. That should be secure."

"Where will you keep the key? Not loose in your pocket, I hope," Celina inquired.

Elara put her hand back in her pocket where she felt two keys. One was the key she just used to lock the drawer and the other belonged to a clothing chest in her room. Smiling almost mischievously, she pulled one of the keys back out of her pocket and motioned for Rhea to come over. Rhea beamed happily and obeyed at once, coming to stand in front of Elara. Celina looked like she might choke on something or punch someone.

"Rhea, can I trust you with this?" Elara pressed the key into Rhea's hand. "It's very important."

"You can trust me! I shall protect this key with my life," Rhea promised, wide-eyed and clearly pleased with her new duty.

"Oh, you can't be serious," Celina grumbled in disbelief. "Elara dear, you met Lady Ravi *yesterday*. Are you sure you really want to trust her with this important task so soon?"

"I can assure you, Lady Oberon, I am more than trust-worthy enough and capable enough to protect a key." Rhea looked at Celina smugly as she put the key in her pocket.

"Well, you didn't do a very good job protecting your things from pirates, did you, Lady Ravi?"

"Celina! What is wrong with you?" Elara couldn't believe her friend had said something so cruel.

After the horrible story of death and destruction at the hands of pirates that Rhea had shared last night, Elara couldn't imagine being mean enough to throw it so unjustly back into Rhea's face.

"Jealousy is an ugly color on you, Lady Oberon," Rhea spat, moving to stand in Celina's face. "It must be so hard for you that despite your best efforts, you can't hate me away. I'm here to stay."

Celina took a deep breath and a step back. "You're right of course, Lady Ravi. I should have been more tactful with my accusations of your shortcomings. I'll remember that in the future."

There was a palpable tension between the two girls that Elara couldn't name. She suddenly felt that she was the odd one out, that it was she, Elara, who did not know the rules to this game they were playing. The way they stared at each other could only be described as pure, unadulterated hatred. It didn't make sense to Elara. They only met yesterday…wasn't it too soon to passionately hate someone you only just met?

"Um, ladies?" Elara called their attention back to her and away from each other. "Care to explain to me what's going on?"

"Isn't it obvious?" Rhea said shortly. "Lady Oberon hates me for no good reason!"

"It is true I have no reason to hate, but I have plenty of reasons to mistrust you, Lady Ravi. I find your presence here *highly* suspicious." Celina spoke more coldly than Rhea did, but with equal amounts of unjust anger.

"Perhaps it would be helpful if you were to call each other by your first names?" Elara suggested gently as she moved to stand between them and loop her arms with each of theirs.

Celina pulled her arm out of Elara's and stormed out of the room. Normally Elara wouldn't condone her friend behaving like a brat—they were adults after all! However, something was obviously going on and she needed to get to the bottom of it.

"*Ti kanies!* What are you doing?" Elara called after her friend. She followed Celina out the door and into the open air. The weather showcased another lovely autumn day, and the people were bustling about as normal outside.

"Countess?" A servant dressed in brown work trousers, cream tunic, and holding an entire basket of vegetables blocked her path.

"Yes… what is it?" Elara asked, trying to keep track of where Celina was going.

"Which storeroom would you like us to use for the harvest?" He gave her a pointed look as if she should know which storeroom was for which.

"I don't know. Which one do you think is best?" Elara tried not to sound annoyed, but she needed to catch up with Celina.

"The count said you would be giving us orders on what to do with this." The servant continued dryly. "Unless there's someone else around here that you'd like to give up your duties to?"

That felt pointed. Elara felt her cheeks turn red as she allowed the implication to wash over her. This random servant had just accused her of being lazy, of being inept, and of passing off her duties to others instead of doing them herself. She looked around and saw other servants and peasants staring at her with the same weariness.

News travels fast.

"I don't like what you're implying," Elara narrowed her eyes into slits. "Can you tell me what I owe this poor treatment to?"

Now it was the servant's turn to look embarrassed. "I'm sorry, Countess. Please forgive me. I only know the whispers from Constantinople."

"And what whispers are those?" she demanded.

The servant looked at the other servants who ducked their heads trying to look busy. He bit his lip and mumbled something inaudibly.

"Speak up, please." Elara waved her hand in his face to get him to look at her.

"They say you refused to marry the prince as was your duty," he muttered. "And everyone was disappointed when it was announced that there would be no royal wedding to celebrate. We have so little to celebrate these days…"

If Elara was braver or more self-righteous, she might have scolded him for gossiping about her, but instead, she merely asked what she really wanted to know: "Does everyone here know about this?"

"Yes. I'm sorry, Countess." He began to say something else, but Elara wasn't listening anymore. The people in her new home knew about her. They knew about her failed engagement. They knew of the embarrassment she had brought to her family, the dishonor she brought to her reputation and to her family's reputation.

The ground felt unsteady beneath her feet as blood rushed to her head. It suddenly felt like everyone was staring at her and judging her. Logically she knew they probably weren't all doing that, but it still felt that way. Her chest constricted and it suddenly became hard to breathe.

They all knew about her failed engagement to Prince Andronikos…Everyone knew about her failings…Everyone was staring at her…Everyone was judging her…Everyone was condemning her… *Women with bad reputations either end up on the streets or dead.* The words of the beggar refused to leave her mind. It was the ultimate condemnation, and she was beginning to see that many of the people here shared the beggar woman's sentiments.

"Stop looking at me!" she screamed as the shame she felt became unbearable.

Some people came toward her, but she rushed off down the hill and toward the beach to get away from them, to get away from them all. Her desire to confront Celina had vanished. Right now, all she wanted was to be alone. The sea seemed like the best and closest place to go.

Chapter Three

The Corsair

Celina needed proof. She knew in her heart-of-hearts that Rhea was lying about *something*. She just needed to figure out what it was and prove it to Elara before it was too late. She didn't understand why Elara refused to see what Celina saw, but then again, she wouldn't consider Elara the best judge of character given what happened with Prince Andronikos.

Even Count Basil had seemingly been fooled by whatever ruse Rhea was playing. The pirate story had been convincing, but Celina had noticed something strange about the way Rhea had told it. The girl seemed to be intentionally leaving out important details.

She walked briskly toward Father Demosthenes' house on the opposite side of the fortress, looking back only occasionally to see if Elara was still following her. She wasn't.

Father Demosthenes' cottage was quite small compared to the estate, but average size compared to the other houses surrounding it. It had a clay tile roof and gray stone walls like all the buildings and had smoke coming from the chimney.

"Father, are you in?" Celina called out as she knocked on the wooden door.

A few moments later, Father Demosthenes opened the door with a pleasant expression on his middle-aged face. He had a dark beard and kind brown eyes. His religious robes had been exchanged for some modest work clothes. Demothenes was clearly baking something as his leather work smock was covered in flour, his hands messy, and his sleeves were rolled up to his elbows.

"Hello. What can I do for you, Lady Celina?" He knew her name, which surprised her, but she didn't take the time to inquire about that.

"Father, I was wondering if you had any record books about Christian peoples living in India or thereabouts?" she asked, trying to sound as nonchalant as possible.

"India?" Demosthenes furrowed his brow. "Whatever for?"

"I need to know if there are any Indian Jacobite nobles and their names and any other information you might have on them. It's very important. I understand you have the only book collection in town. Can I take a look?"

Father Demosthenes motioned for her to come in and moved to the side to allow Celina to enter his dwelling. "I have one book on Orthodox nobles and their staff from a census collection the monks at Mount Athos gave me a few years ago. You can see if what you're looking for is in there."

Celina followed him past the messy kitchen and to his bookshelf which was positioned next to a window and beside a large armchair, the coziest little reading nook Celina had ever seen. He pulled a large brown book off the shelf and handed it to her.

"Thank you, Father." Celina smiled as she excitedly opened the book and hungrily looked for any information about the elusive Rhea Ravi.

- - -

Elara loved the ocean. Ever since she was a little girl, the warm Mediterranean waters had always brought her comfort. She now stood knee deep in the water, not caring about the cold or the fact that her dress was getting soaked. It was nice to be alone and away from prying eyes.

It was devastating that the servants seemed to know about her troubled past. She had hoped that her old life might remain hidden from the people of Tossa de Mar so that she could start over and reclaim her family's good name.

Instead, there was judgment, just as there had been judgment in Constantinople. People staring at her and wondering how she could have been so foolish as to give up marrying a *prince* and future emperor of the Eastern Roman Empire.

They simply didn't know Prince Andronikos Palaiologos the way she did. If they knew him, they would understand why she did what she did. If they knew the way he spoke to her, or the time he threw a vase at her head, they would understand. If they knew that breaking off her engagement with the prince was like cutting off an infected limb—painful, but necessary, then perhaps they would not judge her so harshly.

Water splashed up on Elara's chest and she gasped aloud, startled by the roughness. The sea was churning the way it always did when ships were near. She scanned the horizon and didn't see any. It wasn't a shipping day, so she hadn't expected to see anything, but that still didn't explain the picking up of the waves. The wind was calm and the clouds clear, so it wasn't a storm either. She wondered if perhaps there was a smaller ship hiding on the other side of the cliffs out of view.

Seeing as she was already soaking wet, she decided to slip under the water and swim to the far side of the cliffs to find out. Elara was a strong swimmer, and she knew better than to swim too close to the rocks, but as she swam, the tide picked up and the water got rougher. Her clothes began to feel heavy, but she persisted onward as carefully as possible.

Finally, she reached the other side of the cliffs but couldn't see much over the water smacking fiercely over the rocks. Elara gripped one of the larger cliffside rocks and pulled herself up trying to get a better view of what was out there. To her horror, there was a ship right in front of her, but it wasn't a normal ship. Instead of the Catalonia flag billowing in the breeze, there was a black flag with a white skull and crossbones.

Pirates.

"Hey! Look, fellas!" A voice said behind her. "I found a mermaid!"

Elara shrieked, seeing a group of strange men suddenly right behind her. Two of them grabbed her off the rocks and dragged her to the shoreline where others were waiting. The cliffs and woods were the perfect cover—no one in the fortress would see the ship coming.

"Unhand me!" Elara screamed as they threw her at the feet of a tall, lean man, dressed in mostly black. "You have no right! Let go!"

"What do we have here?" the man in black asked.

"A girl, Captain. She was spying on the rocks," One of the men explained.

"Spying, was she? She looks much too gentle to be a spy." The captain chuckled. "What are we to do with you, Softy? We might be corsairs, but we don't take spying lightly. We're men of honor after all."

Elara's heart pounded in her throat, and her stomach tied in anxious knots. Other than killing her, there was no telling what horrors these men might do to her. She had to play this right if she wanted to get out of this alive and unscathed.

"I can help you get into the fortress," she said firmly. "As long as you promise not to harm me or anyone else, you can take whatever you like."

The captain smiled down at her, clearly pleased by her words. "See, gents? I told you the count's servants would be no trouble at all."

Elara felt herself being hauled to her feet and the men laughed but made no aggressive moves against her. She found herself face to face with the captain now and hated herself for thinking he was a little handsome with his thick hair, long eyelashes, high cheekbones, and full lips. It was almost a sin that a man this heinous on the inside should be so decent looking on the outside. The other pirates at least had the decency to be ragged.

"Go on then, Softy. Lead the way." He gestured to the fortress above them.

Elara led the pirate crew up the path on the side of the cliff that led to the fortress' back door. She knew it would be locked, but one word from her and it would open allowing all these terrible men inside.

She knocked three times on the door and heard one of the servants call out, "Who's there?"

"It is I," Elara said with a shaky voice. "Can you open the door?"

"Are you alone?" the servant asked.

The tip of something sharp poked her side, and she glanced sideways to see the captain was the one holding her at knife point. Any call for help or warning would spell her doom.

"Yes, I'm alone. Please open the door."

The doors opened and the ten or so pirates funneled in with excited yelps. They immediately began breaking things and taking what they wanted, but true to their word, none of the people were touched.

"Elara! What's going on?" Rhea was shaking and once she saw the captain's face she screamed and fled in the opposite direction.

The captain didn't seem to notice or perhaps he just didn't care. "I want to see Count Basil's ledgers of acquaintances and associates, if you please, Softy."

"Why do you want that?" Elara asked, perplexed.

"That's my business." He tapped his knife gently on her shoulder and gestured for her to lead the way. "Show me where they are."

Elara nodded. "This way, Captain."

She felt him staring at her as they walked down the halls to her papou Basil's room. She thanked God her papou was not at home. The captain was still staring at her as she opened the large oak doors that led to the master bedroom.

"Why do you keep staring at me?" she asked.

"You're a very pretty maiden," he said in a low voice.

"Touch me and I'll kill you," Elara spat in disgust.

The captain laughed and turned away from her. "Relax. I never take a girl against her will. Now, show me the ledgers."

"They're over there in the top drawer." Elara pointed to Basil's tall dresser drawers. His room and furniture were much like Elara's room, but larger and more masculine—less decorative, although the large fireplace was more ornate.

"I don't see what I'm looking for, Softy." The captain said as he rummaged through the drawer.

"It's buried deep. Keep looking." Elara picked up a heavy vase as she slowly crept up behind him.

- - -

Celina was practically giddy as she raced back to the estate. She had her proof tucked away in her pocket. Father Demosthenes had been nice enough to let her tear a page out of the book as long as she promised to return it in the coming days. That was plenty of time to show it to Elara and get Rhea sent away for good. She just hoped Elara would have enough sense to believe it.

"Fire! Pirates!" Someone was yelling frantically.

She stopped in her tracks, looking up at the estate in horror. There was fire coming out of two of the windows and people rushing about either to escape or help put out the flames. The sound of glass smashing and more people shouting could be heard from inside.

"Elara!" Celina yelled as she raced up the stone steps to find her friend. "Elara! Where are you?"

Celina swung the door open and charged inside seeing the fullness of the chaos unfold. Servants were running for their lives as pirates ransacked the place, taking whatever they wanted and breaking everything else.

"Celina!" It was Rhea looking out of breath and shaking. "He has Elara! They're in Count Basil's room and he barricaded the door, so no one can get in!"

Without a word, Celina raced up the stairs and toward the portrait of Countess Zoe. She pulled on the frame and ran down the dimly lit secret passageway. She could feel Rhea behind her, but did not acknowledge her as her focus was consumed with saving Elara.

"Get away from her—!" Celina started to shout as she entered Count Basil's room but stopped short at the sight that greeted her.

Elara was there, holding a knife to a man's throat. The man's head was bleeding slightly, he was tied to a chair, and there was a smashed vase at his feet. The countess looked a bit soggy and ragged, but otherwise unharmed. Somehow, miraculously, Elara had gotten the upper hand on this one man at least.

"Friends of yours?" The man tilted his head toward Celina and Rhea. He sounded awfully calm for having a knife at his throat.

"Shut up!" Elara snapped. "I want you and your crew gone. Understood?"

So, this was the captain. He looked fairly young to be a pirate captain, but Celina supposed there was no real age limit on these sorts of things. The man had thick dark hair that swooped slightly over his cheekbones. He had a thin frame, chiseled jawline, and was wearing a tattered black jacket over a stained linen shirt and black trousers. If he was cleaner and had been better dressed, Celina would have assumed he was a part of the noble class.

"How am I supposed to *get gone* if I'm tied up?" The captain spoke as if they were discussing the weather. Perhaps being tied up and having a knife at his throat was a regular occurrence for him.

"I'm going to untie you, but first, I want you to give the orders so that the other pirates leave at once." Elara's hand was trembling, but whether it was from nerves, or the cold was hard to say.

"The ledgers aren't here, are they? The count took them with him, didn't he?"

Celina didn't know what ledgers he was talking about, but he seemed rather peeved that they weren't there for him to steal.

"He always takes his ledger book with him on his travels, yes," Elara admitted, unmoving.

60

"Dammit. That's too bad." The captain smirked, still looking completely at ease. "Will you put the knife down, Softy? You're obviously not going to kill me. You don't have the stomach for it."

"I'm stronger than I look," Elara said, clearly trying to convince herself more than him.

Rhea grabbed Celina's arm and whispered in her ear, "Tell the countess to let the man go. His men will be here soon." As much as she hated to admit it—Rhea was right.

"Dear," Celina moved to stand beside Elara and put a hand on her shoulder. "You're going to have to untie him. It's only a matter of time before the others come looking for him and they won't be happy if they see him like this."

"Yeah, listen to your friend. She's clearly smarter than you." He chuckled again in an arrogant sort of way that made Celina want to strike him.

"Fine, I'll untie you, but then I want you *gone*." Elara breathed, her voice was soft, but confident. She did not betray any of the weakness or fear she must have been feeling.

"Your wish is my command, Softy. You untie me and I'll be out of your hair forever." He grinned, revealing a row of surprisingly nice teeth.

Elara clenched and unclenched her jaw. "My name is not Softy."

"I don't care what your name is," he said, his voice rough now. "*Untie me.*"

Before Elara or Celina or even Rhea could make a move, the door burst open and some of the other pirates burst in. They were not as good looking as the man tied up before them.

"More pretty wenches!" One of the men said with a sinister laugh.

Celina's heart was pounding, and she wished she had a knife too. There was no telling what these men might try to do to them.

"Leave the girls be and untie me!" The captain ordered firmly.

"You heard Captain Kardia. Untie him!" One of the men said to the others.

Celina's heart dropped. *Theodosius Kardia*. The horrid man from Rhea's story and Lord Nekros' nightmares. He was real, he was here, and he was tied up by gentle Elara of all people.

Theodosius' men untied him and helped him up from the chair. Theodosius dusted himself off and turned to smile at Elara who was still gripping her knife for dear life. Celina and Rhea stayed behind her.

"I respect the hustle, Softy. Have to run though. Little time and much to do and all that." Theodosius winked and gestured for his men to follow him out.

"Wait!" Elara said, noticing something. "What's that in your friend's pocket?"

"What? This?" One of the men pulled out Elara's prized necklace from his pocket and laughed. "Finders keepers."

- - -

Elara used the secret passageway out of her papou's room to try to catch up with the pirates. She chased the men up to the lookout rooftop bridge where they could cascade down and exit the way they came, taking her yiayia's necklace with them. Celina and Rhea had run around the other way to see if they could cut off the pirates before they made it to the ship that way.

"Stop!" Elara yelled. She couldn't let them steal her necklace. Any other piece of jewelry wouldn't matter so much, but that one…that was her family's most prized possession. Elara made it to the top walk and watched as the first of the men was cascading down the walls.

Theodosius turned back to look at her, amused. "You never give up, huh? I admire that."

"Give me my necklace!" she said, ignoring him completely as she raced toward the tall, bald man that had the necklace in his pocket. "Give it back!" She pulled on his coat trying to retrieve it, but to no avail.

"Piss off, lady!" The man shouted, shoving her off balance.

Elara stumbled backward, tripping over something she couldn't see. It caused her feet to slip out from under her and send her falling over the high wall of the fortress. Luckily, she managed to grab onto the ledge to keep herself from falling to the depths below.

"Help! I'm slipping!" Elara screamed.

She could hear the pirates laughing and continuing on their way—ignoring her. Her arms strained with the effort to hold herself up, and with each moment, her grip on the rocks was slipping. If she didn't get help soon, it would be only a matter of time before she fell to her death.

"Celina! Rhea!" Elara cried out again for salvation, despite knowing that her friends were too far away to help her. "Help!" She gave one last shout as her fingers started slacking.

Just as she was about to fall, strong hands gripped her wrists, pulling her up to safety. The person placed her gently on the stone floor where she collapsed into a shaking heap. She looked up to see who had saved her and found Theodosius Kardia looking down at her, smirking. The rest of the pirates were gone, and it was just the two of them on the lookout bridge.

Elara opened her mouth and closed it, feeling unsure of what to say or do. Did he expect her to thank him? To tremble in admiration? She knew she would never do that, but he had just saved her life so she should say something.

"Why did you do that?" Elara asked, a bit breathlessly.

"I'm a gentleman." Theodosius winked, looking entirely too pleased with himself.

"You're a *pirate*." She frowned in disbelief, not believing him to be virtuous in any way. Pirates weren't exactly known for their merciful tendencies.

"If I'm being honest, I prefer the title corsair or captain to pirate."

"Semantics." Elara moved closer to the wall in case she had to grab a rock to fight him with. She didn't like how he was standing over her and she was still on the ground. "I knocked you out with a vase and held you at knifepoint. Why would you help me? What do you want?"

"I *wanted* Count Basil's ledger book with the names and details of his associates, but since you don't have that, please know that I don't want *anything* from you." He was clearly aggravated now but made no violent threats. "My crew ransacked your home and stole some of your things. Call it even, Softy?" Without another word, he escaped over the fortress wall as the others had and disappeared out of sight.

Elara stayed on the floor for a few more moments trying to collect herself both physically and emotionally. Her yiayia's necklace was gone, her fortress had been ransacked, she had no idea where Celina and Rhea were, and the infamous pirate Theodosius Kardia had just saved her life. So much had happened in a little over an hour or two.

"Elara! Where are you?" Celina and Rhea were calling for her below. Their voices sounded frantic, but not in a way that suggested any bodily injuries on their part, to which Elara was relieved. Her necklace was one thing, but her friend's lives were another thing entirely.

"I'm here!" she called back, slowly getting to her feet. Her arms were sore from gripping the wall, but, other than that, she was, physically, unharmed.

She made her way back down to the front of the estate where her friends were both waiting for her. The estate and surrounding areas had suffered a lot of damage, but it appeared that none of the people around had sustained injuries. Servants and other townsfolk were already starting to clean things up, but it would take a while for everything to be fixed. Windows were broken, tables tossed over and burned, jars smashed, doors slightly off their hinges, food spilled, valuables stolen...

"Is everyone well?" Elara asked frantically as she passed people by.

"Yes, Countess," they replied, sounding more shaken than anything. They were all looking her up and down and she couldn't help but feel the judgment.

This happened on your watch.

"Elara dear!" Celina hugged her tightly and Elara wanted to cry but didn't let the tears fall. She went to hug Rhea, who was standing a few feet behind, but Celina stopped her by grabbing her arms and holding her there.

"What are you doing? Step aside," Elara told Celina.

"Tell Elara the truth or I will," Celina said over her shoulder to Rhea as she held Elara in place.

Rhea shakenly looked at her feet and it was clear by the stains on her face that she had been crying quite a bit.

"Tell her," Celina ordered sternly.

Elara pulled herself out of Celina's grip and went to stand before Rhea. "You can tell me, Rhea. Whatever it is, I'm sure it can't be that bad."

"It is bad." Rhea choked out a sob. "Really, really bad."

"It's all right. Tell me," Elara said gently, putting her hand on the girl's shoulder.

"I'm not...I'm not..." Rhea stuttered and burst into tears.

66

"Oh, for God's sake!" Celina stomped over and thrust a piece of paper in Elara's hand. "Read this. It will tell you at least part of what Rhea here has been lying to you about!"

Elara frowned as she slowly unfurled the paper. Before her was a record of Indian nobility and their attendants. She scanned the list until she saw it:

Lady Sidra Ravi, Baroness equivalent
Attendants: Calypso Jinnere, Hanni Buban, Lila Peret, and Rhea Alkan

"So, you're not a noblewoman? You're a servant? Rhea Alkan?" Elara frowned as she looked up from the paper.

"Yes," Rhea sobbed. "Lady Sidra died on the ship when the pirates attacked, so I...I replaced her first name on the papers with my own. I knew I couldn't go back to India without her and I—I didn't know what else to do. I'm so sorry, Elara. Please forgive me."

"That's *Countess* Elara to you." Celina looked smug and thoroughly justified.

Elara wasn't sure how she felt, but it definitely wasn't smug.

"Countess Elara." Rhea shakingly grabbed Elara's hands and held them tightly. "I am so truly sorry. Please don't send me away. I'll be on the streets if you do. I can't go back to India without Lady Sidra, and I can't go back to my homeland either—the shame of it. My family would never let me back in."

Family shame. That was something Elara understood well.

"Your homeland? You're not from India?" Elara asked, feeling like she was learning fifty new things about Rhea at once.

Rhea's eyes widened as if she just realized she had given away another terrible truth. "I'm from...Anatolia."

"A Turk!" Celina spat. "Even worse than I suspected! Are you even Christian?"

Rhea burst into tears again as she said, "I'm Muslim."

"Ah-ha! Even more lies!" Celina was clearly relishing the vindication she was feeling.

"Don't be xenophobic, Lady Oberon. It's a bad look." Elara shook her head in annoyance.

Political tensions between the Eastern Roman Empire and the Ottoman State were at an all-time high, so it made perfect sense to her why Rhea might feel safer lying about both her national and religious identities.

"I'm not being xenophobic. I'm merely pointing out that I was right about her!" Celina doubled down.

"So that's what this is all about? Being right?" Elara gave a humorless laugh. "I wish you cared more about being kind than you do about being right."

Celina's shoulders drooped and her cheeks turned red. This was clearly not what she thought Elara was going to say. She sputtered a myriad of excuses but fell silent after she saw Elara wasn't being swayed.

"I'm not happy with you either, Miss Alkan," Elara said, turning to Rhea.

Rhea was still crying and looking at her own feet to avoid making eye contact with anyone, so Elara kept going.

"Today my home has been ransacked by pirates and my things were stolen, broken, and set aflame. I lost a tremendously important family heirloom that I promised my papou *yesterday* I would keep safe." Elara took a shaky breath. "And when I needed you both the most, you were either busy lying to me or scheming vengeance out of what I can only assume was self-righteous jealousy."

"It wasn't jealousy! I was trying to protect you!" Celina protested.

"Yes, and a grand job you did protecting me from the *pirates!*" Elara snarled back.

She was so angry she thought about hitting Celina. Instead, she sat on the lopsided stone bench behind her and began to sob into her hands.

Her friends silently moved to sit next to her, each putting a hand on her shoulder in comfort. It was quiet for a time save for Elara's gentle sobs of despair. She had let her papou down, failed to live up to her family name, got her new home destroyed, and lost her yiayia's necklace—all in one day! She could only imagine how disappointed her papou would be when he returned home from Athens, how hurt and embarrassed he would be by her failings.

Elara wondered how fast the news of the pirate attack would spread and how soon before the entire Mediterranean knew about it.

She imagined Lord Nekros sipping tea on his balcony in Constantinople, talking to his wife about what a disappointment Elara was to have fallen prey to the pirates he had explicitly warned her about. Elara imagined Empress Maria being equally dismayed by Elara's continued missteps and complaining about her former lady-in-waiting to nobles over breakfast in the palace. She imagined Prince Andronikos' smug face, pleased that Elara was floundering foolishly without him.

"Countess?" Rhea's timid voice broke Elara away from her dark thoughts. "I just want you to know I held on to the key. The pirates had to smash the furniture to pieces to get it open."

Elara looked up at her ladies-in-waiting and pulled a small metal key out of her own pocket. "The key I gave you was a fake. I had the real one with me the whole time."

"What?" Rhea gasped, eyes wide with shock and perhaps a little hurt.

"The key was a test!" Celina looked relieved. "I knew you wouldn't trust a girl you just met with the real key to your family heirloom!"

Elara ignored Celina's words of triumph. The test and the keys didn't matter anymore. The necklace was gone, and she had no one to blame but herself.

"It's not your fault what happened, Rhea. Nor yours, Celina. I am the one that has failed." Elara looked miserably down at her feet. "What if...What if when my papou gets home, he's so angry with me

70

that he throws me out? What if my reputation has become so rotten, I end up homeless?" Elara had never vocalized this fear before, but the beggar woman from yesterday had reminded her that it could be an unfortunate reality.

Women with bad reputations either end up on the streets or dead.

"Your papou would never kick you out. He loves you!" Celina reasoned, but her voice betrayed her worry. It wasn't uncommon for badly behaved women to be abandoned by their families.

"I think it's time I start taking the accusations against me and the reality of my situation seriously…" Elara's voice trailed off as hot tears spilled down her cheeks again.

"So, what are you going to do about it? Stay here and cry? Or fix things?" Celina challenged, not unkindly, but in a tone that suggested she had an idea.

"What do you suggest?" Elara asked her, perking up slightly.

"Instead of seeing this as a failure—see it as an opportunity! You get the servants and locals to help clean this place up while we track down the pirates and get your family heirloom back." Celina smiled, clearly proud of this idea she'd come up with. "Once we have the necklace, we race back here and make sure everything looks good before your papou's return."

"Is that all?" Elara replied with a shaky breath.

"Oh, well, we'd also have to be careful not to get caught doing anything unladylike while getting the necklace for reputation's sake, but other than that…" Celina shrugged like it was all so simple.

It wasn't an implausible plan, but it would be extremely difficult to say the least. "We have no idea where the pirates are going and even less of an idea of what they might have done with the necklace."

"That's not true actually." Rhea interjected.

"What do you mean?" Elara said as she and Celina turned to look at Rhea expectantly.

Rhea leaned her face closer to theirs and whispered, "I overheard the pirates saying they were going to Rome next. That pirate, Kardia, is looking for some type of book."

Count Basil's personal ledger. Elara still had no idea why Theodosius Kardia wanted that, but if he did want a ledger full of information on nobility, Rome would be the next closest place to get one.

"Say this plan works—we find the necklace without getting caught and get the fortress cleaned up before my Papou gets home. What then?" Elara asked. "It's still a rather embarrassing situation."

"Oh, but remember, dear, this is an opportunity to change the optics! If you fix everything up and retrieve the heirloom before Count Basil returns home, you can take back control of the narrative. You can turn a difficult situation into a moment of triumph where you—overcame adversity and handled the problem with ease! Everyone will be very impressed!" Celina was good at spinning things, but she was also a practical and logical person. Elara knew her friend wouldn't suggest this if she didn't believe it was possible.

It all sounded much too good to be true to Elara, but perhaps it could work. It wouldn't magically repair her reputation overnight, but it could be a start.

Fix the optics. Change the narrative.

Instead of whispers of her embarrassing blunders, people would talk about how Countess Elara Iliakos saved her family legacy and protected her new home from pirates. The fortress would be all cleaned up and the stolen necklace would be back in its place before anyone would know it had been gone. She would be seen as the perfect countess, one who did her duty and handled the pirate crisis to a tee.

It could work, or at the very least, it could make her papou proud of her again. She wanted that more than anything.

Elara smiled at her friends excitedly, feeling hopeful for the first time that day. "All right, ladies. Let's go to Rome!"

Chapter Four

Rome

Elara, Celina, and Rhea spent the next few hours preparing for their long journey. Elara put the head butler, George, in charge of the estate, and she asked Father Demosthenes to look after the people of Tossa de Mar while she was away. She was confident that they would be more than all right without her, but it was good that she made as many preparations to help them as possible.

Then there was the issue of packing. Elara had never been on a mission such as this before and wasn't exactly sure what she should bring. She knew she had to pack light, and she knew that she and her ladies-in-waiting would probably be safest if they dressed as discreetly as possible so as to blend in with the average peasantry. The less attention they brought to themselves, the safer and better off they would be. The last thing three women traveling alone would need was more attention. Elara had considered asking a male servant to come with them but felt that four people might be too many. Besides, right now Celina and Rhea were the only people she trusted.

"What do you think? Does this look discreet enough?" Elara asked Celina later in her room. She was wearing a long dark black jacket over a cream-colored shirt tied together with a belt. On her legs were brown work trousers and a pair of traditional sailor boots. On her head, she wore a dark brimmed hat.

"Lose the hat," Celina said, wearing a similar outfit, but her long jacket was a dark gray and her trousers were navy blue. "I've never worn trousers before. I'm not sure how I feel about them to be honest."

"Should we come up with boy names? I'd like to go by Justinian," Rhea suggested, her jacket was a muddy brown and her trousers were black with matching boots—the opposite of Elara's color scheme.

Elara chuckled as she tossed her hat aside. "I'll go by Constantine, and Celina can go by Augustus."

"Can I talk to you for a moment, Elara dear?" Celina placed a hand on Elara's arm and pulled her aside.

"What's wrong? If you don't like the name Augustus, you can be Tiberius or something else instead."

"It's not that. Are we sure we can trust Rhea? She did lie to us about her identity. Perhaps we should leave her behind." Celina glanced over at Rhea as she spoke, squinting her eyes in mistrust.

Rhea for her part was putting on a brown belt around her waist and humming innocently to herself.

"She's coming with us," Elara said firmly. "I trust her."

Celina cocked an eyebrow and whispered, "Are you sure?"

"Yes, I am, and that's final. I really wish you'd give her another chance to be friends, Celina. Friendship is a beautiful thing, you know." With that Elara turned on her heels and went back to preparing her satchel for their journey.

Once the girls were in their attire and had packed one small bag each, they made their way to the docks where they could pay for safe passage to Rome aboard one of the many shipping vessels and trade ships. Elara wasn't a big fan of sailing, but they didn't have many other good options when it came to international travel.

"Good morning…" A tall sailor with a balding head and crinkled eyes greeted them at the docks and then squinted at them as they got closer, "…sirs?"

"We'd like to book a ride to Rome, please." Elara made little effort to obscure her voice. She doubted this sailor would care much about what their real genders were as long as he got paid.

"Yes, very good. I'm going to Rome in an hour and you're welcome to come aboard my ship. It will cost you four dinero each," he explained, pointing out his ship. It was a fine-looking ship with two large sails and recently repainted wood planks on the hull.

"Thank you, sir." Elara paid him and then the girls made their way onto the boat.

- - -

"I'm feeling positively seasick," Celina muttered grumpily just twenty minutes into their journey on the high seas.

Celina didn't normally get seasick, but since she hadn't eaten anything, and with the nerves of the journey, her stomach felt extra queasy.

She couldn't believe she let Elara talk her into this, but then she remembered it was actually her idea originally. It was a good idea despite the rocky ocean waves. Get the estate cleaned up, find the necklace, and return home before Count Basil even knew they were gone. Elara would have a chance to prove herself as countess and everything would go back to normal. Celina only wished Elara would see sense when it came to Rhea Alkan. That woman was not to be trusted.

"Want something to eat?" Rhea asked, holding up a pear to Celina's face. "It might make you feel better, Lady Oberon."

"Ugh, get that out of my face." Celina waved Rhea away like she was swatting away a fly.

Rhea's face drooped slightly, and her brow furrowed. "I was only trying to help. A full stomach always helps me when I'm feeling seasick."

"If I need your help, Miss Alkan, I'll ask for it," Celina retorted before marching to sit down by the starboard side railing.

She cupped her head in her hands and closed her eyes, trying to steady her breathing. To distract herself from her discomfort, she paid attention to the sounds and smells around her. The smell of sea salt in the air, the sounds of sailors shouting at each other over the rushing water, and seagulls flying in the air.

"I don't know what I'm doing wrong." She heard Rhea say to Elara.

"Celina just needs time. I'm sure you'll be good friends soon enough." Elara's ever optimistic voice wafted in the air, making Celina feel guilty again.

I wish you cared more about being kind than you do about being right. Elara's words rolled around in her head like a sentence of damnation. She wasn't jealous as Elara had surmised—at least that wasn't her main motivation. Mostly, she was protective of her friend, and she didn't trust strangers. Celina didn't really trust anyone, come to think of it, but she especially didn't trust strangers from faraway places. Still, she could be kinder. She had promised Elara that she would be, but it was hard to trust.

"May I join you, Lady Oberon?" She looked up and saw Rhea had returned. The way the sun glinted off Rhea's skin almost made her look like she was glowing. Her lush dark curls were braided together as part of her boyish disguise, but she still looked much too pretty to pass for a man.

Perhaps I am jealous of her, Celina thought to herself.

"You don't give up, do you?" Celina shrugged, trying to appear as unbothered as possible.

Rhea ignored the jest and plopped down next to her, taking a large bite out of the pear she had offered Celina earlier. The munching sound was grueling, but Celina let it slide.

"Are you sure you don't want some of this pear?" Rhea said with a full mouth. "It's good."

Celina put her face back in her hands. "I'm not hungry. Thank you, Miss Alkan."

Rhea finished it and threw the pear stem over the rail and into the ocean. "When I was a child, the other children would tease me because they thought my eyes were too close together."

"Oh," was all Celina could think to say in reply.

"Did you ever get teased as a child?" Rhea asked, wiping the pear juice off her hands and onto her trousers. "Did they ever say anything to you that made you question your worth?"

Celina considered her question for a moment before saying, "I didn't spend much time with other children growing up."

"Are you not close with your siblings?" Rhea furrowed her brow as one does when they are genuinely interested in what the other person has to say.

"I don't have any siblings."

"Really? That explains so much," Rhea laughed.

"What do you mean by that?" Celina asked, trying to decide if she should be offended or not.

"I have four brothers and two sisters," Rhea continued, not responding to Celina's inquiry. "They are my family's pride and joy."

"But not you?" Celina reclined back against the side of the ship and curled her knees to her chest, getting comfortable.

"No, I am what you might call the 'black sheep' of the family. I was telling Elara—*Countess* Elara—that I'm always trying my best, but..." Rhea trailed off staring somewhere in the distance.

"It's never good enough?" Celina guessed, trying to finish Rhea's thought for her.

"Yes, it always seems that way." Rhea leaned back and turned so she and Celina were facing each other. "But I am going to prove myself to them, to Countess Elara, and to you, Lady Oberon. You'll see. Everyone will see."

"How exactly are you going to do that?" Celina's voice was thick with skepticism.

"I'm not sure, but it's happening." Rhea turned on her back, so she faced the sky.

Celina chuckled before turning away as well. "I'll pray for your success, Miss Alkan."

- - -

Elara was jolted awake by the sound of people running about from one side of the ship to the other, shouting orders, the waves crashing up on the sides of the ship as it pulled into the Roman port. Her back was killing her, and she wasn't sure how long she had slept for. It could have been thirty minutes or thirty hours; she was that groggy and disoriented.

"Oh, you look terrible, Elara dear," Celina said, helping her to her feet.

"Thanks. You're a real charmer," Elara retorted, her voice dripping with sarcasm.

Despite her earlier seasickness, Celina still looked put together with her hair pulled back neatly and her face looking surprisingly refreshed.

"I'm only telling you how I see it." Celina laughed and looped her arm through Elara's. "Come on. Rhea is already off the boat and waiting for us on the docks."

Elara and Celina walked arm and arm off the ship and onto the sturdy docks. Rhea had their bags by her feet and was waving to them enthusiastically as they made their way toward her. Much like Celina, Rhea also looked put together and refreshed.

"*Kalimera*, Countess Elara. How did you sleep?" Rhea asked warmly.

"Just fine, thank you, Rhea." Elara blinked, trying to get her eyes to adjust to the sun.

It was a beautiful day in Rome, warmer than Catalonia and less windy too. The sun glinted off of the majestic marble building before them and she could already see the stone streets were bustling with life.

"So, what's the plan?" Celina asked as she and Rhea looked at Elara expectantly.

Elara swallowed, her mouth suddenly dry. "First thing to do is get some food and drink. Then I'll come up with part two of the plan."

"I know the perfect place!" Rhea smiled, boldly inserting herself between Elara and Celina and linking arms with both of them. "Lady Sidra and I used to go to this lovely little tavern near the Santa Maria Rotonda. You'll love it!"

Elara and Celina let Rhea lead them forward without much protest. She was proud of Celina for letting Rhea take charge like this.

Perhaps the girls had made progress after their conversation on the ship.

"Miss Alkan, is this a real tavern or did you just imagine it?" Celina asked after they had been walking for ten minutes.

"Patience is a virtue, Lady Oberon," Rhea quipped back.

So perhaps they hadn't made much progress after all. Elara was too tired and too hungry to scold them. Instead, she let Rhea keep dragging them toward their destination.

The weather was beautiful, and the sights were exciting, so she didn't mind the walk. Every piece of Roman architecture was more incredible than the last. The tall marble buildings with sweeping roof tops, large stone statues in front of grand stone steps, and gold-plated bridges were all majestic to behold.

"I heard most of this stuff was stolen from Constantinople and Egypt centuries ago," Celina whispered to her.

Elara rolled her eyes, "Can you let me enjoy this, please?"

"What? It's true!" Celina protested.

"Yes, yes, you're always right about everything, but you could have more *fun* every now and again," Elara teased, earning a laugh from Rhea.

Celina's cheeks turned red and said nothing. Elara worried that perhaps she'd hurt her friend's feelings, but she also thought that perhaps it was good for Celina to hear hard truths too since she was so fond of dishing them out all the time.

"Here we are!" Rhea stopped them in front of what appeared to be a nice tavern.

Elara tried to read the wooden sign, but it was in Latin. A couple passed them and went inside. As the door opened, Elara was able to get a quick glimpse of the people sitting inside with their wonderful looking meals.

Taverns were for people of all classes, but there was an expectation that the people inside would look and act appropriately. Back in Constantinople, Elara had seen her fair share of drunk patrons being thrown out for their indecency.

"Are we...dressed well enough to go inside?" Celina asked, looking down at their boyish and now slightly dirty attire. "Perhaps we should find a more grimy, low-life pub instead? The crooks there would probably have more information on pirate activity too."

"It's just a tavern. It might be well kept, but it's not exactly fine dining," Elara reasoned.

She knew Celina was probably right about their attire, but since they had walked all this way, she felt it was only fair to give this place a try. Besides, she was a countess after all, so they would not be turned away, right?

They opened the door and went inside trying to draw as little attention to themselves as possible. As soon as one of the tavern staff saw them, it became clear they were not going to get the kind of service they were used to as members of nobility. This low-profile attire might not have been such a good idea after all. Elara was glad for a moment that no one here would know her and thus no one would judge her or spread nasty rumors about her messy looks.

"Excuse me... uh, madams? We run a nice and safe establishment here. We don't have time for beggars or troublemakers." The barkeep looked at them with a combination of pity and disgust. He probably thought they were homeless or low-life thieves.

"We're not beggars nor troublemakers, sir. We've just gotten off a ship from Catalonia and we haven't had time to freshen up," Elara explained, pulling out her small coin purse. "We'd like to eat here, and we have the money to pay as you can see."

"Fine, you can stay," the man said, eyeing the money. "But no funny business or I'll have you thrown straight out."

As the girls made their way to the table, Elara whispered to her friends, "We probably should have cleaned ourselves up first, I suppose."

"Oh, you think?" Celina muttered back a bit sarcastically.

They ordered three pints of ale and fresh bread covered in basil, tomato slices, olive oil, and pieces of mozzarella cheese. After the long journey they'd had, Elara would have enjoyed any meal, but this one was particularly delicious. The bread crunched loudly in her mouth as she bit into it, creating an explosion of flavors which danced across her tongue.

"Elara," Rhea whispered, her eyes suddenly wide.

"Hmm?" Elara said, her mouth still full of her third slice of bread.

"Don't look now, but... I think Theodosius Kardia is behind you at the table by the back door." Rhea was trembling slightly, but she kept her composure so as to not startle the other patrons.

Elara swallowed. "Do I dare look?"

"I'll look," Celina volunteered, bravely turning to look behind her. "She's right. It's him."

Elara's mind was racing. She wasn't sure how a notorious pirate was sitting amongst the people of this tavern so casually. As scary as the situation was, it might also have been a blessing. Time was running out and she needed to confront him about the necklace before he left and disappeared again.

"What's he doing now?" Elara asked Rhea, who had the best viewpoint.

"He's getting up..." Rhea whispered.

"Oh, he's not coming toward us, is he?" Celina gripped the wooden table, looking understandably overwhelmed by the sudden situation.

"No," Rhea shook her head. "He's going out the other side."

"I can't let him get away," Elara muttered as she gathered her courage to stand.

"Wait—where are you going? Elara, don't!" Celina grabbed her arm, but Elara pulled free.

She walked alone to the back where she could now see Theodosius making his way to the back exit. He was dressed nicely for a pirate, wearing a red tunic, dark trousers, and boots. A long dark coat covered his arms, and he appeared to have cut his hair ever so slightly.

Theodosius was bigger and stronger than her, but Elara's advantage was that he hadn't yet spotted her coming up behind him. As he made his way out the door, down three steps, and into the side alley, Elara knew what she had to do. Heart pounding, she took advantage of the last step she was on to pull out her dagger and grab him from behind, pressing the blade gently to his throat.

"I want my necklace back, you son of a bitch." Elara snarled in his ear trying to sound as menacing as possible.

To her dismay, Theodosius laughed, half in surprise and half in amusement, but clearly not in fear. He grabbed her arm and spun them around, so they were facing each other, the knife still in Elara's hand, but clearly not in her control as he held tightly to her wrist.

"We have to stop meeting like this, Softy." His voice was deeper and richer than she remembered.

"I want my necklace back," she murmured again, her heart pounding so fiercely she was certain Theodosius could hear it. "It was my yiayia's..."

He pushed her up against the wall of the alley and took the knife from her hand, putting it in his own pocket. "I don't have your necklace."

"One of your men stole it, if you recall!" She tried to focus on her anger and not on how close his face was to hers. "I want it back."

"And I want that ledger. You didn't bring it with you to trade by any chance, did you?" he asked, sounding hopeful.

Elara looked down at her feet, saying nothing. She hadn't even thought of bringing something, like a ledger, to try to trade for her necklace.

"Ah, thought not." Theodosius frowned for a moment but then put his signature smile back on again. "Well, it's been lovely seeing you again, Softy, but I have places to be."

Elara grabbed his coat sleeve as he attempted to slip away. "Wait! I can get you a ledger."

"From where?" he challenged her.

"Uh, I could, um…" It was like her brain was frozen as she suddenly couldn't think of where to find another ledger to give him. Her papou was the only one she knew for certain would have one.

Theodosius grew impatient. "I don't have time for this. Goodbye." As he turned again to leave, he saw his path was blocked.

Celina stood with her own knife out, pointing at him. Rhea stood just behind her with clenched fists, looking terrified, but also ready to fight.

He glanced back at Elara, saying, "I see the gang's all here."

"Give her the necklace, Mister Kardia," Celina said coldly. "And I promise I won't stab you."

"It's *Captain* Kardia, and I already told Softy here, I don't have any necklaces," Theodosius grumbled, clearly annoyed.

"We don't care what your title is," said Elara mimicking his words back to him as she picked up a large loose stone that was on the ground to use as a weapon. "I want what's mine."

"There's three of us and only one of you," Rhea chimed in finally finding her voice. "You do the math! Give us the necklace or we're prepared to fight!"

Theodosius burst into laughter and moved his hand as if wiping a tear from his eye. He started making his way to get past Celina and her knife. Elara realized that if she didn't do something quickly, he was going to run and be lost to them, possibly forever, and with him, her necklace would be lost too.

"It's been fun, ladies!" He knocked the knife out of Celina's hand with a swift motion and pushed Rhea into a pile of garbage with little effort. They were simply no match for him. "But I've got to go."

Elara leapt up on his back from behind and threw her arms around his neck, clinging to him like a monkey in a tree. "GIVE ME BACK MY NECKLACE!"

"Agh! Get off me, you lunatic!" Theodosius spun around trying to dislodge her, but Elara hung on for dear life.

"Halt!" came a commanding voice.

Theodosius stopped spinning, his pulse racing under her grip. She looked up and saw a well-dressed guard on a horse staring at them, his hand on the hilt of his sword. Elara hadn't seen a soldier of Rome before, but his uniform was similar to the ones from Constantinople.

"Madam, please dismount the gentleman," The soldier ordered.

"Yes, sir." Elara released her grip on the corsair's neck, slid down his back, and landed gently on her feet. She looked over at her friends and saw Celina helping Rhea to her feet. They looked as scared and shaken as she felt.

"Does someone want to tell me what is going on here in this alleyway?" The soldier asked no one in particular, but she noticed his eyes were on Theodosius as he spoke.

"This woman attacked me!" Theodosius said, pointing to Elara.

"How dare you! This man stole my yiayia's necklace!" Elara retorted angrily.

"Did you steal the lady's necklace?" the soldier asked Theodosius.

Theodosius scoffed as if the accusation was offensive. "I most certainly did not! She's a lying wench! Arrest her for assault!"

"Arrest *him* for theft and piracy!" Elara yelled equally appalled. "Don't you recognize him, sir? He's the infamous *Captain* Theodosius Kardia, the corsair! He ransacked the fortress where I live in Catalonia!"

"Theodosius Kardia?" The soldier said, clearly pleased. "I believe I have a warrant here for your arrest."

Two more soldiers appeared behind them on foot instead of on horseback. They had the same uniform on, and in their hands were ropes for binding wrists. Theodosius gave Elara a look like he wanted to strangle her, but he made no movement toward her.

"Arrest them all," the soldier ordered the other two soldiers who then began tying their wrists together behind their backs. The soldier on the horse dismounted, and to Elara's dismay, began arresting Celina and Rhea as well.

"Wait!" Elara yelped. "Unhand me! We haven't done anything! I'm Countess Elara Iliakos of Constantinople—" She started to explain, but the first soldier interrupted her.

"A countess are you, madam? Well, if you are a countess then I am the Pope." He laughed heartily and the other soldiers joined him.

- - -

"Hello! There's been a terrible mistake! My friends and I aren't supposed to be here!" Elara called through the bars of the cell door.

They were in a dank holding cell beneath a rather majestic marble courthouse. The cell was not majestic and consisted of dim lighting, dirty straw floors, and rusty metal bars. She, Celina, and Rhea were in one cell while Theodosius had been put in an identical cell next to them.

"Is anyone there?" Elara tried again.

"Give it up, Softy. No one's coming," Theodosius said from where he was lounging on the hard ground of his cell with his feet propped up on a bucket. He always appeared relaxed, regardless of the circumstances.

"This is hopeless," Rhea muttered from where she was curled up surprisingly close to Celina.

"Do you want the good news or the bad news, dear?" Celina asked Elara.

"The good news, I suppose." Elara sighed leaning against the cell door.

"The good news is that when you put in for an appeal, they will write a letter to Count Basil to see if he can verify your identification, and when he does come to identify you, we'll be set free." Celina explained it like the Roman three-week appeal process would be a walk in the park, not to mention that Basil would have to come all the way from Athens. Who knew how long that would take?

"And what's the bad news?" Elara felt she already knew the answer but asked anyway.

Celina, still seated on the floor next to Rhea, leaned back against the stone wall as if to put as much distance between herself and the bad news as possible. "The bad news is that when Count Basil comes, and he will come because the court will compel him, he'll be very unhappy with the situation. Our whole plan will go up in smoke, and that necklace we came over for will be truly lost."

"It's going to be so embarrassing," Elara groaned. "I always seem to make things worse, don't I?"

"That's not true. It's not your fault we're in this mess." Rhea shook her head.

"She's right, Elara dear," Celina agreed with Rhea for perhaps the first time ever. "It's clearly *Mister* Kardia's fault."

"I know you're messing up my title on purpose, Miss Whatever-Your-Name-Is." Theodosius stood up and walked over so he was leaning on the bars looking into the girls' cell. "Are you really Countess Elara Iliakos?"

"Yes. I do have the misfortune of being her." Elara looked him up and down, trying to guess why he would care to know.

He looked suddenly excited. "You know you're an absolute legend, right? Everyone in Constantinople knows about you. I really had no idea who you were before, but now, I can say that I met the rebellious countess."

"What are you talking about?" Elara's heart raced as it often did when she learned that people were gossiping about her.

"You ended your engagement with Prince Andronikos. You called him out on his bad behavior and told him you'd rather be alone than with him. That was so amazing of you!" Theodosius gripped the bars of the cell almost gleefully. "I bet you were the first person to say 'no' to him before. I bet he had a temper tantrum. I wish I could have been there to see his smug little face all upset at having to deal with the consequences of his own actions like a normal person!"

Elara blinked, unsure of how to respond. No one had ever congratulated her or praised her for ending her engagement. Even her papou and Empress Maria, who both agreed with her decision and told her she was making the right one, had never praised her for it. It was shameful. Breaking off an engagement to a prince was shameful, and yet, Theodosius Kardia was acting like it was an act of heroism.

"Prince Andronikos didn't seem too upset when I delivered the news." Elara shrugged. "Other than spitting in my face, of course."

Celina and Rhea both flinched at that, neither of them having heard the depths of Andronikos' abusive behavior before. Theodosius didn't flinch or look surprised, instead he nodded like spitting in a fiancé's face was something he knew Andronikos would do.

"Did you hit him back?" Theodosius asked. "Any knives to the throat or what not?"

"No!" Elara was appalled by the suggestion. "I would never attack a prince! That would have been even more scandalous, and I was already up to my neck in scandal at the time."

"Ah, that's too bad. I would pay money to watch you hit Andronikos." Theodosius sighed dreamily like he was imagining Elara giving her former flame a good lashing.

Elara had also spent time imagining what it might be like to hit Andronikos, but she would never admit that out loud.

"How exactly do you know Prince Andronikos, Captain Kardia?" Celina asked, getting his title right.

"I used to attend him years ago." Theodosius looked at Elara as he spoke. "He once stuck a nail in my leg and got *me* in trouble for it. Can you believe it?"

"Yes, that sounds like him." Elara shook her head with a combination of fondness and disgust. "He really was the *worst* at any age. I had no idea you were one of his serving boys."

"It didn't last long. After my brother died, things went south for me rather quickly." Theodosius didn't elaborate but instead leaned against one of the bars of the cell with a forlorn expression on his face.

"I'm sorry about your brother," Elara said softly, breaking the silence.

"Thank you. He was a good man." Theodosius turned back to look at her again. This time he had a more calculating look on his face. "Since you're a countess from Constantinople, you must know the Despot of Constantinople, Lord Nekros Palaiologos, correct?"

"Yes, I know him. He was good friends with my late father, and he was the one who warned us about you literally the night before you attacked the fortress, funnily enough." Elara almost laughed at the timing of it all. Everything had happened so quickly.

"Lord Nekros was at Tossa de Mar?" He gripped the bars with a wild expression on his face.

"The day before you came, he was, yes. Why do you ask?" Elara frowned as she tried to read his body language.

"I'll make a deal with you, Countess! If you can get me an audience with Lord Nekros, I'll get you your necklace back." Theodosius offered suddenly.

"Really?" Elara felt hope spring in her chest. The deal was tempting, and Nekros had given her an open invitation to visit his home in Constantinople. It would be easy enough to get an audience with him, but could she trust the pirate to keep his end of the bargain?

"Why do you want an audience with Lord Nekros?" Celina, the ever practical one, asked pointedly. "No offense, but I don't think Lord Nekros is your biggest fan."

"I—I only want to discuss with him the matter of clearing my good name. I've been accused of some pretty damning things, and I'd like a chance to restore my reputation. You understand that, right, Countess?" Theodosius looked at her with eyes full of hope.

Elara knew that others would call him a liar and perhaps she was being naive, but Elara couldn't help but sympathize with him. If there was a chance she could get her necklace back and restore not only part of her own reputation, but help someone else restore theirs as well, she had to try.

"We have a deal." Elara smiled and shook the corsair's hand through the bars. His hand was gruff from manual labor, but it was warm and comforting somehow too.

"Elara, you can't be serious," Celina predictably protested.

Rhea had objections of her own. "I don't think we should trust him either. He and his men killed Lady Sidra after all."

"Killed Lady Sidra? Lady Sidra *Ravi*?" Theodosius sounded offended. "No, I rescued Lady Sidra! She was supposed to marry some noble boy from Catalonia, but she was in love with someone else, so I helped her fake her own death and escape."

"Lady Sidra is *alive*?" Rhea gasped. "I don't believe you!"

"It's true! She's living in Athens now, I believe. I'd be happy to take you there sometime if you'd like. I'm sure she wants to see you and explain all this herself—*after* I get an audience with Nekros, of course," Theodosius said confidently.

Rhea frowned and her mouth hung open in shock at his declaration. What happened next was even more surprising; Celina put a comforting arm around Rhea's shoulders.

"There's still another problem," Celina reminded them. "How are we going to get an audience with Nekros when we're trapped in these prison cells?"

"Leave that to me!" Theodosius grinned. "I have the perfect escape plan."

Chapter Five

The Vatican

The plan was simple enough, perhaps a little too simple for Celina's liking. Then again, perhaps she was just being negative and overly cautious. She couldn't help it. How could they trust a pirate of all people to keep to his word? His reasoning for wanting to see Lord Nekros seemed a little too close to Elara's motive for getting the necklace. It was almost as if he was already learning how to prey on her emotions to manipulate her.

Theodosius also had this way of looking at Elara that made Celina's blood boil. Elara held her own well enough most of the time, but sometimes, Celina would catch her friend looking back at Theodosius with that same strange look. There was an unspoken tension between the two of them, and as a third-party observer, Celina didn't like it. It wasn't jealousy, she just really didn't trust Kardia to have good intentions. Elara had already fallen for a bad man once; she didn't need to go through that again.

"Ta-da!" Theodosius declared loudly after he successfully picked the lock on his cell. Elara clapped, entertaining him, but Celina and Rhea both stood silently waiting for him to finish the job.

After the cells were open, the four of them sneaked up the side stairwell to the top landing. Luckily for them, the guards on duty weren't facing them, but were instead facing the opposite wall where they could better see the door to the outside. It was dark everywhere with the only light coming from a few small torches that lined the walls.

"How long until our lunch break?" One guard asked the other.

"I don't know. Maybe half an hour." The other guard shrugged. "It's hard to tell in here since it's so dark all the time."

"I'd kill for a proper window, I would," The first guard agreed.

"They think they're punishing the prisoners with little to no light, but they're punishing us as well if you think about it."

"It's inhuman, it is."

"Excuse me, sirs?" Rhea slipped out just as she was told. "Could either of you point me in the direction of the loo?"

"Hey! How'd you get out of your cell?" The guards moved toward her to grab her, but just as they did, Theodosius hit one guard in the head with a large rock, knocking him out cold.

"What the—?" Before the other guard could finish his thought, Elara and Celina helped Theodosius knock him out too.

"Excellent work, ladies!" The corsair complimented them.

"Thank you, Captain." Elara smiled a bit too big at him for Celina's liking.

They dragged the guards over to the side of the room and removed their uniforms. Theodosius put on one of the uniforms and Elara put on the other. The uniforms consisted of long dark shirts under simple breast plates with trousers with chainmail around the waist.

Celina and Rhea did their best to clean themselves up and look as presentable as possible. Luckily the guards had confiscated some dresses from other female prisoners that fit them well enough.

"Here, cover your pretty face with this," Theodosius handed Elara a headscarf. "There's no way people will think you're a man if they can see a face like that."

Elara blushed slightly. "You think you're charming, don't you?"

"Oh, I know I'm charming." Theodosius winked and Celina couldn't help but roll her eyes. She was happy to see that Rhea looked equally disgusted. If only Elara wasn't such a bad judge of character.

After they all had their outfits on, and the guards were properly bound and gagged, they made their way outside and into the sunshine. Elara and Theodosius walked behind Celina and Rhea as if they were two soldiers escorting the ladies to some mysterious new location.

"Before we can go back to my ship, I need to get something first," Theodosius told them as they walked through the streets.

"Get something from where?" Elara asked.

"You'll see." Theodosius had a mischievous look on his face, which immediately set Celina on edge. Elara and Rhea didn't seem to share her concern at this turn of events as the group moved in silence toward their unknown destination.

The weather was still unusually warm for a fall day and Celina couldn't imagine how sweaty Elara and Theodosius were feeling in their soldier uniforms.

"Here we are," Theodosius said in a casual tone.

They turned a corner to see a row of large columns, biblical statues, and an open area surrounded on all sides by tall, elegant buildings. There were large stone statues of robed men perched on the corners of the rooftops overlooking the entryway.

"The *Vatican*?" Elara said in shock. "What on earth do you want from there, Captain?"

"Just a sextant."

"Sorry, a *what*?" Rhea suppressed a juvenile giggle and Celina rolled her eyes.

"A sextant. It's a navigation device that my first mate, Yianni, has been *begging* for." Theodosius shrugged. "So, I'm going to get him one. The best one in fact."

"Surely there are easier and cheaper sextants you could acquire that don't involve robbing the Pope," Elara said with wide eyes.

"Robbing?" Theodosius laughed. "Who said anything about robbing? I'm going to trade for it with one of the guards who works here."

The girls looked at him skeptically, making the pirate laugh again. "Relax, ladies! Countess, you come with me, and the other two can wait here. We'll be back before you know it."

Elara looked at her friends and, to Celina's horror, seemed to be seriously considering going along with the man.

"Oh, Elara dear, you can't be serious!"

"Will it take long? This trade?" Elara ignored Celina and asked Theodosius instead.

"Only a few minutes at most! Then we'll be on our way," the captain promised.

"This seems dangerous. How can you trust him?" Rhea spoke up finally and Celina was glad. If Elara wouldn't listen to her, perhaps she would listen to Rhea.

Before Elara could respond, Theodosius answered, "Don't worry! The countess and I need each other. There won't be any backstabbing from me."

With an annoyed sigh, Elara pinched the bridge of her nose between her pointer finger and her thumb as she said, "Let's get this over with." Perhaps she wasn't as bewitched as she appeared.

- - -

Elara was nervous about leaving her friends behind at the Vatican pillars. Celina and Rhea had only just started to get along and Elara knew one stressful event could send Celina spiraling back into old habits.

"If this is a trick, I'm prepared to fight you, you know," Elara told Theodosius as they walked across the stone courtyard and toward Saint Peter's Basilica.

Theodosius laughed quietly. "Relax. Like I said, I don't backstab. Especially when I have an alliance with a lady as lovely as you."

"Ha." Her face felt hot, but it wasn't from the unusually warm weather nor her uncomfortable clothes.

The doors to Saint Peter's Basilica were magnificent, but after growing up around the Hagia Sophia back in Constantinople, it hardly seemed revolutionary to Elara.

"Who goes there?" a guard asked as they made it to the grand entrance.

"Good to see you too, Paul." Theodosius grinned. "I have something for you, but only if you have what I want as well?"

"Who's the girl?" the guard, Paul, asked with narrowed eyes as he looked Elara up and down suspiciously. Apparently, the scarf hadn't concealed her as well as she had hoped.

Paul was a heavier-set man with wispy brown hair and a goatee. His uniform was much grander and more colorful than the soldiers they had stolen theirs from.

"This is my sister, Angelia," Theodosius said innocently.

"I didn't know you had a sister, Kardia."

"There's a lot you don't know about me."

"Oh really?" Paul scoffed at that. "Do tell."

"I don't have time to give you my full autobiography. Do you have what I want or not?" Theodosius quipped back, growing impatient.

Paul pulled a small silver device out of his cloak. It was rounded on one side and pointed on the other. It couldn't have been much larger than a crow.

"That's it? That's the sextant?" Elara said with a frown. It wasn't exactly as impressive as she had imagined.

"Yes, my lady." It was Paul who answered. "And a very good sextant at that."

"Excellent." Theodosius pulled a small piece of parchment bound together with a leather strap, clearly intending to trade.

Paul seemed to have other plans as he slipped the sextant back into his cloak.

"What are you doing—?" Theodosius began, confused.

"Sorry, Kardia, but the price on your head has gone up." Paul smirked maliciously.

"There he is!" A group of three guards were suddenly upon them with drawn swords. Elara felt her heartbeat pick up as she realized what was happening.

"Son of a bitch!" Theodosius grabbed Paul by his collar and shoved him once before turning to grab Elara's wrist. "Come on!"

"Get them! Before they get away!" The guards were getting closer.

"My apologies again to you and your sister, Kardia!" Paul called after them as they ran, not sounding sorry at all.

Instead of running back toward the pillars where Celina and Rhea would be waiting, they ran further onto the Vatican property.

"Where are we going?" Elara asked, perplexed. "We need to get *out* of here, not further in!"

Instead of answering, Theodosius pulled Elara into what appeared to be a nearby supply shed. Inside the shed were tools used by the guards, including armor, shields, and swords. She realized it wasn't a shed at all, but a large armory.

He locked the armory door with a wooden panel before picking up two swords and handing one to her. "Here."

"No…" Elara's eyes widened as she shook her head and took a step back. "I don't know how to… I mean, I'm not trained in…" She bit her lip suddenly and irrationally embarrassed. No one had ever taught her to use a sword before. Why would they? She was a countess for Christ's sake.

"You know how to use a dagger but not a sword?" Theodosius titled his head, studying her.

She shrugged. "No one teaches girls swordplay at etiquette school."

"Open up, pirate!" There was a loud banging on the door. The guards had found them.

"Ah, well, there's no time to learn like the present." He turned to face the door with his sword raised ready for combat. "If we survive this, I'll teach you how to fight."

"I think we should run," she suggested as the wooden door started breaking apart. There was no way that they could take down three guards on their own, especially when Elara had no combat training beyond some dagger self-defense skills.

Theodosius said nothing but stared at the door as the Vatican guards clawed their way in.

As the guards entered with their weapons raised, the pirate captain began fighting them immediately. Their swords clanged together, and it became much like a dance as they moved about the room.

Elara was both pleased and a little offended that the guards ignored her entirely and kept their attention on subduing Theodosius.

There was a sense of dignity in the captain's fighting style, while the guards were more brutish. It became clear that the guards were trying extremely hard to stop Theodosius by any means possible— including killing him without trial. Meanwhile, Theodosius fought to defend himself and his life.

Even though he was outnumbered three to one, Theodosius was clearly the more skilled swordsman. He blocked their attacks and gave well timed counterattacks of his own. He disarmed and stabbed a guard in the shoulder. It was not a death blow, but one that took the guard out of the match.

Now, it was just two against one. One of the guards slashed his sword at Theodosius, but the pirate parried and riposted with a swipe of his own, sending the second guard to the floor with a string of curses. Elara suddenly felt much more confident about their chances.

The last standing guard, however, was not to be underestimated, as he blocked each of the pirate captain's thrusts and even sent him flying into a suit of armor.

"*Dammit!*" Theodosius grunted as he hit the floor with a loud clang. His sword slipped out of his hands, skidding across the floor far out of reach.

"Do you yield, pirate?" The guard demanded pointing his sword into Theodosius' exposed ribcage.

"Yield?" Theodosius snorted. "I'd rather die."

The guard's upper lip twisted into a cruel smile. "That can be arranged."

"I wouldn't if I were you." Elara pointed her sword into the small of the guard's back.

"You don't want to mess with me, my lady. The Pope will excommunicate you for this treachery!" The guard threatened her.

"I guess it's a good thing I'm Orthodox Christian, then," Elara said dryly, making Theodosius chuckle.

Unexpectedly, the guard twirled around to face her, and their swords clanged together, echoing off the stone walls.

"I'm going to kill your lady friend, Kardia, and then, I'm going to kill you!" The guard thrust his sword at Elara as he spoke.

By some miracle, she managed to block many of his initial attacks but wasn't sure how or when or where to strike back.

"Never fought a real man before, my lady?" The guard taunted her in a way that felt both threatening and vaguely domineering.

"How dare you, sir!" Elara ducked away from his blade in the nick of time. "Does your master, the Pope, know you talk to women this way?"

"I talk how I want to anyone who is beneath me!" The guard jabbed his sword at her again, but she was able to quickly parry out of the way before it stabbed into her flesh.

Elara was fumbling around in the armory, desperately trying to not get killed, but it was only a matter of time before the deranged guard ran her through.

"Anytime now, Captain!" she called out, but when she looked over to where Theodosius had been on the ground, she saw he was gone.

No. Had he abandoned her?

"Left you for dead, did he? Come out, coward!" The guard snarled looking around the room for where the pirate had scurried off to.

That nasty, no good pirate left me for dead, Elara thought angrily. Celina had been right, and she had simply been too foolish, too trusting, too—

"Up here," a deep voice interrupted her thoughts.

The guard and Elara looked up to see Theodosius hanging onto the ceiling banister just above them.

"What the—?" Just as the guard began to speak, Theodosius leapt down and knocked the man out cold.

"Excellent teamwork, Countess," Theodosius grinned at her. "I could not have done it without you."

"I really thought…" she paused to catch her breath and to steady her still furiously beating heart.

"You thought I left you for dead?"

"Well… Yes."

"I told you, Countess, I don't break deals or stab backs. I might be a pirate, but I'm also a man of my word." He gave a little mock bow, and Elara couldn't help but let out a small laugh.

They left the guards tied up as they made their escape back to where Celina and Rhea were waiting for them. Elara wasn't completely sure what had just happened, but she was sure now of one thing: Theodosius Kardia fought with honor, while the highly respected guards of the Vatican did not.

- - -

"Where exactly are we going now?" Rhea whispered quietly to Celina. They hadn't spoken much at the Vatican, and Elara and Theodosius were in a hurry and gave no explanations.

"I'm not sure, but I have a bad feeling we're about to end up on a notorious pirate ship," Celina whispered back. As they walked, Celina could see the docks coming into view. "I hate being right."

"You love being right," Rhea disagreed, before calling softly over her shoulder, "Countess Elara, I'm not comfortable being on *that* pirate ship."

"The ship is perfectly safe," Theodosius promised. "Besides, it's the only mode of transportation that gets us where we need to be in a timely manner."

"Don't worry, Rhea. It's just a temporary transportation arrangement," Elara said, clearly trying to put them all at ease, but it wasn't working.

The closer they got to the ship, the more nervous Celina was becoming. There were so many things that could go wrong, and she was worrying about all of them.

This part of the shipyard felt different than the ship docks on which they had arrived. The pirate ship looked like any other shipping vessel when its signature black skull and crossbones flag was put away. Celina could hear the pirate crew bustling about as they prepared for the journey.

"Welcome back, Captain! Nice outfit!" One of the crew members shouted down to them when he saw Theodosius and the girls approaching.

"Thanks, Gregory! I stole it from a Roman soldier!" Theodosius replied smugly.

The crew member, Gregory, laughed as he swung the gangplank down to them so they could climb aboard the ship.

"After you, ladies," Theodosius gestured for Celina and Rhea to go ahead.

Celina took one last look at Elara, who nodded reassuringly, before ascending the plank. Rhea followed closely behind her. The pirate ship did look similar to the ship they arrived on with its wooden planks and large cream-colored sails. Crew members were racing about preparing to set sail for their next destination.

"Was beginning to think you weren't going to make it back in time," a tall man with a balding head, said to Theodosius as he shook his hand. "Did you get what I asked for?"

"Here you go." Theodosius tossed the man a small object that was most likely the sextant. "Don't say I never do anything for you, Yianni."

"How did you—?" Elara bulked.

"I pickpocketed Paul." The pirate captain winked. Celina didn't know who Paul was, but clearly Elara did as she stared wide-eyed.

"Did you also get a ledger with the information you needed?" The bald man called Yianni asked vaguely. He clearly didn't want to give away the reason why the pirates wanted a noble man's ledger.

"We don't need the ledger intel anymore." Theodosius nodded toward Elara. "I've got something even better."

"Is that so? And who are our lovely new friends?" Yianni raised his eyebrows as if noticing the women for the first time.

"Yianni Drakos, meet our favorite Tossa de Mar girls." Theodosius introduced them with pride in his voice as if he had brought celebrities to a dinner party to impress the host. "This is Lady Celina Oberon of Bulgaria, Miss Rhea Alkan of Anatolia, and *the* one and only Countess Elara Iliakos of Constantinople."

"Wait, you're Countess Elara Iliakos? You're a legend! The story of you ending things with that spoiled Prince Andronikos is the best story I've heard all year!" Yianni looked just as impressed as Theodosius had earlier.

"Yes, and you're the man who stole my necklace and pushed me off the roof, nearly to my death," Elara replied coldly.

Yianni Drakos' face dropped, embarrassed. "Yes. Sorry about that. Won't happen again, I assure you. I'm a nice guy, really. Captain, tell her that I'm a nice guy."

"Yianni is a nice guy... When he's not stealing things and pushing ladies off roofs of course. Speaking of—Yianni, do you still have that necklace on you by any chance?" Theodosius asked.

"Erm, I don't, actually. I traded it for some mead last night to an Athenian woman." Yianni winced regretfully and scratched the back of his head as he spoke. "She was on her way back to Athens last I heard... It was very good mead, mind you."

"You traded my priceless family heirloom for a glass of mead?!" Elara said with an amount of outrage that made Celina proud.

"No, of course not!" Yianni winced again. "I traded it for *two* glasses of mead."

"*Two* glasses? Well, I suppose that's all right then," Elara's voice dripped with sarcasm.

"Really?"

"She's being sarcastic. It's obviously not all right," Celina said as she crossed her arms to join Elara in a defiant pose.

111

"Ah." Yianni looked at his feet, ashamed.

Theodosius clapped a hand on Yianni's shoulder. "Don't worry. We're going to get the necklace back, and in exchange, the countess has agreed to get me an audience with Nekros."

"Nekros?" Yianni's eyes widened, and he grimaced knowingly. "Well, then, I'll finish preparations so we can set sail for Athens as soon as possible."

As she watched Yianni walk off, Celina wondered if they should start worrying for Nekros' safety. It seemed that these pirates had a secret reason for wanting an audience with the despot and she wasn't sure if Theodosius' story could be trusted.

"Follow me, ladies, and let me show you around," Theodosius offered politely.

As he gave them a quick tour of the ship, they began to set sail. Orders were being barked by Yianni, who was Theodosius' first mate. Below deck, things seemed more cramped and chaotic, but Theodosius offered to let them sleep in his captain's quarters so they would feel safe.

"How often do you use the cannons?" Rhea asked, her voice was void of emotion, but it was clear she was remembering something terrible from the night Lady Sidra allegedly faked her own death.

"We only use them when we have to," Theodosius shrugged as they followed him back up the narrow ladder to the deck.

"Captain! We've got company!" Gregory shouted from the crow's nest, pointing to the distance.

Celina scanned the horizon and saw that a ship was following them closely. She wondered if it was a Roman ship angry at their attempted escape or if it was another pirate ship. Either way, not great.

"Get ready! All hands on deck!" Theodosius ordered and his crew sprang into action, getting ready for a fight.

"I knew this was a bad idea! We should never have come here," Rhea whined, and Celina couldn't help but agree with her. It was becoming uncanny how much she and Rhea were agreeing today.

"Elara, perhaps if we grab a lifeboat, we can make it back to shore," Celina suggested.

"I've put you both in danger, and I'm sorry," Elara admitted, looking sullen. "But I can't leave without getting my necklace. If you want to go, I won't argue. Return together to Tossa de Mar and I'll go the rest of the way alone."

"We're not leaving you!" Celina and Rhea said in unison and the two girls looked at each other in surprise.

"For the record, Miss Alkan, just because we've been agreeing a lot today doesn't make us friends." It was important to Celina that Rhea and Elara understood this. Just because she trusted Rhea more than she trusted notorious pirates, didn't change anything between them.

"Understood," Rhea said stiffly. "Thank you for the reminder, Lady Oberon."

"You two could fight through a hurricane," Elara grumbled. "And here I was thinking you had made progress with one another."

"We have made progress," Celina said pointedly as she crossed her arms. "Rhea and I both agree that pirates are bad. Perhaps that is something we can get you to agree with, Elara dear."

"Celina, please try to understand..."

"If you get caught working with pirates your reputation will get *worse*. You understand that, right?" Celina pressed. "If word gets out that you've been traveling with *Theodosius Kardia* of all people... Well, let's just say it won't matter if you get the necklace back and clean everything up. You'll never socially recover from this terrible lapse in judgment!"

"I know you think I am a bad judge of character, but I need Kardia to get my necklace back," Elara argued angrily. "And we won't get caught! I mean, we'll wear disguises and everything. No one ever needs to know!"

She could tell Elara desperately wanted them to see her side of things, but Celina simply did not agree with her. They could have gotten the necklace without Theodosius, somehow, she was certain.

The problem with Elara, in Celina's opinion, was she always thought she knew people's hearts. She always thought everyone was good and that everyone was her friend until proven otherwise. Elara had swapped the keys back at the fortress, not to prove Rhea was up to something, but to prove Rhea was trustworthy. It was a test Elara believed Rhea would pass wholeheartedly. Rhea had technically passed that test, but she had still been lying about her identity.

There was no test to prove Theodosius Kardia's innocence. No matter what Elara might think of him, the pirate was already guilty in the eyes of the Empire. He couldn't be trusted.

It wasn't Celina's job to constantly point out the untrustworthy people to Elara over and over again. One would think that Elara would have learned to see the worst in people after what Prince Andronikos had done to her heart.

"You're right. I do think you're a bad judge of character," Celina retorted in frustration.

She quickly turned away from Elara, not waiting for her friend to respond to her harsh, but true, words. Celina walked briskly to the other side of the ship to get a better view of the oncoming vessel.

It was much closer now, nearly upon them. It was hard to see from here which flag was being flown over the ship, but it was clearly not a pirate flag.

"They're coming up on the starboard side!" Theodosius, now at the helm, shouted to his crew.

The ship made a sharp turn, making the waves splash up and spray Celina's face. The cold saltwater disoriented her, causing her to stumble backward and then forward. At least she wasn't feeling seasick this time around.

"Celina! Be careful!" A woman's voice called out, but with everything else clogging her senses, Celina couldn't tell if it was Elara or Rhea warning her.

The ship rocked viciously again as the other ship got ever closer. Theodosius and Yianni were shouting about something, but Celina couldn't hear what it was. The pirate crew was running back and forth on the deck pulling ropes and shouting various ship terms which Celina didn't understand. There was the sound of cannon fire, a clear warning shot, but from whom, it was also hard to say.

Celina stumbled closer to the starboard side of the ship, trying to get a closer look at the other ship's flag so she could see who they were dealing with. She wrapped her arms around the railing to sturdy herself before sticking her neck out a bit to see better.

"Celina! Get away from the side!" Elara called out from where she and Rhea were standing near the ladder leading to the deck below. "We're going down for safety! Come with us!" Elara was right. It would be safer to go below deck.

Before Celina could move to follow her friend, another sharp turn, accompanied by a large splash of the waves, suddenly dislodged Celina's grip and sent her hurtling over the side of the ship. The cold salt water of the sea greeted her harshly as she sank below its depths. She didn't even have time to scream before her whole body was submerged under water.

Celina knew to hold her breath, but she had never been taught to swim properly, at least not properly enough for waters with two warring ships making choppy waves. She did manage to get her head above water to take in a gasping breath, saltwater burning her eyes, nose, and throat.

"Help! Help me!" Celina screamed before becoming submerged under the waves again.

As she floundered around underwater, she could see that someone else had either fallen in or jumped in after her. The person swam toward Celina, and the last thing she felt before passing out was arms wrapped around her, pulling her up.

Chapter Six

Ship Swapped

"Is she dead?" a male voice asked.

"She's breathing and has a pulse, so I would say no," another, more familiar female voice replied.

Celina slowly opened her eyes and immediately began spitting up water and coughing. She was lying on the wooden floor, most likely the deck of a ship. Seagulls flew above her, squawking loudly to each other. The air and sea were calmer now, the fight between the two vessels was clearly over.

"Are you well, Lady Oberon?" It was Rhea's voice.

Celina turned to see Rhea sitting on her knees next to her. Rhea's clothing was soaked, and her hair was a wet, tangled mess.

"Hmm… Did—did you jump in to rescue me?" Celina asked with a furrowed brow.

"Of course I did!" Rhea said with a strange amount of forced cheerfulness. "I am your lady's maid after all."

"My lady's maid?" Celina sat up, confused. She looked around and realized that Elara wasn't with them, nor were Theodosius, Yianni, or Gregory. "We're on the other ship."

"Welcome aboard the Romanos Navy ship," a man with salt-and-pepper hair and strangely blue eyes greeted her. "We're happy that we could help rescue you from those dreadful pirates."

"Yes, thank you again, Captain Titus." Rhea looked pointedly at Celina. "For rescuing us from those dreaded pirates. We're so grateful. Aren't we, Lady Oberon?"

Celina caught on at once. "Yes! We are very appreciative of your help, good sir!"

"You're welcome, of course. Please tell us which port we can drop you off at?" Captain Titus offered politely.

"Athens," Celina answered. "We're going to Athens."

- - -

To say that Elara was devastated would be an understatement. She'd watched in horror as Celina nearly got swallowed up by the sea and then watched Rhea bravely leap into the water to rescue her, only for them both to be pulled up by the other ship. Now, the other ship was long out of sight, as the pirate ship had maneuvered expertly away and escaped.

"We have to go back for them," Elara was saying to Theodosius as she trailed behind him on the deck.

"There's no time. If they survived, they'll just have to find a way to meet us in Athens." Theodosius kept up his brisk pace as he marched along the deck and didn't even bother to look back at her as he spoke.

"*If? If* they survived?" Elara's stomach lurched. She didn't want to even think that. If anything happened to Celina or Rhea, it would be entirely her fault.

Theodosius stopped walking and finally turned to face her. "I'm sure they're fine. They're both charming enough to deal with Romanos Navy sailors. As long as they stick together and don't say anything outlandish."

"They're smart, and know how to behave, but..." Elara took a shaky breath. "Celina and Rhea hate each other. I'm not sure they can get along without me there to scold them."

"Are you their mother?" he asked with mock concern.

Elara ignored his sarcastic remark. "Things are tense between them for some reason, and I'm worried. Are you sure we can't go back?"

"It'll be safer for all of us if we carry on to Athens." Theodosius crossed his arms and leaned against the wood of the mast. "Once we get to Athens, we can find your necklace *and* your friends."

"And from there, we go to Constantinople to see the despot, Lord Nekros," she said, finishing the plan that she had heard from him so many times already.

"That's right."

"What exactly do you need to discuss with Nekros, again?" Elara asked with slanted eyes.

Theodosius stared at her thoughtfully for a moment before moving to stand closer to her face. "I already told you, Countess. I'm just trying to clear my good name." Without another word on the matter, he slipped by her and started barking orders to his crew.

The day turned into night, and Elara found that the ship really came alive after sunset. Gregory and another crew member set out candles, Yianni began playing music on his basuki, and other crew members danced and sang. Most of the crew were men, but a few of them, Elara noticed, were actually women.

There was a woman who was putting out soup and bread for everyone to eat for dinner at a long table they had set up on the deck. The woman was tall, with dark skin, and around Elara's age. Her full name was Constantina Argyrou, but she went by Tina.

"Can I help you set the table?" Elara asked Tina.

Tina smiled pleasantly. "That would be great! Here, take these bowls and put one by each seat."

Elara did as she was told, putting a wooden bowl neatly and evenly by each seat. "So, Tina, how did you come to be on a pirate ship? I thought pirates believed women were bad luck."

"Captain Theodosius doesn't discriminate like that." Tina shrugged as she put soup in each bowl. "I came aboard with my brother, Jimmy, some time ago."

"I see," Elara said as she put down the last bowl.

"Is it true you're the girl who turned down a prince's hand in marriage?" Tina asked with a curious twinkle in her eyes.

"Ugh! I wish everyone didn't know that about me," Elara grumbled in embarrassment.

"Are you serious? I thought you were very brave." Tina handed Elara wooden spoons to put next to the bowls. "I wish I had been braver when my ex-husband asked me to marry him."

"What happened to him?" Elara asked.

Tina rolled up her sleeve, revealing a long-jagged scar. "Let's just say, if it wasn't for my brother, Jimmy... I might be six feet deep."

"Oh." Elara's eyes widened with understanding. "I'm sorry."

"Don't be sorry! You should congratulate me on escaping! Just as I congratulate you for getting yourself out early as well."

"Well, congratulations, Tina." Elara hugged her. Ordinarily, it might have been strange to hug a stranger she'd just met, but given the circumstances, Elara couldn't help but feel a kinship with Tina and their shared past.

"Congratulations to you too, Countess." Tina accepted the hug graciously.

"Thank you. You can call me Elara if you want." Elara smiled, feeling she had quickly made a new friend.

"Time for dinner!" At Tina's command, every crew member rushed over to grab a seat at the table. Theodosius sat at the head of the table, and no one dared to eat until he had his first bite. Elara found herself wedged between Yianni and Tina, but she didn't mind. Everyone looked at the captain expectantly.

"Before we begin, I must welcome Countess Iliakos to our table." Theodosius lifted his goblet. "Let us toast to her. The girl who defies future emperors!"

"To the girl who defies future emperors!" The crew chanted before merrily clinking glasses and drinking.

Elara made eye contact with Theodosius who winked at her. She had never had a person in her life so openly admire her before. It was both intimidating and flattering at the same time. Elara wasn't sure what to make of it. On the one hand, she really liked it, and hoped he and the others, like Tina, would keep it up for the remainder of their journey. On the other hand, she worried that Celina was right, and perhaps Theodosius didn't mean it, and was just trying to manipulate her. It was hard to say for certain.

"What do you think of the soup, Countess?" Theodosius asked her.

Elara, who had already taken many greedy spoonfuls of it into her mouth despite how hot it was, said, "It's very good. Thank you, Captain, for your hospitality." She tried to project her voice over the merry sounds of the others speaking so he could hear her.

Theodosius leaned his strong yet wiry frame back into his chair. "Yianni, switch seats with the countess so I might have a better conversation with her."

"But this is the first mate's chair," Yianni protested.

"*Now*," Theodosius ordered firmly.

With a defeated sigh, Yianni got up from his chair and switched seats with Elara. The seating arrangement hadn't really mattered to Elara, but she did like the excuse of sitting closer to Theodosius and getting a chance to know him better, even if she'd never admit it out loud.

"So," Theodosius smiled playfully and leaned forward on the table. "Tell me about this necklace of yours, Countess. Why's it so special? Surely a lovely lady such as yourself has no shortage of beautiful jewelry to choose from."

"It was my late yiayia's and it's a very precious family heirloom. We got robbed once when we lived in Constantinople, and we don't have many true heirlooms left," Elara explained, finding herself also leaning on the table, mirroring his body language.

"That's all? You're risking your life for dear ol' granny's heirloom?" He looked at her curiously. "There must be more to the story than that."

"Yes, there's more, but it's a little silly," she admitted, taking another sip of soup.

"Try me," Theodosius challenged. He had this magnetic energy about him and Elara felt it pulling on her. She wondered if he was feeling it too.

I do think you're a bad judge of character, Celina's words rattled in her brain, but she refused to heed them. She wasn't doing anything wrong. It wasn't a crime to think a corsair was charming. It wasn't like anything was going to happen. He seemed to be a gentleman about these sorts of things, and she already had her heart burnt once. She wasn't about to let a dangerous man like Theodosius Kardia anywhere near that.

"Come on then," Theodosius pressed. "What's your silly little secret?"

"The nobles in my circle and the people in Constantinople—and even at Tossa de Mar, if I'm being honest, they... well, they think it's shameful that I broke things off with the prince. It's been," Elara swallowed, choking on the words, then finally letting them spill out all at once. "It's been a very embarrassing and shameful time for my family. My papou... he's in Athens right now, actually, on business... he's had to do so much work to restore our name, and still people talk..."

"So, you think if you get this necklace back and take care of everything before your papou returns from his trip, that he and others will be so impressed with how you handled things and got back the heirloom that your good name and honor will be restored?" Theodosius surmised.

Elara blinked. "I know it won't be entirely restored, but I thought it would be a good start to proving myself to my papou and to my new community."

"An interesting plan." He smiled almost sympathetically. "There must be more than just that?"

"I also..." Elara took a deep breath, trying to steady herself. "I also don't want to be homeless."

"Homeless? How could a countess ever be homeless?" Theodosius raised a questioning eyebrow. Clearly, he wasn't familiar with what could happen to a woman if her male relatives decided they didn't want to deal with her anymore.

"Sometimes, when women get into trouble, they lose... Everything." Elara averted her eyes by staring into her soup bowl.

"Ah, I see," Theodosius spoke slowly. "I understand how judgmental people, and especially nobility, can be. They label you once, and then you feel they define you forever."

"Yes, that's exactly what it's like." Elara had never heard someone speak exactly what she had thought before, and she wasn't sure how to feel about it.

"They care a lot about how they look and how things look. It's very superficial," Theodosius continued on.

Tina interjected, "Yes, if only they cared about *being* good as much as they cared about looking good."

"If only! But those are the rules so what can you do?" Elara took a swig of her drink. These pirates really understood her, and she wasn't sure how she felt about that either. "Do you have experience with nobility, Tina?"

"Just you, Elara." Tina smiled over her glass.

"What about you, Captain?" Elara asked curiously as she turned back to look at Theodosius.

"What about me?" He smirked.

"What are you clearing your name with Lord Nekros about?" She watched his face trying to gauge the pirate captain's expression. Elara wasn't as good as Celina at telling when people were lying, but she felt her instincts were good when she paid attention.

Theodosius took a breath and looked back at her as if deciding how much or how little to reveal. "Remember when I told you my brother died, and my life went downhill pretty quickly after that?"

"Yes, I remember." Elara listened intently, keeping her eyes locked on him.

"That was only part of the story. The truth is my brother was murdered, and when I tried to confront his killer, *I* got blamed for his death instead." Theodosius spoke slowly as if each word was more painful than the last.

"Why would they blame you?" Elara furrowed her brow, trying to understand.

"Politics." Theodosius waved his hand absentmindedly. "It's easier to blame one poor boy than the rich people who are in on it."

"I see." Elara nodded understandingly.

"Do you?" he asked softly.

"Yes, you want to present evidence to try to clear your name with the despot in hopes that he'll pass along your innocence to his brother, Emperor Michael." It was a sensible plan, in Elara's opinion, given that Theodosius was telling the truth.

"Something like that." Theodosius looked into his goblet avoiding Elara's eyes now. "They won't let me take Communion at church—did you know that? The Ecumenical Patriarch of

Constantinople said I wasn't allowed to take Communion at any Orthodox Church until I repent."

"That's common punishment for people suspected of crimes," Elara said sadly. It didn't seem fair to cut people off from God and their community when they needed it the most.

"I miss the halls of the Hagia Sophia Church." Theodosius looked into her eyes again. "I miss the warmth and beauty of the Orthodox Liturgy."

"All the more reason to convince Lord Nekros of your innocence."

Elara and Theodosius were alone at the table now. The other crew members had shuffled off to bed, including Tina who had cleared the table of all the dishes. The candles were almost completely melted but still illuminated the night enough for them to see each other's faces.

"Sounds like this has been a difficult situation for you, Captain," Elara continued. "I would be devastated to lose a beloved family member and to be cut off from my church."

"But you have lost family, Countess," Theodosius surmised. "And you have been cut off from your home church in a way. I mean, when was the last time you were at the Hagia Sophia?"

Elara swallowed suddenly, feeling her throat was strangely tight. "I—I haven't been back since I moved away. But I'm not excommunicated or anything!"

"You might as well be. Prince Andronikos made your own home unbearable for you after you ended things with him, didn't he?"

Theodosius had this way of speaking the painful truth without making it seem like it was Elara's fault and instead laying the blame on Andronikos.

"No, the prince didn't... The situation was painful and shameful for me. You know what people are like." Elara looked away for a moment before her eyes met his eyes again.

Theodosius was studying her intently. "You don't blame Andronikos?"

"I am responsible for my own actions. *I* ended things with him," she told him almost angrily. "I don't need to blame him or anyone else other than myself."

"Why did you end things with him? Was it because he was too handsome and wonderful?" Theodosius leaned back in his chair, his voice condescending. "You want me to believe he was gracious to you, but you were terrible to him? I don't believe that. I know what the prince is like."

Elara stood up, finally having enough. "It's really none of your business. I don't need to be getting into such personal details with a corsair of all people!"

"You're right, of course, Countess." Theodosius stood, heated as well. "I forgot myself. Thank you for putting me back in my place!"

"Well, someone had to do it!" Elara snapped with equal snideness. The past was simply too painful to talk about, like a scab being picked apart over and over again with no time to heal. Why couldn't he just leave it alone? "I'm tired. I think I shall retire for the evening."

While Elara remained in her tense position, Theodosius relaxed back into his calm joking persona. "Of course, allow me to show you where you'll be sleeping."

The captain's quarters consisted of a small bed, two lanterns, one round window on the left side wall, and a small desk by the door. It was private, and Elara was grateful for it. She supposed she might have been too harsh on Theodosius earlier, but it was hard to talk about those painful times in her life.

"Thank you for your hospitality. This room will do nicely," Elara said, trying to sound as sincere as possible.

"It's no trouble," Theodosius folded his arms over his chest and shrugged. He leaned on the doorway watching her for a moment. "I *should* apologize for my behavior tonight."

"You should."

"But I won't." He laughed at his own wit.

Elara rolled her eyes good naturedly before attempting to close the cabin door on his face. Theodosius stopped the door from closing with his hand, leaving the two of them staring at each other, their faces mere inches apart.

Her heart beat a little faster as the idea of him trying something salacious briefly crossed her mind. It was true that there was a sort of connection slowly growing between them, and at times, a palpable tension too, but that didn't mean anything more serious would be happening.

"Countess, I want to say—" Before Theodosius could finish his sentence, Elara pulled out a knife and pointed it at him.

"Don't even think about it. I'm not falling for any of your tricks." She lowered the knife only slightly. "I'm going to sleep in here *alone*, and you're going to make sure no one bothers me, understood?"

"Relax, Countess," Theodosius chuckled. "I was only going to say goodnight, but yes, I understand, and I'll make sure no one bothers you."

"Very good." Elara put her dagger back in her belt.

"Do you have an endless supply of knives in your pockets or...?" he asked, teasing her again.

"Goodnight, Captain." She closed the door in his face.

- - -

"Countess? Are you awake?" Theodosius' voice came through the closed door far too early in the morning for Elara's liking. The sky outside was still a pinkish orange, as the sun had only just begun to rise. Based on the sounds of soft snores from below her, no one else was awake yet.

"What do you want?" Elara grumbled, still annoyed at him from earlier.

"I want to teach you how to fight before the whole crew wakes up." His words surprised her, and he must have suspected as much

131

when she didn't immediately reply. "I promised back in Rome that I would teach you to fight, so get up!"

Elara sat up and stared at the closed door. While she still didn't trust him, Theodosius could have barged in on her or taken advantage of her at any moment, but he hadn't. He had respected her space, and now he claimed he wanted to help her learn to fight just as he had promised he would.

"Come on, Countess. Learning to defend yourself is an important skill to have!" Even though she couldn't see him, she could hear the smile in the corsair's voice.

"Fine! Give me a moment." Elara dressed quickly in the clothes Tina had lent her and braided her hair in a messy fishtail. Her clothes consisted of a dark-gray jacket over a cream-colored tunic, with traditional work trousers, and boots. When they arrived in Athens, she planned on wearing more traditional clothing, but this would do for now, especially if she had to learn to fight.

Placing her dagger under her coat for safekeeping, she opened the door to find Theodosius predictably grinning at her, leaning lazily on the door frame, completely at ease.

"Good morning, Captain," Elara said crossly, her voice still scratchy from sleep.

"Good morning, Countess." His voice was deep and rich like he'd been up and about for hours. Perhaps he had been. "Shall we begin?"

She followed Theodosius to the main deck, which was starkly empty save for a sleepy Gregory in the crow's nest and Yianni silently watching them from the helm.

"So, have you ever sparred with anyone before?" Theodosius turned to face her.

"Obviously not." Elara put her hands on her hips. "I told you I'm a lady, and ladies aren't really taught that sort of thing in school."

"Ah, well, better late than never." He raised his hands into a fighting stance and motioned for her to mimic him.

"No swords?"

"We start with hand-to-hand training—in case you don't have a sword or dagger handy."

Feeling a bit awkward and silly, Elara raised her hands up at chest level and clenched her hands into fists. She'd only ever been in a few fights, most of them with Theodosius, and none of them had been thought out. Most often, her fighting style was about desperation, not form, as could be seen from the fight at the Vatican.

"What do I do now?"

"I'm going to come at you in slow motion, and all you have to do is raise your arm above your head like this—" He showed her with his own arm bent above his face. "And block me nice and strong, understood?"

"I suppose," Elara muttered, unsure. She did not have a good feeling about this.

Theodosius moved slowly, as promised, and she blocked him with ease. He complimented her form which made her happier than was probably warranted. They practiced the block a few more times, and each time Theodosius pushed her a bit faster.

"Very good, Countess. Next, let's try the counter punch." Theodosius took her fist in his hand and moved it slowly to show her how to do it. "You see, you blocked the attack with your left arm, and then, you countered the attack with a right hook to the face or neck."

"Yes, I see," said Elara, trying to sound more confident than she felt.

"Let's practice them both together." They practiced that maneuver a few more times before Theodosius was satisfied with her progress. "Good. Let's go over elbows to the gut and knees to the groin next."

"Like this?" Elara exuberantly plowed her knee into the captain's lower abdomen.

"Agh!" Theodosius doubled over, coughing in pain. "You already know that move, huh?"

Elara smirked, only feeling a little guilty. "Oops, my mistake. Are you hurt, Captain?"

"Hurt? Me? No, I'm just fine. Really." Theodosius had a dark glint in his eyes, and Elara immediately regretted messing with him. "Since you're such an expert on that, let's try an escape move next."

"An escape move?" She chuckled nervously.

"It's probably the most important move you'll learn today." He wrapped his arms around her from behind, holding her in place by clenching her wrists. "Try to get out of my grasp."

Elara struggled for a moment, first trying to elbow him, then trying to stomp on his feet, and finally trying to grab her knife. Every attempt she made was unsuccessful. She strained a bit more before realizing that without the proper training, getting out of this would be impossible.

"All right, Captain," she huffed in defeat. "How do I get out of this?"

Theodosius laughed softly before whispering in her ear, "I want you to know that I could have done this at any point in our other fights, but I didn't. Because, despite what my reputation might suggest, I am a gentleman."

Elara's heart began to beat faster, and her face felt hot, but surprisingly it didn't feel like fear, at least not fear in the traditional sense. It was something else that she couldn't put words to it.

"If you're such a gentleman, teach me how to get out of this," she said through gritted teeth.

"Move your leg out like this." He slowly guided her to the proper position. "Now, twist just so, and you should be able to slip your wrists out. After you slip out, you can *gently* shove me to escape."

It took her a couple of tries, but eventually, she mastered the maneuver and was able to do it quickly enough. She wondered if it was becoming easy because Theodosius was taking it easy on her or if she was actually getting better.

"Well done, Countess. Aren't you proud of your progress?" He beamed at her, and she couldn't help but feel a twinge of pride in her gut.

"I guess I am." Elara glanced at the open waters. "Do you suppose I'm combat ready? Shouldn't I learn to swordplay too?"

"I'd stick to your dagger for now, but if we have time, I can teach you the sword another day," Theodosius promised with a hint of a smile on his lips.

Elara was taken aback by how effortlessly handsome the captain looked in his pirate garb as he pushed his thick hair out of his eyes. The rising sun glinted off his long eyelashes, and his cheeks were slightly rosy from the exertion of sparring.

The sky was almost a proper blue color now, and the crew was up and about, getting ready for the day. She noticed some of the crew members were staring at her and whispering.

"Well, I should, uh… I should finish getting ready for the day, so if you'll excuse me." Elara nodded at Theodosius, not waiting for a response as she slipped away back to the captain's quarters.

Chapter Seven

Athens

Celina looked out at the moon's glow glistening over the water. It was too dark to see much else. She hoped Elara was doing all right on her own and that she hadn't fallen into any of Theodosius Kardia's charm traps.

Now that Celina had dried off, and Captain Titus had given her and Rhea fresh clothes and food, she had plenty of time to lament her situation. It was mostly her fault for standing so close to the edge, and if it weren't for Rhea, she would definitely be dead. Rhea had saved Celina's life even after she had been so terrible to her this whole time.

"Titus has agreed to let us stay in the captain's quarters for the night." Rhea appeared next to her. "How are you feeling?"

"Physically, I'm fine," Celina mumbled, still looking out at the ocean.

"How are you feeling emotionally?" she pressed.

"Why do *you* care?"

"I was just asking."

Silence hung between them, and Celina couldn't help but feel guilty about her outburst. Rhea had saved her life, and the only reward had been continued hostility.

After a moment, Celina swallowed her pride enough to speak again. "I'm worried about Elara."

"Me too," Rhea whispered so low it was almost inaudible.

Celina turned to face Rhea. "The sooner we find her the better."

"We'll be in Athens by the morning, and then, hopefully, we'll be able to track her down." Rhea went to put a comforting hand on Celina's shoulder and then seemed to think better of it, letting her hand fall to her side. "We should get some sleep." The two girls walked to the captain's quarters side by side, saying nothing.

The captain's cabin was standard-looking. It consisted of a small bed, a desk, and a large chair by the window. There was a small red and blue rug on the floor, but it did little to bring the homey feeling the girls were accustomed to.

"Oh, I guess you'll be taking the floor, or you could sleep in that big chair, I suppose," Celina said as she plopped drowsily onto the bed.

"Er, excuse me?" said Rhea with a suddenly sharp tone. "I think *I'll* be the one taking the bed, and you'll be the one in the chair or floor."

"Pardon me? I think not. I'm a noble lady! You're a *peasant,*" Celina said in a derogatory tone.

Rhea glowered at her before grabbing Celina by the hair, pulling her off the bed, and throwing her on the hardwood floor.

"OW! What the hell?!" Celina yelped.

"Looks like the bed is mine, you ungrateful wench." Rhea sat on the bed and began taking her shoes off preparing for bed.

"Miss Alkan, this is most undignified! Get off the bed!" The two girls wrestled a bit, slapping each other and pulling each other's hair.

"You're a spoiled brat, Lady Oberon!" Rhea yelled as she shoved Celina to the floor again.

"Ugh!" Celina grumbled from the ground. She was too tired to keep fighting, but she knew she wouldn't sleep a wink on the floor nor in the lumpy chair by the window. "Perhaps we could share the bed? Would you be agreeable to that?"

Rhea bit her lip considering the offer. "All right, but you better not hog the blanket."

Celina smiled as she got on the left side of the bed, and Rhea took the right. They had their backs to each other, both trying to pretend the other one wasn't there.

"Goodnight, Miss Alkan."

"Goodnight, Lady Oberon."

The water was mostly calm, and with the lanterns out, the room was nearly pitch-black, save a sliver of moonlight that trickled in from the round window. The blankets were a bit scratchy, and the bed a bit lumpy, but otherwise, it was a decent sleeping arrangement given the circumstances. Celina wondered what Elara was doing right now. Was she safe? Without Celina there to protect her, there was no telling what could happen.

"Miss Alkan? Are you awake?" Celina whispered.

"Yes, what is it?" Rhea said back just as quietly.

"Do you think Elara is doing all right without us?" Celina stared at the sliver of moonlight, not having the courage to look at Rhea and gauge her expression.

"I think the countess is stronger than both of us combined," Rhea muttered drowsily.

Celina smiled and finally turned to face the other girl. "Stronger than us both, do you think?"

"Mhmm." Rhea turned on her side to face Celina too. It was too dark to make out her full facial expression, but Celina sensed that Rhea was smiling. "I think we need her way more than she ever needed us. I don't know if you noticed, Lady Oberon, but we're kind of a mess."

This made Celina laugh. "Oh, I've noticed."

"Have you?" Rhea laughed too.

"It's not our fault you know. We've got emotional baggage that Elara doesn't have." Celina surmised as she fiddled with the corner of the blanket.

"Emotional baggage? How do you mean?"

"Well, you're always trying to prove yourself to people like me who don't deserve your kindness," Celina admitted in a suddenly serious whisper. "And as for me... I don't trust people. I was betrayed a few years back, and now there are few people I trust."

"That... was surprisingly deep of you, Lady Oberon. May I ask who betrayed your trust?"

"A couple of my friends were bribed by my father's enemies to assassinate me," Celina whispered, trying not to think too much about

140

that day. Her old friends, two held her down while the third held the knife. "If my father's guards hadn't heard my screams..." Celina shuddered, trying not to think about it, but sometimes, it was hard not to get lost in the pain of the memory.

"That's awful," Rhea whispered back. "I'm so sorry that happened to you."

"Thank you and thank you for jumping in the water to save my life." Celina felt herself curling up and put her head on Rhea's shoulder. "I'm sorry I was so mean to you. You don't deserve it."

"It's all right." Rhea put her arm around Celina and pulled her into a friendly hug. "We're friends. That's why I jumped into the water to save you. Because I want us to be friends."

"I know," Celina whispered. "But I'm scared. Elara...Elara is the only person other than my father that I trust."

"You can trust me," Rhea whispered, sleepiness seeping into her voice. Her arm slackened slightly as she drifted off. "I'd never betray you."

Celina felt sleep overcoming her as well. "Goodnight, Rhea."

"Goodnight, Celina."

- - -

"LAND HO!" The shouts of the bustling pirate ship roused Elara from her slumber. She reached under her pillow to retrieve her knife. Dressing quickly and braiding her hair out of her face, Elara went out to see if she could get a glimpse of Athens. After two and a half days of sailing, she was anxious for land.

Sure enough, she could see the Acropolis on the hill in the distance, and the outline of the city buildings. Her papou would be among those buildings. She wondered what he would do if he saw her traveling alone with pirates in a foreign city. Hopefully, her disguise would keep her hidden from sight.

Her mind then drifted to Celina and Rhea. She hoped they would be able to meet her in Athens—assuming they hadn't killed each other over their petty feud or been actually killed by some other force. Elara didn't want to think about it. All she could do was pray for them.

"Good morning, Countess." It was Theodosius, looking particularly fresh-faced and handsome for first thing in the morning. "How did you sleep?"

"I slept well, thank you," Elara replied stiffly. "How did you sleep?"

"I fared fine." He shrugged and leaned his back on the starboard railing. "Ready to get your necklace back?"

"You know I am." She smiled despite herself. "But how exactly are we going to do that?"

"Well, you, me, and Yianni are going to find the woman he traded the necklace to, and then we're going to get it back by *any* means necessary." He winked.

"I know you've been teaching me to fight, but I really don't want anyone to get hurt." Elara frowned at him and leaned away to show that she was serious.

142

"Relax, Countess." Theodosius moved off the railing to stand closer to her. "Give me a little credit, please. I have my ways of getting what I want without hurting a fly."

"I'm not worried about the flies," she muttered back dryly, as she stared out at the approaching Athenian shoreline.

After the boat docked, Theodosius, Yianni, Elara, and, at Elara's request, Tina, all disembarked and headed into the bustling city of Athens, Greece.

The city was just as she remembered it. There were tall marble buildings with decorated columns, beautiful domed churches, and open-air markets with fresh goods. It smelled delicious, and she hoped they could eat a bit before too long.

"Hungry?" Theodosius asked as if he read her mind.

"I'm starving," Elara admitted, holding her hands over her stomach.

"Me too," said Tina.

"Me three!" Yianni slung his arm over Theodosius' shoulder. "Can we get some spanakopita or souvlaki or something, please, Captain?"

Theodosius laughed. "Fine! I suppose it would be better to negotiate on full stomachs."

The smell of fresh spanakopita, tiropita, souvlaki, gyro, and other Greek foods filled the air, making Elara bitterly homesick for Constantinople. The thing she missed most back at the fortress was authentic Greek cuisine.

They ate spanakopita and other treats as they walked. They were just as savory and delicious as Elara remembered. The last time she'd had spanakopita on the streets like this, she had been with her yiayia...and Celina. Her throat got tight thinking of Celina. She prayed silently again that Celina and Rhea were safe.

"When I was a kid, I wanted to eat souvlaki for every meal," Tina told the group as they walked and ate.

"If you think this is good, you should try the gyro and baklava in Constantinople," Theodosius said, his mouth full of tiropita. "It's the best."

"It *is* the best," Elara agreed. "They don't make food like that in Catalonia."

"My favorite is spanakopita, for sure," Yianni said as he finished shoving the last piece into his mouth. "My yiayia used to make it the best. No one makes it as good as she did."

After finishing their food and walking for a few more blocks, they finally stopped in front of a large stone building with a red door. The windows were small, and there were no signs on the door indicating what or who might be inside.

"Are you sure this is the place?" Theodosius asked Yianni, his tone thick with skepticism.

"She should be here, yes." Yianni gestured for the captain to try the door.

"Who is this *she?*" Elara asked Tina as Theodosius knocked three times on the door.

"The noblewoman Yianni traded the necklace to," Tina told her.

The door opened, and a tall, thin woman in an elegant red dress with reddish-blonde hair pulled into a tight bun, stood there, looking like the mere sight of them disgusted her. "Ew, what are you filthy pirates doing here?"

"Hello to you too, Lady Justine. May we come in?" Theodosius requested with his most charming smile.

"How dare you come here, Kardia. I have half a mind to fetch my butler to throw you in jail!" The woman jutted out her jaw, defiantly not letting them inside.

"Come on, Justine," Yianni laughed good naturedly. "We all know you're broke. You haven't had any staff in nearly five years."

"Screw you, Drakos." Justine flushed as red as her dress, but she stepped aside, letting them enter, nevertheless. They went through the doorway with Theodosius entering last.

Lady Justine's house was beautiful, but clearly in disrepair. She had dusty shelves and empty places where furniture or an elegant rug should be. There were no curtains over the windows and no art on the walls.

"I'd offer you all a seat, but as you can see, I'm short on chairs." Justine gestured to the mostly empty room as if inviting them to sit on air.

"We don't mind standing." Theodosius smiled and put a hand around Elara's arm, pulling her forward so she was standing closer to

Justine. "Where are my manners? Lady Justine, have you met Countess Iliakos of Constantinople?"

Elara jerked out of his grasp, annoyed. She didn't want people to know who she was so that she wouldn't be judged for who she was traveling with.

Justine's eyes widened in surprise. "Countess Iliakos? The girl who refused the prince?"

"The very same." Theodosius nodded before turning to Elara. "Countess, have you met Lady Justine Parakios of Athens? Before Lady Justine's marriage, she was a lady-in-waiting to Empress Maria Palaiologos too, a few years before you were."

Elara suddenly felt self-conscious standing in the presence of a woman of Empress Maria's court, even if she wasn't anymore. "It's nice to meet you. Sorry to intrude on you like this... I don't normally travel with pirates, I swear."

Justine looked Elara up and down. "You're not as pretty as I imagined you to be."

This caught Elara off guard, and she almost laughed. "Uh, pardon me?"

"I thought that a woman who turned down a prince would be prettier, that's all. You're not ugly, of course, and you've got a nice frame about you, I suppose, but you're no Empress Maria." Justine circled Elara like a vulture waiting for a rabbit to die before devouring it.

"No one is as pretty as Empress Maria," Elara agreed, not seeing a point in arguing with the lady.

"You're too plain to be a fool," Justine continued. "Only a fool would ruin her reputation over a man."

Elara's throat tightened, and she suddenly felt like she was looking into a mirror. Justine was penniless because her reputation must also be in shambles, and unlike Elara, she didn't have a wealthy parental figure to take care of her.

"Where's your husband, Lady Justine?" Elara asked, fearing she already knew the answer.

"He left me to rob the cradle. Apparently, he couldn't stomach the life experience I had before I met him." The message was clear— Justine's marriage was getting dissolved. In order to appeal for marital dissolution, her husband would have had to claim she had an affair, which would ruin her reputation. Soon Justine would be on the streets like the beggar woman in Catalonia.

"I'm so sorry to hear that." Elara couldn't help but feel empathetic. If the fallout with Andronikos had been any worse, Elara might have faced a similar fate.

"I don't need pity from someone like you," Justine scoffed, crossing her arms in a defiant pose.

Theodosius opened his mouth to say something, probably unsavory, but Tina beat him to the punch.

"Lady Justine, we've come to discuss a certain necklace. We know you have it," Tina interjected as she moved to stand shoulder to shoulder with Elara.

"God, *Constantina Argyrou*? I almost didn't recognize you. You've gotten fat." Justine smirked almost as if that fact pleased her.

Tina's face turned a slightly darker shade, and her hands balled into fists. Elara felt herself mimicking Tina's body language; neither of them said anything in response to the insult.

"Where's the necklace?" Yianni asked, his hand on the hilt of his sword.

"What necklace?" Justine replied innocently.

"You know which one." Theodosius had a hand on his own sword. "You're not exactly swimming in jewelry, are you? So, if you're done insulting women who are better than you, perhaps you'd like to show us where it is."

"I really don't know what you're talking about!" Justine said defensively.

"Search the house," Theodosius told Yianni and Tina, both of whom obeyed his orders immediately. Elara moved to search the house too, but Theodosius stopped her with his hand. "Not you, Countess."

Normally, Elara would have questioned him or ignored his orders, but this situation was so foreign to her, she decided it would be safer to stand back and let the pieces fall where they may.

"You better not break any of my things!" Justine yelled as Yianni and Tina went upstairs. "Honestly Kardia, I thought we were friends. Why are you coming here to ruin everything?"

"*Friends?*" Theodosius laughed contemptuously. "After all the lies you told in Constantinople?"

"Oh, spare me! That was seven years ago! Get over it." Justine rolled her eyes, but Theodosius wasn't done.

He continued, saying, "...and now the rude way you've spoken to Countess Iliakos and to Tina is completely unacceptable. So, no, we're not friends."

"Ah, I see." Justine smirked. "Captain Kardia still has a soft spot for the ladies. I used to be a lady you had a soft spot for, you know."

"Not anymore." Theodosius kept his hand on Elara's arm, but whether it was to hold her back or himself, Elara couldn't tell. What she could tell was that Theodosius and Justine had a history, and a complicated one at that. She wondered what lies Justine had told in Constantinople that had him so upset.

"I didn't take you as the kind of man who'd want Andronikos' leftovers," Justine sneered.

"You're awfully rude for someone all alone in an empty house," Elara said, finally finding her voice. Justine could call her ugly and plain but calling her Andronkios' leftovers was crossing the line. She did not want to be defined by her ex-fiancé.

Instead of responding to Elara, Justine kept her eyes locked on Theodosius, clearly seeing him as the bigger threat. "There's no way

149

that after everything you've done, you think you can have a *countess*. Especially a countess once engaged to a prince. Clearly, she is just using you to get this necklace."

Theodosius squinted his eyes at Justine, looking as insulted as Elara felt. "The countess and I have an arrangement, and it's all very appropriate, I can assure you."

"Yes, because when people think of Countess Elara Iliakos, they think *appropriate*." Justine gave a little sarcastic laugh as she spoke.

Something within Elara snapped. She pulled out of Theodosius's grasp and rushed towards Lady Justine in an attempt to slap the Athenian woman across the face. Theodosius, always the quick one, stopped her just in time.

"How dare you!" Elara snarled as she struggled to get out of Theodosius' hold. "I am a countess! You cannot speak to me like that!"

"It's not just me!" Justine squeaked, sounding a bit nervous now. "Everyone says it!"

News travels fast.

Elara felt sick as blood rushed to her cheeks. Everyone was talking about her, about her failure, about her shame. She wasn't sure if she wanted to fight, collapse, or both.

"Our situations are not so different, Lady Justine. You know what it's like to have a bad reputation… You know how it can ruin a woman's life." Elara eyed Justine, daring her to see how comparable their situations were. They were both victims of the same unjust system.

"But you are not *ruined*, Lady Elara. Count Basil has kept you safe despite your many moral failings."

"That's enough!" snapped Theodosius. "Yianni! Tina! Got the necklace yet?"

There were loud footsteps coming back down the stairs, too many footsteps for it to be just two people. Yianni and Tina appeared with their hands tied above their heads, and they weren't alone. Three Athenian guards appeared as well, with swords drawn. Elara's heart dropped down to her stomach at the sight of them. She couldn't believe she was going to get arrested again.

"Hello, Captain Kardia," one of the guards said. "You and your crew are under arrest."

"Is that so?" Theodosius unsheathed his sword as he pushed Elara behind him.

It was then that many things happened at once. Theodosius swung his sword and began fighting one of the guards. The other guard stepped forward to help the first, but Yianni broke free of his hand bindings and jumped on the guard's back, wrestling the guard to the ground.

Elara pulled her dagger out of her pocket and helped cut Tina's wrists free. The binding wasn't very strong, and Elara wondered how the guards had so grossly underestimated the pirates.

"Thank you." Tina smiled at her before moving to help Yianni take out the guard he was wrestling on the ground. Yianni looked like he was losing, so it was a good thing he now had Tina there to help him.

Theodosius and the first guard were locked in a sword battle that was way above Elara's skill level. The guard would make a jabbing motion, and Theodosius would duck or block perfectly before thrusting his own sword. They made delicate cuts on each other's arms, but neither seemed to really be able to land a definitive blow.

Elara's stomach twisted into knots as she watched Theodosius fight. If only she had studied swordplay, she might have been able to do something to assist him. She watched in horror as the guard slammed Theodosius against the wall. His body made a loud cracking sound when it collided with the wood and drywall.

"Oh, God!" Elara said aloud, clasping her hands over her mouth.

Hearing her cry, Theodosius briefly made eye contact with her and looked about the room before swinging his sword at the guard again. The two men were evenly matched skill-wise, but the guard had a bit more muscle to him than Theodosius did, and the guard seemed to be less tired than the pirate.

"Countess! Where's Justine?" Theodosius called out to her as he continued his fight.

She looked around and realized that Lady Justine was nowhere to be found. The back door beside the fireplace was swinging slightly, and she realized that Justine must have run that way. Without hesitation, Elara raced out the door with her dagger in hand. Justine was their only clue to the whereabouts of her yiayia's necklace. If Justine disappeared, they would never be able to find it.

Elara raced out of the house and found herself in a corridor of houses on cobblestone streets. She turned to the left and saw a woman in a red dress running in the distance. It was Justine.

"Lady Justine! Stop!" Elara yelled as she raced after the woman. It wasn't pleasant running on cobblestones down narrow alleyways she wasn't as familiar with as Justine was, but she kept going. The alleyways may have been endless, narrow, and difficult to tell apart, but Elara could tell there was a pattern to them just as there was back at Fortress Tossa de Mar. She might not be able to outrun Justine, but perhaps with this knowledge of patterns, she could outwit her. Instead of going straight after her, Elara skidded and took a left turn that looped around to the opposite pathway.

"What the hell!" Justine shrieked as Elara ambushed her from the other side.

"Halt!" Elara grabbed Justine by the shoulders and shoved her up against the walls of one of the houses, pressing her dagger to the lady's throat. "Where is my necklace?"

"I—I don't know!" Justine stammered.

"Yes, you do! Yianni traded it to you just the other day for two glasses of mead. Tell me what you did with it, or I'll kill you!" Elara snarled, as she pressed the dagger slightly into the woman's flesh.

A single prick of blood dripped down from Justine's throat. "I don't know! I swear I don't know!" she sobbed.

Elara loosened her grip slightly, so no more blood was drawn, but she dared not let Justine go. "I'm going to give you one more chance to tell the *truth*. Woman to woman, tell me what you did with my necklace, and I'll let you go."

"Fine! I sold it, all right? I sold it so I would have enough money to pay my debts. My ex-husband took everything and—" Justine began to sputter her excuses, but Elara interrupted her.

"Sold it to who?" She shook Justine's shoulders when she didn't respond. "Who did you sell it to? Tell me now!"

"You can't tell Theodosius," Justine whispered.

"What?" Elara frowned, confused. "What are you talking about? Who has my necklace?"

"I sold it to the despot, Nekros Palaiologos!" Justine sobbed, looking ashamed.

She released Justine's shoulder and dropped her knife back into her own pocket. "Why can't I tell Theodosius about that?"

Justine clinched her jaw and changed the subject. "You were right, Lady Elara. We are the same. Both of us are good women who have been ruined forever by the wiles of faithless men."

"Why can't I tell Theodosius about Nekros?" Elara repeated, not allowing Justine to pull her into a pity party. They didn't have time to wallow over all the ways they had been wronged by men.

"Because Lord Nekros hates Theodosius, of course, and if he finds out I told..." Justine took a shuddering breath. "I can't get between them again... Not after poor Leonides—" Whatever Justine was about to say was cut short by an arrow sailing straight into her throat.

Elara screamed in horror as she watched blood gush from Justine's neck. Then the lady slumped over onto the ground, dead at Elara's feet.

Chapter Eight

Abandoned

Athens looked exactly as Celina remembered it from her visit a few years ago, but she still wasn't familiar enough with the layout of the city to get around without a map.

"I think we should try to find out if there are any nobles who recently bought jewelry in this area." Celina pointed to the paper map she had spread out on the tavern table. "Perhaps we can check out some local merchants as well to see if any of them got a necklace from a pirate named Yianni Drakos."

"A sensible plan," Rhea agreed, her mouth full of spanakopita.

Celina sighed as she rolled up the map of Athens and put it in her satchel. "Do you suppose the pirates are being nice to Elara? She's a very sensitive girl, you know."

"Elara's not a baby." Rhea took a swig of ale and another bite of her food.

"True enough." Celina opened her mouth to say something not so nice about Rhea's eating habits but thought better of it. She was trying to be nicer to Rhea, like a real friend would be. Elara would be proud of her for the effort at least.

"Are you going to finish that?" Rhea pointed to Celina's half eaten tiropita.

"Go for it."

After they ate, the two girls wandered outside to see if they could find any local merchants to talk to, specifically ones that sold or dealt in jewelry.

"What can I do for you lovely ladies? See anything you like?" The merchant asked from behind his stand where he was selling evil-eye bracelets, cross necklaces, and worry-beads.

Celina barely glanced at the jewelry, noting it was cheaply made and not at all in line with the kind of necklace they were looking for. "I think we're looking for something a little more high-end. Do you know where we could find something like that?"

"Of course!" The merchant beamed. "My brother, Takis Alexios, has a little shop down the road—very nice jewelry there. The best in Athens!"

"Better than yours?" Rhea mused.

The merchant laughed, "Well, it's pricier than mine to say the least."

Celina and Rhea walked down the street where they found the shop run by Takis Alexios. The jewelry didn't look that much different than the kind the merchant was selling up the road but being able to talk to an actual shop owner was a good thing, in Celina's opinion.

"*Yasas?* Hello?" Celina said as she and Rhea walked around the shop.

It was a small, dimly lit room with shelves lined with merchandise. There was some jewelry on the countertops but at a glance, none looked like the kind of jewelry they were looking for.

"*Yasas!*" The shop owner, presumably Takis, greeted them. "Can I help you girls find anything?"

"We're looking for a necklace with red rubies bound together by a silver chain—very expensive, very old. Do you have anything like that?" Celina asked, trying to sound as nonchalant as possible.

Takis laughed, looking a bit confused. "I'm afraid not, but we have many other lovely options if you're interested in something a bit simpler?"

"Hmm, I see," Celina tried to hide the disappointment in her voice. "Oh well, very sorry to have bothered you. Are there any other jewelry stores this way or perhaps a noble lady who loves dealing in jewelry nearby?"

"I'm sure we can find you something else you might like!" Takis pulled out a box of red bracelets and necklaces but none of them were what they were searching for.

"Oh no, thank you—" Celina started to say but stopped when she noticed Rhea staring out the shop window, slack-jawed. "Rhea? What do you see?" She had hoped it was Elara outside, and was disappointed to see it wasn't.

Instead, there was a beautiful Indian woman in an elegant lavender dress, surrounded by what appeared to be three lady's maids.

The Indian woman was laughing with the other girls as they strolled casually down the street.

"It's her..." Rhea muttered. "It's Lady Sidra Ravi."

So, Theodosius Kardia had told the truth when he said that she was alive. Rhea was staring in half amazement, half horror, as if the truth was wonderful and horrific at the same time. Celina supposed it was. Finding out that your friend had faked her own death and hadn't told you would be both good and bad—good because she was alive, but bad because she had lied and made Rhea mourn for nothing.

"Are you going to go out and speak to her?" Celina asked Rhea quietly.

"Should I?" Rhea replied, never taking her eyes off the window.

"Oh, come on then," Celina looped her arm through Rhea's and pulled her out of the store and back onto the street.

"Wait! We shouldn't bother her." Rhea tried to pull back, but Celina ignored her as she continued to move toward the Indian noblewoman and her lady's maids.

"Pardon me! Lady Sidra!"

"*Celina!* Don't!" Rhea hissed quietly, sounding mortified.

"Lady Sidra Ravi!" Celina shouted louder now, drowning out any of Rhea's protests.

Finally, Lady Sidra turned toward them, looking confusedly at Celina. Then her eyes widened in surprise as she noticed Rhea on Celina's arm. Her mouth fell open slightly as if this was the last person she had expected to see in sunny Athens.

"Hello, my lady," Rhea said hoarsely when they were standing less than three feet apart. "How—how are you alive?"

"Hello, Rhea." Sidra frowned and shifted on her feet awkwardly.

The other three girls standing with Sidra giggled as if this was a silly situation instead of a serious one, at least in Celina's opinion.

"I'm Lady Celina Oberon." Celina extended her hand for Sidra to shake.

"From Bulgaria? Great to meet you," Sidra said with a surprised smile. "I'm Lady Sidra Ravi from India, as you seem to know already, and these are my maids—Calypso, Hanni, and Lila." The three girls bowed politely to Celina.

"Pleasure." Celina gave them a curt nod. "So, Rhea and I were under the impression that you had been brutally murdered by pirates."

"Right, about that..." Sidra gave an awkward chuckle. "You see—I faked it. I wanted to marry someone my father didn't approve of, so I faked my death."

"How could you not tell me?" Rhea was clearly on the verge of tears, but she held herself together, which made Celina proud of her.

"Rhea, I'm terribly sorry. We needed someone to 'survive' so they could tell people I'd died, and it needed to be believable. So, I picked you." Sidra frowned and fiddled with her hands.

"But why did you not write to me after?" Rhea pressed. "Why did you not let me know? I—I cried for you, I mourned you, I thought you were really gone."

"God, you're still so pathetic, Rhea," one of the lady's maids, Hanni, quipped. "Isn't it obvious by now that we Jacobite Christians didn't want to share quarters with a dirty Turk like you!"

There was a palpable silence, for a moment, as the shock and startling truth of the moment washed over them all. Sidra and her girls abandoned Rhea on purpose because she was different from them. Celina's stomach lurched as guilt settled into her. She suddenly, truly regretted every mean word she ever said to Rhea—now more than ever.

"Lady Sidra, are you really going to let your maid say such rude and hateful things?" Celina chastised her.

"Hanni is just being honest," Sidra shrugged apologetically. "Sorry again, Rhea."

"It's all right." Rhea choked on a sob as the three lady's maids giggled at her again, this time even Sidra smirked. They weren't sorry.

"No, it is not all right!" Celina put her arm over Rhea's shoulder. "None of you are being very Christ-like! Rhea Alkan is the sweetest, bravest, funniest person in the Empire, and if you can't see that then you're as daft as they come!"

Celina, with Rhea in tow, marched off down the street. She didn't much care about the direction they were going as long as they got as far away from those nasty girls as possible.

"Thank you for standing up for me," Rhea said as tears streaked down her face. "I'll be sure to mention your kindness to Lady Elara when we find her."

"I didn't do it for Elara," Celina muttered gently as they walked down a narrow alleyway together. "I know what it's like to be betrayed by people you thought were your friends."

This was meant to comfort Rhea, but for some reason, she started crying harder. Celina didn't know what to do but pat the poor girls back comfortingly.

"You know what the worst part is?" Rhea whispered, her voice barely audible over the sound of the Athenian market life.

"What's the worst part?"

Rhea closed her eyes tightly as if the truth was too painful to witness. "I truly loved Sidra with all my heart—and I meant *nothing* to her."

Celina didn't know what to say to that either, so she just cooed more generic comforting phrases and patted Rhea's back some more. Her throat was tight as she remembered her old friends revealing their true colors. When they had held her down and hit her, she had wanted to die. What was the point of living when the people you loved hated you? When all your friends wanted you dead?

They walked for a bit longer until they saw a crowd ahead of them all surrounding something or someone in an alleyway.

"What's going on up there?" Celina asked a boy sitting nearby.

"Lady Justine Parakios just got murdered by pirate assassins," he said matter-of-factly. "That's her body up there."

- - -

162

"She's dead. The arrow went straight through her neck." Elara was pacing back and forth back at Lady Justine's house, a nervous wreck.

Theodosius, Yianni, and Tina had managed to subdue the guards, so the immediate danger was gone, but there was still the matter of the assassin lurking somewhere, possibly with more arrows.

"There goes your one witness," Yianni muttered to Theodosius, but the captain ignored his first mate, his eyes locked on Elara.

"Countess," Theodosius moved to stand in her path and held her upper arms, forcing her to hold still. "Breathe. I need you to focus. What did Justine say to you before she was shot?"

You can't tell Theodosius.

But she had to tell him; there was simply no other choice. Whatever was going on suddenly felt much bigger than her and her yiayia's necklace.

"She said she sold my necklace to Nekros—and then she started to say something about a person named Leonides." Elara felt Theodosius tense up at the name Leonides. "You know him?"

"Yes," his voice was strained. "Leonides was the name of my late brother."

"Your brother?" Elara frowned. "Why would Justine be talking about your late brother?"

Theodosius ignored her question, and instead, turned to Yianni and Tina who had been watching them silently. "You see? I need to confront Nekros soon. Things are only going to keep getting worse until I do."

"It's risky," Yianni shook his head. "Killing Justine was bold. Bolder than he's been in a while."

"Sorry—you think *Nekros* sent the assassin to kill Justine?" Elara surmised as shock seeped into her voice. She couldn't imagine Nekros, her father's friend, killing anyone, let alone a noblewoman.

"It wouldn't be the first time he's done something like this to cover his trail," Tina said solemnly with her arms folded over her chest.

Theodosius turned back to Elara. "Countess, I know this is a lot, but if what Justine said is true, and she did sell the necklace to him, then our only way to get it back is to go straight to him. Do you think you can still get me an audience with the despot?"

"Nekros was a friend of my late father's." Elara stared at the pirates, realizing that she might have been too trusting of them. Perhaps Celina was right, and she really was a bad judge of character.

"Countess, we had a deal." Theodosius stepped toward her but stopped when she took a step back. "Don't pull your knife out again, for God's sake."

"Elara, you can trust us." Tina stepped forward, holding out her hands to show her she had no weapon. "We're your friends. We want to help you get your necklace back, truly."

"Truly?" Elara scoffed. "And do you want to kill Nekros, *truly?*"

"No, not kill. We just need to talk to him," Theodosius promised. "Please, Countess. Nekros isn't who you think he is. He's a dangerous man, but if I could only speak with him..." His voice trailed off, but the meaning was implied.

Theodosius wanted a chance to talk Nekros out of something or into something; he wanted the chance to plead his case. Elara couldn't fault him for that. She sometimes wished she could talk to everyone who spoke ill of her and plead her case too, to get the chance to beg them to see her truth.

"I suppose..." she said slowly. "I can get you an audience with Nekros, but you can't kill him. You must promise me you won't harm him physically."

"I promise," Theodosius said. Elara looked at Yianni and Tina pointedly.

"I promise too." Tina crossed her heart with her right hand.

"I promise three." Yianni smiled cheekily.

"Very well," Elara sighed, only half-convinced. "Let's go to Constantinople."

- - -

Celina had never seen a dead body before. Now she knew the sight of it would be burned into her mind forever. The poor woman had an arrow sticking out of her throat from which her blood had pooled out. Her skin was a muted gray while her eyes remained half-open and lifeless.

"What do you think happened to her?" Rhea whispered in horror.

"She got shot with an arrow in the neck," Celina replied dryly.

Rhea rolled her eyes. "I know that! What I meant was—who shot her and why did they do it?"

The 'who' and 'why' were the questions of the day, it seemed. Celina thought back to what the boy had said about *pirate* assassins being responsible. Her pulse quickened as she thought about Elara all alone aboard Theodosius Kardia's ship.

"We have to find Elara," Celina said to Rhea as the two girls retreated from the crowd of onlookers. "Before it's too late."

"Too late for what?" A voice asked from behind them, making both girls jump. They turned to see none other than Count Basil Iliakos, Elara's papou. He was dressed nicely in a purple and orange tunic and his mustache looked thicker than before.

"Count Basil! My lord, what are you doing here?" Celina squeaked as she and Rhea bowed to the Count respectfully.

"I could ask you girls the same question." Basil looked worriedly between them. "Where's my granddaughter? Where is Elara?"

"She's—She's uh…" Celina looked at Rhea, trying to decide what they should say.

They had two options: tell the truth and get Elara in trouble *or* tell a lie and risk Elara getting in more trouble later. Either way, they had to say something.

"Elara is…here, my lord." Rhea said, clearly deciding on a half-truth. "She's in the city of Athens is what I meant to say."

"Where in the city?" Basil asked, frowning.

Rhea and Celina looked at each other again before Celina spoke, "We wish we knew."

"She's *missing?*" Basil's face went a ghostly pale, and his hands trembled slightly. "Well, where did you last see her?"

In Rome, Celina almost said, but thought better of it. Instead, she and Rhea said nothing as they looked down at their feet in shame.

"Lady Celina, where did you last see my granddaughter?"

"On the ship," Celina mumbled, another half-truth. "We lost track of her here. I don't know where she is, but we are looking for her, we promise."

"You lost my granddaughter? I must find her!" Basil huffed and set off back down the busy main street, presumably to look for Elara.

"Count Basil, wait!" Celina called after him, but he quickly disappeared into the crowd.

"What do we do now?" Rhea asked Celina. "We still have absolutely no idea where Elara is, and now the count knows!" Elara was not going to be happy with them when she finds out her grandfather had learned about this misadventure.

"The dead woman," Celina said, a sudden idea striking her.

"The dead woman? What about her?" Rhea frowned.

"The boy said the lady was killed by *pirate* assassins!" Celina grabbed Rhea's arm and started pulling back the other way back toward the crowd that was still formed around the dead body.

"Pirates!" Rhea breathed, catching on. "Elara is traveling with pirates."

"Exactly, so if we find the pirates..." Celina turned a corner, dodging people as she walked briskly to get a better look at the scene of the crime. She hoped someone would know the deceased and be able to tell them more information.

Rhea surmised the plan, finishing Celina's original thought. "If we find the pirates, we might find Elara! Brilliant plan, but how do we find these pirates?"

"Excuse me," Celina tapped on the shoulder of an onlooker. "Do you know the address of where this dead lady used to reside?"

The onlooker, a man in his mid-to-late-forties, gave them the address. Thankfully, it wasn't too far away. Just a couple of blocks from where she had been killed. Celina and Rhea walked the narrow cobblestone streets until they reached the house. The door hung open, and there was commotion inside.

"Oh, dear," Celina whispered, feeling her heart rate go up. Perhaps it wasn't safe to go barging into a stranger's home uninvited. There was no telling who could be inside.

"Come on then," Rhea said as she moved to knock on the door frame before stepping inside and disappearing into the house.

"Rhea, wait!" Celina said as she rushed in after her. Rhea did not wait.

Inside there were no pirates and only a few pieces of furniture. Rhea gave a sudden little gasp, causing Celina to look down. There, on the floor, were three Athenian guards, bound and gagged with rope.

"Help me untie them," Rhea said. She and Celina pulled out their daggers and cut the guard's ropes and removed their gags.

"Thank you, ladies," the first guard said.

"What happened to you, sir?" asked Rhea.

"Pirates," the guard spat. "Theodosius Kardia and his evil gang."

Celina and Rhea exchanged excited looks as they asked in unison, "Which way did they go?"

- - -

Elara followed Theodosius and the others back down the main square to get to the ship at the Piraeus port. Her feet were hurting, and she was nervous about the trip ahead, but the hope of seeing her necklace again was putting a pep in her step.

If Nekros really did have it, then he most certainly would give it back to her; he was a family friend after all. Just because he and Theodosius didn't like each other, didn't mean that things would be bad for her as well.

Once she got her necklace back, her papou would be proud of her again, and he would see that she was ready and capable of being a countess.

Her fears of going back to Constantinople were another thing entirely. The city she had once called home seemed foreign in her mind now. Still, there was something nostalgic and poetic about going home again to get her yiayia's necklace and, hopefully, getting the chance to restore her good name in the place where it was first tarnished. That was assuming no one found out that she had worked with pirates to get there. Getting caught working with pirates would most certainly not help her prove she was a respectable countess.

Just don't get caught, she thought to herself. *Get the job done and don't get caught.*

"Can we get some spanakopita to go?" Yianni asked, interrupting her thoughts.

"We have food on the ship," Theodosius said as they kept up their brisk pace toward the docks. They had a long journey ahead of them, and it was only a matter of time before those Athenian guards got loose and came after them. The sooner they left, the better.

"But the food on the ship isn't as good as it is here!" Yianni complained. "No offense to you and Jimmy, Tina."

"None taken." Tina rolled her eyes in annoyance, making Elara laugh.

Even though Elara missed Celina and Rhea, she was really beginning to appreciate her new friends. She wasn't sure calling pirates '*friends*' was a good idea, but it was the truth.

"Kardia! Halt!" It was the guards from before, shouting behind them. Thankfully, they were several feet ahead, but it still made Elara's heart beat nervously. There appeared to be five figures coming toward them: the three guards, and two others behind them that she couldn't recognize from this far away.

Theodosius grabbed Elara's wrist before shouting to his friends, "RUN!"

Off they went, sprinting full speed toward the ship. Elara was glad he had taken her by the wrist, otherwise she most certainly would have gotten lost or separated from them in the Athenian crowd. Theodosius pushed people much more easily than she would have been able to do on her own.

"Stop them!" She heard the guards yell, but their voices seemed to be getting more and more faint as they got further and further away.

"Move! Faster! Come on!" Theodosius shouted as he pushed people out of the way.

The four of them had made it to the docks, but they still needed to find, embark, and set sail on their ship before they really would have escaped.

"This way!" Yianni alerted them, pointing out where the ship was docked.

Elara, panting hard as she ran, had never been so happy to see a pirate ship in her life. They were almost there. They had almost made it.

"STOP! WAIT!" Shouted new voices from the people running with the guards. They sounded like women's voices and Elara's mind must have been playing tricks on her because she could have sworn she recognized those voices from somewhere. "ELARA!"

Elara skidded to a halt and turned back. "Celina?"

"It's a trap!" Theodosius pulled on her arm. "Don't stop!"

"I think my friends, Celina and Rhea, are here!" said Elara as she tried to pull away from the pirate's grasp.

"We can't wait for them," Tina told her sternly. "Elara, I'm sorry, but if we wait for them, those guards will have us all arrested."

Tina was right, and Elara felt her heart plummet into her stomach. She had to leave Celina and Rhea behind…again. Otherwise, the guards would throw them all in jail and with her papou somewhere in the city. It wouldn't take long for her whole plan to fall apart—no family necklace and no chance to prove herself worthy again. Plus, Theodosius, Tina, and Yianni could potentially be hanged for piracy, so there was also that.

"Fine, let's go." Elara tried to push the guilt out of her mind as they continued running.

Once they got on the ship, Theodosius immediately began barking orders to set sail and the pirate crew leapt into action.

"What happened to the necklace?" Gregory asked from the crow's nest.

"We're going to Constantinople to find it," Theodosius told him simply as he went to the ship's helm.

Yianni and Tina worked with the others to lower the sails and make the necessary preparations for send-off. Elara didn't know much about sailing, so she stayed out of the way as much as she could.

"HALT! KARDIA! GET BACK HERE, PIRATE SCUM!" The guards called from the docks as the ship sailed away from port.

"ELARA! IT'S US! WAIT! *ELARA!*" Rhea and Celina called to her. They looked so tiny from this distance, but even from where Elara stood, she could see their devastation. They knew she was leaving them behind, this time on purpose. She hoped that they would one day understand. Celina was the one who had told her before that she couldn't get caught working alone with pirates. It would be disastrous for her already tattered reputation. Surely, Rhea and Celina still understood that and understood why she couldn't get caught by those guards.

"FORGIVE ME AS THE HOLY WISDOM FORGIVES US ALL!" She yelled back in a half sob, watching them until they disappeared from her sight.

Elara hoped that the 'Holy Wisdom' part would be enough of a clue for them to know where she was going next. The name 'Hagia Sophia', the Cathedral in Constantinople, was Greek for 'Holy Wisdom'. Hopefully, they would figure that out and follow her there.

Chapter Nine

Moonlight Clues

"Are you upset with me, Countess?" Theodosius asked from the doorway of the captain's quarters. His voice was surprisingly soft and not as sarcastic or pointed as it normally was.

Elara was curled up in the big chair by the window, sobbing her eyes out. "Not everything is about you, Captain."

"I'm sorry we had to leave your friends behind." He stepped into the room, but didn't dare approach her too closely. "They'll be safe in Athens, and when you see them again, you can explain the whole situation. I'm sure they'll understand."

"No, they won't. I'm a terrible person," Elara sobbed. "I've been doing all this to prove I'm still worthy of the Iliakos name, to make my papou proud, and to—to not be defined by my ex-fiancé, but here I am—abandoning my best friends and consorting with *pirates!* I deserve all the nasty things they say about me."

Theodosius sat on the edge of the bed facing her in the chair. "Huh, you know, Countess, I think your life would be a lot easier if you cared less about what those snobby nobles thought of you and more about doing whatever makes you happy."

"You don't understand." Elara wiped her eyes on her sleeve. "A woman is nothing without her reputation. I'm nothing."

"You're not nothing," Theodosius said in a scolding tone now, sounding slightly insulted.

Elara ignored him and instead continued on. "My papou told me not to lose this precious family heirloom, and what did I do? I lost it one day later!"

"Yianni stole your family necklace. That's not your fault!" Theodosius argued on her behalf as if defending her in court.

"My papou will probably kick me out when he discovers the trouble I'm in now!" She hiccupped. "I'll end up like a beggar woman on the streets, or dead like Justine."

Women with bad reputations either end up on the streets or dead. The words of the beggar woman rattled around her brain in an unbearable rhythm, refusing to leave her alone.

"You won't end up like a beggar or Justine! I know you related to Justine's situation, but you're really nothing like her." His voice was gentle as he handed her a handkerchief to wipe her tears. "And if the count does kick you out, you can always join my crew full-time and live here."

"Why are you being so nice to me?" Elara accepted the handkerchief even though she had stopped crying.

Theodosius smiled, almost shyly. "I don't know, Countess. Call me old fashioned, but my mother raised me to be kind to women— especially when they're upset."

"And where is your mother now?"

"She's probably still serving as a maid for Empress Maria." He shrugged casually. "Or she could be dead. It's hard to say for certain. We haven't spoken since my brother, Leonides, died."

Leonides. Elara had been meaning to ask about him and now seemed as good a time as any. Especially since Theodosius seemed to be in a particularly gentle mood. Perhaps it would still be best to warm up to such an inquiry, just to be safe.

"I used to be a lady-in-waiting to Empress Maria for five years. I might have known your mother. What's her name?" she asked softly.

"Eudokia," he replied fondly. "Eudokia Kardia."

"I don't know her, but she has a very pretty name." Elara sat up.

"Thank you." Theodosius looked at his hands as if to avoid making eye contact with her. He was hiding something, but Elara could tell he wasn't being malicious. He was probably feeling vulnerable.

"Uhm, do you mind me asking how exactly your brother died?" Elara looked intently at his face, trying to gauge the corsair's expression.

"He was murdered," Theodosius whispered, providing no more details than he had the other night, so she decided not to pry further. Knowing the exact details of how Leonides was murdered wasn't her business.

"Yes, you mentioned that at dinner the other night. I'm so sorry." Elara thought about reaching across the space between them and touching his hand in comfort but thought better of it. She had experienced the death of loved ones before but never at the hands of another individual.

"My brother deserves to be remembered for the person he was when he was alive—not for what happened to him at the end." Theodosius finally looked up and made eye contact with her again.

Elara imagined she was catching a glimpse of his soul reflected in his warm brown irises—the real man behind the corsair's facade.

"Leonides was so… He was such a wonderful brother and a dear friend. That's how I want people to think of him."

This time Elara did reach forward across the space between them and touched his hand. "May his memory be eternal."

Theodosius stared at her hand on his, and slowly wrapped his other hand around it, so he was holding her hand with both of his. He looked up at her with an intensity she wasn't expecting and held her gaze for a time, saying nothing.

Finally, when the moment seemingly became too intense for him, he dropped her hand and said, "Want to learn some swordplay after dinner? I believe I promised to teach you."

- - -

That's how Elara found herself out on the top deck of the ship with a sword in one hand and a small glass bottle in the other.

"Sorry, what are the bottles for again?" she asked, still confused.

"To help you loosen up." Theodosius took a swig from his own bottle. "Plus, you need to be able to sword fight with just one hand and not rely on two."

It was starting to get dark out, so the deck was lit only with swinging lanterns. The wind was whipping the sails into a frenzy—a sure sign that a storm was coming.

A crew member she didn't recognize was at the helm, steering the ship, but no one else was on deck with them. Even the crow's nest was empty, as Gregory had retired early for the evening.

"All right, Countess, take the first position," he instructed her with the wave of his sword.

Elara put her right foot in front of the other and raised her sword out to mid-shoulder height, just as he had taught her. "Like this?"

Without warning, Theodosius swung his sword, knocking hers out of her hand and sending it flying to the floor with a loud clang.

He gently tapped the tip of his blade to her chest. "Killed."

"I wasn't ready!" she grumbled, annoyed.

She wasn't sure why she had agreed to this. The likelihood of her getting in a sword fight seemed fairly slim, regardless of what had happened in Athens.

"Pick it up." Theodosius motioned to the blade at her feet.

Elara took a drink from her glass bottle instead, instantly regretting her decision. "Ugh! What is *this*? It burns."

"It's ouzo." He laughed. "Go on. Pick up your sword."

"I think I hate ouzo almost as much as I hate sword fighting," Elara joked dryly as she picked up her sword off the deck.

"You don't have to drink it." Theodosius lunged, swinging his sword at her again, but this time, she was ready. Their blades reverberated against each other, but the hilt stayed firmly in her hand.

"Very good." He smiled, keeping his eyes locked on hers. "Ready for the second position?"

"Is that a rhetorical question?" she mused, trying not to think about how close their faces were to each other.

Theodosius took a step back and made a slightly different stance with his legs. His right leg was still in front, but his left leg was now turned out, slightly bent at the knee. He kept his glass bottle behind his back and motioned with his sword for her to mimic his new stance.

"How's this?" She mirrored him as best she could.

Instead of responding, he swiped his sword at her again, which she managed to block—barely.

Without losing momentum, he twirled and swung at her, this time at a low angle. His blade, mercifully turned to the blunt side, bounced off the side of her upper thigh.

"Hey! You almost cut me!" Elara jumped, nearly tripping on a pile of ropes behind her.

"But I didn't. Although, if this was a real fight, I definitely would have sliced you up good," Theodosius said unapologetically. "I'm going to teach you how to block both high *and* low blows."

She repositioned herself back to the proper stance, trying not to look rattled. "Fine, let's go again."

Sword fighting, Elara was coming to learn, was like a dance. It was rhythmic, and once you learned your opponent's groove, you could use that knowledge to block and counterattack. She watched the captain's feet—the way he effortlessly glided about the deck; his arms appeared to move in tandem with his legs, transitioning from the first position to the second with ease. Their swords clanged together, and Elara was proud of how she managed to block each of his blows and even got in the occasional counter jab.

"Excellent work, Countess." Theodosius beamed at her, and Elara tried not to look too pleased by his praise.

"Thank you, Captain."

"Do you think you could use what I've taught you to try to disarm me?" He challenged, twirling his sword around with the flick of his wrist.

"Uh." She shifted nervously on her feet; the wood of the floorboards groaning a little underneath her. "I can try…"

"We'll make it interesting," he said with the hint of a dare in his voice. "If you can disarm me before I disarm you—I'll let you keep that sword."

"And if you disarm me first?" Elara raised a tentative eyebrow. Her heart was suddenly beating much more quickly, and she wasn't sure why.

"I want my room back," Theodosius said simply. "You can sleep in a hammock below deck with the rest of the crew."

"All right, it's a bet." Elara rolled her eyes. She was not entitled to his room anyway. If Tina slept in a hammock below deck, so could she. "Throwing a lady out of her room though, tsk-tsk. That's not very gentlemanly of you, Captain."

"Well, no one's perfect." Theodosius slashed his sword against hers so quickly and so forcefully, she barely had time to react. Thankfully, she was already in the proper stance to block his attack.

The metal clanging sound of their swords filled the air until it was all she could hear. It was almost as if the ocean waves and creaks of the wooden boards had vanished, leaving only Elara, Theodosius, and the swinging of their weapons.

She was blocking well, but her counter attacks weren't hitting him hard enough to even hint at a disarmament. He was too strong, too quick, and too skilled. If she was going to have a chance at winning this, she would have to find a way to outwit him.

"Don't forget to block and parry if the sword gets too close to your neck," Theodosius reminded her, still in teacher mode despite their bet.

"I won't forget," Elara grunted, slashing her blade at him, but like all the other times, he riposted quickly.

They moved across the deck, attacking, blocking, and counterattacking for what felt like an eternity. She was beginning to feel exhausted, but knew if she stopped now he would win by default.

Elara realized as she parried and deflected another one of Theodosius' blows that she wanted to win. She wanted to prove herself;

prove that she could handle this violent world she'd stumbled into and prove she was a person worthy of respect.

"Getting tired, Countess?" Theodosius teased her as she stumbled and nearly lost her balance after yet another jab of his sword. Her glass bottle of ouzo spilled from her hand and then shattered unceremoniously onto the deck.

"Oops," Elara muttered, eyes wide. "I'm terribly sorry."

"It's fine." He lowered his sword to survey the damage. "I can get Gregory to clean—"

She slashed her sword at him again which he blocked, but just barely.

Theodosius looked at her with a combination of shock and admiration. "Damn! Nice feint!"

"I try." Elara shrugged before thrusting her sword at him again before he had time to recover.

They went back and forth again, but Theodosius was off his rhythm now, probably still in shock over the bottle spill trick she had just pulled.

Elara had a renewed energy as she attacked and pushed their fight to a tight corner of the ship. It was another strategic move on her part; the tight quarters of this part of the ship would give Theodosius less room to maneuver. She'd gotten the idea from watching him fight one of the guards back at the Vatican.

"Who taught you how to fight like this?" he asked with an exasperated huff.

"You did," she replied triumphantly as she sent his weapon sailing through the air, landing on the floor with a clatter.

"Damn."

Elara gently tapped the tip of her sword onto his chest. "Killed."

Theodosius laughed, "You win! Keep the room and the sword."

"You can keep the sword," she said, placing it by a nearby railing. "But yes, I'll be keeping the room."

"Perhaps we could share the room," he joked suggestively.

"Ha! You wish." Elara rolled her eyes.

To that, Theodosius said nothing, but stared at her. His face was red from the exertion of their sparring match, and his eyes were dark with something she couldn't quite decipher. He made no movement toward her, but the slow rise and fall of his chest suggested to her that he wanted to close the gap between them.

Elara felt warmth flooding her cheeks as she opened her mouth to change the subject. Before she could get a word out, the sound of thunder boomed overhead. Large raindrops began to fall from the sky, soaking them and obscuring her vision.

Together, they raced below deck to escape the storm.

- - -

Celina couldn't believe it. Elara had left them behind, choosing those goddamn pirates over them. Still, she couldn't find it in her heart to be too mad. She understood that Elara didn't want to be caught by those guards and have people talking about her, but it still hurt.

"Will you please stop pacing?" Rhea half-begged, half-demanded.

They were still at the docks, even though the ship Elara was on was long out of view. The guards had left, so it was just the two of them standing on the wooden planks. The people of Athens continued on with their day as seagulls flew overhead. If it weren't for the throbbing anxiety tying Celina's stomach in knots, it might have felt like a normal, boring day.

"I don't know what we're supposed to do or where we're supposed to go next," Celina admitted, continuing her pacing.

"Maybe we should regroup with Count Basil," Rhea suggested. "He might be able to guess where Elara is going next."

"No, Elara wouldn't want that." Celina shook her head. "Count Basil knows too much already. Best we don't inform him, so he'll have no choice but to return to Catalonia."

"All right, so what is your plan then?" Rhea grabbed Celina's arm, forcing her to stop moving. "And stop pacing!"

Celina frowned. "Hmm, we have to find out where Elara is going, and we have to do it fast."

"Let's sit down and brainstorm." Rhea led Celina down the pier to a spot where they could sit comfortably staring out at the sea. There weren't many people around, so it was reasonably quiet.

"This was a good idea. Thank you, Rhea." Celina swung her legs as she looked out over the water. The weather was perfect, not too cold and not too hot. It was a shame that they needed to leave so soon.

There was no telling where their next location would be and what the weather there would be like.

"I hope Elara is well," Rhea said. "She must have been so scared to run like that."

"Elara is stronger than both of us combined," Celina replied, echoing Rhea's words from the night before.

"Fair enough," Rhea chuckled at the call back. "So, where do we think she's going next?"

"Hmm," Celina mulled that over in her mind, trying to think of the most obvious place that Elara and those pirates would go next. "She's probably following a lead on the necklace."

"It must be a place where beautiful jewelry is commonly traded or a place where beautiful jewelry is... *kept*," Rhea nodded as she spoke, like she was getting at something, but it wasn't clear what.

"What sort of place is that?" Celina asked, confused. "You can buy and sell jewelry in any city or town in the Mediterranean."

"Yes, I suppose you can," Rhea sighed in defeat. "We could really use some of that holy wisdom that Elara was talking about."

Celina frowned as a sudden idea slipped into her mind. "Wait, what did you just say?"

"I said, *yes, I suppose you can*," Rhea replied, not following what Celina was getting at.

"No, the other thing."

"Use some of the holy wisdom—?"

Celina stood suddenly as excitement overtook her. "I know where she is going! Or I know where she *might* be going."

Rhea stood too. "Where? Tell me!"

"To the Holy Wisdom Church, also known as the Hagia Sophia, the Cathedral in Constantinople!" Celina was practically bouncing on her heels. "Elara's going to Constantinople!"

- - -

"Tina?" Elara went down below deck, looking for the only other woman aboard the ship. "Are you down here?"

"I'm here," Tina said weakly from a hammock where she was resting.

Tina was paler than normal, and she looked sweaty from her fever. The lower deck wasn't particularly well lit, but Elara could tell her new friend wasn't doing well.

"How are you feeling?" Elara asked as she knelt beside her, so she could look at her at eye level.

"I feel like shit," Tina admitted with a cough. "Don't get too close. I hope it's not catching."

"Can I get you anything? More water? Soup?"

"No, thank you. I'm fine for now."

"Do you think you'll be better by tomorrow? Theodosius says we'll be at our destination by late tomorrow, and I was really hoping you'd come along again." She fiddled with her sleeve, feeling selfish for even asking. Tina deserved rest, and here Elara was, asking her to hurry up so she could have company on the next leg of their journey.

"I'm sorry." Tina coughed again. "I think it'll just be you and the boys this time."

"Ugh, I was afraid of that," Elara muttered softly.

"They're not so bad, those boys." She smiled weakly.

"Yes, they'll do, I suppose."

Once again, she found herself missing Celina and Rhea. Elara wondered what her friends were doing right now and if they even still considered her to be a friend at all. Perhaps they had given up on her and gone home. The lonely bitter ache twisted like a knife in her stomach. It seemed like no matter what she tried to do to make things better, she just ended up making things worse.

"What's wrong?" Tina asked, probably reading all the various emotions dancing upon Elara's face.

"I'm—I'm just missing the way my life used to be," Elara admitted. "I used to be beloved and respected by all. Now I'm more reviled by the day, it seems, and I don't know how to fix it."

"Maybe you can't fix it," Tina said simply. "And maybe that's a good thing."

"You think it's a good thing to be broken?" Elara whispered.

Tina closed her eyes and appeared close to sleep. "You're not broken, Elara."

"Thank you, Tina. I'll let you rest. Feel better." She stood and made her way back to the top deck.

Above deck, the other pirates were bustling about, getting ready to turn in for the night. By this time tomorrow, they would be in Constantinople.

"Countess." It was Theodosius.

"Hello, Captain," she greeted him warmly as he moved to stand beside her. "Here for a rematch?"

"A rematch against you, the queen of swords?" he scoffed. "After yesterday, I think I'll spare myself the humiliation and let you keep the room."

"Getting used to your lower-deck hammock then?"

"Something like that." Theodosius was wearing his signature mischievous grin that Elara was coming to learn was more of a nervous smile than a disrespectful smirk. The collar of his dark jacket was turned up toward the sky like a shield protecting his neck. She wondered if he felt the need to shield himself due to his dangerous lifestyle or due to the traumas of his past.

"Do you have news?" Elara asked after a few minutes of comfortable silence, the two of them staring out at the dark ocean. There was nothing to see this late at night except for the streaks of moonlight reflecting off the water.

"You've seen Tina," he presumed.

"I have. She's very ill."

"Yes, Tina needs to see a physician as soon as possible, and we have none onboard... So, if it's all right with you, I was thinking we could make a pit stop in Thessaloniki to get her a physician before we go on to Constantinople." Theodosius didn't look at her as he spoke. Perhaps he was worried she would say no. If that was the case, Elara was a little offended.

"Of course we should get her a physician! That's a wonderful idea. I'm sorry I didn't think of it myself," she admitted.

Theodosius turned and smiled at her gratefully. "Good. Thank you, Countess."

"Were you really worried I would have a problem with that?" Elara frowned and crossed her arms over her chest. "Tina is my friend. Of course, I want her to be healed as soon as possible. I'm not *that* selfish."

"My apologies. I don't think you're selfish, Countess." He bit his lip and took a step closer to her. "Tina's my friend too, like a sister to me, and I'm just really worried about her. She's never been this sick before..." His voice trailed off.

Elara suddenly felt her heart drop as a realization overtook her. "You think she's going to die, don't you?"

"She has the exact same symptoms that a former crew member named Felix had. Felix died in less than forty-eight hours." Theodosius took a steady breath and blinked a couple times in a row.

"Hey." She put a hand on his arm. "What happened to your friend, Felix, isn't going to happen to Tina. We'll get her the help she needs."

"I can't believe this is happening again," Theodosius muttered, more to himself than to her.

"Listen to me." Elara pulled on his lapel, trying to regain his attention. When he didn't budge, she touched his cheek, forcing him to look her in the eyes. "Felix's death is not your fault. You know that, right?"

"But it is my fault." Theodosius turned into her touch like he was grateful for it. "I didn't get him the help he needed. I'm the captain. I was supposed to look after him."

"It's not your fault. You did the best you could, and now you *are* getting help for Tina, so she'll be healthy again in no time." Elara tried not to think about how close together their faces were now. From an outsider's perspective, it might have looked inappropriate, but they were on the sea, in the dark, where only God and the moonlight could see them.

"Thank you, Countess," he whispered, his nose just a few inches from hers.

"You're welcome, Captain." Elara took a step back. "I think I shall retire for the evening. Please let me know when we've arrived in Thessaloniki."

Theodosius nodded. "Very well. Goodnight."

"Goodnight." Elara slipped away toward the captain's quarters without looking back.

- - -

"I think this boat is much more comfortable than the last," Rhea said as she swung happily in her hammock. "The bed on Titus' ship was so lumpy, but this is cozy."

"Oh, you think so?" Celina rolled her eyes from her own hammock, even though it was dark so no one could see her. She found the hammock to be the most uncomfortable thing she had slept on yet, but perhaps she was just acting spoiled.

It had been very nice of the merchant ship to offer them a ride to Constantinople for just a few silver coins each. In less than a day and a half they would be at their destination and hopefully they would finally be able to find Elara.

"So, what's Constantinople like?" Rhea asked, changing the subject entirely.

"It's lovely. It's the Center of Orthodoxy and all that." Celina smiled full of nostalgia. "There are many beautiful churches, tall, glorious buildings, and the food is incredible."

"Did you live there?" Rhea turned in her hammock, and Celina could tell, even in the dark, that she was looking at her.

"No, I've always lived in Bulgaria, but my parents and I would visit every summer. That's where I first met Elara. She was at the Hagia Sophia with her grandparents, and I was there visiting with my parents. We hit it off straight away." Celina remembered it like it was yesterday.

Elara had been her first friend and her last, it had seemed, when Celina's other friends tried to kill her. Now, she had Rhea too, so perhaps her friendship circle was finally growing again. Perhaps Celina was, after all this time, finally healing from her past.

"I'm really glad you came on this journey with me, Rhea," said Celina.

Rhea's only reply was soft snoring and silence. Celina chuckled quietly as she also slowly slipped into slumber.

"*Get up, you vile bitch!*" A harsh voice and a hand over her mouth woke Celina up with a start. It was still dark below deck, so she couldn't see who was grabbing her, and with her grogginess she wasn't sure it wasn't a bad dream.

"Let go! Unhand me!" Rhea was yelling somewhere to her left.

It wasn't a dream. She was awake, and people were attacking her and Rhea in real life.

"Stop! Leave us alone!" Celina struggled against her captors as they dragged her and Rhea above deck. The top deck was lit only by two lanterns and one tall man with a torch.

"Which one of you is Celina Oberon?" The tall man with the torch asked as the girls were thrown on the ground at his feet.

Celina let out a shaky breath, "I—"

"I am Lady Celina Oberon!" Rhea shouted confidently. "Who the hell are you and why have you taken us from our sleep?"

The tall man looked Rhea over, probably wondering why a noblewoman from Bulgaria looked Turkish. He didn't say anything right away but walked around them both in a circle like a vulture.

Celina watched him right back, her heart pounding. She hoped Rhea knew what she was doing by switching identities with her.

Glancing around, she saw that there was a small group consisting of three men and two women gathered around her and Rhea. They were an angry looking group, but only the man moved toward them.

The others remained back as if afraid, or perhaps, they weren't as on board with this man's actions as he made it seem.

"And who are you then?" The tall man stopped pacing and stood directly in front of Celina.

"I'm...Hilda." Celina made the name up on the spot.

"Hilda what?" The man frowned down at her. His eyes had a yellowish hue under them, and his hair was scraggly like a bird's nest. He looked scary, but not healthy. The man wasn't fit like the guards from Athens.

"Well? What's your last name, Miss Hilda?" he demanded with a cough.

"Vandero. Hilda Vandero." Celina made up a random last name to go with her random first name. She doubted this man was smart enough to know that Hilda was a northern Baltic name and Vandero was a southern Spanish one.

"Miss Vandero, there's a price on Lady Oberon's head. I've been offered four hundred silver coins to bring her to her father's political rivals. Dead or alive."

Celina felt her heart plummet into her stomach. Her old friends once had the same idea. It seemed that her father's enemies never slept. That was one of the many reasons her parents had sent her to Elara and Count Basil in the first place. They thought she would be safer at Tossa de Mar in Catalonia than she would be in Bulgaria. Somehow, the enemy had found her, here, in the open water.

"If you think you're taking me anywhere, you're sorely mistaken!" Rhea spat, still pretending to be Celina.

The man laughed. "Calm down, Lady Oberon. I'm here to offer you an opportunity to outbid your father's enemies. Give me more than four hundred silver coins, and I'll let you both go free."

"And what if we don't have over four hundred silver coins?" Celina asked.

"Well, then, I'll have no choice but to kill you, Miss Vandero." He grabbed Celina by the neck and held a sword to her throat. "And take Lady Oberon here back to Bulgaria by force."

"Don't hurt her! We have the money, of course!" Rhea assured him, sounding much less confident than before. "I have more than enough coins to satisfy this deal."

"Wonderful. Fetch the silver at once." The man dropped Celina back onto the floor and put his sword back in its holster.

"Sir, it is very late at night—" Rhea began to stall, but the man saw right through her.

"Now, Lady Oberon! Fetch me my money—*now!*" He put his hand back in the hilt of the sword, but did not pull it out this time. The threat was clear enough without it.

"Yes, right away, sir!" Rhea leapt to her feet and began half-walking, half-running, to the ladder to go below deck.

Neither of them had four hundred silver coins or anything of equal value. Soon the man would realize this, kill Celina thinking she was Hilda, and kidnap Rhea thinking she was Celina. So, it was in her best interest to plan an escape, and quickly.

"Sir, can I tell you a secret? It's something Lady Oberon won't want you to know." Celina stood slowly as she spoke, holding out her hands to show she had no weapon or anything else up her sleeves.

The man stared at her intently as the predicted curiosity overtook him. "Tell me, Miss Vandero."

"The truth of the matter is…" Celina slowly began to get closer to him as she spoke, never breaking eye contact.

"Yes? Go on," he pressed impatiently.

"The truth, sir, is…" Celina pulled his sword out of its holster and held it up to his throat.

"What the—!"

"…I have your sword."

"A trick! Stop her!" Some of the onlookers shouted.

"No, don't move!" The man commanded his men, shaking as Celina pressed the blade so intensely to his skin he nearly bled.

"I'm going to kill you like the dog you are, and then these people can carry your body back to my father's enemies themselves!" She snarled in his face.

"N-no please!" His eyes were wide but, as Celina had predicted, he wasn't healthy or fit enough to fight her off, especially with the blade digging into his neck. "You—you're Lady Oberon. Not the other girl?"

"Nothing gets past you, sir," Rhea reappeared behind Celina, holding one dagger in each hand. "Who else wants to fight?"

Surprisingly, the crowd didn't rush her, probably because they had no idea if she could fight or not, and because Celina might kill their leader if they dared to move. They were all cowards, too afraid to fight two women.

"I'm tired of this ship and all its weaklings," Celina said to Rhea.

"Agreed. Let's take a lifeboat and get out of here," Rhea said, moving toward the lifeboat, and getting it ready to drop in the water.

"Don't follow us or you'll be sorry! I'll finish you off before you so much as look in my direction!" Celina breathed in the man's face before releasing him and sprinting to the lifeboat where Rhea was waiting and ready to go.

"Stop them!" The man yelled as he and the small group of people rushed to the side of the boat as the lifeboat descended into the water below.

"Bye! Tell them to send stronger men next time!" Celina waved up at them as the lifeboat rowed into the darkness. The one benefit of the water at night was how easy it was to disappear. Soon the pitch black of the night would make them invisible to most ships.

"That was a close one," Rhea murmured in the dark as they rowed the lifeboat as far away from the ship as possible.

"Oh, yes," Celina agreed. "We're lucky we were smarter and stronger than them. Had he been a healthier man, I don't think that would have worked, even with two daggers."

"That reminds me!" Rhea dug in her pocket and pulled out one of the daggers. "This one's yours, I think."

"Thank you." Celina didn't grab the dagger but instead kept rowing.

"Do you know which direction we're supposed to go in?" Rhea asked after a few minutes of silence.

"Hmm, I'm not sure." Celina looked around, seeing nothing but darkness. She wished she'd learn how to use constellations to navigate, but she hadn't.

"Great. Love to hear that," Rhea muttered sarcastically. "I'm going to take a nap. Wake me up when the sun rises."

"Oh, all right. I'll keep watch." Celina knew she personally wouldn't be able to sleep a wink, but it would probably be good for Rhea to get some shut-eye.

Hours passed, but eventually Celina also found herself drifting to sleep in the lifeboat. She awoke sometime later to the sounds of seagulls and distant shouts. Sitting up she saw a dock in the distance just in front of a large fortress-like building.

"Rhea dear, wake up!" Celina shook her friend awake.

"Who's dear?" Rhea said groggily as she sat up. "Where are we? Did we make it to Constantinople?"

Celina shook her head as their destination grew slowly closer. "No, that's not Constantinople. That's Thessaloniki."

Chapter Ten

Thessaloniki

Elara finished braiding her hair and tied a leather belt around the waistline of the lavender work-dress she wore, courtesy of Tina's wardrobe. Once she was satisfied with her apparel, she spun around, searching for her satchel to take on the journey. She found it dangling off the bed, with only a dagger, a small coin purse, and a thin shawl inside. Elara hoped that would be all she needed. The only task waiting for them in Thessaloniki was to hire a physician for Tina, and then they could continue on their way to Constantinople.

Easy.

If everything went according to plan, she would be on her way back to Tossa de Mar by dinner time tomorrow. Over the course of the last two days on the ship, she'd been practicing what she'd say to her papou once she returned home with her yiayia's necklace in hand.

"Look, Papou, I handled the crisis perfectly while you were away and saved our most prized heirloom, all while acting in a dignified manner befitting a noblewoman. As you can see, I'm more than prepared to be the perfect countess and restore honor to our family name."

"Who are you talking to?" Theodosius smirked, leaning on the door frame behind her.

Elara jumped at the sound of his voice but quickly composed herself. "Have we docked?"

"Come and see for yourself."

It was a beautiful sunny afternoon in Thessaloniki. The sight of the Thessalonian castle, Heptapyrgion, sitting on the hill just beyond the port, greeted her eyes first. Then, she took in the other beautiful buildings, including the Rotunda of Galerius and the Church of the Acheiropoietos.

She hadn't been back since her engagement had ended. Prince Andronikos had proposed to her here, at the steps of the Rotunda of Galerius. That should have been a sign the relationship was doomed from the start. Any man that proposed in front of a building erected by an emperor who used to kill Christians for sport, probably wasn't as thoughtful as he ought to be.

"Ready to go?" Theodosius' voice once again brought her back to the present moment.

"Ready." Elara smiled and looked around. "Is Yianni coming with us?"

Theodosius shook his head, his smile mirroring her own. "He's staying with Tina. It's just you and me this time, Countess."

"Very well. Lead the way, Captain." Elara tried to keep her voice neutral. A day out with just her and Theodosius Kardia—what could possibly go wrong?

They walked off the ship and headed straight for the town where hopefully a physician or other medical professional might be available.

The city was bustling but it wasn't nearly as crowded as Athens or Rome had been. Elara wondered where everyone was or if this was simply a smaller city.

"It was more crowded the last time I was here," Elara noted aloud.

"That's probably because of the new curfew they're enforcing," Theodosius surmised with a shrug. "Only certain people are allowed out after dark."

"But it's not dark yet," Elara frowned as they walked. She had never heard of Thessaloniki having a curfew before. She wondered what other changes were going on in the area.

"You know how it goes; more rules mean less people want to stick around. They probably moved south or..." His voice trailed off as they came upon a large brick building.

"What's wrong?" Elara asked.

"I—I don't know. This building is all closed off, and it used to be so open." Theodosius looked around with a furrowed brow and hands on his hips. "Something strange is going on."

"You there! Halt!" A guard on horseback suddenly appeared.

A guard showing up should have been alarming. However, with everything they had been through over the last couple days, Elara was confident they could talk, or fight, their way out of an arrest.

"Why is it we run into guards in every city? It's as if they're obsessed with us, truly," Elara muttered dryly for only Theodosius to hear. She watched with satisfaction as he turned away and bit his lip to keep from laughing at her quip.

The guard approached them slowly, his back to the sun. Elara had to put her hand up and squint just to see him properly.

"Who are you two? Do you have permission to be out and about? Hold on, Lady Elara Iliakos? Is that you?"

"Uh, yes, it is." Elara beamed as best she could with the sun glaring in her eyes. "I'm sorry, sir, I can't see you very well with the sun. Do we know each other?"

"It's Dimitrios Milakis, my lady," The man dismounted his horse. "I was in Prince Andronikos' personal guard when you were in Constantinople."

"Oh, Dimitrios! So good to see you." Elara laughed, trying to look pleased to see one of her ex-fiancé's personal guards. She could see him clearly now that he was closer and not on horseback. He had the same long, slender nose and jagged haircut she remembered.

"You as well. Who's your friend?" Dimitrios asked, eyeing Theodosius.

"Uh, this is... my cousin, Lord Theodosius Iliakos," Elara lied.

"Pleasure to meet you, sir." Theodosius stuck out his hand for Dimitrios to shake. When the guard didn't shake it, Theodosius dropped his hand awkwardly to his side.

"I didn't think you had any young male relatives on your father's side. Isn't that why the countess title went to you? Since you are the only heir?" Dimitrios frowned, suspiciously.

Elara's eyes widened. She had forgotten how much the people from Constantinople knew about her family. Dimitrios would not be as easy to lie to as other guards might have been.

"We're related through marriage," Theodosius filled in the lie for her.

Dimitrios looked them both up and down, probably wondering why two nobles looked so undignified. Elara felt her cheeks burn, and something unpleasant coiled in her stomach.

"Sir, we need your help," Theodosius carried on, seeming as comfortable as ever. It was an act that Elara was coming to learn. To the untrained eye, Theodosius appeared confident and unbothered, but his hands buzzed slightly, and his eye gave the occasional twitch. Thankfully, Dimitrios didn't seem to notice, or perhaps he simply didn't care.

"I'm always happy to help, Lady Elara, despite the circumstances. What can I do for you?" Dimitrios asked a bit backhandedly.

"What circumstances, sir?" Elara huffed half-angrily, half-sarcastically. "Do you mean the circumstances of me ending my engagement to Prince Andronikos and everyone I once thought was my friend *punishing* me for it?"

"Countess, please don't—" Theodosius looked at her pointedly, as if to say, *get it together before we get arrested.*

"No, I'm not done! How dare you judge me, Dimitrios? You know as well as anyone what Andronikos was like! You *know* how he treated me! You *know* what he *did* to me! You should be the one who

202

is ashamed. Not me!" Elara screamed at him, her voice echoing off the walls of the sleepy city.

There was a moment of stunned silence where neither Dimitrios nor Theodosius seemed to know how to respond. Elara thought about apologizing. She considered Tina, and how her outburst might delay her friend's medical treatment, but she couldn't bring herself to apologize for how she had felt for so long. It was so deeply unfair that her relationship with Andronikos could still be haunting her after all this time. They always judged her and never him.

"I'm sorry, my lady," Dimitrios bowed his head as if he just remembered that palace guards were not as high ranking as a countess. "I meant no offense."

Theodosius held up a hand. "Please, we need a physician, sir. Our friend is terribly ill, and it's an emergency."

"I know someone who can help. Follow me." Dimitrios went back to his horse.

"That was amazing. You're amazing," Theodosius whispered in her ear as they walked behind Dimitrios' horse.

"It wasn't amazing," Elara disagreed. "I lost my temper. Ladies aren't supposed to lose their temper—especially not in public."

Luckily, there hadn't been any strangers around, and Dimitrios wasn't high-ranking enough to gossip about her freely, but that didn't mean he wouldn't let something slip. Why did she always have to make things worse for herself?

"Well, I thought it was incredible. You really put Dimitrios in his place." Theodosius marveled at her like she had accomplished a feat of great heroism. Even though she didn't agree with his assertion, she liked the way he looked at her.

"I don't want to be defined by Andronikos forever," Elara admitted quietly.

"You're not defined by him," Theodosius promised. "Don't you get it, Countess? You're so much more courageous than that prince. He's probably jealous of you."

Elara doubted the truth of that, but she appreciated Theodosius saying it all the same. "Captain, you can call me Elara. All my friends call me Elara."

Theodosius smiled shyly, pleasantly surprised. "I'm honored, Elara. You may call me Theodosius, if you like."

"Theodosius it is." Elara looped her arm through his as she often did with her female friends. This surprised him as well, but he seemed to like it all the same.

Dimitros glanced back at them with slanted eyes, noting their closeness. Elara dropped his arm, half-embarrassed at the judgment, and half-angry she couldn't touch Theodosius' arm or any man's arm without it being deemed inappropriate.

"What?" Theodosius called up to Dimitrios. "Two cousins can't link arms?"

Elara stifled a laugh as Dimitrios turned around and said nothing.

- - -

Finally, they made it to a tall building that Elara recognized as belonging to one of the local noblewomen, Lady Valerie Karena **Palaiologos**, the Despotess of Thessaloniki. The title, despotess, was the Eastern Roman version of a duchess or princess. Lady Valerie was the sister-in-law of Emperor Michael, having married his late brother, Lord John Palaiologos, the Despot of Thessaloniki. If anyone could get them a physician quickly, it would be the despotess.

Dimitrios opened the grand front door and ushered them inside. Elara had never been in the despotess' manor before, but it looked like a standard noble home, with grand ceiling, ornate decorations, and an open courtyard with a lush garden.

"Lady Valerie? You have company. May I present Lady Elara Iliakos and her *cousin*, Lord Theodosius Iliakos." Dimitrios bowed to Lady Valerie as he introduced them.

"Elara Iliakos?" Valerie looked up from a pamphlet she was reading. "This is certainly a surprise."

Lady Valerie looked exactly how Elara remembered from their brief interactions in the past. She was a fuller-figured woman with a receding jawline and gray-blonde, curly hair pinned back in a tight bun. Her cheeks were one shade too dark from the rouge she wore, and her eyebrows were drawn a little too high to look natural.

"Hello, Your Excellency," Elara bowed to her and got straight to the point. "Our friend is gravely ill, and we need a physician, if you please."

"A physician? Surely, you didn't come all this way for a physician." Valerie fanned herself leisurely with the pamphlet as she leaned back on a gold encrusted sofa.

"Please, Your Excellency, our friend is very sick..."

"Don't they have physicians in Catalonia or wherever it was that you were banished to?" The despotess gave a short, humorless laugh.

Elara took a breath to steady herself. She was not going to yell at the despotess the way she had yelled at Dimitrios.

"And who are you again?" Valerie asked Theodosius before Elara could get another word in.

"I'm Countess Elara's cousin, Theodosius Iliakos. Your Excellency, can I just say, you are even more beautiful than described." Theodosius laid the charm on thick.

"Thank you, sir," Valerie blushed. The despotess had a reputation of liking men's attention, and Theodosius seemed to know it. "You're a fit young man. Have you a wife?"

Theodosius glanced quickly at Elara and then back to Valerie. "I would very much like to have a wife one of these days."

"I thought you said you were related to the countess through *marriage*?" Dimitrios said from the doorway. "Was that not your marriage, sir?"

"It was my aunt's marriage, actually," Theodosius smirked as he continued to lie with ease.

"Leave us, Dimitrios. I wish to talk to my guests in private." Valerie shooed Dimitrios away.

Theodosius gave a sarcastic little wave to Dimitrios as the guard left the room defeated, and Elara elbowed him for it. If they wanted to get a physician for Tina, they needed to be on their best behavior.

Valerie stood and walked toward them until she was standing right in front of Theodosius. She pressed a hand to his chest and slid it down until it rested right above his pelvis.

"So, about that physician...?" Theodosius' voice went up an octave.

"You are very fit, sir." Valerie looked him up and down like he was a piece of lamb she wanted to sink her teeth into.

"Your Excellency, our friend is ill. She needs a physician as soon as possible," Elara said through clenched teeth and forced politeness.

"Fine." Valerie dropped her hand but kept her eyes on Theodosius. "The physician is down the hill. Go fetch him for your friend."

"Thank you, Lady Valerie." Elara and Theodosius bowed and started to leave.

"Not you, sir." She grabbed Theodosius' arm, pulling him back toward her. "You stay here with me and let the countess fetch the physician. It's been so long since I've had good entertainment. Won't you please entertain me until Elara gets back?"

"I—I couldn't possibly." Theodosius laughed awkwardly but backtracked once he saw Valerie's sour expression. "I mean, won't your husband be upset?"

"My husband has been dead for ten years! A woman has needs, you know!" Valerie touched his chest again, moving ever closer to the pelvic region.

"*Lady Valerie—!*" Elara's tone was dangerously close to outraged. She couldn't believe this was happening. The despotess was trying to proposition her friend right in front of her.

Theodosius cut Elara off before she could say anything more. "Cousin, fetch the physician and take him to Tina, please."

"What about you? I'm not leaving without you!" She tried tugging on his arm to get him away from Valerie's wandering hands, but he resisted.

"Don't worry about me. I'll show the despotess a good time, and you can come get me later." He smiled at her, but Elara could see the queasiness in his eyes.

"Really?" Valerie squealed in delight like a spoiled child.

"Uh-huh," Theodosius' forced enthusiasm was hard to watch. He must be really worried about Tina's life to go through with this.

"You don't have to do this, Theodosius," Elara said sternly.

"Yes, you do. Don't listen to her," Valerie pouted, putting one arm on Theodosius' shoulder and the other on his ass.

"Just go and come straight back," he said through a forced smile and gritted teeth. "I'm fine."

"Yes, you are *very* fine." Valerie planted a kiss on his exposed neck.

Elara's blood was boiling. She imagined herself throttling the despotess, but one look from Theodosius stopped her. Without another word, she raced from the room. The sooner she got the physician, and brought him to Tina, the sooner she could come back here to rescue Theodosius.

She knew that men sometimes forced themselves on women, but she'd never seen a woman do it to a man before. Theodosius was not in a high enough rank to refuse her without punishment.

Thankfully, the hill wasn't that steep, and the physician was easy enough to find once she made her way down. The physician, Matthew, was a kindly older man who graciously accepted to come with her back to the ship where Tina was waiting.

"Tina! Where's Tina? I brought the physician!" Elara said as she and Matthew boarded the ship and headed toward the deck below.

"Over here!" Yianni called her over to where a feverish, but still alive, Tina was waiting. There was a man holding Tina's hand that Elara took to be Tina's brother, Jimmy Argyrou.

"What seems to be the problem?" Matthew asked Tina as he immediately got to work.

"Fever, mostly," Tina murmured weakly. "And a cough."

"Sounds like an infection. I've got some vinegar and mint here, add that and some lemon to a cup of hot water..." Matthew mused over different remedies as he shuffled through his satchel and handed various vials to Jimmy.

Following the physician's instructions, Jimmy poured the vials into some water and stirred the concoction for his sister to drink. Matthew dabbed something that looked like mud on Tina's sweaty forehead and pressed a green leaf over it.

Elara nervously waited a moment just to be sure Tina had everything she needed before racing off again. Once she saw Tina sit up to drink the herbal water, she decided it was time to go.

Before she could take a step, Yianni pulled Elara aside. "Where's Theodosius?"

"I have to go back for him." Elara took a deep breath. "I think I might need your help, Yianni."

Elara and Yianni made their way back toward the despotess' home, over the rocky terrain. It seemed that even less people were out now than there were before, if that was possible.

"So, what happened to the captain?" Yianni asked as they made their way.

"I think Lady Valerie is trying to *proposition* him," Elara said through gritted teeth.

"Well, is she attractive?" Yianni had the audacity to laugh.

"She's old enough to be his mother," Elara turned to him angrily. "But even if she were *attractive*, it's never right to proposition people who are in need—to take advantage of him like that—it's sick!"

"Yeah, the despotess does that a lot," a voice piped up, stopping Elara and Yianni in their tracks.

They turned and saw that it was a boy sitting on a large rock. He looked no older than twelve years old.

"Hello there. You know Despotess Valerie?" Elara asked the boy gently.

The boy nodded somberly. "Every boy and young man in Thessaloniki knows her. Even me."

- - -

Celina found it strange how few people were out and about in Thessaloniki as she and Rhea walked around. The town wasn't empty by any means, but it certainly wasn't full of life like Rome, Athens, and even Tossa de Mar.

"Where is everyone?" Rhea asked what Celina was thinking out loud.

"Hmm, I'm not sure. It's so unusual." Celina looked around until her eyes fell on an elderly couple walking arm and arm around what she assumed was the gate to their home. "Oh, pardon us! Do you know where everyone is? It's so quiet today."

The couple saw the two girls approaching them and quickly moved to get back into their home as if they were afraid of them. This was strange behavior for Eastern Roman people to exhibit, especially when Eastern Romans were known for their hospitality.

"Wait! We just want to talk! Can you tell us what's happening here today?" Rhea surged forward and blocked the couple from going back inside their home.

"We're so sorry!" the elderly woman said as she gripped her husband's arm fearfully.

"Please don't hurt us! We know we broke the curfew, but—" the elderly man blubbered, but Rhea interrupted him with a gentle wave of her hand.

"We're not the authorities! We're... tourists." Rhea looked at Celina, clearly hoping her friend had a better plan of what to say or ask next.

"Tourists?" the elderly man scoffed. "You picked a hell of a time to go on a holiday here. Curfew for us peasants started over an hour ago, and we really shouldn't be out here any longer."

"Wait, slow down. What curfew? It's the middle of the day." Celina frowned, confused. She had only heard of curfews being used in times of war, and Thessaloniki didn't look war-torn.

"You haven't heard? Lady Valerie Palaiologos has imposed extremely strict rules on us. Her Excellency is a tyrant..." the elderly woman's voice trailed off into silence with one look from her husband.

"We shouldn't speak ill of the despotess," he said before turning back to the girls. "Want my advice? Get inside somewhere quickly or go be tourists someplace else."

Without any further explanation, the elderly couple pushed past Rhea to go into their home and slammed the door behind them. Rhea and Celina looked at each other in dismay.

"What's a despotess?" Rhea frowned, putting her hands on her hips.

"It's a title. Like a duchess or a princess." Celina looked out at the empty streets for a moment, thinking. They needed to hitch a ride to Constantinople so that they could finally find Elara, but it seemed that most of the fishermen and sailors were away or also observing the curfew.

"Celina, we only have a few hours before dark." Rhea was right. If they were breaking curfew now, it would only be worse for them after dark.

"I have an idea, but you're not going to like it." Celina turned to look at her friend. "I think we should pay this Lady Valerie a visit."

Rhea scowled, "You think we should visit the lady that this elderly couple called a *tyrant?*"

"Yes. The despotess controls the ships going in and out of this place. We need a ship to get to Constantinople," Celina explained it like it was simple, but she was nervous as well. This curfew situation, and the fear that the couple had shown didn't bode well for anyone.

Rhea sighed, rubbing her temple. "So, what's the plan? Shall I pretend to be your maid again?"

"No, I think I should pretend to be *your* maid." Celina took a breath, almost as surprised by her statement as Rhea was. "My father's enemies are still after me, so it might be best if I pretend to be Hilda Vandero, and you pretend to be Lady Sidra Ravi."

Rhea half-smiled, half-frowned at the idea. "All right, if you're sure you want to."

"I want to." Celina grinned and gave a little mocking bow. "Happy to serve you, my lady."

After they cleaned themselves up in a nearby fountain and fixed up their hair as best they could, the two girls made their way up the hill where they knew the despotess lived. It was a large manor house that was probably just as big, if not bigger, than Count Basil's estate, Tossa de Mar, back in Catalonia.

"Are you going to knock, or should I?" Rhea asked.

"You can do it. Go on," Celina nodded encouragingly.

Rhea lifted her hand and knocked three times on the tall, oak door. There was no response. Rhea knocked again, louder this time. Still, no one came to the door.

"Maybe the butler and the maids are on curfew too," Rhea shrugged, but just as she finished the thought, Celina grabbed the doorknob and pushed her way inside.

"Oh, good; it's open." Celina walked in, not waiting for an invitation.

"Wait! Celina, wait!" Rhea rushed in after her. "You can't just walk into the despotess' house!"

Celina was getting tired of waiting and playing by the rules. The sooner they got a ship, the sooner they could set sail for Constantinople to finally find Elara.

Lady Valerie's home was gorgeous, with high cathedral ceilings, exotic plants, rich mahogany furniture, and an open-air courtyard in the center.

"Hello? Despotess Valerie? Are you at home? We're sorry to intrude, but we need your help!" Celina called as they walked about the courtyard.

"You have to love an open-air courtyard. I wonder if the despotess ever eats out there," Rhea noted pointedly as they walked.

"Oh, very cheeky." Celina remembered the conversation to which Rhea was referring. Their arguments about open air courtyards seemed forever ago.

Her friendship with Rhea had made so much progress since then that it was hard for Celina to remember why she had acted so bitterly in the first place. She wished she had been nicer to Rhea from the beginning. Elara had been correct when she said she wished Celina cared more about being kind than about being right.

Celina walked over to Rhea and touched her friend's arm. "Rhea dear, I want to apologize again—"

"Can I help you, ladies?" A man's voice asked behind them, making them both jump. The man was clearly a guard, with a long, slender nose, and jagged haircut. Celina thought he looked vaguely familiar, but she couldn't quite place where she had seen him before.

"Are you...?"

"I'm Dimitrios Milakis from Constantinople," he said, studying her for a moment. "You're friends with Lady Elara Iliakos."

"Yes, I am!" Celina smiled, completely forgetting she was supposed to be in disguise. "I'm Lady Celina Oberon, and this is my friend, Miss Rhea Alkan."

"A pleasure." Dimitrios gave them a little bow, which the girls respectfully reciprocated.

"I'm sorry that we're intruding, sir, but we really need to see Lady Valerie," said Rhea.

"Her Excellency, Lady Valerie, is *indisposed.*" Dimitrios pronounced the word 'indisposed' like it was causing him physical pain. "Perhaps you could come back tomorrow?"

Celina shook her head. "That won't work. We need a ship today. It's very important, and with this curfew, Lady Valerie is the only one who can help us."

Dimitrios frowned, clearly confused. "A ship? Why don't you just get a ride with Lady Elara? She came in on a ship earlier this afternoon with her...*cousin.*"

"Wait, Elara is here?" Celina could scarcely believe her ears. "Where is she now?"

"And who is her cousin?" Rhea asked no one in particular. Celina shot her a look.

"You just missed the countess. She went to fetch the physician for a sick friend," Dimitrios told them, gesturing to the door that Elara had presumably left through.

Before the girls could ask where this physician lived, or any other details they might need to find Elara, there was suddenly a loud thump-sound coming from above them. All three of them looked up in surprise.

"What was that?" Rhea asked in a whisper.

"I'm not sure. Please excuse me for one moment, ladies." Dimitrios drew his sword and headed toward the back staircase.

Rhea and Celina exchanged looks, clearly having the same thought. There was another staircase in the front foyer that they could slip up and explore. Perhaps they could find Lady Valerie up there and get more information on Elara or the physician she had gone to fetch. Celina knew they were probably just asking for trouble and that there was a chance that Valerie would be cross with them, but they had to try to investigate if it meant finding Elara.

The girls climbed to the top landing of the marble staircase, which led out to a long hallway. There were paintings and windows on the walls, giving the perfect combination of light and ambiance. They continued quietly down the hall, listening intently for any more thumping sounds. About halfway, they heard it again, followed by some muffled arguing from behind a closed door at the end of the hall.

Rhea gripped Celina's arm and whispered in her ear, "Maybe we should go back downstairs."

Celina didn't move, but instead, stared intently at the door, as if something was about to spring from it. She took a shaky breath as the arguing grew louder, and the door handle rattled. Perhaps Rhea was right. They shouldn't be here. It was too dangerous.

"All right, let's go." Just as Celina turned and said it, the door burst open, and a partially naked man ran out from the room. Rhea and Celina gasped in a combination of horror and surprise as he whizzed past them and bounded down the stairs.

"Stop that man!" yelled a woman's voice from the room. Celina was so shocked that she froze in place. She and Rhea made eye contact as if they weren't sure if they should laugh or scream.

Dimitrios finally made it to that part of the hall from the opposite stairwell. "Your Excellency? What happened? Are you hurt?"

A woman emerged from the room, fully clothed, but clearly upset. "That man is escaping before I was finished with him! Get him back here at once!"

Dimitrios ran toward the stairs, and this time, Celina and Rhea followed him. The naked man was just getting to the bottom of the stairs as they followed him down. He probably would have escaped by now, but he was holding up a thin cloth to cover his private parts, which slowed him down.

"Halt!" Dimitrios yelled but the man kept going.

The naked man took one last look back as he approached the front door, but that was a mistake on his part. While his head was turned, the door opened and two people, a woman and a man, rushed inside. Unable to stop in time, the naked man ran right into the woman, unintentionally scooping her up in his arms to keep his balance and dropping his one cloth, so his naked bits pressed up on her lavender dress.

"Oops! I'm... I'm very sorry, Countess." The naked man laughed.

"What—where are your clothes?" the woman demanded in a familiar voice that Celina would recognize anywhere.

"Elara!" Celina said in delighted surprise as she and Rhea made it to the bottom of the stairs.

Elara, still wrapped up in the naked man's embrace, looked over at her friends and grinned excitedly. "Celina! Rhea!"

Their reunion was short lived as Dimitrios, with sword in hand, pulled the naked man's hair, yanking him away and throwing him to the floor.

"Unhand him!" the other man, who had entered with Elara, shouted as he unsheathed a sword of his own and began to engage Dimitrios in a fight.

Celina's eyes widened as she understood who these men were. The one fighting Dimitrios was the corsair, Yianni Drakos, which meant the naked man on the floor was Theodosius Kardia.

While Yianni fought Dimitrios, Celina and Rhea raced forward to hug Elara. It was all happening so fast, and there was a lot going on, but Celina felt a swell of joy in her chest at being reunited with her friend.

Elara was here and she was safe. There was so much Celina wanted to tell her, and so many questions she wanted to ask, but it would have to wait. Elara accepted their embrace only briefly before pulling back.

"I'm so happy to see you both!" She beamed and then glanced over to where Theodosius was crouched on the floor. "Help me find something to cover him."

Elara kneeled beside the pirate, touching his shoulder gently. "Are you hurt? What happened?"

"Nothing happened," Theodosius huffed, clearly making an effort to keep his exposed parts as invisible as possible. "The only thing that hurts is my pride."

"Here!" Rhea had found a long cloak hanging by the door and she threw it on Theodosius' lap.

"This is a lady's cloak." Theodosius scrunched his nose, like he'd rather walk around naked than be seen in women's clothes.

"We don't have a lot of options, Theodosius," Elara reminded him sternly. "Put it on."

"Very well, but you must promise not to laugh at me," he said as he slipped the cloak over his shoulders. Once tied, the cloak fell to his knees but otherwise covered him completely.

"Could use a little help over here, Captain!" Yianni shouted from where he and Dimitrios were still locked in combat. Their swords clanged together as Dimitrios shoved Yianni up against the far wall, clearly going in for the kill. If Theodosius didn't help Yianni soon, he'd be dead.

"Here. Use this to help Yianni." Elara pressed her dagger's hilt into Theodosius' hand.

"Thanks." He looked at her fondly for a quick moment before rushing to help his friend.

While the boys fought, Elara turned back to Celina and Rhea. "Where is Lady Valerie?"

"Upstairs, I believe," Celina told her. "Why?"

Without answering the question, Elara moved past her friends and raced toward the staircase they had just descended. Celina had no idea what Elara was up to or what she wanted from Lady Valerie, but she followed her up the stairs, nonetheless. Rhea followed close behind them.

"Lady Valerie?" Elara called. "Are you up here?"

A woman, whom Celina presumed was Lady Valerie, emerged from her room. She was wearing a gaudy, dark green gown, her hair pinned up in a messy, gray-blonde bun, and had makeup caked haphazardly all over her face.

"Lady Elara, you're back. How's your sick friend?" Lady Valerie asked contemptuously.

Then Elara did something that truly shocked Celina—she slapped the despotess across the face with such force that Lady Valerie stumbled backward, falling over onto the floor.

Chapter Eleven

Reunited

"Don't! She's nobility!" Rhea squeaked, sounding as horrified and surprised as Celina felt.

"What the hell was that for?" Valerie asked, holding her cheek.

"You shouldn't have touched him." Elara began hitting Valerie repeatedly where she lay on the floor. "You shouldn't have touched anyone! I know what you did. I know what you've been doing to this place, you controlling witch!"

"Stop!" Celina grabbed Elara around the stomach trying to pull her off the despotess.

"Listen to your friend! I've done nothing wrong!" Lady Valerie spat as she held her arms above her head defensively.

"Let go of me!" Elara elbowed Celina in the stomach.

Celina dropped her immediately as a combination of shock and pain overtook her. She couldn't believe that her friend, sweet Elara, the girl who cared about doing the right thing, was lashing out at a despotess of all people.

"I know you've been hurting people all over Thessaloniki," Elara yelled in Valerie's face, but she made no more attempts to hit the despotess. "A boy told me...I know you keep them all under curfews and lockdowns so they can't leave, and if they try to leave, you have the boys and men brought to you—!"

"Shut up!" Valerie stood up and grabbed Elara by the collar, shaking her. "If I want a young boy under me, then I shall have them! I'm the despotess of Thessaloniki! I can have whatever I want!"

This time Valerie attacked, and unlike Elara, the despotess was going for maximum damage. They wrestled, slapped, and punched each other as they got dangerously close to the railing of the staircase. Elara had the anger, but Valerie appeared to be the more skilled one when it came to hand-to-hand combat.

"Be careful, Elara! You're close to the stairs!" Rhea called out, hiding her face behind her hands.

Celina couldn't decide if she should jump in or not. Having had no proper combat training, she would be of little use in a fight and might just get in Elara's way. Still, she desperately wanted to help her friend, but she didn't know how.

The front door opened down below, and three more guards entered the manor. Two of them ran to the left to help Dimitrios, and the other one ran upstairs to help the despotess. That was when Celina decided that doing nothing but watching was no longer an option.

"Do you have your blade?" Celina asked Rhea as the guard ascended the stairs.

Rhea pulled her dagger out of her pocket. "I'm ready to fight if you are."

Celina smiled as she pulled out her own dagger. "Let's do this."

Once the guard made it to the landing, the girls sprung on him while Elara and Valerie continued fighting next to them. The guard was a more skilled fighter than the two of them, but he was outnumbered and lacked the adrenaline that they had coursing through their veins. That being said, he also had a sword, which was much longer than the girls' daggers.

Their best bet, in Celina's opinion, wasn't to beat him in the traditional sense, but to get him to tumble back down the stairs, where, hopefully, he would be too sore to come after them again. Celina and Rhea took turns trying to stab him, push him, and get him to stumble backward. The guard shoved Celina into a nearby wall, causing her to lose her knife near the side of the railing.

Finally, Rhea managed to get him to drop his sword, but she was also forced to drop her knife at the same time. She pushed him again, but he was stronger than her. He put his hands around her throat in an attempt to choke her out. Rhea slapped him as hard as she could, but he was too strong.

Celina knew she had to act quickly as Rhea's face was turning an alarming shade of dark purple. Slowly getting back on her feet, Celina pushed herself off the wall and jumped on the guard's back.

"LEAVE HER ALONE!" Celina shouted as she clung to the guard's necks, squeezing as hard as she could.

The guard dropped Rhea, so he could focus on flinging Celina off of him. She miraculously managed to hold on. Finally, Celina got him to stumble close to the stairs. Hopping off his back, she gave the man a good push, sending him flying down the stairwell to the foyer below. His body landed with a thud, and he groaned loudly but didn't get up to go after them again.

"Good shove!" Rhea's voice was raspy as she clapped Celina on the back.

Even though she too was pleased with the turn of events, Celina didn't feel much like celebrating. She hoped the man was only injured and not dying on the floor below.

"AHHH!" Elara screamed suddenly.

Celina and Rhea whirled around to see that Elara was dangling from the railing over nothing but the marble floor several feet down. Valerie stood menacingly above her.

"ELARA!" Theodosius shouted from below, but he was too consumed by his own fight with the guards to be able to help her.

"You're going to fall to your death, Countess Elara," Valerie snarled as she pressed her foot onto Elara's right hand, causing Elara to scream in pain.

"Don't!" Celina rushed forward but halted when Valerie turned around holding her own dagger.

"One more step and I'll have all your throats slit." Valerie's eyes were dark, and Celina could tell she meant it; the despotess was in a killing mood.

"You don't want to do this, Your Excellency," Rhea pleaded. "We're sorry about all this mess. If you just let Elara up—!"

"Shut up! God, don't you young people ever stop talking?" Valerie turned back to Elara, "After you die, I'm going to send word to Empress Maria about what a rotten woman you've become."

"No!" Elara's voice was strained with effort.

"Your papou, poor Count Basil, will never be able to show his face in public again! He will die of shame!"

"NO!" Elara yelled, and mustering the last of her strength, she pulled herself up a bit more and stabbed Valerie in the foot with Celina's discarded dagger.

"AGHH!" Valerie screamed before tripping and falling through the broken railing herself.

Celina and Rhea ran forward and pulled Elara back up to the safety of the landing. They looked over the edge to see Lady Valerie's crumpled body below, blood pooled on the floor by her head.

"Oh, God!" Elara sobbed. "She's dead!"

- - -

"I—I didn't mean to kill her," Elara was shaking. She couldn't believe what she had just done.

After that boy had briefly told her and Yianni about the despotess harming young men and boys, sometimes boys as young as ten, Elara had become so angry. Her anger had only grown when she saw Theodosius naked, clearly running for his life. Elara knew that Theodosius was physically stronger than the despotess, but that didn't change the fact that Lady Valerie had used her authority, her power, and her threats to coerce his consent. It was sickening when it happened to young girls in other parts of the world, and it was equally sickening when it happened to boys here too.

"You were defending yourself," Rhea said, trying to soothe her as the three girls made their way back down the stairs.

Celina said nothing, which made Elara especially worried, since she had just minutes ago elbowed Celina in the stomach and seemingly abandoned her in Athens a few days ago.

"I'm so sorry about everything," Elara started to say as they reached the foyer.

"There you are," Theodosius said cheerfully. "You see, it's a good thing I taught you to fight, isn't it, Countess?" He was dressed in one of the guards' clothes now, and he didn't seem to react at all to Lady Valerie's dead body on the ground.

"Where are the guards?" Celina asked, looking around the empty room. Even the guard that Celina had knocked down the stairs was gone.

"We took them out of commission and threw them in the cellar," Yianni said, sounding a little too pleased. "We can put Lady Valerie down there as well, but then we should get back to the ship."

Elara put her hands on her face trying to steady her breathing. She couldn't believe what a mess this whole trip was becoming. Everywhere she went, things seemed to get worse, and she was no closer to getting her necklace back or returning home.

"Elara." Theodosius put a hand on her shoulder, and she noted how good he looked in the guard's uniform. "Everything that happened today—it's not your fault."

"Yes, it is," she whispered. "I killed the despotess."

"You *accidently* killed a dictator and a defiler. Some might say that makes you a hero." Theodosius shrugged as he dropped his hand back to his side. "Plus, with the despotess dead and the guards out of commission, there's no one left here to further ruin your reputation or your family name."

"Huh, yes, I suppose that's true." Elara bit her lip, feeling guiltier than ever. She appreciated that Theodosius was trying to make her feel better, but she was starting to feel worse.

"Elara, can I speak with you?" Celina motioned for her to come over alone.

She followed Celina into the open-air courtyard where Rhea was waiting for them. Elara didn't know what to say to them. This wasn't exactly the reunion she had imagined.

"Girls, I'm really sorry about Athens. This whole journey has had so many unforeseen challenges and I'm… I'm really sorry." Elara fiddled with her hands, unable to keep eye contact with them.

"Oh, Elara dear." Celina wrapped her up in a tight hug. "We're not mad at you."

"You're not?" Elara's voice muffled into Celina's shoulder.

"We're not," Rhea promised as she joined the hug.

The hug ended, but they kept their arms around each other loosely. Elara looked at her friends, they were a bit disheveled and bruised but otherwise appeared whole and relatively unharmed. She didn't even want to know how bad she herself looked.

"What are we going to do now? What comes next?" Celina asked her softly.

Elara nodded, "I'm going with Theodosius to Constantinople. I found out from a woman in Athens that Despot Nekros Palaiologos has my necklace, so I'm going to get it from him."

"I told you she was going to Constantinople." Celina smiled at Rhea in a friendly way that surprised Elara. "All right, when do we leave?"

"You still want to come with me?" Elara perked up, pleased.

"Of course we do!" beamed Rhea. "You clearly need us."

The girls laughed and hugged again. It was wonderful to have her friends back.

"Hey, Countess!" Theodosius called from the other room. "You should see this!"

Elara, Celina, and Rhea quickly made their way back to the main room where Theodosius and Yianni were staring at something on the mantel.

"What is it?" Elara asked as she approached them.

"It's Nekros' coat of arms," Yianni said, pointing it out to her.

"So?" She wasn't sure what they were getting at. It was normal for nobles to display coats of arms for their family members. Nekros and Valerie were brother and sister-in-law after all.

"So that means Nekros has been here in the last few months," Theodosius said simply.

He didn't need to explain further. It wouldn't be the first time Theodosius and Yianni accused the despot of bad behavior. While Elara still didn't want to believe bad things about her father's friend, Nekros, it wasn't a good sign that he had visited Valerie recently and done nothing to stop her assault on the people of Thessaloniki. As the despot of Constantinople, and a man, he outranked her.

"I'm sure there's an explanation," Celina piped up from the back, but Elara said nothing. Once they got to Constantinople, the truth would be revealed.

- - -

After cleaning up the manor and moving the despotess' body out of sight, the group set off back to the ship. Elara hoped Tina was recovering well after seeing the physician. She wondered if perhaps the physician, Matthew, would consider coming along with them in case Tina needed more care.

Gregory greeted them as they arrived back on the ship. The other crew members were getting ready to set sail under Yianni's orders as Theodosius made an excuse to rest for a bit. Elara watched the captain walk away and considered following him, until she noticed Tina was up and about with Matthew.

"Tina!" Elara, followed by Celina and Rhea, walked over to the side rail where Tina was.

"Hello. Who are your friends?" Tina smiled. She still looked tired, but in much better spirits than when Elara had last seen her.

"This is Lady Celina Oberon and Miss Rhea Alkan, my ladies-in-waiting," Elara introduced them. "And this is Constantina Argyrou, but she goes by Tina."

"Nice to meet you, Tina." Rhea shook Tina's hand.

"How are you feeling?" Celina asked, shaking her hand as well.

"I'm doing much better thanks to this man." Tina looked over at Elara again and almost did a double take. "You look a little bruised up. Maybe Matthew should look at you too?"

"No, I'm fine." Elara shrugged off her friend's concern and turned her attention back to the physician. "Sir, I was actually going to tell you that we'll be leaving soon, so if you wanted to go back to Thessaloniki—"

"I'll stay on," Matthew said, interrupting her. "Every ship needs a physician—even a *pirate* ship." He gave a wink.

- - -

While Tina chatted with Celina and Rhea, Elara slipped below deck to find Theodosius. She found him in a back room she hadn't seen before. It looked almost like a smaller version of the captain's quarters she was staying in, with a small bed and a round side table with two chairs. Candles lit the room well enough to see, but it was still a bit dark without any windows.

She smiled to herself, remembering his complaints about sleeping below deck in a hammock when he had a room here all along.

Theodosius was dressed like himself again and had combed his hair back out of his face. For a pirate, he was always surprisingly well groomed. He was fixing the cuff of his sleeves, his back to the open door, seemingly unaware that she was there watching him.

"How are you doing?" Elara asked him from the doorway.

Theodosius turned to look at her with the look of a man who hadn't slept in a long time. "Spying on me, are you?"

"I'm just checking in. Are you injured at all from your...encounter with the despotess?" she asked, feeling like she needed to speak in innuendo to protect his privacy.

"My *encounter* with the despotess? Is that what they're calling it these days?" he chuckled darkly. "I swear I got away before anything happened."

"I know." Elara stepped further into the room, so she was standing in front of him, but she was careful not to encroach upon his personal space. "I'm... I mean if you wanted to talk about it—you know I'm here for you."

"You're probably wondering why a bloodthirsty pirate like me allowed myself to be *violated.* You're probably wondering why I didn't just kill her myself." Theodosius sounded disgusted with himself. The shame seeped into his voice, and Elara recognized the self-hatred at once. She often spent time hating herself for things that were outside of her control.

"You couldn't have killed her. You were in her house, under the watch of her guards. If you'd hurt her, they would have killed you." She paused, thinking. "Besides, playing along was the only way to get a physician for Tina."

He took a step forward and gently traced a thin cut on Elara's left eyebrow. His hands were warm, and Elara found she liked the touch. Over a week ago, she might have pulled out her dagger and threatened to kill him, but now things were different.

"You were really worried about me, weren't you, Countess?" Theodosius whispered softly, his hands resting gently on her arms now. She suddenly remembered earlier when his arms had been wrapped around her, his nakedness exposed.

A shiver ran down her spin and there was a slight tingle of something in her stomach. "I told you—you can call me Elara."

"*Elara.*" Theodosius leaned his face down close to hers, but just before their lips touched, Elara put her hand on his chest stopping him. He immediately pulled his face away but kept his arms around her. "Sorry. Did I do something wrong?"

"No." Elara's breathing was shallow. "I just haven't kissed anyone since my engagement ended, and I'm a bit nervous."

"It's fine." He dropped his arms and took a small step back. "We don't have to."

"I want to," she blurted out, moving toward him again before she could stop herself. Her heart was pounding as she moved to put her hands in his. "Do you—do you want to?"

He scoffed but was clearly enjoying himself. "Elara, I've wanted to kiss you since the first moment I saw you. I think you are absolutely fantastic—"

Before he could finish complimenting her, Elara stood on her tiptoes and gave him a small peck on the lips. It was a silly little kiss, almost juvenile, but perfect for breaking the tension between them.

The captain grinned, taking her face in his hands, and kissed her deeply. It was a warm kiss, passionate, yet surprisingly gentle. Elara's heart felt like it might explode out of her chest. She wound her arms around his waist trying to get as close to him as possible.

"Theodosius?" Yianni barged into the room causing them to jump apart. "Ah sorry, Captain. I was just... I was uh..."

"Out with it!" Theodosius snapped at him. Elara felt her cheeks get hot with embarrassment.

"Jimmy made dinner, and I was sent to fetch you." Yianni snickered uncomfortably. "Sorry, I didn't realize you were already eating."

Theodosius glowered at him, but then his face softened. "Elara and I will be there in a minute. Thank you, Yianni."

"Anything for you, Captain." Yianni gave another awkward chuckle before he slipped out of the room.

"Sorry about him. He never knocks." Theodosius gave her that shy grin he sometimes did when he wasn't feeling confident but didn't want to show it. "How are you fairing?"

She took a deep breath and then smiled. "I'm grand. Are you well?"

"Uh-huh, I'm very well." He beamed, looking incredibly relieved.

"Good." Elara laughed. "We should—we should go join the others for dinner before Yianni starts a gossip mill about us."

"Yes. Good idea. Allow me to escort you." Theodosius held out his arm as a good gentleman would.

She took his arm and allowed him to guide her back above deck. The whole way there, they laughed quietly and whispered jokes to each other. In the back of her mind, Elara knew this wasn't the kind of relationship that could last, but for now, she was determined to enjoy their connection.

Dinner passed in a blur of laughter and good company. Celina and Rhea took turns telling stories from their travels, and Elara was impressed with how their friendship had blossomed over the past week. Occasionally, she would look over at Theodosius, and she would catch him looking back at her, smiling.

"Let's have a toast!" Yianni held up his glass. "To our victories across the Mediterranean, and to our future victories in Constantinople." He glanced at Elara and Theodosius as he spoke but gave nothing else away. It appeared that Yianni hadn't told any of their friends about the kiss, but Elara suspected it was only a matter of time.

Everyone clinked their glasses together and cheered to their successes so far. Late tomorrow, they would be in Constantinople, and she would finally be able to retrieve her necklace and go home. She was happy about that, but there was a part of her, deep down, that didn't want the adventure to end. There was a part of her that didn't want to say goodbye to her new friends, Tina, Yianni, and especially Theodosius.

- - -

"I call dibs on the left side of the bed!" Rhea said as she, Elara, and Celina all piled into the captain's quarters to sleep for the night.

"Does it matter which side? It's going to be cramped either way," Celina kidded her as she and Rhea flopped on the bed.

"I can sleep in the chair," Elara offered, gesturing to the cozy armchair by the window.

"No!" both Celina and Rhea said at the same time.

Elara rolled her eyes and went to sit on the bed on the right side, so Celina was in the middle. "Are you sure it won't be too cramped?"

"It'll be like the sleepovers we had as kids!" Celina pinched Elara's arm ruefully. "Remember when we stayed up all night, and Countess Zoe came in and yelled at us for making too much noise?"

"I remember! Yiayia was so cross with me the next day!" Elara laughed.

"You would have loved Countess Zoe." Celina turned to Rhea. "She was cross, but also the best old lady you could ever meet."

Rhea lit up, looking happy to be included in the nostalgic conversation. "If Countess Zoe was anything like Elara, I'm sure I would have found her to be delightful!"

"No, my yiayia was so much more magnificent than me—I'll never be as great as she was," Elara said, looking at the floor like she suddenly found the wooden paneling interesting. Her throat became tight as she thought back to how strong and amazing her yiayia was. When she remembered all the times her grandmother had been there for her, and now Elara had let her down.

"Elara dear, what is it?" Celina put a comforting hand on her shoulder.

"I can't believe I lost my yiayia's necklace just *one day* after my papou gave it to me, and who knows if we'll actually be able to get it back." She shook her head in dismay.

"We'll get it back," Rhea swore determinedly. Elara remained unconvinced. Even if she did, by some miracle, manage to get the necklace back, could everything she'd broken in her life really be fixed?

"You know what?" Celina said, bumping Elara's shoulder. "I don't recall your yiayia ever wearing that necklace, so how precious could it have been really?"

- - -

No matter how hard she tried, Elara could not get her brain to let her sleep. Too many thoughts of Constantinople, her yiayia's necklace, and her kiss with Theodosius swirled in her head. It didn't help that the bed was, in fact, very cramped. Celina snored too, but Elara would never tell her that.

She turned on her side, facing her friends. They were both sound asleep, and their heads were touching. Elara was grateful that her friends were becoming close, but it did make Elara feel...lonely? She wasn't sure she could put words to it. It didn't really make sense, but even in this cramped bed, her friends felt far away.

Elara turned again, this time on her other side, so that she was facing the far wall. She wondered if Theodosius was awake, and if he was planning what they would do once they got to Constantinople. If he was awake, would Theodosius be thinking about her and their kiss as he lay in bed, or was that just something girls did?

Trying to sleep was starting to feel futile, so Elara got up and put a shawl around her shoulders. She slipped soundlessly out of the room, being careful to shut the door so as to not wake her friends. The ship was so quiet and so still at night with the crew almost all asleep. The only person awake on deck would be Gregory in the crow's nest and another crew member on helm duty.

Elara tiptoed down the ladder that led below deck, and made her way past the snoring pirates in their hammocks to find the back room where she knew Theodosius was staying.

The captain's door was shut, but she could see lantern light filtering in from under the door frame. He was still awake too. She made her way toward his door to knock, but before her hand could touch the wood, she heard voices inside.

"...As your first mate, I'm worried is all," Yianni's voice was saying.

"What? You don't trust me?" Theodosius' voice said back, and even though Elara couldn't see him, she could tell he was smiling and acting relaxed.

"Of course I trust you! It's Elara I don't trust." Yianni's voice sounded strained, and Elara felt her heart plummet into her stomach. She thought Yianni was becoming her friend, but now he didn't trust her?

"*Elara* is who you don't trust? Are you serious?" Theodosius laughed humorlessly. "She's the kindest person I know. Why do you not trust her?"

"Her family is close with Nekros. Perhaps she's working for him, giving him information about you." Yianni's footsteps echoed off the walls; he was clearly pacing. "I mean, don't you think it's strange that people seem to know where we're going before we get there? That guards and nobles want us dead in every town and city we visit?"

"We are notorious corsairs, Yianni. Perhaps it's not Elara but our *reputations* that precede us," Theodosius countered, still sounding unfazed.

"Just because Elara let you stick your tongue in her mouth doesn't mean you can trust her," Yianni argued, and Elara's stomach became more and more bunched together. She couldn't believe Yianni really thought this about her. It was hurtful, to say the least, and she had to keep her hand over her mouth to remind herself not to make a sound.

"I wish you wouldn't be so crass about that," Theodosius sounded angry now, and the sound of his chair scraping against the wood floor suggested he was standing up. "You know, if you hadn't stolen, and then gambled away Elara's necklace in the first place, we wouldn't have this opportunity to finally confront Nekros. So, perhaps I should say thank you, Yianni."

"I wasn't gambling! You know I traded that necklace to Justine to get information about Nekros!"

"Yes, and instead of information, you got a glass of mead. A lot of good that did us."

"It was *two* glasses of mead!" Yianni spat. "And Nekros killed her for it!"

Elara thought about Lady Justine dead in an alley in Athens. The woman had known something about the despot, and it had gotten her killed.

"You're upset about Justine's death? Is that it?" The captain's voice sounded closer now, and she wondered if he was standing near the door.

"No! I'm worried about *you!*" The first mate's frustration was palpable. "You're so besotted by your lust for the countess—it's going to get you killed!"

"Without her, I would still be searching for useless ledgers in Rome and wasting my time kissing ugly women, instead of the beautiful...*eavesdropper!*" Theodosius suddenly pulled the door all the way open, catching Elara in the act.

"Uh, sorry," she said awkwardly. "I wasn't—I didn't mean to interrupt."

Theodosius looked more amused than angry, but Yianni looked as pale as a ghost, his eyes widened in surprise. Elara rocked on her feet and heard a creaking sound coming from the floorboard beneath her. That sound must have been how Theodosius caught her.

"Countess, this is such a lovely surprise. Please come in." Theodosius pulled her inside by the arm and shut the door behind her.

"See!" Yianni regained his composure. "She is spying for Nekros!"

"How dare you!" Elara snapped back. "I spy for no one! After everything...Yianni, I thought we were friends."

Yianni glanced down at his feet a bit ashamedly, but he wasn't done insulting her, "You can seduce the captain, but not me—I don't trust anyone outside of the crew!"

"Get out," Theodosius ordered Yianni coldly. The captain wasn't shouting at his first mate, and somehow, that made his words even more intense.

"Captain, be reasonable. Her family is close friends with Nekros!" Yianni argued again and, to be fair, if Elara heard someone's family was close friends with someone she didn't like, she probably wouldn't trust them either.

"I said *get out!*" This time Theodosius did shout as his anger spilled to the surface.

Yianni looked crestfallen that his captain wasn't listening to him, but followed orders, nonetheless, slamming the door behind him.

"I'm so sorry. I heard voices, and I don't know what I was thinking. I really wasn't spying, I swear!" Elara blurted out as soon as Yianni was gone.

"Relax," he whispered, closing the space between them and kissing her. This kiss was just as passionate as their first, but now it was tangled with a sense of urgency, as if he was worried she could disappear at any moment.

Elara felt her heart beating wildly, and her arms instinctively wrapped around him, holding him in a tight embrace. She had never been kissed like this before.

When they broke apart, Theodosius kept his face near hers as he said quietly, "Why are you here?"

"I couldn't sleep, and I wanted to see you," she breathed.

"Well, here I am," he grinned teasingly. "Anything else I can do for you?"

Elara was quiet for a moment, deciding on the best course of action. There were things she wanted to discuss with him, but it was hard to concentrate with his body so close to hers.

"We should talk about our plans for Constantinople, and... I think you should tell me more about your conflict with Nekros." She watched his face, trying to gauge his reaction.

"Ah, is that all?" Theodosius took a step back much to her dismay. "You should probably sit down. This story takes some time to tell."

Chapter Twelve

The Brothers

Seven Years Ago…

Theodosius wasn't sure what he was supposed to be doing with the tapestry he was holding, but he was determined to figure it out. Prince Andronikos had given him orders to help set up Emperor Michael's birthday feast, but Theodosius hadn't been given specific instructions on what should go where.

"You look lost," Leonides commented with a chuckle as he approached his brother.

Leonides was dressed in the same servant's uniform that Theodosius had to wear. It consisted of a white tunic under a dark embroidered vest and matching trousers. Unlike Theodosius, who was clean-shaven with short wavy hair on his head, Leonides had dark, curly hair and a thick beard on his face.

"Leo, thank God! I was given this monstrosity of a tapestry, and I have no idea where to put it!" Theodosius held the tapestry like it was on fire and he'd die if he couldn't drop it soon.

"Always so dramatic, little brother." Leonides rolled his eyes as he helped his brother lift the tapestry and put it on the far wall of the banquet hall.

The banquet room was set up with three long tables connected to each other on their corners, so that they made a square horseshoe shape. Emperor Michael would be sitting at the head table, facing the center. Musical performers would be situated on the left-hand side where they could be out of the way but still heard and seen by the noble guests. Theodosius and Leonides would be in the back of the room with the rest of the servants, only coming toward the feast if someone from the royal family beckoned for them.

"See, that wasn't so hard. Mother will be very proud of us, I think." Leonides clapped Theodosius on the back approvingly.

"Yes, thank you, but there's still so much to be done." Theodosius looked around the room trying to decide which task to tackle next. Last year, he had been scolded by Prince Andronikos for moving too slowly, so he wanted to make sure everything went smoothly this year.

"Calm yourself, Theo," Leonides said, pulling him back to the present moment. "Look up and see who's just arrived."

Theodosius followed his brother's instructions and saw Empress Maria Rita Palaiologos gliding on the balcony hallway above them. Her ladies-in-waiting followed closely behind her, along with some footmen carrying several boxes.

Every year, on the emperor's birthday, the empress would prepare a surprise gift for the emperor, something no one else could get. Last year, she'd gotten him a giraffe from Ethiopia, and the year before that, she'd gotten him a padparadscha sapphire gemstone, the rarest gemstone in the world, from Tanzania.

"I wonder what the empress is going to get the emperor for his birthday this year," Theodosius said.

Leonides smirked knowingly. "I already know what she's getting him. Found out yesterday."

"Really?" Theodosius raised his eyebrows. "Tell me!"

Leonides shook his head, "I promised Lady Justine I wouldn't tell. She'll get in trouble with Empress Maria if the secret gets out before tonight."

"Fine, keep your secret." Theodosius raised his hands in mock surrender.

He'd just get Justine to tell him herself, or perhaps he could get Yianni to spill the beans with enough prodding. Yianni worked directly for the emperor, so he'd have some inside knowledge, surely.

After preparations were finished in the banquet hall, Theodosius set off to find Lady Justine. Knowing her, she was probably sitting with the other ladies-in-waiting in the relaxation room of the palace. The relaxation room consisted of comfy sofas with soft pillows and lush rugs, which a person could walk on barefoot and feel like they were walking on air.

"*Christos anesti*, Theodosius," Lady Justine Parakios greeted him with a teasing look. The other girls sitting with her giggled at his approach. The ladies-in-waiting were dressed richly in brightly colored satin robes. Their long hair was styled perfectly in curly tendrils.

Justine was no exception, with a satin red dress and amber curls to match.

"*Alithos anesti*, Lady Justine." Theodosius bowed his head respectfully. "I hear from my brother that you know what the empress's mystery gift is this year. Can you tell me what it is, please?"

Justine lifted a goblet to her lips, taking a dramatized sip. "I'm not sure I'm allowed to do that, but perhaps we could come to an agreement?" The other ladies giggled again.

"What would you like?" he asked, a bit perplexed.

"I want what every girl wants." Justine stood and waltzed over to him, so they were standing face to face. She reached up and caressed his cheek. "Put in a good word for me with Prince Andronikos?"

Surprised, Theodosius recoiled from her touch. "You want an audience with the prince?"

"Do you know another Andronikos?" Justine smirked.

"Well, the prince's grandfather is also called Andronikos..." Theodosius mused, knowing perfectly well which Andronikos she was referring to. "He's a bit old, but I suppose I could ask him—"

"Be serious, Kardia! Do we have a deal or not?"

Theodosius pursed his lips into a grimace. Justine had always been ambitious, but she'd never directly asked to talk to Prince Andronikos before. He had a feeling that Andronikos wouldn't be receptive to the conversation, but he supposed he could give it a shot. Justine was a friend after all. After Andronikos most likely rebuffed him, he could go back to Justine with a simple apology. Then, she could move on and be spared Andronikos' cruelty and smugness. Theodosius feared for any woman Andronikos actually liked and set his eyes on.

"All right, I'll put in a good word with Andronikos for you and see if he'll meet with you," Theodosius agreed with a shrug.

"Splendid!" Justine clapped her hands together happily before whispering to him, "So, the empress is giving the emperor a solid gold bible, handcrafted by holy monks on Mount Athos in the eleventh century. It's supposedly the most expensive, and one of the oldest bibles in the whole world."

"Wow, a bible. Thank you for telling me," Theodosius said, trying to keep the disappointment out of his voice.

The empress was giving the emperor a bible? That felt a bit boring compared to years past. Surely, the emperor already had plenty of high-quality bibles lying around.

"You're welcome. Don't forget about our deal." Justine gave him a peck on the cheek, causing Theodosius to blush. Lady Justine was beautiful, and she knew it. He knew she thought he was handsome too, but he was not in high enough standing economically to tempt her in that way.

"I—I won't forget, my lady." He bowed to her and heard the other girls giggle one last time as he left the room.

Theodosius made his way down the hallway as he decided his next course of action was to find Andronikos, see if the prince needed anything, and then name drop Justine as promised.

Before he could make it to Prince Andronikos' quarters, he heard two men arguing. He slipped behind a nearby pillar to listen in without being seen.

"I won't be spoken to like this, Mister Kardia! I am a despot! Know your place!" a man with a gruff voice snapped angrily.

Leonides spoke next, "Your Excellency, I apologize for the situation, but the point stands that I have evidence of your—"

"*Evidence!* Bah!" the despot snarled. "How dare you! I am a nobleman! Emperor Michael is my older brother. You can't accuse the emperor's brother of such things! It's treason!"

"Treason? Lord Nekros, please be reasonable about this. I only want to do a quick search of your quarters—"

"I refuse! Get out at once! Don't come back until you have a warrant from Emperor Michael Palaiologos himself!" With that, Nekros shoved Leonides into the hallway and slammed the door in his face.

"*Dick*," Leonides muttered under his breath so low that Theodosius almost missed it.

"What was that about?" Theodosius asked, stepping out from where he was hiding.

Leonides jumped, and then relaxed seeing it was his brother. "It's nothing. Just Lord Nekros refusing to let me search his stuff when there's evidence that he's been *stealing* from the emperor."

"Stealing? Why would a despot need to steal? Isn't he wealthy enough?" Theodosius asked in confusion.

"You'd think so!" Leonides put his hands up in exasperation. "Come on. There's still so much to do before tonight."

As the brothers made their way back down the stairs, Theodosius completely forgot he was supposed to speak to Prince Andronikos about Lady Justine. The air in the palace couldn't have been more electric as servants and nobles alike moved about, preparing for the emperor's feast.

"Theo and Leo! The Kardia brothers! Just the two boys I wanted to see." Yianni Drakos appeared behind them, putting his arms around their shoulders in a jovial manner.

Theodosius grinned as he always did when his best friend Yianni was around, but Leonides, being nearly four years older than them, was less than enthused.

"*Yasou*, Yianni. What can we do for you?" Leonides asked, sounding slightly annoyed.

"For me? Nothing. The real question is what can I do for you? The emperor wants everyone doing their best when it comes to his celebration tonight," said Yianni matter-of-factly.

"We're doing well, thanks. Everything is going perfectly so far," Theodosius assured his friend. The last thing anyone wanted was for the emperor to think they weren't up to the task of throwing a party.

"Ah, all right. Well, keep me updated." Yianni winked at him before slipping down a side hallway and out of view.

"He's an interesting fellow, that friend of yours," Leonides commented as they continued down the hallway toward the kitchens.

"Yianni's a good guy once you get to know him," Theodosius chuckled. "He grows on you." He wasn't sure if that was exactly true for everyone, but Yianni had certainly grown on him over the years.

Leonides said nothing to this as he pushed the door of the kitchen open. The kitchen was even more crowded than the banquet hall. Cooks, maids, and serving boys were everywhere, doing a million tasks at once.

"There you are, loves!" Eudokia Kardia, their mother, called out to them. "I've been looking all over for you two. Can you help me move these wine jugs?"

"Of course. Happy to help." Leonides picked up one jug, and Theodosius picked up the other one. They carried the wine to the back of the banquet hall where the jugs would be out of the way but easy enough to access for anyone who wanted a drink.

"Perfect! Bless you both for your strong arms," Eudokia beamed at her sons. Their mother was a short woman with a large bosom and graying hair, but her gracefully carved features and hazel eyes kept an air of beauty about her.

"Anything for you, Mama." Leonides gave her shoulder a squeeze. "The feast tonight is going to be grand, and I'm sure the emperor will be well pleased with our work."

"Perhaps they'll even let us dance this year," Theodosius said jokingly as he pushed the wine jug into place against the wall.

"Don't be silly, Theodosius. Servants don't dance at these sorts of things—it's not proper." Eudokia shook her head at him, not finding him the least bit amusing.

Leonides and Theodosius exchanged looks as brothers do when their mother has absolutely no sense of humor.

- - -

The emperor's feast was grand. Musicians played the lute and the basuki, while nobles from all over the empire wined, dined, and danced merrily. Theodosius and the other servants weren't allowed to take part in any of it. They were there to work and to serve the needs of the nobility around them.

"*Christos anesti!* Might I have a refill on my wine?" Count Basil Iliakos asked, holding out his glass for Leonides to refill.

"*Alithos anesti.* Yes, here you go, my lord." Leonides filled the count's glass to the brim.

"Don't give him too much! I don't want him to get sick again!" the count's wife, Countess Zoe Iliakos, said from her seat at the table.

"Don't worry, my darling. I can handle it!" Count Basil grinned at them before returning to his wife at the table to finish his meal.

Theodosius smiled to himself, enjoying the show, even if he wasn't permitted to partake. His eyes scanned the room, looking at the various party guests. Prince Manuel, the youngest son of the emperor, was begrudgingly being sent to bed for the evening. He watched two servants dragging the young boy out of the room in the midst of a tantrum. Despite the spoiled display, Theodosius could already tell that Manuel would grow to be a better man than his pompous, older brother, Andronikos. Anyone would be better than Andronikos.

At the other side of the room, Empress Maria was talking to Lady Valerie Palaiologos, who had a glass of wine in one hand, and her other hand in a young boy's lap. Lady Valerie, Despotess of Thessaloniki, had a reputation for liking boys much younger than herself. Theodosius' stomach lurched and he quickly looked away when Valerie appeared to glance in his direction.

He saw Yianni next, putting another slice of lamb on Emperor Michael's plate. Yianni looked up, making eye contact with Theodosius, and gave him a wicked grin with his signature wink. Theodosius couldn't help but chuckle in amusement.

"Have you seen Nekros tonight?" Leonides asked, drawing back his attention.

"Huh? No, I haven't. Why?" Theodosius scanned the room quickly but saw no sign of Nekros, nor Nekros' wife, for that matter.

"No reason." Leonides sighed a bit too loudly for it to really be 'no reason'. Theodosius wondered what his brother suspected the despot was guilty of now.

"Theodosius!" It was Justine again.

"Yasas, Lady Justine—" Theodosius started to greet her, but before he could finish, she slapped him across the face. "Ow! What the hell was that for?"

"You didn't talk to Prince Andronikos about me!" she whined angrily.

252

"Oops, sorry." He scratched the back of his head. "Must have slipped my mind. I can talk to him now if you'd like?"

"Don't bother! I've already made an absolute fool of myself!" Justine huffed angrily before stalking off in the other direction.

"*Dammit*," Theodosius muttered under his breath.

"Forget about her," Leonides chuckled in amusement. "She'll find another rich man to marry her soon enough. You truly did her a favor by not talking to Andronikos."

"I know, but I promised her I would. I like to think I'm a man of my word." He pressed a hand to his stinging cheek, pushing it up toward his eyes.

"You are a man of your word. Try not to worry too much about it." Leonides suppressed a grin and stifled another laugh, still looking a little too amused by Theodosius' predicament. His brother was always laughing at him, it seemed, but Theodosius didn't really mind.

"You think me getting slapped is funny?" Theodosius asked, pretending to be offended as he rubbed his sore cheek.

"Funny? You? No, never!" Leonides laughed again, and this time, Theodosius joined him. No matter the circumstances, he and his brother always found time to laugh together.

"Attention, everyone!" Empress Maria clinked her goblet loudly to get the partygoers to settle down and listen to her. "It's time for the emperor to open his gift!"

The crowd murmured in anticipation and took their seats. Theodosius scanned the room, looking for the guards who would bring in the golden bible for the emperor to unwrap. Sure enough, two guards entered the room, holding a large rectangular box about the size of an old Roman shield.

"What could it be?" Emperor Michael said in delight as the box was placed before him. Everyone waited with bated breath as the emperor slowly opened the lid, revealing...

Nothing.

The crowd gasped in confusion, and some looked around as if to see what other surprise the empress had planned. Guessing by how unusually pale Empress Maria looked, there was no other surprise.

"It's empty," Lady Valerie stated the obvious.

"Where is my husband's gift?" Empress Maria questioned the guards, who looked just as bewildered as she did.

"*I knew it,*" Leonides muttered quietly under his breath. "I'm going to find Nekros." He disappeared into the crowd, leaving Theodosius alone with the wine jugs.

The room erupted into chaos as the nobles tried to figure out what had happened to the emperor's gift. There was a lot of arguing and none of it was productive.

There was an uncomfortable twist in Theodosius' stomach as he looked back at the door through which his brother had disappeared. Leonides was a smart man, and a strong one too, but would he be safe confronting a *despot* of all people for the second time in one day? He should go after his brother to see if he needed backup.

Silently, Theodosius slipped out of the party and down the hallway, unseen. All he had to do was take the stairs up one floor to Nekros' guest chamber and, assuming Leonides needed him, he'd improvise from there.

"Are you stalking me now?" A disgruntled voice asked.

Theodosius turned to see Lady Justine standing with her arms crossed, glowering at him. Clearly, she was still upset about Andronikos.

"I'm looking for my brother," he said shortly, not having time for whatever she wanted now.

Justine followed him up the stairs, clearly not taking the hint. "You know, I really trusted you to help me out, and this is the thanks I get?"

"So sorry to disappoint you, my lady, but I did offer to speak to Andronikos now or perhaps tomorrow, if you wanted," he reminded her as they walked.

"It's too late now," she bemoaned. "The prince already thinks I'm a fool."

"He's not the only one," Theodosius grumbled, not looking at her.

"What was that?" Justine asked with slanted eyes.

Before he could reply, the sound of arguing could be heard from Nekros' chamber. "I know you stole it! Give the bible back, and we'll forget this whole thing!" Leonides' voice was saying.

"I have no idea what you're talking about!" Nekros shot back.

Theodosius sped up his pace, making his way to the door, which was wide open. What Theodosius saw inside would change him forever. Just as Theodosius and Justine made it to the doorway, Nekros, with a knife in hand, slashed open Leonides' throat, killing him.

"NO!" Theodosius screamed, lunging down to catch his brother's falling body. "No, no, no, no! Leo!" He cradled Leonides' head in the crook of his right arm, and pressed his left hand to his brother's throat, desperately trying to stop the bleeding.

Justine was screaming for help while Theodosius kept his eyes on his brother. Leonides was already gone, but Theodosius still clutched his body tightly as if he could will him back to life. This couldn't be real. It wasn't. It had to be a bad dream.

"Please, don't go, Leo. Don't go. Stay with me!" He pleaded with his brother's lifeless form, tears streaming down his face.

"What's going on in here?" Two guards demanded as they entered the room.

"Thank God you're here!" Nekros sputtered to the guards. "Theodosius Kardia has murdered his own brother in cold blood!"

- - -

"Let me go! I'm innocent!" Theodosius yelled as the guards chained and dragged him back to the banquet hall. All the guests had left with only the emperor, the empress, and a handful of servants remaining in the hall. The guards threw Theodosius to his knees at the foot of Emperor Michael's throne.

"What is the meaning of this?" Emperor Michael asked in a disgruntled tone.

"Your Majesty, this man is a murderer and a thief!" Nekros said as he handed the emperor a rectangle-shaped object. "Theodosius was trying to steal your birthday gift from the empress, and when his brother confronted him—he killed him!"

"No! It's not true! Nekros is lying to you, Your Majesty—!" Theodosius yelled but was silenced by a guard slapping him across the face with such force that his ears rang.

Even though he couldn't see him, the sound of Prince Andronikos' smug laughter could be heard in the shadows to Theodosius' left. This meant that Andronikos would not only not be helping him, but the prince also seemed to be gleefully enjoying watching Theodosius suffer.

"Do not speak to the emperor unless spoken to!" the guard snarled, kicking Theodosius in the stomach for good measure.

"This is a gorgeous bible," Emperor Michael said to Empress Maria.

"Do you think so?" Empress Maria beamed, pleased. "I got it from Mount Athos. It was made by the monks there in the eleventh century."

"Amazing! You've outdone yourself again, Maria." The emperor then turned to Nekros. "Thank you, brother, for returning this. I am indebted to you."

"It was my pleasure." Nekros bowed deeply. "You know I would do anything to protect the sanctity of the empire."

"Nekros killed my brother. He slit his throat," Theodosius trembled as he spoke with his face to the floor, but he had to speak. They had to know the truth.

"Shut up!" the guard snapped, kicking him like a dog.

Theodosius felt like he had turned into a dog. No one in the room was looking at him like he was human. They assumed his guilt with absolutely no proof just because of a nobleman's word against his own. He tried to lift his head to look around to see if his mother was present, but the guards wouldn't let him look.

"Do we have any witnesses of the incident?" Empress Maria asked. It was the first reasonable request of the night, but Theodosius had little hope that anyone with high enough rank would defend him, especially now that the despot had dehumanized him to such a degree.

"I was there, Your Majesty. I saw what happened." Everyone turned to see Lady Justine standing timidly behind Nekros.

A wave of relief washed over Theodosius. Justine had been there! She had seen the whole crime as he had. She was a noblewoman and could help clear his name. "Lady Justine, thank God. Tell them what really happened. Tell them what Nekros did to Leonides."

Justine looked down at him with watery eyes and a pale face. "I saw... I saw Theodosius Kardia kill his own brother over the golden bible."

"*No!*" Theodosius' heart dropped into his stomach. "Don't lie! Justine, you know the truth! Please!"

Justine was not done slandering him. "Lord Nekros tried to stop him, but it was too late. Look at Theodosius—his hands are covered in poor Leonides' blood."

After she was finished speaking, Justine looked at her feet almost ashamedly, while Nekros had a smug smile stretched across his face. Nekros had bribed her, Theodosius realized. He'd bought her silence and her complicity.

"My hands are only covered in blood because I was trying to save him! Nekros is the one who killed Leonides and stole your bible, I swear to you!" Theodosius yelled, outraged, but it was clear that no one believed him. Without another noble person around to defend him, he would be found guilty.

"Guards, take Mister Kardia to the holding cells to await sentencing for his horrific crimes," Emperor Michael ordered, his mind made up.

"No! No! I'm innocent! It was *Nekros!* Nekros killed Leonides!" It took two guards to get Theodosius to his feet and begin dragging him away. Still unseen, Prince Andronikos' laughter seemed to grow louder from the shadows.

- - -

No one believed Theodosius. Even his own mother, Eudokia, was refusing to see him. Most of his friends, once they had heard about Justine's testimony, had decided that he was guilty too. His former master, Prince Andronikos, seemed happy at Theodosius's demise, regardless of whether or not he was guilty.

Now, Theodosius sat alone in his cell, curled up in a ball on the hard stone floor, waiting for sentencing. It seemed likely that the emperor would sentence him to death, and then the truth of what had really happened to Leonides would die with him. At least Theodosius might get to see Leonides again in the next life. Surely Christ and the Saints would know the truth of what had happened and would send him to Heaven to be reunited with his brother.

A loud clanging, and the sound of men shouting interrupted Theodosius from his depressive thoughts. He sat up and looked around, but didn't see much in the dark. Suddenly, a torch light appeared as a man in a dark cloak came toward the cell door.

"Yianni? What are you doing here?" Theodosius asked in disbelief when the man's face came into view. Yianni had a small cut on his upper cheek but otherwise looked like his regular smiling self.

"I'm here to spring you!" Yianni said as he opened the cell door and unlocked the chains on Theodosius' wrists and ankles. "Let's go!"

The young men ran together down the tunnels and out the side of the palace walls. The bells began to ring, signaling that the nobles knew of their escape attempt.

"Stop them!" a guard yelled as he raced after them.

"We have to keep going!" Yianni shouted, grabbing Theodosius' wrist and pulling him along the cobblestone streets. It was late at night, so the streets were mostly empty, but there were still enough people around to point and look at them as they passed by.

"Where are we going?" Theodosius asked as he and Yianni continued to race down the streets toward the harbor.

"Halt! Stop Kardia!" One of the palace guards was nearly upon them. Theodosius realized, with a horrified feeling in his stomach, that they were likely to be captured if they didn't find safety soon.

"Quick! In here!" Yianni pushed him into the side door of a building.

The smell of incense and sound of Orthodox Christian chant filled Theodosius' senses. The most beautiful mosaic iconography covered the walls and ceilings. They were in an Orthodox Church, and it appeared to be in the middle of a late-night Compline Service. This meant no guards or soldiers would be allowed inside until it was over.

"This way," Yianni whispered, pulling Theodosius behind one of the large pillars. "We'll hide here for a bit and then run to the ship from there."

"What ship?" Theodosius asked, confused.

"A ship to get us out of here, of course. I've only been planning it for ages." Yianni smiled, pleased with himself.

"You've been planning to escape from Constantinople for *ages?*" Theodosius asked, surprised.

"Well, maybe not ages, but you know things have been corrupt with the royal family for a while now. It seems they only care about themselves, and I knew it was only a matter of time before they started framing us lower class gents for their own crimes. Anyways, I was thinking of escaping just me, but I couldn't leave you behind." Yianni shrugged as if it was all no big deal, and as if what he was saying was not at all treasonous.

"Why couldn't you leave me behind?" Theodosius asked, trying not to sound ungrateful. "You'd be safer if you had."

Yianni shook his head. "Well, I might have been safer, but we're best friends, you and me. I couldn't leave you behind when you needed me most. That's what friends are for, right?"

"Right." Theodosius grinned. "So, you believe I'm innocent then? You know I didn't kill Leonides."

"I know you loved Leonides very much, and you'd never have hurt him." Yianni put a comforting hand on his shoulder and Theodosius thought he might cry.

"Thank you, Yianni. You are a true friend." He choked on his words as he wrapped his arms around Yianni's neck in a tight hug.

"There's no need to get all sappy," Yianni said, patting him on the back.

After an hour or so had passed, the boys slipped back out into the night. The guards were long gone now, and the hour was so late that almost all were sleeping. As quietly as they could, they made their way down to the harbor and aboard the first ship they could find. It was a merchant ship that belonged to Creten merchants on their way to trade goods in Athens.

Theodosius took one last look at the place he had always called home. Now, in the darkness, it looked no different than any other port city in the world.

Chapter Thirteen

Honor Bound

Present Day...

Elara let the story Theodosius was telling her wash over her until she was consumed by it. All the hostility toward Lady Justine back in Athens made sense now. She had to admit she was impressed by Theodosius and Yianni's restraint when seeing Justine again. If Justine had done to Elara what she had done to Theodosius, Elara might not have been so kind.

The animosity toward Lord Nekros also made sense, assuming it was all true as Theodosius had told it. Elara had no reason to think that Theodosius was lying, but she found it difficult to believe that her family never knew that their friend, Nekros, was a thief and a killer.

"That's the whole story." Theodosius lounged in his chair, much more confident and mature than he had seemed in his story. The Theodosius of present day was all grown up, no longer the naive boy who watched his brother die in his arms. He was smarter now, and more guarded.

"I'm so sorry about your brother," Elara said softly. "May his memory be eternal."

"You said that before." Theodosius looked at her pointedly, as if waiting for her to say something more, to give her opinion on the matter a little more decidedly.

"I can't even imagine what you went through, losing him like that, and then being blamed for it…it's so awful." She stretched her hand across the small table to touch his arm.

"Sometimes…" He took a shaky breath. "Sometimes, I think Leonides is the lucky one, and I wish it had been my throat that had been ripped open so that he could be here mourning me instead."

Elara blinked back tears and said nothing. What could be said to that? Instead, she stood and pulled him to his feet. She wrapped her arms around his waist and buried her face in his chest. He smelled like the ocean.

They stood there hugging for a few more moments before Theodosius gently disentangled himself from her embrace. He kept his hands on her shoulders and looked into her eyes with a serious expression.

"Elara, do you understand now why I have to confront Nekros when we get to Constantinople?"

She nodded. "Yes, of course…but you're not going to kill him, are you? We could explain what happened and get you a pardon so that you won't need to fight Nekros."

Theodosius grimaced and shook his head. "They're not going to pardon me. To pardon me would incriminate Nekros, and they can't have that. Nobility always protects their own."

"I'm nobility—I'll protect you!" Elara offered without thinking. "I can speak on your behalf and then…" She trailed off as she realized she couldn't do what she was offering. To speak against Lord Nekros, a despot, would be social suicide. To speak on behalf of a corsair would render her reputation permanently irreparable.

"There's no need for that. I think we both know it would never work. Thank you for the offer anyways." Theodosius kissed her cheek, then the side of her mouth, then her lips again.

Elara moaned into the kiss, wishing there was more she could do for him without destroying herself and her family name in the process.

"We have a big day coming up, so you should probably get some sleep." He led her to the doorway, opening the door for her. "Goodnight, Elara."

It was a clear dismissal. Elara was glad he hadn't tried anything more than kissing but she hadn't expected him to send her away so soon. Perhaps he was just tired.

She stepped through the doorway, but turned to look back into his eyes as she said, "You're not going to kill Nekros, are you? You know that won't make things any better."

"Can't you ever just say goodnight?" he kidded her with a teasing look. When she didn't reply, he added, "I won't kill him. I just want to confront him is all. Perhaps get him to make a retraction about me—so that I can be vindicated, but he won't have to incriminate himself."

"There's an idea." Elara smiled, satisfied with his answer.

- - -

Celina awoke to the sound of the wood panels creaking under the pressure of the waves. The sky was still dark, so the only light came from the candles on the desk, one by the chair and one by the bed. She turned on her side to see Rhea still soundly asleep, but Elara wasn't anywhere to be found. Sitting up, Celina looked around the room to see where her friend might have gone. The big chair was empty, and the floorboards were clear, with no sign that anyone had been sleeping there.

That's when the door suddenly creaked open, causing Celina to jump. It was Elara, still in her night clothes, with her hair pulled back in a messy fishtail braid.

"Sorry, did I wake you?" Elara whispered as she tiptoed into the room and moved to sit on the side of the bed next to Celina.

"No, I heard a noise," Celina explained as she lay back down. "Where did you go?"

"I had to pee," said Elara as she pulled the covers over herself and lay down too.

"Oh, all right. Goodnight, dear." Celina closed her eyes and promptly fell back asleep before she could hear if Elara replied or not.

Hours passed, but it felt like mere seconds as Celina was once again jolted awake by the sound of crashing waves on the hull. This time, however, the sound was joined by the commotion of people walking and talking on the deck, along with the sunlight now fully streaming through the window.

Rhea and Elara were still asleep on either side of her, so Celina had to move carefully to get out of the small bed without waking either of them. Once her feet touched the floor at the end of the bed, she got up and began to quickly dress to get ready for the day. After she dressed and pulled her hair part-up, part-down, she made her way to the deck to see if Tina or anyone had prepared anything to eat.

The warm sunshine and sea air greeted Celina as she moved about the deck. Above her, Gregory was shouting about a bird in the crow's nest, and some of the other crew members were laughing about something as they toiled along with their morning tasks.

"Celina! Good morning!" Tina shouted and waved from where she was standing at the side of the ship. There was a man standing with her that Celina assumed was her brother, Jimmy, from how similarly they looked from their hair to their dark complexions to their long noses.

"Good morning, Tina dear. You look well today," Celina greeted her with a smile.

"Thank you. I feel much better today than yesterday. How'd you sleep?" Tina asked with her hands on her hips and her shoulders back, conveying a confident pose.

Unlike Celina, who wore a simple work-dress, Tina was dressed like the men with tall dark boots over cream-colored trousers and a short sailor's jacket.

"I slept well, thanks. I hate to ask, but is there anything to eat? I'm absolutely famished." Celina didn't want to be presumptuous about who the main cook was on the ship, but seeing as Tina was the only other woman there, she had to ask.

Tina smiled knowingly before turning to the man next to her. "Did you make us anything good this morning, Jimmy?"

Jimmy nodded. "There's eggs, bread, and some fruit in the kitchen if you want some."

"Thank you very much," Celina beamed at them before making her way to the ladder that led below deck where the kitchen and food storerooms would be. She walked confidently toward her destination, but when she made it to the kitchen door, she paused as she heard argumentative voices inside.

"It's not my fault you can't keep it in your trousers!" Yianni was saying to someone out of view.

"For the last time, you crass dick—I didn't bed Elara," Theodosius replied hotly. "I don't have any intention of bedding her and impeding on her honor like that. I'm not that stupid."

"Well, you were stupid enough to kiss her, so forgive me for assuming," Yianni said grumpily. Celina nearly gasped but quickly put her hand over her own mouth just in time.

"Grow up! I didn't realize kissing was a crime!" Theodosius snapped.

"It is when it's distracting you from your mission. What's the point of kissing her, and getting all distracted by her, if you're not even going to bed her, and you're not planning on seeing her after the mission is complete? What is the point of it?" Yianni continued.

Celina stood frozen just outside the door with her hand still firmly clamped over her mouth. She couldn't believe what she was hearing.

"I'm tired of having the same argument with you over and over. I thought we settled all this last night." Theodosius moved something as he spoke, making a clanging sound. "Dammit! I dropped my breakfast."

"Answer my question, Theodosius," Yianni pressed in a commanding voice. Celina had never heard a first mate talk to their captain like that before.

There was a moment of silence before Theodosius spoke softly, "Forgive me, Yianni, for wanting a small moment of happiness before I face my brother's killer. I like her. Is that so wrong?"

Yianni sighed a bit dramatically, in Celina's opinion, "Just make sure you know what you're doing. I still think the countess could be working for Nekros."

"She's not. Elara is a good person."

"Unlike us corsairs, I suppose. Our morality is so small, it could get lost in a clam shell," Yianni said, sounding bitter.

"Very funny. I think you missed your calling as a court jester. It's never too late to switch career paths, you know," Theodosius quipped.

"Don't tempt me, Captain. You know I'm great with crowds."

The sound of food and dishes being scooped up brought Celina back to the moment at hand. Her stomach rumbled quietly, and she knew she couldn't stay here for too long.

"Oh, good morning," Celina said innocently as she made her way into the kitchen. She did her best to make it appear as if she'd just arrived and heard nothing.

"*Kalimera*, Lady Oberon," Theodosius greeted her with his signature cheeky grin. "Here for some breakfast? Jimmy made eggs and some biscuits."

"There's also apples over here if you want some fruit," Yianni said as he tore open a sack of apples that had been leaning against the wall.

"Wonderful! I'm starving." Celina picked up a bowl and scooped some eggs into it, along with a biscuit and an apple for good measure. Theodosius and Yianna said nothing more but watched her get her food silently. Her heart thumped nervously as she worried the men might suspect that she had been eavesdropping on them. Keeping her eyes on her bowl, she started back toward the door to leave.

"Is Elara awake?" Theodosius asked just as Celina's hand grasped the latch on the door.

Celina took a breath to steady herself before she turned to look at Theodosius. "The countess was still asleep when I got up."

"Ah, all right." Theodosius leaned on the far wall with his arms crossed casually. "Will you tell her to come find me when she gets up? I want to go over the plan for Constantinople."

"Of course." She forced a smile, but she wasn't sure it was convincing. With a respectful nod, she slipped out the door and headed back up to the above deck.

271

As she made her way back to the captain quarters, Celina shoveled some eggs into her mouth and finished the biscuit before discarding the bowl on a nearby barrel. The eggs were mushy in her mouth, and the biscuit was flavorless, but she was so hungry and so upset that she didn't care.

Celina burst through the door to the captain's quarters to find Rhea and Elara getting ready for the day. Rhea was further along than Elara, indicating that she had gotten up first.

"Good morning," Rhea greeted her. "Where have you been?"

"You kissed him," Celina accused Elara, ignoring Rhea all together.

"W-what?" Elara laughed awkwardly.

"Don't deny it. I overheard Theodosius and Yianni talking. I know you kissed him." Celina felt the words tumbling out of her mouth with a weighty emotion, but she wasn't exactly sure what that emotion was. Whether she was more upset that Elara had kept this secret from her, or that Elara had stupidly kissed a pirate, which threatened to ruin the very reputation that they were working so hard to help restore, Celina wasn't sure, but she suspected it was a combination of both.

"Wait, you kissed Yianni?" Rhea asked with a furrowed brow.

"No, she kissed Theodosius." Celina glowered down at Elara who was sitting in a crumpled heap at the end of the bed. "Do you deny it?"

"I do not deny it." Elara wrung her hands. "But it's not what you think!"

"God, how could you be so foolish! He's a pirate!"

"He actually prefers to be called a corsair—"

"I don't care! It was an idiotic thing for you to do! You're lucky he didn't try to take your honor right then and there!" Celina scolded her harshly, causing Elara to flinch as if she'd been slapped.

"Celina! That's a terrible thing to say!" Rhea said, coming to Elara's defense.

"It's the truth! She needs to be smarter about these things!" Celina snapped back. "Why are we bothering to help fix your reputation if you're just going to throw it away for *him*, anyway?"

"Theodosius didn't take my honor, but even if he wanted to, he couldn't..." Elara choked on a sob, a few tears fell from her eyes, and she covered her face. "I already gave it to Andronikos."

A silence settled over the girls as Elara's words flowed over them. All the shame Elara had been feeling suddenly made a lot more sense to Celina. Elara had slept with Prince Andronikos out of wedlock, and the royal court probably knew it, or at least suspected it. None of that would have mattered if she had married him, but she had called it off.

"Oh, Elara dear," Celina said softly as her friend continued to weep. She sat on the bed and wrapped Elara up in her arms.

I wish you cared more about being kind than you do about being right. Elara's words from a few weeks ago continued to haunt Celina.

If only she had learned them, but once again, Celina had been caught up in righteousness, and not in kindness or compassion for her friend.

"I'm sorry, dear," Celina whispered as Rhea sat on Elara's other side and joined their hug.

- - -

"There you are," Theodosius said as he slipped beneath the stairwell where Elara was hiding.

"*Yasou.*" She tried to echo his sunny demeanor the best she could, but found it was difficult to muster, given her mood.

"Didn't Lady Oberon tell you I was looking for you?" He stood next to her against the wall, so they were shoulder to shoulder. Theodosius was dressed in a long dark jacket with matching boots with his hair swept handsomely to the left side of his face.

"Must have slipped her mind," Elara said dryly.

"Uh-oh, are you two in a fight?" he asked with a raised eyebrow.

"No, Celina is just..." she laughed humorlessly. "Celina is like Yianni. She's a bit overprotective of me, just like Yianni is overprotective of you."

"Ah," Theodosius smiled knowingly. "Yes, that makes sense."

"So, what did you need to talk to me about?" Elara asked, trying not to think about how close their faces were to each other.

"We'll be in Constantinople later tonight." He traced a finger gently across her jaw, and Elara felt her heartbeat pick up. "I thought you might want to go over the plan for when we get there."

She blinked. "Truthfully, I don't have a plan. Do you?"

274

"No plan? Well, we should make one. Where in the city does Nekros live?" Theodosius asked softly, never taking his eyes off her face, her lips.

"Nekros lives in a mansion just a few blocks north of the Hagia Sophia Cathedral." Elara let her hand drift softly over his collar as she spoke. She was tempted to place her hand over the spot on his neck where she might be able to feel his pulse and see if his heart was racing as fast as hers was. She resisted the urge.

"Do you think he'll be home?" he asked.

"I'm not sure, but he'll most likely be somewhere in the city. I can request an audience with his attendant, and we'll go from there." She shrugged, feeling more confident now that she had spoken the plan aloud.

Nekros had once told her that she could visit him any time she was in the city. Elara just hoped he would give her necklace back and wouldn't be too angry to be face-to-face with Theodosius Kardia again.

"That plan sounds like a good one to me." Theodosius cupped her face in his warm hands and pressed his lips to hers. She kissed him back without caring what Celina or anyone else thought. Just a few more hours, one more adventure, and then they might never kiss again. She was determined to enjoy it until then.

"Captain? You out here?" Yianni's voice interrupted them from above, most likely standing by the helm of the ship. His voice was like a blade slicing Elara and Theodosius apart from one another.

"*Dammit,*" Theodosius muttered under his breath before calling out, "I'm here. What is it?"

"You're gonna wanna see this!" Yianni shouted back in a nervous tone. Elara couldn't tell if the nervousness was excitement or fear. Either way, it sounded important enough to drag Theodosius away from her for the time being.

Theodosius sighed and pinched the bridge of his nose. "I'll be right there!"

"Never a dull moment around here," Elara teased him.

He eyed her for a moment, and then said, "You're coming with me, aren't you?"

She shook her head. "I don't think Yianni would like that. It would probably be better if you went alone but call for me if you need me."

"All right, I'll see you later then." Theodosius gave her one last peck on the corner of her mouth before slipping out and going up the steps to the helm.

After he was gone, Elara leaned back on the wall to wait a few minutes. She wanted to wait a while before venturing out to make sure people wouldn't see her and Theodosius too close together and suspect they had been locking lips. It was mostly quiet now that she was alone. There was the gentle sound of the water lapping on the ship planks and muffled voices above her, loud enough to hear, but too quiet to make out what they were saying. She hoped whatever Yianni was telling

Theodosius about wouldn't be too dangerous. Whatever it was, she suspected she'd find out soon enough.

"I've looked everywhere for her. It's like she disappeared." It was Rhea's voice, speaking just out of sight. Elara stayed still and quiet, not wanting to see her friends right now. She was still upset with Celina, and some alone time felt warranted.

"Don't say that," said Celina, also out of sight. "If Elara's disappeared, that could mean she's gone overboard or something else equally horrible."

"She's probably avoiding you because you were mean to her this morning," Rhea pointed out coolly.

Elara smiled despite herself. Now that the girls were getting along, Elara was glad Celina had Rhea to give her the hard truths she was so used to dishing out.

"I said I was sorry!" Celina grumbled in exasperation.

Her friends must have walked off after that because there was only silence now. Elara closed her eyes and leaned her head back on the wood. Soon they would be in Constantinople, and this stressful adventure would finally be over.

- - -

The sea wind kept sweeping Celina's hair in her face so furiously, it was starting to feel intentional. Everyone seemed to be mad at her today, so the wind might as well be too.

Leaning back against the port-side railing, Celina huffed an exasperated sigh. It was fine if Elara was avoiding her, she didn't care. She just wished she knew if her friend was safe or not.

"I'm sure Elara will turn up soon enough," Rhea said soothingly as she joined Celina by the port side railing.

Celina was beginning to see that Rhea and Elara were very much alike. Both of them were eternally optimistic at times, and both refused to agree with Celina on just about anything.

"Hmm, yes, I suppose." Celina looked out at the crew bustling about their day without so much as a pause to look in their direction.

Looking up, she saw Theodosius in what appeared to be a heated conversation with Yianni. The men were taking turns pointing at a large piece of paper, most likely a map, and using the sextant on it, which Theodosius had acquired for his first mate at the Vatican.

"What do you suppose those two are going on about?" Celina asked, pointing to Theodosius and Yianni.

"Looks like they're arguing over a map. Do you think we're lost or something?" Rhea had an equally confused look on her face.

"Only one way to find out." Celina pushed herself off the railing and slipped her arm through Rhea's. "Let's go ask."

Together, the two of them glided across the deck, and up the staircase, to the helm of the ship.

"I can't believe you pulled me away from—from what I was doing, for *this*," Theodosius was saying to Yianni as the girls approached.

His tone was harsh, but not loud; his brow was furrowed but his face was not red. This suggested to Celina that the captain was frustrated, but not too exorbitantly angry, so he was safe to talk to.

Yianni appeared far more relaxed. "I think navigation is an important part of a captain's job. Who's gonna make sure we're really staying on course if not you?"

"We have a navigator! Am I expected to do everything?" Theodosius looked like he might throttle his first mate. Before anyone could throw a punch, Rhea announced her and Celina's presence.

"Excuse me, Captain Kardia? Lady Celina and I were wondering if we might have a word with you?"

"Of course, Miss Alkan. What can I do for you two?" Theodosius' face transformed into a pleasant smile as he greeted them. It looked disingenuous to Celina.

"We wanted to know when we would be arriving in Constantinople. We're still on course, aren't we, Captain?" Celina asked innocently.

Theodosius narrowed his eyes at her for a moment but recomposed himself quickly. "Yes, we're still on course, Lady Oberon. We should be in Constantinople by this evening."

"Lovely to hear." She smiled back at him with equally passive aggressive energy.

"Have either of you seen Elara recently?" Rhea asked.

Yianni shook his head, but Theodosius remained silent and glanced past them at the staircase which the girls had just ascended.

"Captain Kardia?" Rhea regained his attention.

"Sorry, I haven't seen her yet today," Theodosius said. "Now, if you two will excuse us, Yianni and I have some important navigation things to attend to."

"Oh, of course," Celina said as she and Rhea nodded their heads respectfully. Theodosius and Yianni followed suit. The girls turned to descend back down the staircase.

"He's lying," Celina whispered to Rhea when they made it to the bottom of the stairs.

"About what?"

"About Elara. He's *definitely* seen her." Celina pulled Rhea toward the mast so that they were farther out of earshot. "Kardia is up to something. I don't know exactly what, but I'm going to figure it out."

- - -

The first thing Elara saw, as her beloved Constantinople came into view, was the shimmering marble and glittering gilding of the Hagia Sophia Cathedral walls. Even from a distance, it was extravagant. The plain stone buildings that surrounded it were dwarfed in comparison. She couldn't believe she was this close to her old home. A nervous knot of excitement and fear coiled in her stomach.

"I've been looking all over for you!" It was Rhea, unaccompanied by Celina for once. "Where have you been?"

"Sorry, I just needed some space to breathe." Elara leaned on the starboard railing as she looked out at the cityscape of Constantinople.

280

"It's a beautiful city," Rhea said, not pressing the issue further.

"Yes, it is." Elara turned and smiled at her friend. "I'm really glad you came on this journey with me, Rhea. I hope Celina hasn't been giving you too much grief."

"It's been my great honor helping you." Rhea beamed. "You'd be proud of Celina and me. We've made good progress, and I think we've become real friends."

"That's wonderful news." Elara grinned back. Rhea's mood was infectious.

Perhaps she should talk to Celina and make things right with her. Elara knew Celina hadn't meant to upset her; she was just looking out for her. Before Elara could ask Rhea where Celina was, a shout sounded above them.

"LAND HO!" Gregory called down from the crow's nest. They were coming into port, so any discussions would have to wait.

"Ready for the last leg of our adventure, Countess?" Theodosius said as he walked down from the helm toward her.

The captain was a vision of handsomeness, and Elara found herself wishing this wasn't the end of their journey. Sailing around from place to place with these pirates had brought her more contentment than she had ever thought possible, but she needed to get her necklace back and get home as soon as possible. As much fun as she was having, she couldn't forget the importance of her mission. She'd come this far to retrieve her yiayia's necklace and make things right, she couldn't back down now, not when she was so close to achieving her goal.

"You're going to miss me when this is all over, Captain," Elara teased him, trying her best to hide her own mixed emotions.

Theodosius smiled his signature grin, but there was a hint of shyness and something else shimmering behind his eyes. "Yes, I most certainly will."

Once the ship docked, only four of them: Elara, Theodosius, Rhea, and Celina, went to disembark. Tina, Yianni, and the others stayed behind to watch the ship and get everything ready in case they needed to make a quick getaway.

"It was so lovely meeting you and spending time with you, Tina," Elara said, pulling Tina in for a fierce hug.

"You're not coming back?" Tina asked, perplexed.

"Once I get my necklace, the girls and I are headed back home to Catalonia," Elara explained, feeling a lump in her throat.

"I'm sure we could give you a ride back to Catalonia." Tina turned to Theodosius, who was waiting patiently by the gangplank. "Right, Captain?"

"We have business elsewhere, unfortunately," Theodosius said shortly.

"It's fine. We have friends in Constantinople who can give us a ride home," Elara assured Tina.

Tina frowned unhappily, but didn't argue the subject further. Instead, she pulled Elara in for another hug and then hugged Rhea and Celina as well.

"Uh, Countess Elara?" It was Yianni. He had an apologetic look on his face.

"Yes, Yianni?" Elara said stiffly. She hadn't forgotten the way he had spoken about her to Theodosius the night before.

"Good luck with everything. Hope this necklace thing works out for you." He scratched the back of his head and cast his eyes downward. It wasn't an apology, but it was a kind remark, nonetheless.

"Thank you." Elara looked around at the faces of the other pirates she had come to know. Gregory waved to her fondly from the crow's nest. Matthew and Jimmy stood in the back, smiling softly. "Goodbye, everyone."

Without another word, the four of them descended the gangplank and made their way onto the shoreline of Constantinople.

Chapter Fourteen

Constantinople

The group quickly and quietly made their way into the city. They had dressed themselves in unassuming dark cloaks and basic traveler garb. From the outside, they would blend in perfectly with the lower-class locals. The four of them walked in a straight line with Theodosius leading the way, followed by Elara, with Celina and Rhea bringing up the rear.

The familiar smell of fresh spices and the hum of the vibrant bazaar almost made Elara teary eyed with nostalgia. It had only been a few months since she was last here, but it felt like a lifetime. Now, seeing the local shop owners, the meats and fresh cheeses, the jewelry, and newly spun clothes, she had never felt more at home.

"Are you feeling well, Elara dear?" Celina asked from behind her as they made their way through the narrow streets.

Elara wiped a tear out of the corner of her eye, stopping it from slipping down her cheek. "I was worried that it would be hard being here again after…well, I'm happy to be home."

Celina squeezed her shoulder comfortingly. They didn't exchange much more than that, but things were already feeling better between them. Celina had said she was sorry, and Elara had forgiven her. There wasn't much more to say than that.

They walked for a couple more blocks before Theodosius stopped them with a raised hand. They were entering the wealthier part of town that led to the mansions where the nobles lived, the Hagia Sophia Cathedral, and the palace where the emperor and royal family resided. Elara had only been here for church, and in the palace, where she used to live as a lady-in-waiting.

"So, which one of these does Nekros live in?" Theodosius asked her.

"Uh, that one." Elara pointed to a large house with clay roof tiles and walls made of brick and stone. It looked like it was the biggest house on the square with the biggest plot of land attached to it.

"Are you certain it's that one?" he pressed, clearly not wanting to risk approaching the wrong house.

"I think it's that one. Most of the mansions look alike though," she shrugged, not seeing the issue. If they went to the wrong house, it wouldn't be the end of the world.

Theodosius sighed, anxiously wringing his hands. "I wish we could be certain…"

"Hey." Elara grabbed his hands to stop him from wringing them and forced him to look at her. "It's going to be fine. We'll go knock on the door, and you can stand back, so if it's the wrong house, it won't be a problem, all right?"

"All right." He relaxed slightly as he always did under her touch.

She tried not to feel too pleased that her touch had that effect on him. Theodosius' dark eyes met hers, and a moment of connection and understanding passed between them.

"I can knock first," Rhea offered, interrupting their moment.

"Yes, thank you, Rhea." Elara dropped her hands and turned to look at her friends.

Rhea had a shy, bashful look on her face, like she'd seen something she shouldn't have. Celina had a more worried look, her arms folded over her chest and her eyes slanted slightly.

"For Christ's sake!" Elara grumbled as she barreled past them toward the house she hoped was Nekros'. She was getting really tired of people judging her, and it was especially disheartening when those people were her friends.

"Wait for us!" Celina called as she and Rhea raced to catch up.

Not slowing her pace in the slightest, Elara marched down the long, wide corridor of houses, finally stopping in front of what she suspected was Nekros' property. She walked straight up to the large wooden doors of the mansion and loudly knocked three times.

Even from the outside, she could tell that this mansion was larger and more majestic than Despotess Valerie's house. Despot Nekros Palaiologos was the highest ranked noble in the land, after the emperor and empress. If this was his house, it wouldn't be his only one. Most nobles had a city house and a bigger summer home in the countryside. It was too late into the fall season for Nekros to be at his summer home, so he had to be here.

"Maybe no one is in?" Rhea said with a shrug after a few moments of no movement.

Elara glanced back at her friends and noted Theodosius' absence. He was most likely hiding somewhere out of sight. Turning back to the door, she knocked again, more loudly this time, her fist turning pink from the impact on the wooden frame.

Nothing.

"I guess we could try a different house or come back later—" Just as Elara was finishing her thoughts out loud, the door creaked open slightly.

"Who's there?" A woman's voice asked from the thin opening.

"*Yasas*, my name is Lady Elara Iliakos. I'm here to see Lord Nekros Palaiologos. Is the despot at home?" Elara peered in, trying to get a good look at the woman, but she was hard to see in the dimly lit doorway. The only thing that could be clearly seen was the woman's face, which had a thin nose, blue eyes, and pale complexion.

"He's out," the woman said shortly.

"I see." Elara tried to hide her disappointment. "Do you know when he'll be back?"

"The despot should be back later tonight. He's hosting the emperor's ball, after all." The woman's words immediately perked Elara up immediately.

"The emperor's ball is tonight?" Elara asked excitedly. The emperor's ball had been her favorite social event of the year back when she lived in Constantinople.

"Yes, but it's for nobility only," clarified the woman sternly, clearly worried that Elara and her friends might try to show up uninvited.

"But we are nobles!" Celina interjected from over Elara's shoulder, but the woman was already closing the door in their faces. "Well, that was awfully rude."

"We must go to the ball! Nekros will definitely be there, and I bet his wife, or one of his other female acquaintances, will be wearing my necklace!" Elara exclaimed as she squeezed her friends' arms.

"I don't think we're dressed properly for a ball," Rhea pointed out the obvious as they made their way back toward the road.

"So, we'll get ourselves cleaned up and wear new attire then!" replied Elara unworriedly. "I bet Empress Maria will be there too!"

"What if the empress' and emperor's son, Prince Andronikos, is there?" Celina questioned pointedly.

Elara felt her heart drop into her stomach. She hadn't considered that her ex-fiancé might be at the emperor's ball, despite it being in his father's honor.

"I'll—I'll just avoid him if I can," she reasoned.

"Avoid who?" Theodosius asked, reappearing from wherever he had been hiding.

"Nekros is hosting the emperor's ball tonight," Elara ignored his question entirely. "It's for nobles and royals only, but if we all dress up nicely, we should have no problem getting inside."

Theodosius smiled his signature grin, "And will you be introducing me as your cousin again, like you did in Thessaloniki?"

Elara felt heat rising to her cheeks as she suddenly remembered seeing the pirate's naked form up close. The circumstances of that moment hadn't been ideal, but she still thought of it from time to time.

"Perhaps you could accompany me as my special guest?" Elara felt suddenly self-conscious as the offer hung in the air between them. She could almost feel Celina's eyes burning a judgmental hole in her skin. It was unheard of for a noblewoman to ask a man into a courtship-like situation, especially a man of less than noble status.

"Andronikos is going to *hate* that," Theodosius stated, grinning wider than ever. "I'm in."

- - -

The group made their way to a local dress shop that Elara had been to multiple times before with the other ladies-in-waiting during her time serving Empress Maria. They had picked up fabrics from the local dressmaker and worked with him to make their gowns for every occasion.

"Simon? Are you in?" Elara called as they entered the shop. The stone walls were almost completely covered in different fabrics.

The dressmaker, Simon Metakis, stepped out from the back. "Elara mou? Is that you?"

"Surprise! How are you?" Elara greeted him with the traditional kiss on each cheek.

Simon was a short, older man with crinkled eyes and a round belly. "I'm so pleased to see you. When did you get back into town?"

"Just an hour or two ago." Elara smiled as she eyed the rows and rows of fabrics. "My friends and I need your help."

Simon didn't ask any questions or show any suspicions. After briefly meeting Celina, Rhea, and Theodosius, the dressmaker immediately got to work taking their measurements for the garments.

"With the emperor's ball being in just a few hours, I won't have time to make you anything from scratch, but I have some pre-made things in the back I can stitch up to fit you," Simon offered the group.

"Really? That would be wonderful. Thank you!" Elara sighed in relief. Things were looking up after all.

Simon brought out three gorgeous gowns for the girls and one dark burgundy tunic with black flecks on the sleeves and shoulder for Theodosius. The dressmaker handed the red-and-gold gown to Elara, the ocean-blue with accents of silver gown to Celina, and the lilac gown with olive-green around the sleeves and hem to Rhea.

There wasn't much time to spare, so the dressmaker had three helpers come out from the back to assist. They were older women, all dressed in black with cream-colored smocks.

Elara was fitted by Simon himself, and she was pleased to find that the dress was almost a perfect fit. There would only need to be a bit of stitching at the waist, and it would be good to go.

"Very lucky this fit so well," Elara beamed at Simon as he went to work stitching the waistline.

"Luck didn't have much to do with it." Simon kept his eyes on her hem, but his voice was fond. "I made this dress for you over a year ago. It was supposed to be an engagement present."

Oh.

Elara's stomach churned and embarrassment heated her cheeks. "You heard about what happened?"

"Yes, the empress told me about it at her last fitting at the palace."

"And?" Elara pressed, wishing to know the old man's opinion.

Simon looked up from his work. "And I'm proud of you for making such a hard, but ultimately good, decision. It can't have been easy, and a lesser woman wouldn't have done it."

She blinked, surprised. "Thank you for saying that."

"You're welcome." He focused again on her dress. "So, who's the handsome fella you came in with?"

"He's a good friend," Elara laughed softly, not wanting to give away too many details about Theodosius' identity.

"Just a friend?" Simon pressed, teasingly. To this, she smiled shyly but said nothing more on the subject.

Once Elara was finished getting fitted, she sat patiently in the front room, waiting for her friends. Since everything was pre-made, and assuming it was close enough to people's sizes, the outfits would be ready in plenty of time for the party.

"What do you think?" Theodosius stepped out of the changing area in his gorgeous burgundy and black tunic.

"You look…" Elara trailed off, unsure of the most appropriate way to finish the sentence. It looked like Simon wouldn't have to make many alterations on his outfit either.

"If I look silly, you can say so," Theodosius laughed, misreading her facial expressions as negative instead of positive.

"No. You look nice," Elara finished, lamely.

"Thanks, Countess," he said in a way that suggested he didn't believe her. "The dressmaker gave me two tunics, so I'm going to try the other one on."

"You *do* look nice, I swear!" she called after him as he slipped back in the changing area.

The second tunic was also burgundy but had gray accents instead of black on the sleeves. It also didn't fit him nearly as well. It hung on him sloppily, and didn't bring out his best features like the other one did.

"The other one is much better, and will take less alterations," Elara said, letting her opinion be firmly known this time.

"Fine, tunic *ena* it is." Theodosius retreated once more behind the changing curtain.

"Elara dear, what do you think of mine?" Celina stepped out in her ocean-blue dress. It was a little short on her, nearly exposing her ankles, but it would have to do given the little time that they had.

"It fits perfectly around your waist and arms," Elara said.

Celina nodded in agreement as she looked down at her attire. "Yes, it's just a bit short, don't you think?"

"Perhaps a little bit, but there's not much you can do about that."

"True enough." Celina retreated behind her changing curtain.

"I have the opposite problem to Celina," Rhea said as she slowly emerged from behind the other curtain. Since she was the shortest of the group, the dress was way too long on Rhea's small frame. It dragged heavily onto the floor as she tried to walk.

"I can cut it for you," Simon assured Rhea. "It won't take long."

True to his word, Simon and his team finished their outfits within an hour or two. They weren't completely perfect, but given the circumstances, they would have to do.

"Thank you, Simon, for your help and for your kindness." Elara handed him a pouch full of coins, which would be more than enough to cover the outfits.

Simon shook his head and handed the coins back to her. "Keep it. I was going to have to throw these outfits out anyway, so you saved me the trouble."

Elara felt a lump in her throat as she leaned down to give the man a hug. "I'll never forget this."

- - -

The city was quiet as all the peasantry and lower class retired for the evening. The only noise and sound of life was coming from Nekros' mansion. There were many candles, torches, and fire pits that seemed to be illuminating the place. The sounds of excited chatter and faint music could be heard from outside.

"Any questions about the plan?" Elara asked her friends.

"I have a question," Celina said. "Will the nobles not recognize Theodosius? He is a famous corsair, and he used to work for them."

"Don't worry. They're too self-absorbed to notice anyone other than themselves and they definitely wouldn't recognize me in this outfit anyway." Theodosius gestured to his new tunic, which was probably much fancier than anything he had ever worn before.

"Hmm, I suppose." Celina narrowed her eyes at him and shrugged, not looking convinced.

Elara knew then that Celina still didn't trust Theodosius, and unlike Rhea, wasn't even willing to give him the benefit of the doubt. It didn't seem fair. If only Celina knew Theodosius like Elara did, then she would see the truth.

"Shall we go in?" Rhea suggested, drawing the group's attention back to the moment at hand. "It's getting late."

Elara was the one to knock again, with her female friends flanking her on both sides, and Theodosius standing behind them. This time, the door swung open, widely welcoming them.

"Hold on! Lady Elara Iliakos? Is that really you?" The small, skinny man at the door yelled excitedly. Elara recognized him by his tufts of blond hair and high-pitched voice, the result of being a eunuch.

"*Yasou*, Panagioti," Elara greeted him, trying to appear warm, but her words came out as stiff and rigid as the nerves in her shoulders. Thankfully, he didn't seem to notice as he ushered the four of them inside.

Panagioti was one of Andronikos' servants. His main job was opening doors and making sure the entrance ways looked presentable to nobility. It was also his job to make sure no undesirables entered the premises, lest the nobility have to deal with people beneath them.

"Who's with you? Is that Lady Celina Oberon?" Panagioti asked, sounding absolutely tickled. "Do you remember me? We met once a few years ago."

"Oh, yes!" Celina beamed, doing a much better job looking at ease than Elara was. "Of course I remember you, Panagioti. You greeted me and my parents at the door of the last emperor's ball."

"Yes, I did! That was me. I'm so pleased you remember. You know, most people don't remember us door-greeters."

"Really? That's a shame. You always do such a good job!" Celina said, buttering him up. It was working.

"Thank you." Panagioti blushed before recomposing himself. "And who's this?"

"I'm Lady Rhea Alkan, lady-in-waiting for Countess Elara." Rhea held out her hand for Panagioti to shake.

"A pleasure to meet you!" Instead of shaking her hand, Panagioti planted a kiss upon it. Now, it was Rhea's turn to blush and look pleased. Elara wondered if any man had ever kissed Rhea's hand before. She suspected not.

Panagioti finally turned to Theodosius. "Your name, my lord?"

"Lord Theodosius Krymenos of Crete. I'm Lady Elara's special guest for the evening." Theodosius was taller, and his voice was much richer and deeper than Panagioti's. It became obvious right away that Panagioti was intimidated by him.

"A special guest?" Panagioti eyed Elara questioningly.

"Yes, Lord Theodosius is a good friend of mine from Crete," Elara said stiffly. "It's still all right to bring guests, is it not? He is noble."

"Yes, it's fine… but you are aware that Prince Andronikos *is* in attendance this evening, right?" Panagioti sounded quieter now, and Elara understood at once that Panagioti wasn't intimidated by Theodosius, but by Andronikos' possible reaction to him.

"Yes, I'm aware. I intend to avoid the prince all evening, if possible," Elara explained, trying to comfort him with her casual tone.

Panagioti laughed, more out of awkwardness than humor. "Good luck with that, my lady."

No further words were exchanged as the group went past the main entrance and into the main hallway.

Many intricate polycandela, metal lighting devices, which held multiple candles, lined the rug-covered stone hallway. There were large mosaics, depicting the life of Christ on the walls between the arched windows. It was gorgeous and completely overwhelming at the same time.

"Relax," Theodosius whispered in her ear from behind as he gently gripped the sides of her shoulders. "You're way too tense for a girl who's just here to get a necklace."

"You're right, of course. I'm just nervous is all." Elara could hear the party from where they stood, and it would only be a few more moments before they were in the ballroom in front of everyone.

"If we see Andronikos, I can punch him for you if you'd like," Theodosius offered with a teasing grin. She knew him well enough by now to know he was only half joking.

"No, thank you, Captain." She shook her head. "I would prefer to avoid violence tonight if we can help it."

"We've got your back too, you know," Celina said as she looped her arm through Elara's. Rhea linked her arm through Celina's on the other side so that they were standing in a row, the perfect image of a united front.

Elara returned their kindness with a smile of her own. She felt fortunate to have friends as supportive as them. "All right, no more wasting time. Let's go."

Together, side by side, in a row, they walked down the hall and entered the ballroom.

The ballroom was huge. Not as big as the one Elara remembered in the palace, but still, quite large. The room had tall cathedral ceilings and large arched windows adorned with stained glass. The walls were painted gold, and torchlight filled the space, bathing it in a warm glow.

In addition to the decor, the room was packed with nobles in their best attire, twirling across the dance floor or conversing politely by the windows. Nekros' staff had set up two diamond-encrusted throne-like chairs at the front of the room for the emperor and empress, but they were empty.

"Shall we dance?" Theodosius asked Elara. It would be easier to find Nekros if they were participating and mingling with the crowd.

"I'd like that." Elara nodded, trying to steady her breathing. It had been a long time since she had last danced in a setting like this. She glanced at Celina and Rhea, both of whom looked apprehensive, but supportive, nonetheless.

Theodosius took Elara's hand and pulled her out to the dance floor. They joined in on a traditional circular-line dance called the kalamatiano. Everyone was holding hands in a circle and doing the steps to the music. Celina and Rhea joined too, farther back in the line.

"Do you know the steps?" Elara whispered to Theodosius.

"Of course, it's the kalamatiano. Everyone in the empire knows that one." He looked over at her curiously. "Wait, Countess, do you not know the kalamatiano dance?"

"It's been a long time!" she quipped as they stumbled along.

"Here. Follow my feet," Theodosius instructed her. "One…two, three, four…five, six, seven…eight, nine, ten…eleven, twelve. And repeat—you got it!"

Elara didn't feel like she got it, but she was getting by. The dance felt like it went on longer than necessary, but the fun was infectious. As they glided across the floor, Theodosius wore what appeared to be a genuine smile rather than his usual cheeky grin. From across the way,

Elara saw Celina whispering something to Rhea that made both girls laugh.

"Walk with me?" Theodosius asked her when the song ended.

Elara took his arm and let him guide her to a secluded staircase in the back left corner of the room. It was roped off, clearly restricted. Nekros obviously didn't want any of his guests to be looking around upstairs.

"See anyone you know?" Theodosius, back to the staircase, gestured to the ballroom.

"A few people, but no Nekros," Elara replied as she glanced again around the crowded ballroom, making sure she hadn't missed him by mistake. The despot was nowhere to be seen. Neither was the royal family for that matter.

"I bet he's in his office upstairs. He was always hiding with his treasures in his room at the palace," Theodosius suggested.

She bit her lip, unsure of the best course of action. "The stairs are roped off. We could get in a lot of trouble if we're caught going up them."

"Well, I guess we better not get caught then." Theodosius winked at her before slipping under the rope and making the ascent up the stairs.

Elara fiddled with the hem of her sleeves nervously. It was a big risk, but they might never find Nekros if they didn't do this. She glanced back at the room to make sure no one was watching her before slipping under the rope and following Theodosius to the top.

The second floor was just as grand as the lower level, but not nearly as decorated or as well lit. There were only a few torches on the wall lighting their path. It reminded Elara of the hallways back at Fortress Tossa de Mar, which made her think of her papou. She hoped he was doing all right, and that he wasn't too worried about her.

"How do we know which room is Nekros' office?" Elara asked Theodosius as they made their way down the hallway.

"It will most likely be the door at the end there." He pointed straight ahead, showing her where he meant. Unlike the other doors they passed, the door he pointed to was slightly ajar, and the light of a fireplace was glowing out of it. It didn't guarantee that it was Nekros' office, or that Nekros would be inside, but it was a good place to start.

Before they could make it to the door, however, they suddenly heard voices coming from the other end of the hallway. It was impossible to hear what they were saying, but it sounded like two men. Elara felt panic slipping into her throat and down to her stomach. Someone was coming toward them, and the hallway provided no cover.

"Go!" Theodosius hissed quietly as he pushed Elara into one of the side rooms.

It was a guest bedchamber, with a four-poster bed, a fireplace, and a large chest of drawers. The voices were getting louder, and it sounded like they might be coming into this room next.

"Under here." Elara pulled on Theodosius' sleeve, and the two of them crouched to hide under the bed. It was a snug fit, and they were pressed closely together, but thankfully, the bed frame was big enough to hide them both. Just as they got situated on the floor under the bed, the door opened, and two sets of boots stepped inside.

"Huh, I thought for sure I saw someone come in here," a voice murmured. Elara knew the voice at once was Panagioti's.

"Could have been a ghost, I suppose," a second, much deeper, voice said teasingly.

Feeling dizzy, Elara pressed her hand over her mouth to keep herself from gasping. She recognized that voice. It belonged to her ex-fiancé, Prince Andronikos.

Chapter Fifteen

Revelation

After Elara and Theodosius disappeared to who knew where, Celina kept her eyes peeled for Nekros and the necklace. Elara might have trouble focusing, but she did not.

"Do you think Elara and Theodosius are in love?" Rhea asked as they stood together on the outskirts of the dance floor.

"I don't know," Celina answered truthfully. "Elara might be, but the pirate is hard to read. I still don't trust him."

Rhea chuckled, "You don't trust anyone."

"Fair enough." Celina smiled back at her friend.

Truthfully, Celina hoped against hope that Elara and Theodosius were not falling in love, but she had an aching suspicion that they might be. It seemed to Celina that Elara was like a moth to a flame, always falling for men who weren't good for her.

At least Theodosius was helpful, and mostly kind, two things Andronikos never was. That didn't change the fact that Celina felt in her heart that Theodosius was up to... *something*. If only she could figure out what that something was.

The band of bouzouki players continued to play more music for the gathered nobles to dance to. As she watched people dance, she wondered why she wasn't recognizing most of them. The royal family was clearly absent, as was Nekros and his wife.

"It's strange that the emperor is missing at the emperor's ball. I wonder where he could be..." Celina noted with a frown as she continued to look around the room.

"This is my first ball, you know," Rhea changed the subject.

"And what do you think of it?" Celina asked, keeping her eyes on the people waltzing about the room. She didn't want to miss any important clues that might lead them to the necklace.

"Everything is so much shinier than I imagined it would be." Rhea sighed dreamily, but there was a hint of sadness in her voice too. Her eyes appeared to well up with tears that didn't fall.

"Are you well, dear?" Celina asked, turning to look at her friend with concern.

"Yes..." Rhea kept her watery eyes on the dance floor. "I'm a little homesick is all."

She wasn't sure how to respond to that other than to pat Rhea on the shoulder. The memory of running into Lady Sidra Ravi in Athens replayed in Celina's mind, making her suspect that Rhea was missing her old friend and mistress.

Irrationally, Celina suddenly wondered if Rhea would ever love her as much as she had loved Lady Sidra. Celina pushed the thought away and turned back to look at the dance floor. It didn't matter if Rhea loved her that much or not. They were only friends because of Elara after all, weren't they?

"Celina, look!" Rhea grabbed Celina's sleeve, pulling her attention to a noblewoman in a black and white dress. Around the woman's throat was a very large, very distinctive ruby necklace.

"Oh my! It's Elara's necklace!" Celina gasped in shock.

"What do we do?" Rhea asked, excitedly. Neither of the girls could believe their luck.

"We confront her of course. Come on! Before she gets away!" Celina moved quickly to follow the woman.

- - -

It had been a long time since Elara and her ex, Andronikos, had been in the same room. Now they were, and even though *he* didn't know it, it was unbearable for her. Still hidden under the bed, Elara kept her hand clamped over her mouth, but her eyes were wide open as she watched Andronikos and Panagioti's boots walk about the room. Theodosius tensed up beside her, but she couldn't bring herself to look at him.

"Now that we solved our ghost problem, can you please tell me about it again?" Andronikos said to Panagioti.

"I promise I already told you everything, sire," Panagioti replied. "Lady Elara showed up with two ladies-in-waiting and one gentleman. That's all."

"Did she look the same?" Andronikos asked. "I mean—how did she look?"

"Elara is still a beauty if that's what you mean." Panagioti stopped pacing and turned on his heels, perhaps to look at the prince. "The man she was with was gorgeous too."

"Don't tell me that!" Andronikos groaned and the mattress above squeaked slightly as he sat on the bed. "Is she betrothed to him? This mystery lord from *Crete* of all places."

"No." Panagioti was pacing about the room again as he spoke, "Not that I could tell, Your Highness. Seemed like an early courtship to me. No marriage or betrothal or anything serious like that."

"Hm, I just can't believe she would dare come back here after— well, I'm sure my mother will be most pleased to see Elara. You know my own mother likes her better than me. If it wasn't for her favoritism, Elara would still be mine." Andronikos always blamed his mother for things that were his own fault; Elara rolled her eyes in dismay.

"Shall we return to the party, sire? You don't have to speak to her if you don't want to," Panagioti spoke to the prince gently now, as one speaks to a pouty child.

"I don't think my mother would allow me to speak to her even if I wanted to." The bed squeaked again, suggesting that Andronikos had stood up.

"Come on." As Panagioti spoke, the sound of the door creaking open echoed off the walls. "We don't want to miss your brother's toast to your father."

"Ugh, the last thing I want to do is listen to Manuel wax poetic for half-an-hour, but I suppose you're right." The boots moved toward the door and then disappeared from sight. An uncomfortable silence rested over Elara. She could hear her own heartbeat pounding in her ears, and wondered if Theodosius could hear it too.

Finally, after a few agonizing moments of making sure the men were really gone, Theodosius crawled out from under the bed, and Elara followed.

"How are you fairing?" Theodosius asked softly, as he helped her to her feet.

"My leg is a bit cramped from hiding, but it'll be fine in a moment." Elara avoided his gaze and shook out her right leg.

"You know that's not what I meant."

"I wonder what Prince Manuel's speech will be about—he must be nearly eighteen by now," she rambled on in a strained voice. "I remember when he was thirteen. Just a little child desperately chasing after Andronikos' affections..."

"Elara." Theodosius tenderly touched her chin, forcing her to look him in the eyes.

"I'm really fine," she said with a shaky breath. "The prince is the one that's clearly not over it."

He shook his head like he wasn't sure if he believed her or not. "If you say so."

"I say so. Let's move on from this room." Elara pushed past him and back out the door into the now empty hallway.

Truthfully, she wasn't sure how to feel. On the one hand, she was still grieving what once was, but on the other hand, she was grateful.

Andronikos still sounded as whiny and terrible as ever. It was a blessing he hadn't caught them under the bed, and an even bigger blessing that she had never married him.

"I have an idea," Theodosius said, coming up beside her. Thankfully he seemed to be dropping the talk of her ex all together.

"What is it? Aren't we still going to Nekros' office?" Elara stopped walking to look at him.

"Yes, we are, but I just remembered that every nobleman's wife has a separate bedchamber, and her jewelry would be in there." He made a face to further allude to what he was implying.

"You think Nekros' wife might have my necklace in her chamber?" She frowned. It felt impracticable to go searching for a lady's bedchamber when they were so close to the door they had originally planned on.

"I think the lady's chamber is just a few doors down the other hallway here. Let's split up—you go to the lady's bedchamber, and I'll look in Nekros' office. Then, we can meet up later with what we've found," Theodosius said his plan with a tone of practicality, but it still sounded strange to Elara.

"You want to split up? Isn't it safer and more practical to stay together as a team?" she asked, trying to keep the hurt out of her voice. It suddenly felt like he was trying to get rid of her.

"Think of the time we'll save and all the ground we'll cover if we spread out," he explained.

That still made no sense to her. "Look, I know I seem emotional from that almost run-in with my ex-fiancé, but I promise I'm not a liability."

"It's not that." Theodosius glanced at the door at the end of the hallway, avoiding her gaze.

"Wait." Something clicked in Elara's mind. "You want to confront Nekros alone, don't you?"

"No! No, I'm trying to help you find your necklace… faster." It was so clear that he was lying, it was almost comical. Elara would have laughed if she wasn't pissed off.

"Theodosius, you can't kill Nekros. That's not what we agreed upon. You can confront him and try to clear your name, but you can't kill the despot!" This had been his plan all along, Elara realized. Theodosius had never intended to *talk* to Nekros—his goal had always been to kill him.

"You killed Lady Valerie," he said coolly. His words made Elara flinch like she'd been struck.

"I regret that. You know I do. And it was in self-defense, not murder!" She couldn't believe he had the audacity to bring that up and compare it to the current situation.

"Nekros killed my brother!" Theodosius snapped; pretenses finally dropped. "He murdered him in cold blood and ruined my life! And you—you want me to have a nice *chat* with him? To plead my case before my brother's killer? Come on, Countess! I know you are not that naive."

Elara shook her head, unswayed by his outburst. "There has to be a way to resolve this without you becoming a killer yourself. There must be some other course for justice and peace you can take."

"There is no other course!" Theodosius took a step away from her. "There was never another course."

"Don't say that. We'll think of something together. I'll help you." She reached out to touch his hand, but he jerked away from her.

"You can help me by understanding why I have to do this. He *killed* my brother," he said, pleading with her now.

"I know what Nekros did was wrong but killing him isn't going to magically bring your brother back to life. You won't have peace until you let this go. Forgive him, so *you* can be free of him." Elara refused to budge on this point, and she could see he knew it. They were at an impasse.

"You should go back downstairs to your friends. Tell Celina she was right about me." Theodosius pulled a blade from his belt before bolting down the hallway toward Nekros' door.

"Stop! Theodosius, wait!" She raced after him, but her legs were shorter than his, and it was hard to run in her ballgown.

He made it to the door first and shut it in her face, effectively locking her out. She didn't know if anyone else was in the room with him or if he was alone, but either way, she needed to get in.

"Don't do this! Open the door!" Elara pounded on the wooden door until her hands were red from the effort. "Theodosius! Open the door! This isn't you! You don't need revenge! Open the *damn* door!"

There were male voices coming from the other side of the door. Someone was in there with Theodosius. Muffled arguing could be heard, and the crashing sound of something falling off a desk or table infiltrated her ears. She had to do something quickly if she wanted to stop a murder.

Just as she was about to turn around, Elara felt a hand firmly grip her arm, yanking her away from the door. Looking up, she saw it was a guard.

"Can I help you, my lady?" The guard asked sternly. He was tall, with a scruffy face, and a pointed nose.

"Uh, hello sir. I think my friend has accidentally locked himself inside this room, and I was just trying to help him—" Before she could finish her rambling excuses, the arguing on the other side of the door grew louder.

The guard dropped her arm, and moved to kick in the door, breaking it off its hinges. With the door now broken down and open, Elara raced past the guard and into the room. The scene that greeted her was of two men locked in a brawl in the middle of a small messy office. Bookshelves lined the walls, and the only light came from the candles on the desk and one torchlight hanging on the back wall of the room.

"Oh, Elara Iliakos! Thank God! Get help! This crazy man is trying to kill me!" Nekros said from the shelf he was being shoved against. Theodosius was standing over him with a blade in his fist. Both men were looking at her, pleading at her with their eyes for two very different things.

Elara stood there, dumbfounded, unsure of what to say or what to do next. It didn't seem possible that she could help one without hurting the other. She didn't want Theodosius to kill Nekros, but she knew if Theodosius stopped now, he would be arrested and killed. It was a no-win situation.

"Your Excellency!" The guard entered the room and unsheathed his sword.

"Don't come any closer or I'll kill the despot!" Theodosius shouted at the guard, who immediately stopped in his tracks.

"Elara!" Nekros pleaded in a half-sob. "Tell the pirate to leave me alone."

"Look away, Countess. He killed my brother—you know I have to do this." Theodosius didn't want to kill the despot in front of her. He didn't want to make her watch the bloodshed; that was the only reason he hadn't dealt the death blow yet. Elara kept her eyes on him, using this insight to her advantage.

"Theodosius, listen to me. You don't want to kill Nekros," Elara said, trying to sound as soothing as possible. "It's true he has hurt you, but this isn't going to make you feel better. It's only going to make things worse."

"Yes, listen to her, Kardia! She speaks wisely!" Nekros pleaded.

"Shut up!" Theodosius snarled in his face. "You killed Leonides. You killed him in cold blood, and then you blamed me!"

311

"Lies! Slander! I have no idea what you're—"

"You turned my own mother against me!" He pushed the blade closer to Nekros' throat.

"Stop! I did no such thing! Elara, help me!" Nekros screamed.

Perhaps if she could get Theodosius to drop his weapon now, and not hurt Nekros, they wouldn't kill him for this. Perhaps they could still work out a deal, and no one else would have to die. Elara raised her hands and slowly made her way toward the men.

"Theodosius, you don't want this. I know you don't. It's not going to fix anything. Let me help you find a better way to get justice for your brother." She got about a foot away from him before Theodosius stopped her.

"Don't—don't come any closer!" he said, sounding more worried than angry now.

Elara raised her hands again in surrender. "I didn't know Leonides, but if he was as great as you say, then I know he wouldn't want his brother to be a killer."

"Listen to your *friend*, Kardia," Nekros said like he was catching on to something. "Don't be a fool."

"I am not a fool!" The anguish in Theodosius' voice echoed around the room. "And I'm already a killer. Most pirates are."

"If you don't release the despot at once I shall have you torn to shreds!" The guard threatened from the back of the room. He had been so quiet, Elara had nearly forgotten he was there.

"Why did you kill him? Why did you take Leonides away from me?" Theodosius asked Nekros, completely ignoring the guard's threats.

Elara expected Nekros to rebuff Theodosius, to accuse him of lies and slander again.

Instead, Nekros gave a heavy sigh, "Leonides was going to report me for theft… I couldn't risk my reputation and my good standing in the court. I had to get rid of him. You understand? If you hadn't walked in on it, I never would have blamed you for it."

"Good God," Elara whispered, shocked that the despot had actually admitted it out loud.

"Nekros, you have to tell the court the truth. I want my name cleared," Theodosius said, sounding more relaxed, but just as determined now that Nekros had admitted it out loud. "You do the right thing, and I won't kill you. Do we have a deal?"

"Well, I don't ordinarily make deals with *pirates.*"

"Fine." Theodosius pressed his blade harder on the despot's throat. "Death it is."

"Wait! Fine! I suppose I have no choice," Nekros choked out defeatedly. "Yes, we have a deal."

"Good." Theodosius released the despot and slowly lowered his blade. He watched Nekros recompose himself for a moment before turning to look at Elara. The corsair had done the right thing, he had listened to her words of reason, and she was proud of him.

313

She smiled approvingly at Theodosius. "See? I knew we could find a compromise—"

Before she could finish what she was saying, she suddenly felt a hand grab her hair from behind and yank her back, causing her to scream.

A thin blade pressed to her throat, and the harsh voice of the guard snarled in her ear, "Don't move, traitor!"

"Stop! Let her go!" Theodosius yelled, but he was ignored.

"Lord Nekros, tell him to let me go!" Elara pleaded with the despot.

"Very sorry, but I can't have a noblewoman defending the dreaded corsair, Theodosius Kardia, when I accuse him of trying to murder me." Nekros scoffed menacingly. "So, I'm going to have you locked away for a little while."

Elara felt her heart plummet into her stomach as the realization of what was happening overtook her. She realized Nekros had never intended to do the right thing. He was never going to admit what he had done to Leonides, and he would continue to vilify Theodosius by using him as a scapegoat.

"You're insane! You can't do this!" she yelled frantically.

"Lady Elara, you shouldn't speak to me like that!" Nekros scolded her. "It's shameful! What would your parents say?"

"They would tell you to let me go!"

"Release her at once, or I'll gut you like the slimy weasel you are!" Theodosius pulled out his blade again, but this time, Nekros stopped him with a wave of his hand.

"Touch me, and the girl dies." Nekros laughed as he watched Theodosius stop dead in his tracks. "Oh Kardia, did you really fall for a *countess?* That's so pathetic. As if someone like her would ever be with someone like you."

"I'm going to tell them!" Elara snapped, recapturing the men's attention. "When I get out of wherever you lock me up, I'm going to tell the court you killed Leonides, Nekros! I swear to God, I will! Let me go!"

"No, you won't. It would bring shame and dishonor not only to you, but to your entire family. The Iliakos family would be forever ruined if you dared to speak against the emperor's beloved brother." Nekros gave a tittering little laugh, but it lacked the confidence of his normal vibrato.

"True," Elara huffed, feeling like the guard was really going to yank her hair out. "It would ruin me, but it would also ruin *your* reputation. No one walks away unscathed when two nobles go head-to-head."

"I outrank you!" Nekros spat.

"Yes, but I'm high enough to take you down with me—especially if Empress Maria is present," Elara grimaced, trying to appear confident.

315

She hoped that Nekros and the guard couldn't hear the bluff in her voice nor the pounding of her nervous heart. The idea of taking Lord Nekros Palaiologos, Despot of Constantinople, to court over the dead brother of a pirate, was not something Elara could ever imagine herself doing. He was right that the shame of it would destroy her, but Nekros didn't need to know her doubts.

Her false confidence and idle threats worked a little too well, as Nekros said, "Foolish girl! I wish you would see the reason. Now, I must kill you and blame Theodosius for another murder. A shame really, but at least both our reputations will remain unscathed."

"*No!* You can't do this! I'll end you!" Theodosius said, but he was powerless to stop it, and they all knew it. If he rushed the guard or Nekros, Elara would get killed in the process. There was nothing he could do to save her.

"Kill her," Nekros ordered the guard.

"But, Your Excellency... She's a countess, a noblewoman of the court," the guard sounded as bewildered by the order as Elara felt.

"I don't care if she's the empress herself. Kill her now!" Nekros snarled angrily.

Elara knew she had to act quickly if she wanted to live. Glancing down, she saw papers, quills, and a jar of ink on the despot's desk, but no obvious weapon. She would have to improvise.

"What are you waiting for? Finish her!" Nekros ordered the guard again.

"If you kill her, I'll kill you!" Theodosius threatened. "And no one will be here to talk me out of it this time!"

"Sorry about this, my lady. Orders are orders." The guard raised his blade to strike, but before he could make the death blow, Elara threw the jar of ink in his eyes. "AHHH!"

As the guard shrieked in pain, she was able to slip out of his grasp. Without a word, Elara grabbed Theodosius's hand and the two of them bolted out the door.

"Go after them! Stop them!" Nekros could be heard yelling in the distance, but she didn't slow her pace. They needed to get out of there as quickly as possible.

- - -

The woman in the black and white dress was briskly walking down the hallway that led to the front door. Celina knew she and Rhea needed to stop the woman before she slipped away into the night, disappearing with Elara's necklace.

"Excuse me! Miss!" Rhea called out to the woman, trying to get her to stop, or at least, slow down to speak with them.

Without so much as turning around, the woman began to sprint toward the door. Celina and Rhea ran after her, neither girl sure why this random woman would be running away from them.

"Wait! Stop! We just want to talk!" Celina yelled, but the woman continued to move at a brisk pace away from them.

"Where is she going?" Rhea panted as they sprinted. "Why is she fleeing from us? We haven't done anything!"

"Probably because she knows she's wearing stolen merchandise," Celina guessed, but truthfully, this behavior from a stranger was odd. She wondered if it might be a trap.

"She's getting away!" Rhea pointed to the woman who was now opening the large front door.

Just as Celina feared, they needed to hurry to stop her before the cover of night hid her from view in the mostly unfamiliar cityscape.

"Here's the plan," Celina said to Rhea once they made it to the door. "I'll follow her directly, and you can run around the other side to cut her off from escaping."

"Good plan." Rhea nodded approvingly before running off in the direction Celina had directed her.

Celina did her part by charging after the woman who was nearly slipping from view. The partial white design on the woman's dress kept her illuminated, but the further away they got from the lights of Nekros' house, the harder and harder it became to see her. The other houses around were dark and the moon was a mere sliver, so it didn't do much to illuminate her path.

"Stop! Please wait!" Celina kept up her pace, noticing that the woman was slowing, either due to exhaustion or the pain in her feet from her shoes. Celina felt proud of herself for choosing sensible footwear.

Just as the woman was about to turn around a dark corner, Rhea suddenly appeared, cutting off her path.

"Holy God!" The woman shrieked as she skidded to a halt.

318

"Not God. Sorry." Rhea smirked apologetically. "We just want to talk about your necklace."

"Leave me alone! I didn't do anything wrong!" The woman took a shallow breath, looking ready to fight. She was dressed regally, but her face looked worn, and her hands held no rings, only calluses and dirty fingernails. No noblewoman would be caught dead with hands like those.

"Oh, you're a thief!" Celina said as the realization hit her. "That's why you ran away!"

"How dare you! I'm not a thief!" The woman shouted, sounding outraged, but there was desperation in her eyes.

"Where did you get that necklace, then?" Rhea asked pointedly. "It doesn't exactly go with your attire."

"This is my necklace. My father gave it to me years ago." The woman clutched the necklace protectively.

"You're lying," Celina stated as she pulled her small knife out from the hidden folds in her dress.

The woman squeaked as Celina came toward her with the blade. "Wait! Stop! You caught me! I stole this necklace from a noblewoman at the party. But she didn't need it! Those nobles have plenty of jewelry—she won't even miss it!"

"You're right. She won't miss it, but our friend, who *actually* owns that necklace, will miss it a great deal. So, hand it over, and we'll let you go," Celina commanded the woman, pointing the dagger directly at her chest.

The woman glanced back at Rhea, and then turned her head to look past Celina, clearly assessing her options. Deciding she had none, the woman unhooked the necklace and placed it in Rhea's outstretched hand.

"Wise choice, thief." Celina put her knife back in the folds of her dress before motioning with her head that the woman was free to go.

Without wasting another second, the woman raced off down a dark alley and disappeared into the night.

"She seemed friendly," Rhea noted sarcastically after she was gone.

"Hmm, yes, an unsavory character to be sure." Celina frowned. "Let me see the necklace."

Rhea held out the necklace for her to examine. In the dark, it really looked exactly like Elara's necklace, but they wouldn't know for sure until they brought it back to her and examined it under the light.

"Put that someplace safe, and let's go back to the party to find Elara," Celina said.

"Good idea. Probably best to hide it away until we can give it to Elara directly," Rhea agreed, slipping the necklace into her dress pocket.

The two girls started off together back toward Nekros' mansion. Before they had gone more than a few paces, the sound of heavy footsteps came from behind them.

"That's them! Those are the girls that took the necklace!" The woman appeared again, this time accompanied by three men. The men weren't guards, but they still looked dangerous.

"Time to run!" Celina said, grabbing Rhea's arm. The two of them wasted no time sprinting off as fast as they could.

Chapter Sixteen

The Chase

Elara and Theodosius raced down the same stairs they had come up, but instead of racing across the ballroom to get to the main entrance, they took a sharp right into an opposite hallway.

"There's a door down there!" Theodosius pointed out a back exit as they ran. Even though the door most likely led out to a dark, and potentially dangerous, alleyway, Elara knew they didn't have many other escape options. They needed to get as far away from Nekros and his guards as possible before they could relax and plan their next move.

"Pirates! Stop them!" Nekros' voice could be heard shouting from behind them, as if on cue.

"I can't believe he used to be one of my father's close friends," Elara muttered as they came upon the back door.

Theodosius grabbed the door handle and pushed his shoulder onto the wood, but the door didn't budge. "It's locked."

"Try pulling," Elara suggested as she glanced over her shoulder and saw the guards getting closer. Thankfully, they hadn't seen them at the door yet.

"I already tried that." Theodosius pushed and pulled, jiggling the door handle every which way with no change. "Dammit! It won't budge!"

Oh God. Elara felt her heart pounding in her throat. Looking around for another exit, her eyes landed on a double arch-shaped window, to the left of the door. It should be big enough for them to fit through, and being on the first floor, it wouldn't be too high of a fall.

"I can break the glass," Theodosius said as if he had read her mind. He used his elbow to smash the window glass open. "Careful not to cut yourself on the way down."

"Halt!" One of the guards had seen them, and was closing in.

"There's no time to be careful, Captain," Elara said as she sat on the windowsill and swung her legs over to drop feet first onto the grassy lawn below. It was higher than she had anticipated, but she still landed with relative ease, and without any serious injury.

Theodosius landed next to her with a gentle thud. "Are you hurt?"

"I'm fine. Are you injured?" she asked, looking him over for any glass shards. Before he could respond, the guards had made it to the window.

"There they are!" one of the guards shouted, moving swiftly to leap after them from the windowsill.

Wasting no time, Theodosius grabbed Elara's hand, and the two of them were off running again into the night. Constantinople was poorly lit at this late hour, but much to Elara's dismay, the sun was beginning to rise, turning the sky a light pink. She couldn't believe they had been at the party all night, and now, in the wee hours of the morning, they no longer had the cover of darkness to protect them from Nekros' men.

"Are they still following us?" Theodosius asked as they ran down another alleyway.

"What do you think?" Elara said back, a bit sarcastically. The guards weren't directly behind in their line of sight, but they could be heard from not too far away. Any moment, they would be upon them.

Even as the sun slowly rose, the streets remained empty as it was still a little too early for the working class to be up and about. That wouldn't last long. Elara predicted that any minute now, people would start flooding the streets, which would make their escape more difficult than it already was.

"Halt!" A guard suddenly jumped out at them, seemingly from nowhere, brandishing a sword.

Elara gasped loudly and froze, but Theodosius reacted quickly. He wrestled the guard to the ground and knocked him out cold with a nearby rock. Theodosius then took the sword from the guard's hand and another off his belt.

"Catch!" He tossed her the second sword. "Use it just like I taught you."

"I—I don't know if I can..." She grasped the hilt of the sword as if it was a completely foreign object. They only had one real sword-fighting lesson, so she didn't feel comfortable using it.

"Trust yourself. You can do this." No sooner had he spoken the words of encouragement when two more guards found them.

"You're under arrest, Kardia!" one of the guards shouted.

"Sorry, now's not a great time. Could you arrest me tomorrow instead?" Theodosius asked slyly. When the guards didn't laugh or look particularly amused by his attempted humor, he continued, "All right, let's do this." He got into the first position, ready to fight.

Elara mimicked his stance, her heart in her throat, and her stomach tied in knots. Fighting Constantinopolitan guards had not been on her to do list for the evening. Yet, here she was, once again acting more like a corsair than a countess.

The guards ignored her completely and charged at Theodosius with their weapons raised above their heads. Their swords clashed together, and it became clear to Elara that if she wanted to help Theodosius, she was going to have to attack one of the guards.

Or run away.

She could run now and save herself from both physical harm and more social embarrassment, but then Theodosius would be fighting multiple guards all alone. Even with his advanced swordsman skills, he wouldn't be able to hold them off forever. They would cut him down eventually and kill him. Theodosius never abandoned her in a fight, so it wouldn't be fair to abandon him now. They would escape together as planned or not at all.

Making up her mind, Elara swung her sword at one of the guards, getting his attention. He blocked her attack with ease, but there was surprise written all over his face.

"What are you doing, girl?" he demanded.

The guard had probably never fought a woman before, especially not a woman dressed in a ballgown. Him calling her *girl* was a good sign that he didn't know who she was, and therefore, wouldn't be able to tell anyone about her bad behavior later.

"Sorry about this, sir," she muttered apologetically before swinging her sword at him again.

Fighting the guard was different from the practice fights with Theodosius. The guard wasn't as quick on his feet as the pirate captain, but he was hitting her a lot harder.

It's all about rhythm, she reminded herself. She just had to learn the guard's fighting pattern if she wanted to disarm him and get away before more guards showed up to arrest them. Their swords clanged together loudly, and Elara grunted under the pressure. Clearly, he knew his size was his best advantage against her. She would have to be quicker and more nimble if she wanted to win.

"Stop this foolishness! Surrender!" The guard demanded as he jabbed his sword at her shoulder, barely missing her flesh as she parried away from him.

"Can't stop now," she replied, as she blocked another one of his blows. Using all the strength she could muster, she double counterattacked with a swing to his shoulder first, followed by a slice across his upper thigh.

"Damn you!" the guard screamed in pain as he fell to his knees and dropped his sword, sending it skidding across the stone ground. Blood pooled out of his leg much more quickly than she had expected.

"So sorry!" Elara tore the bottom hem of her gown and wrapped it around the man's leg. Hopefully, Simon, the dressmaker, would forgive her for ruining his beautiful design. "Hold pressure here."

"Lord Nekros is going to kill you," the guard whispered. His voice wasn't menacing or even threatening anymore. He was warning her.

News travels fast.

She wanted to ask him exactly what he meant, and what he knew, but she could hear Theodosius fighting behind her and knew that more guards would be there soon. They needed to escape—quickly.

"Sorry again!" Elara huffed, racing to pick up his dropped weapon. The feeling of guilt slowly dissipated and was replaced with satisfaction. She had defeated the guard all on her own, and now she had two swords to fight with.

"Elara!" Theodosius called out to her. She whirled around expecting to see him in a fight, but instead, he was standing on a four-wheeled cart with a mule drawn at the front. The guard he had been fighting with was lying unmoving on the ground beside the cart.

She frowned, trying to figure out what he was planning. "What are you—?"

"Come on! Take my hand!" He held out his hand to her and pulled her up on the cart with him. The cart was small, and covered in hay and dirt, but it seemed sturdy enough to hold them.

Elara propped her swords up on the inside of the cart before helping Theodosius with the reins on the mule.

The sound of more guards coming could be heard all around them. Theodosius slapped the ass of the mule, and the cart lurched forward, sending them off down the narrow, stone street. It was a bumpy, noisy ride. Even though the cart was faster, Elara wondered if it would be more practical and safer to stay on foot.

"Let me steer." Elara tugged on the reins, but Theodosius held on tightly.

"No, it's fine. I can steer."

"I know these streets well, so I should steer—"

"Excuse me, Countess, but these are the *lower-class* quarters, so I probably know the streets better than you—"

One of the wheels hit a raised part of the road, jolting them into the air for a second. Elara let out a yelp as she was involuntarily thrown into Theodosius. Luckily, he caught her, so they didn't spill into the street as the cart continued down the road.

"That was a close one," he laughed with one hand gripping the reins, and the other around her waist. His signature grin was plastered across his face, and his eyes sparkled despite their dire circumstances.

Heat rushed into Elara's cheeks, but she was too shaken from their misadventures to do something stupid, like kiss him in broad daylight. It was probably a sin to like a pirate as much as she liked Theodosius. Her reputation would really never recover if anyone ever found out.

"Kardia! Halt!" Another guard had caught up with them and leapt up on the back of their cart.

"New plan—you steer, and I'll fight," Theodosius said, tossing her the reins.

Elara tried to keep her eyes on the road, but she kept glancing back to make sure Theodosius was doing all right in his fight. The two swords she had acquired rattled at her feet, ready for her to use at a moment's notice.

The sound of swords clanging and men grunting could be heard as the guard and Theodosius wrestled with each other. Each bump in the road threatened to throw one, or both of them, off the cart.

A swordfight was difficult enough on steady land, or even a rocking ship, but to do it on a bumpy, high-speed cart seemed insane. Somehow, Theodosius was making it look easy as he moved expertly in the small space, blocking each of the guard's offensives with counter attacks.

Finally, the pirate captain dealt the last blow, sending the guard and his sword tumbling onto the stone ground.

"Good hit!" she said, relieved.

He turned to look at her, and his eyes became wide. "Look out!"

Elara whipped her head around just in time to see they were barreling toward a wall. She tried pulling on the reins, but the mule wasn't listening to her as much as she would have liked. The side of the cart skimmed the wall, making a terrible screeching sound.

"We have to jump!" Theodosius shouted when the mule refused to slow. "The road's too narrow! We're going to crash!"

"Jump? Onto the hard *stone?*" she asked, horrified at the thought.

"Trust me!" He held out his hand to her.

Without thinking about the consequences, Elara took his hand and jumped. By the grace of God, and Theodosius' good planning, they landed safely in a large pile of hay. The mule-drawn cart didn't crash too badly, and instead, whizzed away without them, leaving dust in its wake.

"I forgot the swords," she groaned as the cart disappeared from view.

"It's fine," he promised her, taking her hand again. "We have to keep moving. They're still after us." It seemed that no matter how far they ran, or where they hid, the guards were always right on their tail.

"What are we going to do?" she whispered as they stopped in a narrow, covered passageway to catch their breath. "We can't outrun them forever. They will catch us eventually."

"You're right." He looked around desperately before finally making eye contact with her again. "I have an idea, but you might not like it."

Elara frowned, not liking the sound of it already. "What is it?"

"Come here." He opened his arms like he wanted a hug.

"What?" If she wasn't so flooded with fear and confusion, she might have laughed. "I don't understand."

"Come here." Theodosius wrapped his arms around her from behind, but it wasn't a hug in the traditional sense. He had her arms pinned behind her in the embrace, almost like being restrained. It reminded her of the practice fights they had done on the ship before arriving in Athens.

"What—?" Elara began again, but he cut her off.

"Scream for help," he whispered in her ear.

Realization hit her then. Theodosius was going to make it look like he had kidnapped her, and forced her to go with him, so that when they got caught, she wouldn't get into trouble.

"I appreciate the sentiment, Captain, but I'm *not* doing that," she hissed. "They'll kill you if I accuse you of something like that."

"They're going to kill me either way," Theodosius gave a short, humorless laugh before twisting her arm behind her back. "Now scream."

"Ow! Stop it!" Elara couldn't help but yell loudly as he twisted her arm behind her back. "Don't!"

"There!" The guards were upon them.

Elara clenched her teeth together, determined not to incriminate Theodosius any further. However, it seemed the corsair wasn't done with the theatrics.

"Don't come any closer or the countess dies!" Theodosius said dramatically. He was playing the part of an evil pirate surprisingly well. When she didn't play along as the helpless victim, he pinched the fleshy part of her arm, causing her to yelp in discomfort.

"Easy there, Kardia." One of the guards held up his hands. "There's no need to hurt anyone else."

"Back off!" Theodosius yelled. "Or I'll kill Countess Iliakos! I swear I will!"

"The pirate is bluffing." Nekros appeared on horseback, accompanied by three more guards.

Elara's heart was stuck in her throat as she watched him dismount. She bit her lip to stop herself from crying, not from the pain, but from the fear of what the despot was going to do to them. Whatever Nekros had planned would be a thousand times worse than Theodosius twisting her arm, she was sure.

"Are you certain, Your Excellency? Kardia appears to have kidnapped the countess, and is now hurting her," The guard closest to them said apprehensively.

"He's doing none of those things," Nekros scoffed, pulling a sword from the holster on his belt.

"I'm being serious! I'll kill her!" Theodosius said roughly, but mercifully, he didn't twist or pinch her arms this time.

Elara kept silent, keeping her eyes locked on Nekros. The guards seemed to be buying Theodosius' charade, but she knew Nekros never would.

"So, do it," Nekros taunted. "Kill the countess. We'll arrest you after she's dead."

"Your Excellency!" Some of the guards protested, but Nekros waved them off lazily before returning his gaze to Theodosius, calling his bluff.

"Filthy pirate! Let go of the poor countess!" an older woman called from a nearby window above them. More people were starting to come out, awakened by either their normal routine or by the commotion going on in the alleyway.

"Yeah, leave her be! She's done nothing to you!" a middle-aged man yelled from a doorway behind them.

Nekros started to look ill-at-ease as more townspeople came leaping to Elara's defense. Even though Elara couldn't see Theodosius' face, she could feel him smiling; his plan to save her was working. She was grateful people cared enough to defend her from what they perceived as an attack against her, but she knew this would not end well for Theodosius.

"Lord Nekros, please—" Elara began, intending to plead for Theodosius' life, but he twisted her arm again causing her to yell out. "OW! Stop doing that!"

"We have to help the countess!" Another one of the guards said, now fully taking her side.

"Yes, someone help the poor girl!"

"He's going to kill her! Someone do something!"

"Don't let that nasty pirate hurt the countess anymore!"

"Stop him, Lord Nekros! Do *something*!"

Now, a large group of people were all yelling out, defending Elara. Everyone, except Nekros, was on her side and she could tell that he knew it. The despot's expression turned bitter as he seemingly realized he would not be able to frame her as easily as he had thought.

"Have I foiled your plans, Your Excellency?" Theodosius said gloatingly.

"Listen to me! The pirate is bluffing!" Nekros told the crowd of onlookers. "He's not really going to hurt her."

"What makes you think I won't hurt her?" Theodosius challenged him, darkly. "I am the dreaded corsair, Captain Theodosius Kardia! According to you, I've killed many before today! What makes you think I won't kill the countess?"

"You won't hurt Lady Elara," Nekros smiled. "Because you are in *love* with her."

Theodosius's arms stiffened around her as the crowd gasped at this accusation. It certainly wasn't an accusation Elara or Theodosius had been expecting, as they both stared at Nekros, dumbfounded.

She wondered what game Nekros was playing now. Her gut told her it probably had something to do with ruining her honor and reputation, by accusing her of sleeping with a pirate, or something like that. While she had refused to play victim in Theodosius' fake kidnapping plan, she would have no problem denying that any relations had passed between them.

"*In love?* With *her?*" Theodosius scoffed, finally finding his voice. "That's absurd! The only person I love is myself! I'm very selfish like that—ask anyone!"

"Very well, let's ask the countess, shall we?" Nekros looked at Elara in a patronizing way.

"Ask her! She'll tell you exactly how terrible I've been!" Theodosius gave her arm a squeeze. His grip was more pleading this time than painful, as he silently begged her to play along.

"Lady Elara, why in all this time have you not screamed for help? I've heard you say 'ow' and 'stop' but you never asked to be released or rescued. You never screamed for help. Why is that?" Nekros questioned, looking much too pleased with himself.

He continued, "Could it be that you don't want to frame Theodosius for this charade he's concocted? Could it be that you're in love with him too, or at the very least, that you have become the pirate's loyal friend and want to protect him?"

Love and friendship or hateful enemies. Those seemed to be the only options Nekros was offering. Elara wasn't exactly sure how deeply she felt for Theodosius, but it didn't really matter. Whichever way she answered, things would not end well. If she played along as Theodosius wanted, Nekros would have him arrested and executed. Then, he would probably accuse her of being damaged goods, ruining her reputation forever. If she refused to play along, and told the truth about Theodosius' good character, Nekros would declare she was traitor, and she would probably be hanged alongside him. It was a lose-lose situation.

Before Elara could decide what to say or do, a horse-drawn carriage pulled up to the entrance of the alleyway. A tall woman, dressed in a golden evening gown, with tight dark curls on her head, swung the carriage door open.

"What on God's green earth is going on here?" the woman demanded furiously. Elara recognized her at once.

"Empress Maria! It's me! It's Elara Iliakos!" She exclaimed, nearly in tears as something within her cracked. "Help me, please! Help me!"

- - -

Celina looked behind her as she ran to see the men chasing them were catching up fast. The sun was beginning to rise, so they could more easily see the path in front of them.

"Quick, the church!" Rhea yelled to Celina as it became clear that they wouldn't make it back to Nekros' mansion before the men caught up with them. The girls sprinted up the steps of the church and pushed their way inside.

They shut the doors quickly, and Rhea placed a nearby chair under the door handle to keep it secured. As soon as she did that, the men could be heard banging on the other side, shouting at them.

"That won't hold for long. We have to keep moving," Celina said, gesturing for Rhea to follow her further into the church.

It was a traditional-looking Orthodox Church, with ornate iconography covering the walls, and stained glass covering the windows. The Icon of the Mother of God with Child hovered above the altar and seemed to be pointing to a place below.

"Let's hide under the altar table," Celina suggested.

"Um, am I allowed to do that?" Rhea sounded concerned. "You remember I'm Muslim, not Orthodox Christian, like you."

"Technically, no women are allowed inside the sanctuary, but God makes exceptions in times of crisis, I believe," Celina said as she slipped behind the sanctuary doors and moved the communion goblet off the altar so she could lift the skirt of the table, exposing the small hiding place underneath.

The girls were lucky that the church was otherwise empty. The last thing they needed was a clergyman or priest to oust them.

"Open the door!" The men shouted from the outside, sounding dangerously close to breaking down the church door.

"Come on!" Celina gestured frantically for Rhea to go under the altar table first. Rhea had the necklace in her pocket, so it only made sense that she should hide first.

The two of them made it under the altar and pulled the tablecloth down just in time as they heard the doors burst open.

"Spread out! Find them!" One of the men ordered. The sound of heavy footsteps echoed off the marble floors.

Even though Celina couldn't see them, she estimated that there were at least three men, and perhaps that one woman, in the church now looking for them. She hoped they would be respectful enough to not mess up the sanctuary too badly and expose them.

Rhea kept her hand tightly pressed over her own mouth to avoid making any sudden and unwanted noises. It was a tense situation, and Celina couldn't help but feel guilty that they were in it. Perhaps if she hadn't been so hasty to run after the woman with the necklace, or if she had asked someone like Panagioti, or another trusted male servant, for help, they wouldn't be in this predicament.

As quietly as she could, Celina stretched out her hand to gently clasp Rhea's shoulder in what she hoped was a comforting gesture. Rhea relaxed a little under her touch, so it seemed to work.

Suddenly, Celina felt a callused hand grab her leg, yank her out from under the altar table, and drag her across the floor.

"Got ya!" A man with a deep voice shouted triumphantly.

"Unhand me, you brute!" Celina shrieked.

There were four men standing around her with large arms, messy hair, and five o'clock shadows. The largest man, with blue eyes, and a jagged scar across his face, was still holding her leg. He grinned down at her with ugly yellow teeth.

"Give us the necklace, and we'll let you go," he said with a thick Venetian accent. The other three men stood back slightly, looking at her menacingly.

"I—I don't have any necklace," Celina shifted her palms to the cool marble floor, desperately trying to find something that could be used as a weapon to help her.

Nothing.

"I know you and your friend took it. So where is it?" the man demanded, his grin quickly turned to a frustrated frown.

Thankfully, none of the men had further investigated the sanctuary, and therefore, had not yet found Rhea. Celina intended to keep it that way.

"Your lady friend stole the necklace, not I." Celina shrugged, trying to look passive. "Perhaps you should go ask *her* what happened to it. She's the thief after all."

"She told us you took it!" The man jerked her leg forward, causing Celina to yell out in pain. "Stop playing games, girl! Where is the necklace?"

"I already told you—I don't have it!" Celina yelled.

"Where's your friend?" Another one of the men asked.

"What friend?"

This remark earned her a slap across the face. Her ear was ringing from it, and a slight trickle of warm blood ran down her nose and to her lip. The taste of blood came next, causing Celina to spit upon the floor to get the rusty flavor out of her mouth. She prayed God would forgive her for spewing blood droplets in his house.

"Ow," Celina muttered as she was hoisted to her feet.

"I'm going to ask you one more time. Where is the necklace?!" The first man jerked her around by her collar to make his point.

Before Celina could muster the strength to tell him to *piss off*, a voice called out in her defense.

"Leave her alone!" It was Rhea.

Celina felt her heart drop to her stomach as she realized her friend had exposed herself to save her, Celina, from further abuse.

"*No!* Rhea, run!" Celina said in horror as she watched one of the men approach Rhea with a drawn weapon.

"The necklace, please." He held out his hand.

"If I give it to you, will you let us be?" Rhea asked shrewdly.

"Of course," the man said, but Celina didn't believe him.

"Don't trust him! Run!" She pleaded with her friend.

Ignoring her, Rhea reached into her dress, pulled out Countess Iliakos' necklace, and placed it into the man's sweaty palm.

"Perfection." The man held the necklace up so that his cohorts could see it sparkling in the light. They laughed happily and clapped each other on the back at the sight of it.

"All right, you got what you came for. Now you can go and leave us be!" Rhea told them sternly.

The men laughed arrogantly, and shoved Rhea, so she was on the floor next to Celina. Blood rushed into Celina's face as a combination of fear and outrage consumed her. As predicted, these horrible men had no intention of letting them go, and she thought Rhea was a fool for thinking they would. Just because Theodosius and Yianni hadn't been bloodthirsty, didn't mean all thieves were so kind. How could they have been so stupid as to let this happen, Celina wasn't sure.

"Sorry, ladies, but you've seen our faces, and we can't have you reporting us to Lord Nekros," the first man said as the group surrounded the girls on all sides.

"Well, we're not going anywhere with you, you fiend!" Celina grasped Rhea's hand and pulled her more firmly beside her as she spoke. If there was any chance to escape, they would need to act as one.

"Going with us?" The men laughed again as they pulled weaponry from their belts. "No. We'll be killing you."

Celina's brain was desperately trying to work out an escape, or a distraction, or something they could use to defend themselves, but there was nothing. As the men advanced toward them, Rhea pressed her face into the crook of Celina's neck, clearly not wanting to watch. Celina kept her eyes wide open, vowing silently to fight until the very end.

Right before the men could skewer them to death with their blades, a woman's voice shouted out from the church doorway.

"Get out of my church at once! The guards are on their way!" It was an older woman, wearing dark black robes and a black head scarf that mostly covered her silver hair. The woman appeared unarmed, but her voice carried a tremendous amount of authority.

"Run!" The men shouted frantically, and sprinted for the back door, leaving Celina and Rhea alone and unharmed in their wake.

"Are you girls hurt?" The woman asked as she made her way over to them.

"We're fine. Thank you, my lady," Celina said, heart still racing. "We're so sorry to intrude like this. I'm Celina, and this is Rhea."

"I'm Eudokia. I'm a monastic from the old monastery attached to this church." the woman said simply, offering no last name nor an explanation as to why the men were afraid of her.

"You saved our lives, Eudokia. How can we repay you?" Rhea asked.

341

"You can start by helping me clean this place up." Eudokia grabbed a broom that had been leaning against a nearby pillar and attempted to hand it to Celina.

"Oh, yes, we will certainly help you cleanup, but first, we need to catch those men before they disappear with the necklace…" Celina motioned for Rhea to follow her to the door.

Rhea, however, was unmoved. "Celina, we can't leave without helping Eudokia clean up first. It's only fair—she did save our lives."

"And we will help, but first, we have to catch up with those men before Elara's necklace is lost forever," Celina argued. She didn't understand why Rhea would prioritize helping a monastic nun sweep dust over getting the necklace they had so desperately been searching for.

"What are we supposed to do if we catch up with those men?" Rhea scowled defiantly. "They already nearly killed us once. We can't fight them!"

"Rhea dear, I don't have time to argue about this. We have to go," Celina stood in the doorframe, waiting for Rhea to move.

When Rhea didn't, Celina continued, "I'll go without you if you won't accompany me!"

"Fine. Go." Rhea took the broom from Eudokia who had been silently watching them as they argued and began to sweep the marble ground.

Celina grumbled, "Fine! I'll clean up your mess alone, and you can stay here and clean up the church."

"My mess?" Rhea spat. "What do you mean, my mess?"

"I mean, it's your fault we lost the necklace in the first place!" Celina said back harshly.

"Why? Because I traded it just now in an attempt to *save your life*?" Rhea frowned.

"Ladies, please stop arguing. This is a holy place," Eudokia interrupted them gently, but the girls ignored her.

"Elara put you in charge of the necklace back at the fortress! It was stolen under your watch!" Celina knew the accusation wasn't completely fair, but she didn't care. It was imperative to her that Rhea understood that this whole mission would never have been necessary if she had guarded the necklace as Elara had entrusted her to.

"The pirates smashed the drawers, and I didn't have the real key anyway!" Rhea's eyebrows pinched together, and her lower lip quivered. "What was I supposed to do?"

"You were supposed to do your job! And now look at the mess we're in! We're so close to fixing everything, but you're ready to give up, so now I have to fix it myself, like always!" Celina shouted.

"Because you've never made a mistake before, right?" Rhea scoffed. "You weren't even there to help when the pirates attacked because you were too busy trying to discredit me!"

"Oh, you are irritating! It's no wonder Lady Sidra would rather be dead than spend time with you!" Celina's voice echoed loudly off the walls of the church and the room lapsed into stunned silence.

Rhea's eyes welled with tears, but she made no retort to Celina's harsh words. Celina instantly regretted saying it. She hadn't meant it. Elara's words, '*I wish you cared more about being kind than you do about being right*,' echoed in Celina's mind.

"As I said, this is a holy place. If you're going to keep being unchrist-like to each other, please do so outside," Eudokia said, breaking the silence.

"We won't be yelling anymore," Rhea promised, her voice soft but clearly hurt. "Lady Oberon was just leaving."

"Yes, yes, I'm leaving. Goodbye!" Celina stormed off into the morning light.

Chapter Seventeen

Darkness

Elara awoke to warm sunlight on her face and the sound of servants bustling around her. The bed she was lying in was the most comfortable bed she had been in since leaving home. The sheets and blankets were soft, and the pillows were plush. The thought of getting out of it made her shudder with dread.

"Time to get up, my lady." A woman's voice said from above her.

"Five more minutes, Yiayia," Elara muttered, still half-asleep or at least trying to be.

"Empress Maria Palaiologos wants to see you as soon as possible." The woman pulled the covers down to Elara's waist. "And I'm not your yiayia."

Elara jolted up, half in shock from remembering where she was, and half from the cold seeping through her exposed nightgown and onto her flesh.

"What shall I wear? I didn't bring any proper clothes to see Her Ladyship in," Elara told the woman, whom she could now see was a serving lady, most likely on loan from the empress.

"We have clothes for you here." The serving lady pulled Elara out of bed and walked her over to the changing area. Three other maids and some garment pieces were waiting for her there.

They were in one of the largest guest rooms in the emperor's palace. Empress Maria was being generous to her as per usual. After everything that had happened lately, Elara felt almost guilty being taken care of by servants in a majestic room with golden tapestries. She wasn't sure anyone deserved such luxuries, especially when so many others were suffering with little to no comfort at all.

"Could someone tell me what happened to Captain Kardia?" Elara asked as the maids dressed her in a dark blue dress.

"The corsair was arrested for treason, murder, and kidnapping," the serving lady told her nonchalantly.

"Is that all?" Elara asked rhetorically, trying her best to keep her voice void of emotion. She thought back to the early hours of the morning and remembered her last moments with Theodosius.

As they had dragged Theodosius away from her, he had whispered a quick apology to her for twisting her arm. His handsome smile, much more somber now than cheeky, was the last thing she saw of him as she was put in the empress's carriage, and he was taken elsewhere.

Theodosius Kardia, the notorious pirate captain, had sacrificed himself for her. She didn't know if it was because he loved her, or because Theodosius was, and had always been, that heroic. Either way, he would be dead soon, and there was nothing she could do to save him without causing more chaos in the process.

Elara felt like she was going to be sick. The guilt would surely eat her alive before she even had a chance to speak to the empress about any of this.

"Sit here, my lady." The serving woman guided her to a small dining area where a round table with light breakfast foods and a kettle of hot tea sat waiting.

"Thank you." Elara took a seat at the table.

A servant poured her a glass of tea, and another made her a plate, containing a large slice of bread with drizzled honey, a small chunk of cheese, and some fresh apple slices.

After they were finished tending to Elara, the serving lady and the other maids bowed their heads and then quickly exited the room.

Once alone, Elara wasted no time chowing down into her meal. It had been many hours, if not a full day, since she'd last eaten anything substantial. The palace food was just as fresh and delicious as she had remembered. The hot tea burned her tongue, but it was so well made that she didn't care.

"Hello, Elara, my darling! So sorry to keep you waiting." Empress Maria Rita Palaiologos strode into the room, unannounced and unattended, which was unusual for nobility.

"Hello, Empress," Elara tried to say as she leapt to her feet, but her mouth was still so full of food that it came out more like: "Huglow, Embess." Instead of trying to speak again, and risk further embarrassing herself, Elara gave a silent, customary bow.

347

"Please sit! There's no need for such formalities," Empress Maria said as she took a seat opposite Elara at the table.

The empress was just as beautiful as ever. Her dark hair was pulled up in delicate curls, yesterday's ballgown exchanged for a simpler, yet equally elegant, navy-blue dress.

"How have you been, my darling?" Empress Maria asked as she poured tea into her own cup.

"Exhausted. I've been on the longest, most difficult journey to get here," Elara admitted, not wanting to sugar coat her experience.

"I can imagine," the empress nodded sympathetically. "You poor thing. It must be so terrible to be settling into a new home and role, only to be kidnapped and extorted by pirates!"

A lump formed in Elara's throat. The lie, while less scandalous, was almost as embarrassing as the truth. How could she possibly explain the truth without further pulling herself into ruin?

"That's not exactly what happened—" Elara started to explain the real situation, but didn't get more than a few words out before the door burst open again.

"My apologies for my tardiness, Your Majesty!" It was Nekros.

Time seemed to freeze as Elara's stomach twisted into fearful knots at the sight of him.

"Nekros, darling, so good of you to come!" Maria smiled warmly and gestured for him to join them at the table.

Lord Nekros strode into the room like he owned it. Perhaps he did, being brother to the emperor had its advantages.

Elara's heart pounded furiously against her rib cage in a combination of fear and rage. *How dare he come here?* What was the purpose of his presence other than to slander her further before the empress?

Empress Maria stood and greeted him politely with an air kiss on the cheek. The two nobles spoke a few words to each other, but Elara couldn't process what they were saying over the rushing blood in her ears. Nekros sat to Elara's right and the empress's left at the table and poured himself a cup of tea. He seemed perfectly at ease, and that enraged Elara even more.

"I've been so worried about you, Countess Elara. I heard from the guards that Kardia forced you to *swordfight* of all things." Nekros shook his head and innocently took a sip of his tea. "Most dreadful of him. How are you fairing?"

"Better than dead, I suppose," she muttered darkly.

"Elara, my darling, you mustn't say such things!" Maria's voice was scolding. Elara wasn't supposed to talk to a despot like that, but she didn't care.

"It's fine." He waved Empress Maria's concern away. "I know Lady Elara is upset with me for not being able to rescue her from that horrid pirate sooner. I do apologize. I worked as quickly and diligently as I could."

Nekros' face broke into the most disgusting, self-congratulatory grin she had ever seen. He was baiting her, confident in his position as the powerful and untouchable brother to the emperor.

Elara took a shaky breath to steady herself before speaking. "I accept your apology, of course, Your Excellency."

"Very good." Nekros, pleased, turned to the empress. "See? All is well now. You worried for nothing."

"Yes, I suppose you're right." Maria smiled, unaware of her brother-in-law's treachery.

"What happens now?" Elara asked no one in particular. The royals were playing a game with her, and she didn't know the rules. The only thing Elara knew for certain was she needed to watch her tongue if she wanted to get out of this interaction unscathed.

"I've sent a letter to your papou, Count Basil, so he knows you're alive and well," Maria replied. "And tomorrow morning, you'll be back on a ship to Catalonia."

Elara felt like she was going to be sick. Now her papou would definitely know all the trouble and harm she'd caused over the past few weeks.

"And Theodosius?" she pressed on dreading the answer. "What's going to happen to him?"

"Who?" Maria frowned, confused.

"The pirate." Nekros nodded pensively. "Obviously, Mister Kardia is to be put to death as soon as possible."

Elara's eyes widened, but she did her best not to react too strongly. "He's already had his trial?"

"His trial is later this evening. The pirate's fate will be decided then." Maria gave Nekros a disapproving look. She was probably annoyed that he wasn't even pretending that the royals were following the law.

"Yes, and Kardia will be found guilty of kidnapping and murder, and will be sentenced to death," Nekros doubled down, confidently.

"You know the outcome before seeing the evidence or hearing any testimonies?" Elara challenged him with narrowed eyes.

Nekros leaned back lazily in his seat, still unbothered by her. "Do you have some evidence to give in the pirate's *defense*, my lady?"

The room suddenly felt much colder than before. Both the empress and the despot looked at her expectantly. To defend Theodosius now would be social suicide, regardless of his innocence.

Women with bad reputations either end up on the streets or dead.

"No," Elara swallowed, hating herself. "I only meant that...I believe in fair trials. The empire's justice system should be as just and merciful as our Lord Jesus Christ is to us."

There was a moment of contemplative silence before Empress Maria spoke, "That was well said, darling. Every trial in Constantinople should be fair. I'll be attending the pirate's trial, so I'll make sure it is just."

"Thank you, Your Majesty." Elara smiled, but the empress' words did little to comfort her. Nekros was going to have Theodosius killed one way or another.

- - -

Empress Maria dismissed them both with promises that she would reach out again in the near future, and that she hoped to see

351

Elara again before she left in the morning for Catalonia. Elara wasn't sure she believed her. The empress had once been her closest confidant and mother figure, and had nearly been Elara's mother-in-law, but now they were painfully estranged.

"Countess Elara! Wait a moment!" Nekros' voice echoed off the walls of the palace's grand spiral staircase as Elara made her descent.

She stopped mid-step and turned to look up at Nekros who was several steps above her. His beady eyes gleamed maliciously at her as he leaned gloatingly on the stair railing.

"You were my father's friend," Elara said before he could get a word out.

"Yes, and I am truly sorry. I'm hoping we can put this all behind us." Nekros' voice sounded remorseful, but she didn't trust it.

"Behind us? You tried to have me killed!" Elara gripped the railing so tightly her knuckles turned white. The despot's audacity knew no bounds.

"A regrettable decision on my part. I did it to protect my reputation, you understand. We are nothing without our reputations." He smiled as if he expected her to agree that protecting one's reputation justified murder.

"Your reputation is forever ruined with me, Your Excellency," she spat angrily.

"That is unfortunate, however, you are but one person, so it hardly matters. Now we are both in good standing with the royal court, and it only cost one man's life." Nekros gave a sickening little laugh before disappearing back up the stairs.

And it only cost one man's life.

Elara felt like the world was spinning around her as she continued down the stairs. Never in her life had she felt this low, this disillusioned, this disgusted with herself and her place in society.

And it only cost one man's life.

Theodosius was going to die, and it was all her fault. He was not a perfect man, but he had kept her alive, and had taken the fall so that her reputation would remain intact. His payment for his heroics would be a painful death and an unmarked grave. No Orthodox clergy would give a funeral to a convicted pirate.

Elara stumbled outside the palace doors, blinded temporarily by the blazing sun. Constantinople was in full swing now and bustling with life. The city folk moved around the busy streets with their wares, chatting loudly as they went. On the outside, it looked like a day like any other. No one seemed to be enveloped in their own personal dark cloud like she was.

Before she could continue to wallow in self-pity, Elara suddenly heard the sound of a liturgical march. The Orthodox chanting grew louder, and she turned to see a procession of Orthodox Christians marching diligently toward the Hagia Sophia for Divine Liturgy. They carried gold crosses on wooden poles, a few held icons of Christ and the Theotokos, and they were dressed in mostly black robes. The priests leading the way were dressed in red and cream garments while holding the Holy Bible. The congregation marched behind them, singing along joyously to the hymns.

After the day—no, after the week—that Elara had, she could use the comfort of Divine Liturgy in her favorite church, the Hagia Sophia. She followed the procession down the street for a few blocks before making it to the grand entrance. The doors were even taller than she had remembered, but the inside was just as beautiful. The iconography of Christ and the Saints was like nothing in this world. It put all other churches to shame.

Elara lit a candle in the narthex and did her cross before entering the nave. Not wanting to draw too much attention to herself, she stayed toward the back, next to a large pillar. The smell of incense, the beautiful iconography, and the sound of Orthodox chant enveloped her senses, making her feel like she was truly in another world, a better world.

Surely, Heaven didn't discriminate against people based on class, and people were punished for lying, not praised. Heaven would be a place where you didn't have to constantly prove your worthiness, nor worry about anyone's reputation. There was a sudden lump in her throat again, and she tried to swallow it down. Her emotions were not going to get the better of her now.

"Oh, thank God! I've been looking for you everywhere, Elara dear," a soft voice said to her right.

Elara quickly wiped the corner of her left eye before turning to see Celina standing before her. Poor Celina was still dressed in her ballgown from the night before, and she looked rough with dark circles under her eyes, and her hair a tangled mess, but Elara was so happy to see her that it didn't matter.

"Celina!" Elara choked on a sob as she threw her arms around her friend's neck and pulled her in for a bone crushing hug. "Where have you been?"

"Oh, you know…running around," Celina gave a half-laugh, half-sob. "I almost got your necklace back, but there were these thieves, and—"

"Wait, where's Rhea?" Elara interrupted her, noticing their friend was nowhere to be seen.

"Rhea is fine. I—I left her at the other church across town." Celina wiped her nose on her sleeve and looked down at her feet, as if ashamed to make eye contact with Elara.

"All right, as long as she's safe. What were you saying about thieves?" Elara whispered quietly, trying her best to not disrupt the service further with their chatter.

"Rhea and I found your necklace on this woman, and we tried to get it from her, but these really buff thieves chased us into a church and took it back, and then Rhea and I argued, and now…" Celina took a breath. "Now your necklace is lost…again. And it's all my fault. I'm so sorry, Elara."

Elara blinked as she processed Celina's confessionary ramble. She'd never admit it to Celina or anyone, but Elara had forgotten about her yiayia's necklace until that moment. With everything that had happened over the past few hours, a piece of jewelry, even one as important of an heirloom as Countess Zoe Iliakos' necklace, seemed trivial now.

"It's all right." She gave Celina's arm a comforting squeeze. "Honestly, the important thing is you and Rhea weren't hurt. I'd never want you to risk your safety for me, especially not over a necklace."

Elara had meant for her words to soothe and comfort Celina, but they seemed to have the opposite effect, as her friend burst into tears. Thankfully, her sobs were quiet enough that they didn't disrupt the service.

"Oh no!" Elara wrapped her friend in another hug. "Was it something I said?"

"N-no, I'm just a bad person," Celina's voice trembled as tears streamed down her face.

"No, you're not! Don't talk about yourself that way." She frowned, trying to figure out the best way to comfort her friend without unintentionally making her cry more.

"But I am!" Celina bemoaned. "I've been so cruel to Rhea, and then we were finally getting along, and...I was mean to her *again*. I'm always mean to everyone because I constantly need to be right. It's no wonder all my friends hate me!"

"Your friends don't hate you, Celina." Elara shook her head in exasperation. "I'm your friend, and I love you."

"You love everyone," Celina half-joked, as she wiped her tears away on her upper sleeve. "You even love that pirate. Where is Theodosius anyway?"

"He's..." She swallowed. "He's been arrested."

"Arrested?" Celina balked in surprise.

"Yes," continued Elara. "They're going to execute him."

"Oh, dear...oh, I'm so sorry to hear that."

"It's my fault."

"How is it your fault? He was committing piracy long before he met you," Celina scoffed as she leaned back against one of the wide marble columns behind her. It occurred to Elara that Celina was probably due for a well-earned rest.

"You're tired. Come back with me to the palace. I'm sure Empress Maria will let you stay in one of the guest rooms," Elara offered her friend, ignoring her question completely.

"Don't change the subject." Even exhausted Celina was on to her. "Why do you think the captain's arrest is your fault?"

"I know he has his flaws, but Theodosius saved my life and then protected my reputation. He sacrificed himself so I could escape punishment. Now Nekros is going to have him executed." Elara miserably slunk down to sit on the marble floor. It wasn't proper to sit at church like that, but she doubted anyone would care enough to notice.

"Sorry, Nekros is doing what?" Celina moved to join her on the floor. "What exactly have I missed?"

Elara told Celina the whole story of what had happened with Theodosius' brother years ago, of Nekros' villainous murder attempt against her, and of her tea conversation with the empress and the despot. Celina listened to the story patiently, and didn't interrupt once as Elara told her tale. When Elara was done, it was clear that Celina was slowly taking it all in.

"This is shocking to say the least, but also, not as surprising as you'd imagine..." Celina's words sounded contradictory to Elara, but she let her friend finish. "Royalty always has a darkness within it. *It is easier for a camel to go through the eye of the needle than a rich man to enter Heaven*, as they say."

"That's my papou's favorite bible quote," Elara smiled, but then her stomach twisted up again. "Empress Maria sent a letter to my papou, letting him know where I am, and what I've been up to. Now he'll know what a mess I've made."

Celina looked away from her and kept her eyes on the front of the church. "He already knows."

"What?"

"Your papou... already knows." She looked at her hands, still not making eye contact with Elara. "Or at the very least, he knows part of it."

"What are you talking about?" Elara almost laughed, even though it wasn't funny. "How—how could he know?"

"Rhea and I saw him in Athens, and we may have let some information about you slip… I'm so sorry," Celina grimaced apologetically, finally making eye contact with her again.

"You saw him in *Athens?*" This time, Elara did laugh, but without humor. It bubbled out of her throat against her consent like she was vomiting up her feelings, unable to contain the absurdity that was her life. She tried to choke the sound back down before anyone in church could catch her and give her a judgmental stare.

"I meant to tell you sooner…" Celina wrung her hands. "I thought I could help you get the necklace back before your papou got home, so it wouldn't matter if he knew."

"It's fine. I don't blame you." Elara traced the mosaic tiles on the floor with her finger. "How did I screw up this badly? Honestly, there should be an award for how horrendously I've handled this entire trip."

"Oh, don't be so hard on yourself. I've done my share of ruining things on this trip too." Celina gave her an affectionate slap on the shoulder.

The girls lapsed into silence as the Divine Liturgy continued. They seemed to have spoken softly enough that none of the congregation was looking at them in annoyance for talking. Elara looked up to the left side of the dome and saw some iconography of the Crucifixion of Christ. A Roman soldier was depicted sticking a spear into Jesus' exposed chest as His Mother looked on in despair.

"There's a person who never cared about his reputation," Elara whispered as she pointed to the icon above. "Christ always did the right thing, and He didn't care what anyone thought."

"Yes, and they killed him for it," said Celina.

"They did." Elara nodded. "But then, he defeated death by death, and rose on the third day, according to the Scriptures..." Her voice trailed off as she found her eyes moving to other bible scenes: Jesus healing the blind man, which upset the Pharisees, Jesus carrying his own Cross after his friends betrayed and abandoned him, Jesus freeing the dead from Hades, taking Adam and Eve with him...

"I know what I have to do." Elara stood. "I have to defend Theodosius in court."

"Hmm?" Celina looked up at her in shock. "You can't! That would ruin you."

"I think I'm already ruined...in here." She pointed to the left side of her chest where her heart was beating with renewed urgency.

"Elara dear, I know you're upset about the injustice happening to Theodosius, but there's nothing you can do for him without destroying your reputation *and* your family name. You could be thrown out onto the streets or imprisoned! Be reasonable!" Celina scrambled to her feet as Elara headed for the door.

Women with bad reputations either end up on the streets or dead.

"I don't care! The only way a person like Theodosius could win their trial is if a nobleperson or a respected member of the clergy spoke on their behalf," Elara said as they made their way back outside. "If I defend him and tell the truth…they might still punish him a little, but they won't kill him."

Celina moved to block Elara's path. "Speaking up for Theodosius is one thing, but you can't tell the emperor that his brother is a killer. It'll be your word against his, and Nekros outranks you!"

"I won't mention Nekros. I can defend Theodosius' good name without dragging anyone else down." Elara pushed past Celina; she needed to get to the palace as soon as possible.

The sun above them was still glowing bright and hot, but it was hitting at an angle now, signaling that it was close to late afternoon. The outdoor merchant stands were starting to pack up for the day, and families were being called in for an early supper. As it grew closer to evening time, Elara knew the trial could begin at any moment, if it hadn't already. She picked up her pace, praying silently that she wasn't already too late.

The girls briskly walked toward the palace in silence. Celina was seemingly done challenging her on this decision. Knowing her friend well, Elara suspected that Celina would make at least one more objection to her plan before they entered the courtroom.

"Elara! Celina!" Someone shouted their names.

Looking around expectantly, Elara saw that it was Yianni Drakos and Tina Argyrou racing toward them.

"Oh, hello!" Celina greeted them first. "Is Rhea with you?"

"Rhea? She's not with you?" Tina replied with a confused frown.

"No…" Celina shook her head guiltily but said nothing more.

"What are you doing here?" Elara asked. It was always good to see Tina, but Yianni's presence confused and worried her. He wasn't exactly her biggest fan.

"Elara," Yianni panted, out of breath. "Theodosius has been arrested!"

"Yes, I'm aware—"

"He's going to be executed!"

"I know—"

"You have to testify for him! Please, you're the only noble who has enough goodness and knowledge to save him!" Yianni pleaded. His eyes were frantic, and his voice trembled.

"Yianni—" she began again to try to explain her plan, but he wouldn't let her finish.

"Please, Lady Elara! I'm sorry about the things I said about you, but Theodosius trusts you...he needs you! Please, you have to help him! He'll die!"

"Yianni!" Elara yelled loudly, finally silencing him. "I'm on my way to his trial to defend him right now! Feel free to come along."

"That's great to hear." Yianni relaxed slightly.

"Told you she'd do it," Tina said with a bemused chuckle.

"Right as always, Tina." Yianni turned back to Elara. "Shall we go? There's no time to waste!"

- - -

Theodosius wished he could remember sunlight. Well, that was an exaggeration. Obviously, he remembered sunlight. But it was so dark and cold in his cell, it made him long for the sun, for the warm rays on his skin. That had been the best thing about being a corsair—being on the open water and feeling the sun on his face. He wondered if it was sunny wherever Elara was.

When Nekros had accused him of being in love with Elara, Theodosius had publicly scoffed. Privately, he knew Nekros was right. Once again, Nekros had managed to use Theodosius' heart against him. The despot had never loved anyone but himself, so it was impossible to hit him back in the same way.

Despite his dire circumstances, Theodosius wasn't angry. Elara and her friends would be safe with the empress. Yianni, Tina, and the rest of his crew were safe at sea. He'd done the right thing for once, and soon, he would be reunited with his brother in Heaven. That was all that really mattered.

His only regret was that he would not be able to feel the sun one last time. The cell had three walls of stone, with no windows, and one wall of bars that shed no light. The only light source was a torch down a side hallway, much too far away for his liking.

Theodosius' ankles and wrists were bound in chains, hooked to the floor like a dog. On top of that, the cell smelled of rot and piss. His trial and execution could not come soon enough.

"I was wondering when they'd finally catch you," A voice said from the darkness.

Lifting his head to try to get a look at who had spoken, Theodosius replied, "Yes, it is about time. Wouldn't you agree, Prince Andronikos?"

Elara's ex-fiancé, who was also Theodosius' ex-employer, stepped into the torch's dim light. He was hard to make out in the darkness, but Theodosius recognized the prince's broad shoulders, blond hair, round face, and small, cool eyes. Andronikos looked bulkier than Theodosius remembered, but perhaps it was a trick of the light. The prince had always been wider than him, whereas Theodosius was taller, more lean.

"I won't be at your trial today," Andronikos said with his signature bored tone. "Want to know why?"

"You didn't do much at my first trial, so I never imagined you'd be at this one either." Theodosius shrugged, causing the chains that restrained him to clink noisily on the stone floor.

"My Uncle Nekros told me about your little...*escapade* with Elara." Andronikos' eyes narrowed, and his jaw tightened slightly, but his tone gave nothing else away. "I shall be having dinner with her this evening during your trial. By the end of the night, you'll be sentenced to death, and the countess shall be mine again."

Theodosius clenched his fists, but took a deep breath before saying, "Your mother won't let that happen. The empress is very protective of Countess Iliakos, you know."

"Oh, I know," Andronikos smiled, revealing emotion for the first time. "Mother loves Elara...perhaps even more than she loves me.

When she sees me and Elara together again, and getting along, she will be most pleased."

"Keep telling yourself that," Theodosius said dryly.

"Are you jealous? Uncle Nekros said you wanted Elara for yourself. Is that true?" Andronikos asked, sounding almost hopeful, like a neglected child wanting to be seen as enviable.

"I'm not jealous of you, Andronikos. I pity you. I shall be dead soon, but you—you will have to live without her. The countess won't take you back." Theodosius' voice sounded confident but, on the inside, he worried that if the prince forced her hand, Elara might have no choice but to take him back.

Andronikos' smile wavered, but his tone remained neutral. "We shall see."

Before Theodosius could ask Andronikos what he meant by that, the sound of metal doors squeaking open filled the air and out marched two guards to the front of his cell.

"Time for your trial, Kardia," One of the guards said in a nasally, taunting voice.

"That was fast," Theodosius muttered as the guards dragged him to his feet and pulled him out of the cell. They unbound his legs, but his wrists remained chained together behind his back.

"Ensure the corsair doesn't try anything," Andronikos told the guards as he slipped from view. It would most likely be the last time Theodosius would ever see his old master, and that was a relief. The prince was still as cruel and callous as ever. Theodosius just wished he could warn Elara about her former flame's intentions before the prince accosted her later that evening.

Elara's smart, Theodosius thought to himself as they dragged him down a hallway that he didn't recognize. *She'll be able to tell if Andronikos is up to his same old tricks or not.* Surely, there was no need to worry about her. Elara was a wealthy woman, in a position of power, with the favor of the empress, which, arguably, made the countess the second most powerful woman in the empire.

Yet, Theodosius was still worried about Elara. Here he was about to be sentenced to death for crimes, most of which he hadn't even committed, and all he could think about was Elara Iliakos. Was she safe? Did she ever find her yiayia's special necklace? Was she already sailing back home to Catalonia?

"Keep moving!" One of the guards clearly thought Theodosius was walking too slowly and shoved him forward.

"I'm going! I'm going!" Theodosius grumbled as he tried to regain his footing after being jostled about.

They turned a corner, and Theodosius recognized his surroundings again. They were in the back of the entrance hall of the palace. Large marble columns lined the walls, and in between them and, on the floor, were the most elegant mosaic art pieces. His favorite floor mosaic was of the two-headed-eagle, a representation of the empire he had once loved, but that had never loved him back.

He looked to the left and saw the open courtyard and open hallways that he used to roam when he and his brother worked there seven years ago. There were the stairs that led to Nekros' old chamber, where his brother had been slain, and there was the door that led to the throne room, where Theodosius had met his fate the first time around. This time, without Yianni, he doubted he would be able to pull off another grand escape.

The thought of Yianni and his other friends made Theodosius' throat feel tight. He hoped his crew had the good sense to sail far away by now. It wasn't safe for them in Constantinople.

"Stop here." The guards came to a halt, forcing Theodosius to stop just outside the throne room door.

The tall and majestic doors were shut, but he could hear people bustling about inside. He imagined the emperor getting situated on his throne, ready to pass judgment, the noble lawmakers sitting to the far left with their scrolls, and at least one local bishop sitting on the right to represent Ecumenical Patriarch Athanasius.

It was all for show. They had already decided that he was guilty. Nekros was probably whispering all sorts of lies about Theodosius into Emperor Michael's ear right now. Of course, Emperor Michael would believe Nekros over Theodosius. Nekros was a despot and the beloved brother of the emperor, whereas Theodosius was a lower-class pirate, with no titles, and nothing to his name but scandal and slander.

The doors finally opened, and a short man stuck his head out, saying, "We're ready for him."

Wordlessly, one of the guards shoved Theodosius forward into the burning, judgmental light of the courtroom. His fate was sealed, and there was nothing left for him to do but to accept it.

Chapter Eighteen

The Trial

"Shall I recount any of the crimes again, Your Majesty?" Nekros asked his brother, Emperor Michael Palaiologos IX, after he had finished the list of things that he claimed Theodosius was guilty of.

"No, thank you. That will suffice," Emperor Michael said in a bored tone. "How does the defendant plead?"

The emperor was stocky, like his son, Andronikos, with dark stubble on his chin and wrinkles around his eyes. He was dressed in a regal, multi-colored tunic, with a bejeweled crown on his head. The emperor sat alone on his golden throne. Evidently, the empress hadn't thought this sham of a trial was important enough to attend. Theodosius couldn't blame her.

"How do you plead?" Emperor Michael repeated sternly.

Of the seventy crimes read, he estimated that he was only truly guilty of three of them. This included theft, the ransacking of Tossa de Mar, and threatening the life of a state official. That wasn't too bad, some light confessions before his execution should clear him before he went to Heaven.

"Does it really matter how I plead?" Theodosius was forced to stand at attention before the court, but if it had been up to him, he'd be sitting with his feet propped up, enjoying the show. It was all theater after all, like performing an Ancient Greek tragedy. The hero always dies in the end, so what was the point in pleading for a different outcome? He'd done his pleading last time, and it hadn't made any difference.

"You plead guilty then, Kardia?" Nekros goaded him slyly.

Theodosius sighed dramatically, "Fine, I plead innocent. Not that it matters much to any of you."

"You can't plead innocent," one of the lawmakers said. "You can only plead guilty or not guilty."

"I plead *not* guilty then." Theodosius shrugged in exasperation.

"And your defense?" Emperor Michael pressed on coldly.

"I have no defense, Your Majesty, other than my word."

"Any witnesses to call upon who might speak on your behalf?"

Theodosius thought of Justine and her lies the last time he had tried to call upon a witness to defend him. There was no one in the kingdom who would defend him now, or at least, no one who had any real power or sway over the situation.

"No, Your Majesty. There's no one." He made the mistake of making eye contact with Nekros, who was grinning like a sick mad man. There was truly no justice in this life, but perhaps in the next...

Before Theodosius could finish the thought, the large doors burst open, clanging loudly. Everyone turned to look in shock at who would dare to interrupt a trial like this without the permission of the emperor. At the door was a beautiful woman standing confidently, powerfully, and auspiciously unannounced. She wore a dark-blue gown, and her long brown hair fell gracefully on her shoulders.

"Oh, *no*," Theodosius muttered quietly under his breath, his heart dropping to his stomach as he recognized the woman immediately.

"My name is Countess Elara Iliakos of Catalonia, and I am here to defend Captain Theodosius Kardia!" she announced, her voice echoing off the marble walls.

There were shocked murmurings from almost everyone in the room. No one could believe what they were seeing—a respected countess defending a notorious pirate captain—that was unheard of. Surely, no noblewoman in her right mind would be foolish enough to try it, but here Lady Elara Iliakos was, risking…no, *sacrificing* everything to clear his name.

Theodosius couldn't believe it. Evidently, neither could Nekros nor Emperor Michael, who both stared at her in shock, their mouths agape, saying nothing.

Elara kept her head held high as she walked down the aisle, followed closely by Lady Celina Oberon and two others. Theodosius' stomach dropped again as he realized the two others were his best friends, Yianni Drakos and Tina Argyrou.

"What are you doing here?" Theodosius demanded quietly when the group made it to the front.

"Defending you," Elara shrugged innocently.

Yianni winked at him, and Tina gave a shy, apologetic smile. They had defied his orders to sail away, and thus, put themselves and the whole crew in even more danger.

"Have you all lost your minds?"

It was a rhetorical question that Elara didn't dignify with a response. Instead, she walked past him to stand in front of the emperor's throne and bowed deeply. Celina followed Elara, while Yianni and Tina moved to stand behind Theodosius.

Yianni clapped him on the shoulder and whispered, "How's the trial going so far?"

"Not great," Theodosius hissed back through gritted teeth as he watched Celina bow and introduce herself to the emperor. He noted that Elara was looking at the empress' empty throne.

"Bet it'll be much better now that we're here." Yianni sounded a little too proud of himself.

"I can't believe you talked the girls into pulling this ridiculous stunt. Honestly, Yianni, you're going to get everyone killed!" Theodosius grumbled, keeping his eyes on Elara.

"I didn't have to talk anyone into anything," Yianni chuckled. "This was all Elara's idea."

"Quiet in the court!" one of the lawmakers snapped, looking at Yianni pointedly.

"*Sorry,*" Yianni mouthed silently as he moved back to stand next to Tina.

"Emperor Michael, I apologize for the interruption, but I could not let you sentence an innocent man to death," Elara said loudly with the perfect mixture of respectfulness and confidence in her voice.

"Innocent? Please!" Nekros said shrilly, but it was clear he was a bit shaken for once. "Kardia is many things, but innocent is not one of them!"

Emperor Michael held up his hand to silence his brother. Nekros' face turned cherry red, but he followed orders and fell silent.

"Lady Elara, are you or your lady-in-waiting under duress?" Emperor Michael asked her gently as he eyed both her and Celina.

"No, Your Majesty."

"Are you being threatened or compelled by some unknown force to be here today?"

Elara shook her head, "I am not. I am here of my own accord."

The emperor blinked, confused. "I don't understand... why would you risk so much for a man who kidnapped you?"

"Because he did not kidnap me, Your Majesty. I traveled with the captain of my own free will." Elara's voice trembled as the truth fell from her lips, but she kept her head held high, even as the judgmental whispers grew louder.

"Silence, please!" Emperor Michael ordered the room.

The room became quiet, but even the emperor couldn't stop the staring and contorted faces of the onlookers.

Despite this, Theodosius could see there was no shame in Elara's body language, only fear of what the truth might bring. That made him

373

feel proud of her, but he still wished she wasn't doing this for him—he wasn't worth it.

"Why would you defile yourself by traveling with such a disgusting man as Theodosius Kardia?" Nekros spoke in a much angrier and more judgmental voice than the emperor.

"*Defile?* You want to talk about what's been defiled, Lord Nekros?" Elara's voice was calm, but there was something simmering under the surface.

"Elara, don't..." Celina whispered a warning, but something told Theodosius that Elara was past caring what anyone thought of her.

"Please enlighten us, Lady Elara. I didn't realize you were a law expert," Nekros egged her on, clearly trying to get her to say something reprehensible in her angered state.

Thankfully, Elara was smarter than that. She took a calming breath before returning her attention away from Nekros and back to the emperor. "Emperor Michael, will Empress Maria be joining us? I was told she would be here, and I would rather wait to give my full testimony when she arrives."

Emperor Michael glanced almost nervously at Nekros, and then looked back at Elara, saying, "No, I'm sorry. She won't be here. If we had known you were going to testify, the empress would have been here instead of..." The emperor's voice trailed off as the doors burst open again.

"Sorry I'm late," a man's voice said.

Everyone turned to look at who had spoken, except for Theodosius, who kept his eyes on Elara. He already knew that voice and knew that the countess would be troubled by it.

Elara's face had gone ghostly pale as she stared at the person marching down the aisle toward her.

"Hello, Lady Elara. You look well."

"Hello, Prince Andronikos," her voice was noticeably less confident. "I didn't think I'd be seeing you."

"Surprise! Here I am," Prince Andronikos smirked, seemingly pleased to have caught her off guard.

Before Elara could say anything else, Andronikos waltzed past her and moved to take a seat beside his father on his mother's throne.

Elara made eye contact with Theodosius, and it was suddenly as if they were reading each other's minds. Prince Andronikos was presiding over the case, and neither of them were happy about it.

Theodosius knew he couldn't say or do anything in that moment, but he gave what he hoped was a comforting and supportive look to Elara. He was confident that she could handle her ex-fiancé. Andronikos and his antics were no match for the countess' sharp wit.

"What have I missed? Anything interesting?" Andronikos asked his father.

"Behave yourself," the emperor replied sternly.

Andronikos scowled at that, his face turning as red as a strawberry, but he said nothing else.

The prince looked out of place among the Mediterranean nobility with his blonde hair, light eyes, and pale skin. He was even paler than Celina, the only other blonde in the room. Leonides once joked that if Andronikos stood next to a cloud, he'd blend right in, until he got angry, and his redness gave him away.

"Shall we continue the trial?" Nekros asked impatiently. "I believe there was some more *testimony* that Lady Elara wanted to give."

Everyone turned to stare at Elara, who suddenly looked like she'd rather be anywhere else. Her face was calm, but Theodosius could tell by the way she clenched her hands together, and the uneven rising of her chest, that she was dangerously close to panicking.

"I would like to say something," Theodosius spoke up. "If that's all right with you, Your Majesty?"

Emperor Michael looked over at him as if he had just remembered that the pirate was in the room. "No, you may not speak, pirate. Go on, Lady Elara."

Elara looked at Celina, a silent, but clear, cry for help. Andronikos showing up had really shaken her, but Celina wouldn't, or rather, couldn't, help her. No one could help her now. She had to finish her testimony on her own.

"The late Countess Zoe Iliakos' necklace was stolen," Elara began, conveniently leaving out that it had been Yianni that had taken it. "I knew I had to get it back, and that Theodosius, with his connections, could help me. So, I asked for his help, and he obliged.

He never forced me or hurt me. Theodosius Kardia is a good man, and he...he doesn't deserve to die."

There was a moment of silence before Andronikos asked dryly, "Is that it? We're just supposed to take your word that he's a good man? Have you no evidence?"

"Does the word of a countess mean nothing?" Elara asked, perplexed.

"Not when that word is spoken so unsteadily," Nekros said in an almost chastising tone. "Look at her hands, brother. See how she shakes! Clearly, she is afraid of Kardia and his wrath."

"I am not afraid of anyone! I speak the truth!" Elara's hands clenched into fists.

"Watch your tone please," Emperor Michael ordered. "If you are done with your testimony, you may step back while we deliberate."

"I'm begging you to have mercy, Your Majesty. Do you really think I would risk my reputation and my safety for a man of low moral character? If you must punish him, give him a chance to reform. He can work for the Church!" She turned to the bishop sitting nearby. "Surely, the Church could use some help?"

"Christ forgives even the worst sinners and offers second chances to all," the bishop said with a twinkle in his eye, giving Elara the first piece of outside support she'd gotten since entering the room.

"You see!" Elara smiled. "I implore the court to forgive Theodosius Kardia, as Christ our Lord and Savior forgives us all."

Emperor Michael frowned, considering this. "Well, I suppose we could think of a punishment more befitting—"

"But Kardia is a killer!" Nekros interrupted. "He killed his own brother, Leonides Kardia—!"

"That's a lie! Nekros is the one that killed Leonides! He killed my brother, and I will not take the fall for it!" Theodosius shouted, unable to keep silent any longer.

There was a collective gasp from the people around them as his accusation toward the despot floated around the room. No one accused the emperor's brother of a crime, let alone a murder.

Elara looked at Theodosius with cool annoyance as she probably felt she had been so close to getting him a reduced sentence before his outburst. It didn't matter to Theodosius; he did not want his brother's death on his record.

"This is outrageous!" Nekros said as the chaos in the room subsided. "What motive would I have for killing a man I didn't even know!"

"But you did know him! He was killed in *your* chamber!" Theodosius spat.

"Pah! You are making such a spectacle of yourself, Kardia! What would your poor mother, Eudokia, think of you now?" Nekros scoffed cruelly.

His face became hot with anger, but this time, he held his tongue. Bringing up his mother was a low blow, and Nekros knew it.

"We shall deliberate on sentencing now if there are no further statements—" Emperor Michael began but was interrupted by Celina of all people.

"Wait, please, Your Majesty, there's one more person that still needs to testify!" Celina said.

"Who would that be?" Michael asked, sounding as confused as Theodosius felt.

Elara looked at her friend, equally confused. "Yes, who do we have to testify next?"

"I need to fetch them…" Celina started before whispering to Elara, "Stall them as long as you can. I'll be back."

- - -

Celina raced back toward the little chapel where she and Rhea had angrily parted ways. There was much that Celina needed to apologize to Rhea for, and she hoped this good deed would set things in the right direction.

Thankfully, by some miracle, the church wasn't more than a few minutes away by foot. Celina wasted no time racing to find Rhea, and hopefully, Eudokia the monastic nun.

"Rhea?" She called as soon as she stepped inside the church. The church looked the same as before, except it was much cleaner now. The furniture pieces that the assailants had knocked over were sitting upright again, and any dirt or glass left behind had been swept away.

"You're back." Rhea was finishing sweeping the marble floor next to an Icon of Saint George. She had exchanged her ballgown for a more conservative work-dress, and her dark hair was pulled back into a messy braid. "Did you find the necklace?"

"No, forget the necklace." Celina took a breath to steady herself before rushing to her friend's side. "Listen, first I want to say that I'm so sorry about before. I was wrong, and you were right."

"Celina—"

"I should have been kinder to you—"

"Celina—"

"I want to be your friend. I want to be best friends—"

"Celina, you really don't have to—" They were talking over each other.

"I don't ever want to hurt you like Lady Sidra did," Celina said, effectively getting Rhea to be quiet and listen. "Rhea dear, I promise to be better and kinder because that's who I want to be. You are kind, loyal, and brave, and you deserve a friend who is all of those things to you too—"

"Celina!"

"Yes?"

"I forgive you," Rhea laughed as she set the broom down to give Celina a hug. "We're friends! Calm down."

Celina smiled, but pulled away quickly so that Rhea could see that it was urgent. "Sorry, I can't calm down just yet. In addition to this apology, I have urgent business with the nun, Eudokia!"

"What business is that?" Eudokia appeared behind them.

Celina could see it now. Both Eudokia and Theodosius had the same hooded eyes, round cheekbones, and slanted smiles. The relation between mother and son was so obvious, she couldn't believe she hadn't seen it before.

"Your son, Theodosius, is on trial for all sorts of heinous crimes. Will you testify?" Celina pleaded.

- - -

"...And another reason I think the death penalty is a bit extreme..." Elara had been talking nonstop for nearly twenty minutes. Most of the room was annoyed, but Theodosius was both entertained and impressed.

"Enough!" Emperor Michael groaned. "We can't wait any longer. I'm sorry, Lady Elara, but we must sentence—"

The doors opened again, and three people walked into the courtroom. Theodosius recognized them at once as Celina, Rhea, and a familiar looking Orthodox Christian nun.

No, it couldn't be.

"Is there still time for us to testify?" Eudokia Kardia, Theodosius' mother, asked pointedly.

"The more the merrier, I suppose," Emperor Michael grumbled, most likely annoyed by the lack of decorum this trial was showing.

Theodosius watched in shock as his mother walked decidedly down the aisle toward him. He hadn't seen nor heard from the woman in years, and she hadn't even attended his last trial. *What was she doing here, and when did she become a monastic?*

381

"Hello, my son," Eudokia said, her eyes were wet, but the rest of her face remained just as stoic as he remembered.

"Hello, Mother." Theodosius bowed his head respectfully, unable to look her in the eye.

"I love family reunions." Rhea smiled widely as she and Celina took their place next to Elara.

"Your Majesty, I have a letter." Eudokia pulled a piece of parchment out of her pocket and handed it to the emperor. "It's from Leonides to his spiritual father. He mailed it exactly one day before he was murdered, and his spiritual father gifted it back to me at my son's funeral."

"It has the Seal of the Ecumenical Patriarch," Emperor Michael noted, his eyes wide.

"Yes, Ecumenical Patriarch Athanasius was Leonides' spiritual father," Eudokia explained. "They often exchanged letters."

The Seal of the Ecumenical Patriarch implied that Orthodox church leadership had a copy of the letter, and possibly more of Leonides' letters as well.

Evidence. Theodosius smiled despite himself.

"Michael, you're not honestly going to listen to—" Nekros began to protest, but his brother silenced him again with a wave of his hand.

"What does it say, father?" Andronikos asked what everyone was thinking.

Emperor Michael grimaced and motioned to one of his guards. "Bring Mister Kardia to me, please."

Two guards were on him then, dragging him to the foot of the emperor's throne.

"Mister Kardia," Michael said slowly. "I've decided I'm going to be merciful and pardon you."

"What?" Theodosius was sure that he must have misheard him.

The emperor continued without addressing any of Theodosius' confusion, "I will pardon you of all crimes if, and only if, you retract your accusation about Lord Nekros."

"But Nekros killed my—!"

Emperor Michael held up a hand. "Retract your accusation against the despot, on the record, and you and your friends will be free to go."

It was then that Theodosius finally understood; Emperor Michael was protecting his brother. Whatever was in that letter had scared him, and like always, the crown would do anything to protect their own—even letting a pirate go free, assuming that pirate agreed to play along.

Theodosius' stomach churned, and his mouth tasted like dirt. Obviously, he would be a fool not to take the offer, but to lie about what he knew had happened to Leonides was unfathomable. His brother had been murdered by Nekros, and there would be no justice if he retracted his accusation.

He thought back to the night before, when he'd held a knife to Nekros' throat. If it wasn't for Elara's interference, he would have killed the despot then and there.

However, Elara had been there, and she was here now, risking everything to save him. He looked at her, and she looked back at him with her soft, kind eyes.

"...*You won't have peace until you let this go. Forgive him, so you can be free of him.*" Elara had said to him, and she was right. The countess was always right, and he loved her for it.

Perhaps his brother's letter, conjured seemingly out of thin air by his mother, was a second chance for him to finally move on. A final gift from Leonides.

"You have a deal," Theodosius told the emperor. "I'll recant my accusation against Lord Nekros, but I want one more thing in addition to my freedom."

"And what is that?" Emperor Michael asked with slanted eyes.

"I want Countess Elara's reputation to be fully restored. She's a good person and a loyal servant of the empire. Please don't punish her for trying to help me."

"Very well." Emperor Michael smiled, probably pleased he would have an excuse to forgive his wife's favorite former lady-in-waiting. "So, will you recant your accusation now?"

"Yes, I recant my accusation against Lord Nekros." Theodosius bowed respectfully to all the royals present and the deed was done.

"You're just letting him off the hook?" Nekros sounded outraged.

"That's right," the emperor said simply.

"But Kardia has committed many—!"

"Oh, be quiet, Nekros!" Michael stood, revealing himself to be taller than his younger brother. "I tire of your antics. We will be having words later in private."

"But—!"

"Enough! This trial is over!"

Theodosius' friends, along with his mother, erupted in celebratory cheers. Elara threw her arms around Theodosius' neck and pulled him into a tight hug. He inhaled the scent of her soft hair and enjoyed the feeling of having her in his arms again. Andronikos' eyes bore into them from across the room, but neither of them cared. Theodosius was finally free for the first time in seven years. The shackles of his past had evaporated, and a renewed sense of peace took hold.

Chapter Nineteen

Home Again

Elara couldn't believe her luck. The emperor was going to pardon her of all transgressions, and Theodosius' life had been spared. Everything had worked out. Now, the only person she still needed to face was her Papou when she got back to Tossa de Mar. She hoped he wouldn't be too angry with her.

"Sorry we couldn't get your necklace back," Rhea linked her left arm with Celina's right as she spoke to Elara. It was good to see Celina and Rhea were on good terms again.

"Forget about the necklace. I'm just happy we're all well and safe," Elara replied with one arm hooked through Celina's left arm, and the other looped around Theodosius' waist. Theodosius had his right arm wrapped around Elara's shoulders in a way that felt intimate without being too inappropriate for a public setting.

The group made their way outside into the dark autumn evening air, but with the mood they were all in, it could have been broad daylight in July.

"We should celebrate! Drinks on me!" Yianni whooped loudly, earning groans from the group, except from Tina, who laughed.

"You need to have money to buy drinks, Yianni," Theodosius reminded him, but he was smiling too. Elara loved that smile. It was warm, mischievous, and kind, all wrapped into one.

"This is where I must leave you," said Eudokia, changing the mood back to somber.

"You're not coming with us?" Theodosius sounded crestfallen.

"I have to get back to the church," she smiled at him softly. "You'll be all right now, love."

"Wait, I'll walk you." He disentangled himself from Elara but turned back before leaving with his mother. "Meet me at the local tavern for dinner? Then we can set sail back to Catalonia."

"Of course. We'll see you there." Elara nodded encouragingly, letting him know they would wait for him while he spoke with his mother privately.

Theodosius grinned at her, before slipping down a side street with Eudokia, and out of sight.

"Eudokia is so sweet," Rhea told the group as they made their way to the tavern to eat. "She loves Theodosius so much."

"She saved him. Whatever she had in that letter saved his life." Elara thought about how lucky it was that Eudokia had kept that letter, and how lucky it was that she was able to produce it at exactly the right moment to help save her youngest son.

"It was a true miracle," Tina agreed.

"Not sure the letter was a miracle, but it was lucky, nonetheless," Celina, ever the realist, concluded. "Perhaps a little *coincidental,* but..."

"Can't you just be optimistic for once?" Rhea teased Celina.

"Oh, I'm sorry." Celina's cheeks turned pink. "I'm working on it, truly."

"Good." Rhea beamed at Celina, and Celina beamed back with equal affection.

Elara was, once again, overcome with a feeling that Celina and Rhea had a connection that she wasn't a part of. It was a special connection, filled with tension that she couldn't quite define. It almost reminded Elara of the connection she shared with Theodosius. Almost.

"Here's the tavern!" Yianni pointed excitedly to a small wooden establishment. A warm glow came through the little windows and the door frame. It was the perfect spot to grab a bite and a drink before they set off on their journey home.

Before they could make it to the door, a voice called out, stopping them. "Elara, may I have a word with you?"

It was Prince Andronikos.

The prince was alone, which was unusual when it came to royalty. Usually, he would be surrounded by guards and servants, but now, he stood seemingly alone. To the untrained eye, his simple cloak, and unkempt hair, made him appear almost like an ordinary person, harmless. He was anything but.

"She doesn't want to talk to you," Celina snapped, standing protectively in front of her.

Yianni, Rhea, and Tina also moved to stand protectively in front of Elara, blocking her from the prince's view.

Elara's heart was racing, but she was feeling much braver now than before. She could face her ex-fiancé. He held no power over her anymore.

"It's fine." Elara pushed past them. "Go inside and order some food. I'll meet you all in there after I talk to him."

"Are you sure?" Tina frowned.

Rhea chimed in, "You don't have to talk to him if you don't want to."

"Yeah, I can beat him up for you, if you'd like," Yianni offered eagerly.

"Very funny," Andronikos rolled his eyes and pouted in a way Elara had once found endearing. Now, she found it annoying and childish.

"I wasn't joking," Yianni said in a serious tone. "I *will* beat him up, if you want me to."

Elara laughed at Andronikos' discomfort. "No need. I'll join you all in a minute." Her friends shrugged and made their way, one by one, inside the tavern.

Celina, the last one to the door, turned back midway, to say, "Elara dear, if I don't hear from you in exactly five minutes, I'm coming back out here to get you, understood?"

"Yes, my lady," Elara nodded with the ghost of a smile on her lips.

Then, Celina was gone, leaving Elara and Andronikos alone in the night. She shifted uncomfortably on her feet as he stared intensely at her. The prince always had a way of making her feel small and insecure under his gaze.

"What do you want?" Elara asked her former flame.

"I want to fix things, little bug," Andronikos said slowly. "Can you please give me time to fix things between us? You never gave me enough time to make things right."

When she first met him, he had nicknamed her 'little bug' in response to the way he said she scurried about the palace hallways. At first, it had been an endearing thing, being called 'little bug'. Now, she saw it for what it was—an insult; a way to make her feel small, like a beetle under his boot.

"Fix things? What's to fix? You hurt me, and now we're done." Elara folded her arms, trying to keep herself from shaking. He had no power over her anymore, she tried to remind herself.

"That's not fair! So, I screwed up one time, and now it's over forever? You really aren't going to give me another chance?" Andronikos was whining in the way she always hated. It made him sound like a bratty child. She couldn't believe he came all this way, without his guards, after all this time, just to whine at her.

"You verbally and physically abused me for over a year," she retorted coolly.

"I was going through a tough time! Can't you just forgive me?" he pleaded, still whining.

"No, I can't."

"Don't you want to come home again? Be welcomed back into court at Constantinople? Don't you miss how things used to be?" His words painted a nostalgic picture, but she simply didn't long for the old days anymore. Her home was wherever her church was, wherever her Papou was, wherever her friends were. Constantinople wasn't home anymore.

"Goodbye, Andronikos. I won't be seeing you again." Elara turned to leave, but he grabbed her arm aggressively, stopping her from moving.

"You're being cruel! How could you hurt me like this?" he shouted angrily in her face, his tight grip on her arm would surely leave a bruise.

"Let go of me!"

"It's because of Kardia, isn't it? He's bedded you, hasn't he?"

"No! Let go!" She tried to pull herself free, but he held on tightly, keeping her trapped there. Her heart was beating agonizingly against her rib cage as she suddenly worried that Andronikos might try to kill her. Perhaps he would try to squeeze her neck like she really was a 'little bug'.

"I can't believe you would ruin yourself with a pirate of all people! You *filthy* little...!"

"Stop! Get off me!"

"I'm going to tell them!" Andronikos' eyes were wide with sudden insanity. "I'm going to tell the whole court what a *slut* you are!"

"No!"

"I'm going to tell everyone all the things we did last summer. The places you put that whorish little mouth—all the places you let me touch you! You'll never be able to show your face in public again!"

As he threatened her, something in Elara's mind clicked into place. She suddenly felt like she was seeing herself from an outsider's perspective. Almost like she was a dove, perched in a nearby olive tree, watching the prince mistreat her below. It was, miraculously, a more sympathetic perspective. Elara was simply a girl doing her best. She deserved better than this treatment.

When she and the prince were together, she had always been good to him. He would push her around, and she used to let him, but things were different now. Elara was different now. Andronikos was, once again, trying to shame her into submission, but this time, she wouldn't be swayed. After all, the world was so much bigger than her reputation.

"Go ahead! Tell them all! I'm not a slave to shame anymore! I don't care what anyone thinks!" Elara raised her free hand and slapped the prince across the face.

The surprise of her slap forced Andronikos to drop her arm, and as soon as she was free, Elara raced into the tavern to safety.

- - -

"Is this your church?" Theodosius asked as they made their way to the doors of a small, but beautiful, Orthodox chapel.

"It is," Eudokia replied softly, fondly. Her eyes lit up, just as he had remembered from his childhood, before his father and brother had died. It was a bright joy he hadn't seen nor felt in a long time.

"You like being a monastic nun here, then? Does it bring you happiness?"

"It's my life's calling," she smiled. "Thank you for the walk. I really missed you, love."

There was a knot in Theodosius' throat, but he swallowed it down. "I'm glad I got to see you, Mother. I thought you hated me."

"Hated you?" Eudokia's eyes widened in surprise. "Why would you think that?"

"You never showed up for my first trial, and there were whispers… I thought perhaps you believed I was guilty." Theodosius looked at his feet as blood rushed to his cheeks.

"I'm sorry I wasn't there for you at your first trial, but you must know, I *never* thought you were guilty! I know how much you loved Leonides."

His eyes were glossy, but no tears fell, as he whispered, "If that's true, why weren't you at my first trial? Where were you?"

"I was gathering evidence to help prove your innocence." She took his hands in hers and forced him to look at her. "You fled before I could do anything to help you."

"I'm sorry," he sniffed.

"No, love, I'm sorry." Eudokia pulled him in for a big hug. "I'm sorry I ever made you think I didn't love you or didn't believe in you with all my heart!"

Theodosius burst into tears as his mother held him and rubbed his back, just as she had done when he was a child. It was a cathartic moment that he wasn't expecting.

Once he finished crying, they made plans to see each other again the next time Theodosius sailed near Constantinople. He wasn't sure when that would be, but he had faith he would see his mother again one day.

"You saved me today, Mother. Thank you."

"All I did was offer you a lifeline. By accepting the emperor's offer, and choosing love over your hate for Nekros, you saved yourself," Eudokia said with pride in her eyes.

Theodosius smiled and opened the church door for her. "Ah, well, thank you for bringing Leonides' letter, then. It's lucky you found it."

"Found it? I wrote it." Eudokia grinned mischievously as she stepped through the doorway.

"But, the Patriarch's Seal...?"

"You're not the only one with pirate skills." His mother winked at him and closed the church door behind her.

After parting ways with his mother, Theodosius walked as quickly as he could to the tavern where his friends would be waiting for him. He was especially excited to see Elara, with whom he hoped to share a tender embrace and a kiss before they inevitably had to part ways.

For the first time since Leonides' death, Theodosius felt hopeful about the future. Perhaps Elara would write to him and invite him to visit her in Catalonia when her papou, the count, was out of town. They could meet up under the cover of darkness so as to not bring her shame. He wouldn't mind as long as he got to hold her, be near her.

"Kardia! Halt!" A loud voice shook him from his daydreams.

He turned to see a handful of guards with drawn swords standing behind him. Was this Nekros' doing? Surely, the emperor, and by extension, his family, were done hunting him.

"We have orders to bring you in, Kardia." The closest guard said sternly.

"But I've been pardoned by the emperor. Haven't you heard?" Theodosius laughed weakly.

One of the guards snarled back, "Our orders don't come from the emperor!"

- - -

Celina had just finished ordering the food and drink she wanted when Elara burst into the tavern with a pale face and scared eyes.

"What happened, Elara dear? Did he hurt you?"

"We have to find Theodosius and get out of here as soon as possible!" Elara looked around the dank, wooden tavern, like a frantic mess of a woman on the run.

"Hey, slow down. Take a deep breath." Yianni gently took Elara by the arm and guided her to a nearby stool.

"Tell us what happened," Celina said, taking Elara's shaking hands in hers. Instead of saying what had happened, Elara just kept repeating that they needed to leave as soon as possible.

"The prince is gone now," Tina reported from the side window. "He's not following you, Elara. You're safe."

"Here—have some of my tea," Rhea handed the countess a hot cup of tea. "It'll soothe your nerves."

Elara took a grateful gulp of the tea, and did seem, at least a little, soothed by it.

Celina watched worriedly as Elara took a few breaths to steady herself. "I told you we never should have let her speak to him alone!"

"Yes, yes, you're right about everything as always," Rhea grumbled, annoyed, but the truth was clear. Prince Andronikos was dangerous and letting him speak to Elara alone had most definitely been a mistake on their part.

"What exactly did the prince say to you?" Yianni pressed. "Did he threaten you? Did he threaten Theodosius?"

"I thought I could handle him..." Elara took a deep breath. "He's even worse than I remembered."

"Memories are funny like that," Tina said darkly.

"We'll leave as soon as Theodosius gets here," Rhea promised. So much for their last dinner in Constantinople.

They didn't have to wait long, as just a few minutes later, Theodosius burst into the tavern with an equal amount of tense emotion.

"We need to leave now!" he shouted to them before anyone else could say anything.

There was a loud commotion on the other side of the door. Celina could hear what sounded like the angry clanging of swords and shields. The guards were back, and they sounded out for blood.

"And we need to go out the back!" The pirate captain grabbed Elara's hand and pulled her off the bar stool. "Come on!"

The group moved quickly to the other side of the tavern and slipped out the back door into the cold, dark night.

- - -

By some miracle, they all made it back to the ship unscathed, but the guards were still on their heels.

Elara felt like she was going to be sick, and if it weren't for the support of her friends, she knew she would not have been able to keep going. She could almost hear Andronikos' threats bouncing off the walls of every solid surface they passed.

"Hoist the flag! Time to set sail!" Theodosius shouted, rousing the remaining crew.

"Why are people always chasing you everywhere we go?" Was Gregory's grumpy greeting to them as they boarded the ship.

"Good to see you too, Gregory!" Theodosius clapped him on the shoulder before turning to shout more orders to the crew.

Soon, they were off, speeding out to the open sea, leaving the guards to shout angrily on the shore. Without the support of the emperor, the guards wouldn't be able to chase them. Prince Andronikos' authority ended at the docks. The crew celebrated with loud, excited shouts, once it became clear that they weren't going to be followed.

"I'm making dinner down here, if anyone wants some!" Jimmy shouted from below deck.

"We're starved!" said Yianni as he and others started to climb below deck. The crew were chatting excitedly as they went, and no one appeared apprehensive about leaving Constantinople. No one appeared to be held back by the sense of dread that Elara was feeling.

"Aren't you coming?" Celina asked Elara.

"I'll be there soon. You go ahead."

"You sure? We can wait for you, if you want," Rhea offered, looking concerned.

"No, you both go ahead. I'll catch up." Her friends shrugged and slipped below deck.

The rushed nature of their departure had left Elara feeling even more uneasy. Emperor Michael and Empress Maria would not live forever. One day, Andronikos would be the emperor, and she doubted she would ever be welcomed back at court in Constantinople. She might never be allowed to return to Constantinople at all.

Swallowing her sadness, Elara watched the shoreline shrink further and further away. The outline of the Hagia Sophia shimmered beautifully, even in the darkness. That was the place in Constantinople she would miss the most.

"How are you fairing?" Theodosius appeared next to her. She had been so busy concentrating on the outline of the city, she hadn't heard him approach.

"I'm fine," she lied.

"You don't look fine."

Elara huffed a humorless laugh at that and turned away from the city to look at him directly. His face was covered in shadows, but the concern he had for her was clear as day.

"And how do I look to you?" she asked, holding back tears.

Theodosius smartly didn't answer the question, but instead, pulled her to his chest in a comforting hug. His arms were firm, but gentle, as they wrapped around her, holding her in place.

Elara had lost one home when she ended her engagement with Andronikos. However, here, now, in the dark on a pirate ship, she realized she had gained a new home, a better home. Even if her reputation was forever ruined, she knew now she wouldn't be alone like the beggar woman, and she wouldn't be left for dead, like Justine. Her friends had proved that they would be there for her. She hoped that they knew that she would always be there for them too.

"Thank you for standing up for me at my trial," Theodosius murmured into her hair. "It meant the world to me."

"You didn't seem that pleased to see me when I first entered the courtroom," she teased him.

"What makes you say that?" Theodosius chuckled and pulled back slightly so that he could look her in the eyes. His arms were still wrapped tightly around her, holding her steady in a tender embrace.

"You asked if we'd lost our minds."

"Did I?" he smiled innocently. "You know, I really don't recall. I only remember being eternally grateful for your heroism."

"You think you're charming, don't you, Captain?" Elara rolled her eyes but leaned up and planted a peck on the corner of his mouth all the same.

"Can I have a proper kiss, Countess?" Theodosius whispered, his eyes were dark like he was drinking in the fact that she was still here with him. Perhaps, like her, he was grateful to be alive, grateful for this moment together after they were nearly torn apart forever.

Instead of responding with words, Elara pulled him by the lapel of his jacket and pressed her lips to his. It was a deep kiss, the kind that she didn't want to end.

- - -

It took them three and a half days to get back to Catalonia. In that time, they had few troubles.

Elara spent most of her remaining time on the ship with Theodosius. He taught her how his sailing instruments worked, and how he used a variety of different maps and compasses to navigate the Mediterranean Sea.

In the evenings, Jimmy would prepare a huge feast, and the entire crew would eat together merrily. Celina and Rhea were always seen laughing and gossiping together about something. They would stay up late, giggling together, keeping Elara awake until the wee hours of the morning, but she didn't mind. Her friends getting along was one of the two things that Elara was most grateful for at the end of this hellish journey.

The other thing she was grateful for was her budding relationship with Theodosius, of course. She hoped he wouldn't sail too far away after dropping them off. They still had so much to talk about and to figure out; she wasn't ready to say goodbye.

"Where will you go?" Elara asked him as the ship docked in Costa Brava.

"I'll sail around the coast, I think. Might make a pit stop in Rome." Theodosius shrugged.

"When will you be back?"

"When do you want me to be back, Countess?" He had a mischievous, hopeful gleam in his eye.

"Soon, obviously!" Elara glanced at the fortress in the distance; it looked exactly the same as she had left it. "Perhaps give me three days to get things squared away with my Papou? I can only imagine the terrible mood he must be in."

"Three days it is." Theodosius kissed her and then he and his crew were gone, leaving Elara, Celina, and Rhea alone on the docks.

"That was fun," Celina said as the three of them walked up the hill toward the fortress. "We should go sailing together again sometime."

Elara looked at her friend with raised eyebrows. "Fun? Who are you, and what have you done with Celina?"

"What? I had fun!" Celina smiled and shrugged nonchalantly.

"I like the new Celina. She's much more relaxed than the old one." Rhea's proclamation earned a laugh from all of them. Even Celina, whose ears turned a little pink, couldn't help but laugh along.

The townspeople were staring at them as they made their way closer and closer to Tossa de Mar, but it didn't bother Elara anymore. They could look and judge her if they wanted to; it really didn't matter. She knew who she was and was confident in herself now. No one would ever make her feel less than again. All that mattered now was that she and her friends were home safe, the weather was beautiful, and the only thing left to do was to find her papou and apologize to him. His opinion was the only one that still mattered.

Elara had just reached the top step when she saw him sitting on the stone bench by the fortress door.

"*Yasas*, Papou mou."

"Welcome home, koukla mou." Count Basil did not get up to greet her as she hoped he would. His white hair had been recently trimmed, and he was dressed in a blue tunic, and wrapped in a black shawl. It was a comfortable day-look for the count, suggesting that he had been back from his trip for at least a day or two, maybe more.

"We'll be at the bakery if you need us, Elara dear," Celina said as she and Rhea quickly left.

Now that they were alone, it became clear that he was waiting for her to speak first. The count was obviously waiting for her to explain herself, to tell him where she had been, and what she had done.

Elara had been imagining this moment for the past few days. The different scenarios of what she would say to earn his forgiveness had been rehearsed and re-rehearsed over and over again in her mind. However, now that she stood before him in the flesh, only one phrase came to her mind.

"Papou, I am so sorry—"

Before she could finish her sentence, Basil stood quickly and threw his arms around her in a warm, loving hug. It was the kind of hug he used to give her when she was a child and scraped her knee, or when her yiayia had died, or when she had first told him she was ending things with Andronikos.

"You're not angry with me?" she mumbled into his shoulder.

"I'm furious," the count chuckled as he released her. "Tell me what you've been up to and why."

Elara wiped a tear from the corner of her eye. "It's a long story."

"I want to hear it all, Elara mou, and don't lie—I already know *some* things."

She told him everything; she told him about Rome, she told him about Athens, she told him about Thessaloniki, and finally, she told him about Constantinople. Elara only left out the harder details about Lady Valerie's death and the kisses she had shared with Theodosius.

There were some secrets she intended to take to her grave, or at least, keep quiet about until her next confession with Father Demosthenes.

"...And after all that, I didn't get Yiayia's necklace back," Elara sighed as she finished her long-winded story. "I'm so sorry about that, Papou. I know how much that necklace meant to you and to our family."

Basil shook his head and wrapped an arm around her shoulder as he said, "Don't worry about the necklace. All that matters is that you are safe."

"I know. I just feel terrible losing it after you entrusted me with it! The necklace was our family's most prized possession."

"Elara, you are my most prized one," her papou said with tears in his eyes. "There will be other necklaces, but there will never be another you."

"Me? But I've done such scandalous things! I'm afraid I really embarrassed the family, and I know I let you down."

Elara wasn't ashamed of her actions as she had been in the past. Everything she had done lately was to right wrongs and save lives, but that didn't change the fact that she would never be allowed in Constantinople again. It also didn't change the fact that she had consorted with pirates and acted unladylike. She had lost her yiayia's necklace, and there was no salvaging her reputation now, even with the emperor's pardon. It didn't bother her anymore. She knew who she was, but she had hurt her papou, and he must feel let down by her. She only hoped he would be forgiving enough to not kick her out, even if she knew a certain pirate ship would give her refuge, if he did.

To her surprise, Basil laughed and hugged her again. "Koukla mou, you didn't embarrass anyone, and you didn't let me down."

"Truly? You mean it?" Tears streamed down her face. "I thought—all this time, I thought you were disappointed in me, and I thought you might not want to keep me anymore. I worried I might end up on the streets!"

"Oh, Elara mou, no, never. I would never throw you out! I am, and have always been, so proud of the woman you have become." His eyes brimmed with tears, but unlike hers, they didn't fall. "I'm very sorry if I ever made you think I wasn't proud of you."

She choked on a sob, unable to respond to his kind words. Her papou was proud of her. He had always been proud of her and had always loved her unconditionally. All the time she had spent trying to prove herself and to repair herself, when all along her papou was already proud of her. When she had thought that all was lost, he had already accepted her. She had never been broken to him nor been a disappointment in his eyes. He wasn't judging her for any of her sins as she had assumed. All that insecurity about her worth had been in her mind and her mind alone. Count Basil would never throw her out onto the streets.

"I love you, Elara mou." Basil wiped the tears off her cheeks with a small handkerchief.

"I love you too, Papou."

The sound of the Orthodox Church bell chimed in the distance, signaling that evening vespers was about to start. Basil held out his arm for Elara to take, and together, granddaughter and grandfather set off to attend the service.

The End

Sophia Sempeles grew up with a love for storytelling. She especially loves telling stories that feature her Greek heritage and Orthodox Christian background. Sophia is currently living in the DC area and plans to write more adventure stories in the future.

Follow the author on Social Media:

Instagram: @sophia.writing.books

TikTok: @sophia_writing_books

www.ingramcontent.com/pod-product-compliance
Lightning Source LLC
Chambersburg PA
CBHW020651110726
47901CB00001B/148